OPENING SHOT

The day it happened Travis drove north. The back of the Land Rover held a spare fuel tank and five jerricans, filled years ago and now a standing violation of several laws; an air rifle; an air pistol; a first-aid kit; stacks of bottled water; MREs; camping gear; and a stash of trade goods: a wad of euros, twenty gold coins, and ten kilos of rolling tobacco. Travis kept the radio switched off. He didn't need the information and he didn't want the distraction. He watched the road and the sky, and the crawling blip on his phone's Galileo monitor. From his seat he could see over the hedgerows. Early May morning mist obscured the distance. The mist lay low, around trees and in hollows, under a clear sky. The only contrails visible were high up. No civil aviation was landing or taking off. Now and then a fighter jet flashed above the damp fields, vapor trailing from its wingtips like cartoon streaks. He saw helicopters often, their throb a seldom absent background. Some were big twin-engined, tandem-rotor troop carriers; most were ground-attack choppers. He avoided looking at them. If you looked too long at an attack helicopter, someone might look back.

It took him a while to realize why so many military aircraft were airborne. They were being kept off the airfields.

The
Execution
Channel

KEN MACLEOD

TOR®

A TOM DOHERTY ASSOCIATES BOOK
NEW YORK

This is a work of fiction. All of the characters, organizations, and events portrayed in this novel are either products of the author's imagination or are used fictitiously.

THE EXECUTION CHANNEL

Edited by Patrick Nielsen Hayden

A Tor Book
Published by Tom Doherty Associates
175 Fifth Avenue
New York, NY 10010

www.tor-forge.com

Tor® is a registered trademark of Macmillan Publishing Group, LLC.

ISBN 978-0-7653-5178-4

Our books may be purchased in bulk for promotional, educational, or business use. Please contact your local bookseller or the Macmillan Corporate and Premium Sales Department at 1-800-221-7945, extension 5442, or by e-mail at MacmillanSpecialMarkets@macmillan.com.

First Edition: June 2007
First Mass Market Edition: February 2017

Printed in the United States of America

0 9 8 7 6 5 4 3 2 1

To Andrew J. Wilson

ACKNOWLEDGMENTS

THANKS to Carol, Sharon, and Michael, for lots. Thanks to Johan Anglemark, Farah Mendlesohn, Svein Olav Nyberg, and Charles Stross for comments on the draft.

PART ONE

Opening Shot

1

THE day it happened Travis drove north. The back of the Land Rover held a spare fuel tank and five jerricans, filled years ago and now a standing violation of several laws; an air rifle; an air pistol; a first-aid kit; stacks of bottled water; MREs; camping gear; and a stash of trade goods: a wad of euros, twenty gold coins, and ten kilos of rolling tobacco. Travis kept the radio switched off. He didn't need the information and he didn't want the distraction. He watched the road and the sky, and the crawling blip on his phone's Galileo monitor. From his seat he could see over the hedgerows. Early May morning mist obscured the distance. The mist lay low, around trees and in hollows, under a clear sky. The only contrails visible were high up. No civil aviation was landing or taking off. Now and then a fighter jet flashed above the damp fields, vapor trailing from its wingtips like cartoon streaks. He saw helicopters often, their throb a seldom absent background. Some were big twin-engined, tandem-rotor troop carriers; most were ground-attack choppers. He avoided looking at them. If you looked too long at an attack helicopter, someone might look back.

It took him a while to realize why so many military aircraft were airborne. They were being kept off the airfields.

————

Two calls had come in the middle of the night. The red numbers on his alarm clock read 4:13. On the bedside table his mobile buzzed and jittered, then stopped as he reached for it. Text message, he guessed. Down the hall the landline phone was ringing. Landlines triggered an older reflex of urgency. Travis jumped out of bed, stubbed his toe on the door, and stumbled down the hallway in streetlight.

"Yes?"

"Dad, I'm all right." Roisin didn't sound all right at all.

"What? What's wrong?"

"I'm just ringing to say I'm all right."

"That's good, that's good." Travis licked his dry lips with a sticky tongue. "Why should—?"

"There's been a bomb—"

"Oh, Christ! Are you all right?"

"I just said—"

"Just hang tight and call the cops, okay? Stay where you are, lie low. Whoever attacked you might still be out there."

"Dad," said Roisin, in a pitying, patient tone that took him back about five years, "it wasn't a bomb on the *camp*. It was a bomb on the *base*."

"Shit! What kind of bomb?"

Roisin took a deep, sniffling breath and let it out shakily. "I think it was a nuke."

Travis almost dropped the handset. He heard beeps and the sound of coins being shoved in.

"Still there?" Roisin asked.

"Yes, yes, if you run out of money just stay and I'll call you back. Where are you?"

"Some wee village gas station. I can't stay. We're just going."

"Why do you think it was a nuke?"

"Dad, I'm looking at a fucking mushroom cloud. I saw the flash."

"Are you all right?"

"Yes, I told you. I have to go."

"Was the camp—?"

"We weren't in the camp. Nobody was, thanks to . . . thank God. We're on the road."

"Where are you going?"

"Wherever."

Travis paused. Wherever. That word had been agreed between them.

"I'll come for you."

"Don't, Dad, please don't. I have to go. I'm all right. Take care. Bye."

She'd put the phone down. Travis dialed 1471 and heard a chip voice. "You were called . . . today . . . at oh four fourteen hours. The caller withheld—"

He slammed the phone down and ran back to the bedroom. He speed-dialed the number for Roisin's mobile and got another chip voice, telling him the number was unobtainable. Travis guessed that if there really had been a nuke the mobile might have gotten fried by the electromagnetic pulse. As he ended the call he saw the flashing envelope symbol and keyed up the text message:

sell apls buy orngs

Travis stared at it for a moment in blank puzzlement, then recognized it. His hand shook a little. He knew better than to call or text back. It wasn't even worth memorizing the number before he deleted it. After he'd deleted it he ran a soft wipe: it was the best he could do short of trashing the chip. For a while he sat on the side of the bed and stared at the phone's blank screen. The text message had left him more disturbed than the phone call. The bomb, assuming it wasn't an opening shot in the big one, would in time become another date that marked a *before*. Before 9/11. Before the bombing. Before the Iraq war. Before 7/7. Before the Iran war. Before the nukes. Before the flu. Before the Straits. Before Rosyth. Before . . . and so you could go on, right up to now: 5/5, the first nuke on Britain. Yet another date that changed everything.

The text message was different. Every new shock, no matter how long dreaded, was unexpected when it came. Travis had been expecting this text message for a long time. It was no surprise.

He thumbed the phone to television and tuned it to Sky News. The two presenters looked grave.

". . . confirmation of an incident at RAF Leuchars . . ."

The caption read BREAKING NEWS: BASE EXPLOSION. The scrolling update read *so far no reports of casualties*.

The male presenter glanced down and said, "Ah, we're just getting the first pictures . . ."

A digital low-res image. He couldn't make it out on the phone screen. Travis grabbed the remote and flicked on the television on the far wall.

". . . viewer on a North Sea oil rig . . ."

A crescent moon high above the sea. Faint background voice, male, Newcastle accent: "Look at the moon, love, and—"

The screen went white, then faded to a glare reflected on the sea, the rig's shadow long and skeletal.

"What the *fuck!*"

A glimpse of the roustabout as he whirled around, turning his phone camera to—

"Holy fucking shit!"

Travis had seen enough onscreen nuclear explosions to recognize a kiloton yield. So, it seemed, had the roustabout.

"Tac nuke on Leuchars, love," he said. "Best I get inside. Stay safe . . . love you too . . . bye."

"As yet there has been no official confirmation," said the presenter.

Travis turned the television off. He could hear a faint ringing sound from outside. Wallingford at night was normally so quiet you could hear a snail climbing the window. After a while he worked out that the ringing sound came from his neighbors' phones. After another while the ringing was drowned out by a deeper tone that came from the sky. The heavy bombers were lifting from Brize Norton.

Time to move.

———

This was what had happened.

Roisin Travis crept among dark conifers, toward a light. She carried a heavy camera with a long-range lens. She had to make an effort not to laugh: she felt like some daft UFO chaser, following a light seen through trees. She knew she looked like an alien herself, in a thin, hooded coverall, with gloves and face-masking scarf of the same insulating black material. Even worn over nothing but jeans and T-shirt, the coverall was far too warm to be comfortable. The notion was that, by containing her body's heat, it made her less visible in the infrared. She suspected a flaw in this reasoning.

She stopped just before the edge of the forest. The trees and undergrowth remained dense right up to that line, beyond which they had been clear-cut some years

earlier. The base at RAF Leuchars had expanded along
with the war; though it had kept its name, it had long
since been turned over to the USAF. The rent was unknown but was rumored to go a long way to mollify
any objections from the Scottish Executive. The only gesture of independence from that quarter was to tolerate a
token peace-protest camp a kilometer away from the
base's eastern perimeter, on the other side of what was
left of the forest. From that huddle of shelters and vans
a fluctuating dozen or so people made sorties to monitor activity at the base and to wave indignant placards
at indifferent motorists. Roisin had spent six months
with this ineffectual crew and had accomplished little
beyond learning how to live rough through winter. With
the Gulf Stream halfway to shutdown this was useful for
the foreseeable future, but nothing to her purpose. Others
had drifted off; the camp was down to six.

The other thing she had learned was how to take photographs on film and develop them. She had learned this
from Mad Jack Armitage. It was a thing he did. He was
quite old and he mistrusted digital cameras. He was not
actually mad. In fact he was not even Armitage. His real
name, he claimed, was Norman Cunningham. "Mad Jack
Armitage" was what he said was his pirate name, and he
insisted on answering to no other, including during his
appearances in court. He was given to attributing his politics and his persistent petty offenses to attention deficit
disorder. It was not that he refused to hold down a job,
pay taxes, vote, pay utility bills, or always put his clothes
on before going out. He merely forgot. In a similar manner he claimed to be not actually a peace campaigner
but a plane-spotter. This was not one of the claims he
made in court. Plane-spotting was not in itself illegal but
almost all the activities involved in it were.

Roisin flattened herself on the ground and crawled forward on elbows and knees until she was lying under the overhang of a gorse bush on the very edge of the clear-cut area. A hundred meters ahead of her was the fence, then some grass, and beyond that the tarmac of a runway. Hangars and towers a kilometer away. She checked the viewfinder and the settings and waited. A perimeter patrol paced by, behind the wire. Twenty minutes later, another. A surveillance drone buzzed overhead, then landed like a toy. Each time Roisin lowered her head and held her breath.

Something *was* in the air. Roisin heard it above the surf and the sound of the wind. She rolled on her back, opened her mouth wide, and eased the sides of the hood from her face and turned her head this way and that until she identified the sound. A big heavy jet aircraft, coming in low over the North Sea. A bomber—no, a transport plane. A C17 Globemaster. It was surprising how much she had learned from Armitage. She rolled prone again and lost her night-vision as the runway lights flared. Roisin heard the change in the engines' sound as the aircraft banked, way out over St. Andrews Bay, and then another change as it dug in the flaps for its approach. She could hear it behind her and felt a tension in the back of her neck; she was lying right under its flight path. It passed over her in a rush and flash and she heard the rubber hit the tarmac.

Before the aircraft had come to a halt she was looking through the viewfinder and zooming the lens. It was almost as if she was hauling the plane back as it moved away. So she saw what happened after the aircraft came to a halt, outside the hangars. The tailgate opened, the ramp lowered, and an object whose main component was a black cylinder that looked about a meter in diameter and four meters long was rolled out on a gurney. A utility vehicle drew up, and the gurney was towed away into the nearest hangar.

Roisin kept clicking the shutter until the film ran out. She replaced the spool and waited. A couple of jet fighters took off and screamed away over the North Sea. A Chinook landed and a dozen soldiers deplaned. They took up positions in front of the hangar. Somewhat later a few cars drove up and a handful of men, some in uniform, some not, passed through the cordon into the hangar. She photographed all that. Two military policemen with dogs passed in front of her, a hundred meters away behind the perimeter fence. The next such patrol followed a few minutes later. She heard voices.

Guessing that security had been stepped up, Roisin backed away into the bushes then rose to a low crouch which she maintained until she was deep in among the trees. With relief she threw back her hood and took off her scarf and unzipped the front of the coverall. Her T-shirt was damp and sticky with sweat. She let the faint breeze from the west cool her for a moment. The stars were very clear overhead in the darkness, the Milky Way like a cold breath hanging. A satellite crawled across the firmament from south to north. A meteor rushed down the sky.

Roisin had no difficulty making her way through the wood. The floor was springy with pine needles. She walked slowly and carefully.

When her phone vibrated she nearly dropped the camera. She ducked to put the camera on the ground. The phone was in her back pocket and if she didn't catch it in five seconds it would start ringing. She tried to reach through the open front of the coverall, then swore under her breath and tugged her right arm up out of the sleeve. Her hand darted to her pocket and she slid the phone out just as the vibration stopped. It was only a message after all. But it was tagged as urgent: the little bead that glowed on the side of the casing was red. She flipped the screen open. It showed her brother Alec's standard e-card shot of himself grinning in his beret in front of a mountain range. Scrawled across it was the text:

> Get away from that base asap Rosh
> expect big security sweep any minute
> I mean NOW!!! xxx

Roisin stared at it. If it was true, how would Alec know? Of course he would—he worked in comms.

Away to her left, to the north, she heard the baying of dogs.

———

The camp was located in a clearing that had once been a picnic-area car park, at the end of a single-track road off from the back of the military housing and the civilian part of town. A concrete litter-bin that they used for the fire. Half-rotted tables with built-in benches that should have been put on the fire long ago but were never quite dry enough. Two vans, one a plain white Transit, the other an ancient VW camper painted with rainbows and peace signs. Two timber-and-plastic shelters and Mad Jack's bivouac. The old man was sitting cross-legged outside it, smoking, when Roisin ran out of the trees.

He stubbed the roll-up and stood up, quite limber.

"What's up?"

She told him. He showed no surprise about her brother.

"You take this seriously?"

"Very," she said. "Listen."

He cocked his head and cupped his ear. "What?"

"Drones, dogs, a chopper lifting . . ."

"Fuck. All right."

He strode to the nearest shelter, the one that held three students from St. Andrews, and rattled the plywood door. Roisin heard raised voices as she stepped inside the shelter she shared with Claire Moyle. She shook her friend in the sleeping bag.

"Where you been?" Claire asked, drowsy.

Roisin swung the camera. "Night photography. Doesn't matter. We got to go before we get chased out."

"Why?" asked Claire. "We haven't done anything wrong."

It took too long to explain. By the time Roisin and Claire had come out of the shelter Mad Jack's bivouac and belongings had vanished into the back of the Transit and the students were slinging things into the camper. The sounds of search hadn't come closer, they seemed to be in the woods and farther along the perimeter.

"Move!" Jack said, not too loud.

"I still think we should just wait," Claire grumbled, then dashed back into the hut and emerged with an armful. "Okay," she said. "Okay." She grinned at Roisin like she was suddenly in full agreement, threw her stuff in the Transit, and walked over to talk to the three students, who sounded like they needed more explanation than they'd gotten.

Roisin grabbed up some gear, food, two-liter bottles of water. She used one to douse the fire then took the driver's seat of the Transit. Claire climbed in on the passenger side, Mad Jack jumped in the back and slammed the doors. The sound seemed to echo.

"Sorry," he said. "Forgot." They were worn words from him. Roisin glared over her shoulder.

The two-van convoy lurched up the potholed track,

the Transit in the lead. They reached the junction to a back road.

"Take the right," said Claire, looking up from a map. "I've worked out a route."

"Good work," said Roisin.

Claire laughed. "Johnny, Mike, and Irena"—the students—"were going to drive straight through Leuchars!"

Roisin checked the wing mirror. The camper had followed them.

"Uh huh. So what's the route?"

"Head up for the Point then cut across past Newport. We can head west on the back roads, then south to the coast. Park in a back street in Pittenweem or another of the wee villages. The camper's going to go on to Dundee. They have friends there."

"They'll get picked up," said Mad Jack.

"Yes, if there's anything to this at all." Claire glanced across at Roisin, who looked straight ahead. "But we won't," Claire added.

"There's a lot to be said for a white van," said Mad Jack.

"Can you see anything back there?" asked Roisin.

Mad Jack shuffled on his knees through camping gear and photographic equipment and peered out the back window.

"Lights in the sky," he reported. "Flashing light back where we were, I can just make it out. No signs of pursuit." He crawled forward. "It's ahead you have to watch out."

"Yeah, yeah," said Roisin.

But there was no pursuit and no roadblock. Within half an hour they had reached their turning point, parted from the northbound camper, and were making their way along a maze of back roads through farmland.

Claire, in the passenger seat, was exchanging text messages with the students. Jack, behind her, was also intent on his phone, no doubt online and browsing conspiracy sites. Roisin was negotiating a corner blind with hedgerows and dipping the headlamp beams when Claire said: "Shit, the phone—"

The road, the hedge, and the whole landscape around became for a moment bright as day.

———

The day it happened was not the day it began. For Travis it began two and a half years earlier, in the Red Lion in Westminster. He'd spent the day investigating the feasibility of a large-scale software project with Alain Gauthier, who was over from Paris looking to outsource various tasks that had overloaded the IT department of the French state electricity company, EDF. The company for which Travis worked, Result, had made a strong pitch; Travis and his colleagues had answered every question. There had been many questions. At seven in the evening Travis and Gauthier had at the same moment stepped back from a much-scrawled whiteboard, nodded, then looked at each other and laughed. Each man's drawn face mirrored how the other felt.

"Call it a day?" Travis said.

"Yes," said Gauthier. He thumbed a line or two into his PDA, nodded to himself again, then closed the device with a click of finality. "As far as I am concerned, the deal is as good as done. But of course . . ."

"I know. Over to the bean-counters."

"Pardon?"

"The guys who count the costs."

"Yes. Still . . ." Gauthier shrugged. "Until then, let us presume."

"Sure." Travis brushed flecks of dried ink from his hands. "Do you have a plane or train to catch?"

"No, no, a hotel for the night. Red-eye from Heathrow in the morning."

"Fancy a drink?"

"That's very kind. You do not wish to go home?"

Travis shuffled papers into his briefcase. "No rush," he said. He blinked, spun the locks, looked up, and smiled. "Let's go."

The Red Lion smelled of sweat from suits and steam from food. Travis bought a bitter for himself and a lager for Gauthier and made his way to the pillar with a shelf on which the Frenchman had positioned an elbow. On the big screen in the corner boys capered around a burning Humvee in Aleppo. At the nearest table a thin fortyish English guy in heavy-framed glasses, with a gold pound sign on his lapel, talked in rapid monotone to a stout young American in T-shirt and combat pants. As Travis sidled past the American's seat-back he caught five seconds of a long story involving Muslims, heroin, and Soviets.

Gauthier stopped giving that pair the evil eye and took his pint.

"Thanks," he said. He glanced sideways again. "Cunts."

Travis flinched and backed away a little around the pillar, toeing his briefcase.

"What?"

Gauthier re-closed the gap. "Sorry." He smiled across the top of his glass. "Five minutes of overhearing these liberales mouthing off about the French."

"I thought it was all about the Muslims and the Soviets. I gathered the guy thinks the latter still exist."

"Indeed, and supposedly controlling France and . . ." Gauthier jerked a thumb at the television.

"The man's a nut. Ignore it."

Gauthier sighed and sipped. "I would," he said, "but I hear that canard too often."

"You do? I've never heard it before."

"Ah." Gauthier looked embarrassed for a moment. He spread his fingers and waggled his left hand. "Well."

"You're married," said Travis, catching a gold glint. Gauthier took the opportunity to change the subject and displayed photos of his wife and small son.

"And yourself?" he asked, slipping his wallet back.

"I was," Travis said. "Until the flu pandemic."

"I'm sorry."

Travis nodded. "It's all right. Well, no, it's not, but . . ."

"I understand," said Gauthier. "I lost my mother to it, and . . . but I know, it's not the same."

They agreed it was not the same.

"Any children?" asked Gauthier.

"Two," said Travis. "Son in the Army, daughter at university. Both doing well."

"Where is your son?"

"Iranian Kurdistan."

Gauthier's glance flicked to the television, and back. "It must be a great concern."

"I worry more about my daughter, to tell you the truth," said Travis, not telling the truth. "She's at SOAS. It's a bit of a hotbed."

Gauthier smiled. "Explain, please."

"School of Oriental and African Studies. Full of noisy Islamists, Zionists, antiwar agitators. Roisin—that's my daughter—she likes getting into all these arguments. She's a pacifist, at the moment."

"And therefore hated by everyone?"

"That's about it, yes."

"What do you think about . . . all that? If that is not too direct a question!"

"I disagree with both my children," said Travis. "If that is not too indirect an answer."

"It's very precise," said Gauthier. "You are against this war, but not against every war?"

"Nah, I just hate the Yanks," said Travis, in an idle tone.

The young American, standing up and pulling on a big padded jacket, overheard him and gave him a look. Travis held his gaze until the American turned away. About a dozen other people joined the American and his English companion in a sudden hubbub as they made their way to the door. Off to a meeting or function, Travis guessed.

"Ah," said Gauthier. He placed his empty glass on the shelf. "Permit me to buy you another drink."

And that was how it began.

———

"Something to show you," said Mad Jack.

Roisin stirred in the front seat. Her joints ached and her skin felt gritty. A distant yellow streetlight illuminated the van through the windscreen. The cobbled street in front was empty, the houses dark, the harbor still. From the sky came the beat of a chopper and the scream of a jet, but that had been going on all night.

"What?"

"Claire, wake up," said Mad Jack. His head poked out under the folds of a blanket Velcro-tacked to the sides and roof of the van. "This is important."

Claire unbundled herself and sat up, yawning. Roisin saw in her eyes the moment when she realized it hadn't all been a nightmare.

"God, what is it now?"

After the explosion they'd had a few minutes of fierce argument, and had eventually decided to stick to their original plan of driving to one of the coastal villages and lying low until daylight. Their phones were unusable, as was the van radio. Most of the surrounding countryside had been empty of any lights from village or farm: power cuts, most likely. Blundering about wouldn't have been a good idea.

"I've developed your pictures," said Mad Jack, his grinning head turning from Claire to Roisin. He ripped the blanket down in a rasp of Velcro and turned to face the back. "Look."

Dozens of prints were clothes-pegged to lines strung across the back of the van. Beneath them, enlargers, lights, and other equipment stood precariously on drop-down shelves. Trays of liquid were spread on every available spot on the floor. With the blanket down the air reeked of chemicals. The big plastic water bottles, Roisin noticed, were still full.

"Where did you get the water?" she asked.

"There's a tap down at the pier," said Mad Jack.

She hadn't even heard him going out.

"What about the fallout?"

"Wind's from the west," said Mad Jack. "Sky's clear."

"Jesus wept."

"Anyway," said Claire, "what did you get?"

"This is the best one," said Mad Jack. He reached for a print, unclipped it, and leaned into the front again, the balls and pads of his thumbs holding the still-damp photograph's edges, his curled fingers cradling it underneath. There was a sort of reverence about his posture. But it was the picture that made Roisin think of the Holy Grail.

There, in not-too-grainy shades of gray, was the object she had glimpsed. It was in side view, the shot taken in a split second when none of the soldiers maneuvering it obscured it. The aircraft's open hatch and ramp were just visible on the left, the hangar door on the right. Bang in the middle of the frame was the object, lashed to a low four-wheeled gurney like a flatbed trailer, being pushed by two men at the back and hauled by two at the front. These figures gave it scale: a stubby cylinder about a meter across and four long, mounted between two triangular frames big enough to let it swing to any angle in the vertical. The base of the frames was flat, scored with vertical lines whose spacing suggested the teeth of a geared wheel lying on its side. From beneath that base a cable coiled to a separate stand with a tilted fixture at the top, like a podium.

"Looks like a telescope," said Claire. "Or a searchlight."

"Or a gun," said Roisin.

The others laughed.

"What?" she said.

"Recoil," said Claire. "I mean, if that's a gun, or even a mortar, these frames must be a lot stronger than they look."

"I didn't mean that kind of gun," said Roisin. "A laser or something."

"Martian heat-ray," said Mad Jack. "Maybe. Or a rocket launcher. But for sure it's not a conventional gun, or a bomb—conventional or otherwise."

"It *could* be a nuke," said Claire. "On some kind of test rig."

"Damn short cable for a test."

"A suicide nuke?"

Mad Jack frowned at the photo for a few seconds. "Now there's a point. But in that case, why the fancy gimbal?"

"Maybe it's just what it looks like," said Roisin. "A searchlight. Well, some kind of detection device."

"You saw what happened," said Mad Jack, jerking his head back at the pictures behind him. "That's a hell of a fuss for a detection device. Even assuming the explosion was a coincidence."

"It could have been," said Roisin. "We don't know."

"Come on," said Claire. "You're just being stubborn for the sake of it."

Roisin had to acknowledge that. She admitted to herself a fear that what lay on Mad Jack's hands was too big to grasp.

"So what do we do with this?" she asked.

"I suppose," said Claire, "we could just hand it in at the nearest police station."

"Fine anarchist you are!" Roisin said. She hadn't expected this from Claire, of all people.

"Well, sure," said Claire, turning her head so that she faced into shadow. "But this might be just too hot for us to handle, you know?"

"That doesn't mean we have to hand it to the police!"

"Um," said Mad Jack, like he was considering it. "There is the wee problem that just having photos like this is illegal, let alone taking them. I mean, they must know it goes on, but technically they could sling us all in jail for being in possession of information 'of a kind likely to be useful to a person committing or preparing an act of terrorism.'"

Claire shrugged. "We could post it. The film and the negatives and everything."

"With our DNA all over it?" said Mad Jack.

"You could make new copies with a mask and gloves on," said Claire.

"Aye, I could," mused Mad Jack. "Then destroy the originals."

Roisin stared at them in disbelief.

"Are you two serious?" she said. "Hundreds of people have died back there. Leuchars must be rubble. We could be sitting under a fallout plume right now. And all because these bastards secretly flew in some secret thing, some fucking dangerous thing. That's how it looks, anyway. If they keep whatever this is secret, which they will if they can, they could blame the explosion on anyone they want. The terrorists, the Russians, the Chinese. They could blame it on us, for fuck sake."

"All the more reason to get this off our hands," said Claire.

"Yes, sure," said Roisin. "Get it off our hands, yes. But not straight back to theirs. Get it out."

"Out to where?" Claire asked. "Press and Parliament? Newsnight? Sure, that'll get it in the public domain all right."

"No need to be sarcastic," said Roisin. "I mean get it out to one or two good journalists, the antiwar movement and the bloggers."

"Now *you're* being sarcastic," said Claire. "That's just a slower and more expensive way of sending it to the police. Your Pilgers and Palasts and Fisks won't even see it."

"As soon as we buy new phones," said Roisin, "we can take close-ups of the prints and splatter them across the Net."

"Yeah, right," said Claire. "Digital pics, right up there on the Net with flying saucers and celebrity arse."

Mad Jack balanced the print across the gearbox and put his fists to his forehead.

"You're both right," he said. "Give me a minute to think."

After a minute he needed another minute. He clambered over the clutter at the back and out of the van. He strolled around to the front, squatted on the curb and rolled a cigarette. He stood up and gazed out across the Firth and lit the cigarette. Roisin and Claire watched the flare and the repeated red glow.

"That's some addiction he's got," said Claire.

"For him it's not an addiction," said Roisin. "It's self-medication."

Claire took a water bottle from the glove box and sipped. "Is he sane, do you think?"

"He's too sane," Roisin said. "That's his problem. Too much reality."

"Overload." Claire nodded. "You know, I kind of feel that way myself."

"You and me both," said Roisin. "Half the time I want to stay here and find a hole to hide in, and the other half it's all I can do not to turn the key and drive like fuck."

"This is the biggest thing," said Claire. "Worse than anything before. God, suppose it's the start of the war."

"If it was the start of the big one," said Roisin, "we'd be seeing a lot of flashes by now."

"Or we wouldn't be seeing anything at all."

Mad Jack stubbed his cigarette and returned to the back of the van. He closed the doors behind him with no more than a click and sat down on a folded blanket.

"All right," he said. "Here's an idea. Nobody knows we have the photos. If there was a security sweep around the camp—and it sure sounded like one—I doubt it's top of the list at the moment. We don't know what the spin on the explosion's going to be. But some fucker's going to claim it for sure. So anyone who might know anything about what happened can expect to get some questioning at the very least. I wouldn't be at all surprised if our friends the students aren't examining their consciences, let's say. Us running away isn't going to look good. So we have a choice—"

"We know that," said Claire. "Sure you don't need another smoke?"

"We have a choice," Mad Jack went on, as if he hadn't heard. "We can turn ourselves in, with the photos and everything. If we do that we might face doing some time, but not a cage in Gitmo. The down side of that is whatever it is Roisin saw vanishes behind official secrecy. Yes?"

They agreed with him about that.

"Okay," he said. "Now, I don't know about you, but I think letting that happen would be a crying shame and a waste of a stroke of luck. Something the gods frown upon, in my experience. To say nothing of making all we've tried to do at the camp a load of wank."

"Yeah, that's how I see it," said Roisin.

There was a short silence.

"Uh-huh," Claire said at last. "All right. I'll go with that."

"You're in?" Mad Jack asked. "You're sure? There's a door beside you, you know. You can walk away."

No hesitation this time. "I'm in."

Roisin wasted an encouraging grin on the side of Claire's head.

"Good," said Mad Jack. He stepped forward, stooping, and crouched behind the front seats. His breath was sour with tobacco and lack of sleep. "I have a plan."

———

Mark Dark's mother came back from her charity stint at the FEMA camp midevening. She looked exhausted. Mark stuck a pizza in the microwave for her, cleared up and trashed the remains of his own and took a Bud from the fridge.

"Back to work," he said.

She smiled from the kitchen table. "Good night, Mark."

She knew him too well.

"Good night, Mom." He blew her a kiss and went downstairs to the basement. He picked his way through the maze of angle-iron shelving to the table in the corner where the servers hummed. A knock on the tabletop as he sat down nudged four out of the five flat screens out of screen saver mode. Mark popped the Bud and scanned as he sipped. To his left was the news on multiple split screen: CNN, Fox, Al Jazeera, BBC. Midwest tornadoes, none of them near Evansville and therefore of no immediate concern to him. Missing white kid. Syria, Saudi, Iraq, Iran, Kazakhstan, Xinjiang: same shit, different day. Next along, the Execution Channel. Straps, gurney, lethal injection, Georgia. Yawn. Right in front of him was the screen with his current project, an ugly spatter of HTML code, much of it pointing to yet-unwritten Javascript applets. Sigh. The screen to his immediate right showed the latest posts linking to his blog (which was called Mark Dark). The other, once he'd keyed a password, displayed a rolling trawl through the porn sites that partially financed it. He appreciated them for the two minutes it took for the screen saver to lock in again—a precaution that had saved him and his mother many misunderstandings—then knuckled down to his coding.

He was knocking back the last warm dregs from the Bud when the news screens cut, within five seconds of each other, to the same news flash.

"WTF!" he said.

He saved his work, cut the porn Web ring and brought up Google, and on the Mark Dark screen tabbed through to his blog posting site and began to write, his glance

flicking between the news screens, the keyboard, and the
text:

Breaking: Tac Nuke on Scotland, England

A tactical nuclear device approx one kiloton has
detonated on [quick Google for the URLs] <u>RAF
Leuchars</u> in <u>Scotland</u>, a base used by and partially
leased to US forces. Claims of responsibility as of
22.25 PST from:

Al Qaeda in Europe
People's Mujahedin-e-Khalq of the British Isles (note:
hitherto unknown org)
Scottish Republican Socialist Army (note: <u>*known MI5*</u>
black op)
Hezbollah of Syria

Mark paused and added: *Analysis to follow,* then posted
what he'd written so far, to put down a marker. He went
back up the stairs and found his mother dozing in an
armchair in front of the muted television. He picked up
the remote and turned off the picture.

"Mom," he said. He shook her shoulder. "Sandra."

She woke, blinking. "I fell asleep again."

"Yes, Mom. I woke you because, uh, I didn't want you
to get a fright . . ."

He waved a hand at the blank screen.

"What is it now?"

"A *small* . . . nuclear explosion in England."

She reached for the remote. "Give me that."

After a few minutes she said: "It's started, hasn't it?"

"No, Mom, it hasn't. Either it's an accident like they're
saying, or it's the terrorists."

"You're not just saying that?"

"No, Mom, I'm not just saying that. I think you should go to bed."

"Those poor people."

"Yes, Mom. We'll know more in the morning. We'll know what to do."

"If there is a morning."

"This isn't the big one, Mom. Really. See you in the morning."

She stood up and gave him a hug. "Good night, Son. Remember to pray."

"Yes, Mom."

She went up one stair and he went down the other.

Analysis: The above claims are laughable. None of the sand nazis have nukes and all their state sponsors with nuke capability have been stomped. The only remaining nukes are in the hands of major players. The joint Brit MoD and US DoD claim that it was a "weapons handling accident due to failures of procedure" is likewise a sick joke. Tac nukes DO NOT go off by accident!!!

This was a precision strike by a state. The only question is which state.

Conclusion: it's started. This is the opening shot in the big one.

———

- Burt Franks; California; lethal injection; murder.

- Orlando Alarcon; Venezuela; firing squad; counterrevolution.

- Axele Curbelo; Venezuela; firing squad; counterrevolution.

2

JEFF Paulson stood under a blank UK ARRIVALS screen and watched both exit gates for UK arrivals. There was only one plane coming in and it wasn't going to appear on the board. Every so often he tried to blink away a dark speck that swam across his eyeball, but it kept coming back until he took his glasses off. It returned when he put them on again, and he realized that it was a refraction of a shadow from the overhead fluorescent light fixture. With that niggle solved, the focus of his annoyance shifted to the flicker of the lighting on a big advertisement to his right, on which WELCOME TO THE BEST SMALL COUNTRY IN THE WORLD was just legible through graffiti and scorch marks. His earpiece murmured news, none of it good. A cleaner ambled past pushing a mechanical broom. Yellow-jacketed policemen cradling Heckler & Koch carbines picketed the glass doors. The terminal at Edinburgh Airport was awake and smelling of coffee but he was the only person standing on the concourse.

A woman came around the corner and out of the exit in front of him, carrying a shoulder bag. She had to be the one he was waiting for. He guessed she was about thirty-five. Height about five-six, in heels. Her short black hair was a mess and the skin under her eyes was blue with lack of sleep. She wore a purple velvet jacket over a pink chiffon dress whose double layers were set fluttering around her ankles by her brisk step. It looked like she'd been wakened up and had pulled the jacket on over a nightgown in the dark.

She stopped in front of him.

"Jeff Paulson?" she asked.

"Yes," he said.

"Maxine Smith." She stuck out a hand.

"Pleased to meet you, ma'am. Any luggage?"

She patted the side of her bag. "This is it."

"Very well, ma'am. We can go straight to the car."

"Not before I've been to the ladies'."

She returned with her hair kempt and her face washed and made up a little. He could see the powdering under her eyes.

"I was at a party," she said. Her breath smelled of alcohol.

"I see," he said.

"It was business." Her heels clicked across the floor beside him.

"Of course, ma'am."

"Call me Maxine. And less of the prissy tone, Mr. Paulson."

"Uh, Jeff. Yeah, okay, sorry. I guess I was surprised. You don't look like—"

"I should hope not."

The glass doors slid back. The policemen glanced over their shoulders and nodded. Paulson's shades darkened in the early morning sun. Maxine Smith stared with open curiosity at the row of light armor lined up on the taxi rank.

"This way."

He led her across the road and through the covered walkway, and paid at the machine. His car was close by, one of the few in the parking area. Smith settled into the Hyundai biodiesel's passenger seat and fussed with her hems.

"Sorry it's a bit grubby," said Paulson. "It's in character."

She looked at him. "You're wearing a suit and tie and shades and you're driving a new-man daddy car. What's your cover—small-time drug dealer?"

"Music journalist," said Paulson. "Local indie scene."

At the roundabout just past the car-park exit scores of vehicles whose drivers had managed to miss or ignore the road signs and the radio bulletins were being waved away. Paulson slid the car into the outward stream and wove in and out, accelerating and overtaking and looping around bends and underpasses to join the motorway into town. That lane was slow and busy, the outward lane almost empty.

"Funny," said Smith. "I'd have expected people to leave."

"Not this way," said Paulson. "It's the road south that's jammed."

"Ah." She noticed his earpiece. "What's the latest?"

"Fallout's drifting out to sea. Search and rescue ops in the town. Sensing equipment helicoptered in. A lot of buildings down. Ninety-seven fatalities confirmed so far."

Smith glanced at the clock. The time was 9:16.

"It's been just over five hours," she said. "That means, I reckon, the final figure is in the thousands."

Paulson knew the algorithm.

"Sure," he said. "The living-quarters on the perimeter housed hundreds of families. All flattened. Gone."

For a moment he felt his composure slip. He found his hand banging the wheel. Cars in front of him had stuff lashed to their roofs.

"This isn't traffic," he said. "It's a refugee column. It's like over there."

"Ever been over there?"

"Just the stint," Paulson said. "Couple years, three years ago. Dodging IEDs in Tehran. You?"

"A few months, a long time ago. My first assignment. Coalition Provisional Authority."

"Wow," said Paulson. "Present at the creation."

Two helicopters hovered over the Gyle intersection. Most of the traffic was turning off to the City Bypass, on which the crawl was even slower. Paulson checked the GPS on the dash and took the lane to the shopping center, avoided the choked car park—the mall entrance was already crowded—and circled around until he found the right exit. Five minutes later the car nosed into a housing estate. Smoke rose from a corner.

"What the fuck!" said Paulson.

Small crowd, some holding up phones to take pictures; no fire engines or cops. The Spar mini-market had burned for some time. Paulson accelerated past it and slewed the car around the next corner, took the next right and the third left and pulled up outside a low-rise block. Cracked concrete fascia and spray-painted graffiti.

"This is the consulate?" Smith asked.

"Hah," said Paulson. "It's a safe house."

Smith had trouble with her heels and hems on the stairs to the third flat.

"I must get some proper clothes," she said.

"There might be something in the corner shop."

A doorbell and a spyhole lens. Paulson faced the CCTV on the lintel.

The door opened. The thin young man inside had a straggly beard and spiky hair. He wore very new black jeans and a faded green T-shirt with SMOKE CRACK IN-STEAD in big letters on it.

"Ah, come on in," he said. He led them through a narrow corridor with a bike in it to a front room with a television, a sideboard, a sofa, and a pair of armchairs, none of them new. Newspapers, magazines, books, and pamphlets lay in neat stacks on the worn carpet. The sound was off and the picture was on. On the screen a man in pajamas tugged at a chunk of broken wall. It didn't move.

Paulson waved toward Smith.

"Maxine Smith," he said. "MI5."

"Pleased to meet you." The man shook her hand, smiling. "Andrew MacIntyre, Lothian and Borders Special Branch. Tea or coffee?"

"I could murder a black coffee," said Smith. "No sugar."

"Jeff?"

"The same. And yeah, I know it'll be instant. That's okay."

"He's going native," said MacIntyre, giving Smith almost a wink. Her grin of response faded as MacIntyre went through to the kitchen and the television resumed its dominance of the room. The pictures coming through were among the first. An eerie aspect of this disaster was that there had been no pictures for hours. Every cell phone within about ten kilometers had been fried by the EMP. Smith stared at the televison images and looked away.

"Fuck," she said. "This is all so fucking unreal."

She threw off her jacket, sat on one end of the sofa, and swung her legs up on it, skirt overhanging. She hugged herself with bare arms.

"Cold?"

"I need drugs," she said.

"There are cigarettes somewhere," said Paulson. "He has a license."

"No need." She fingered a small round tin from her bag and took two pinches of snuff. "Ah, that's better. Christ."

"Very louche," said MacIntyre, in an admiring tone, as he arrived clutching mugs. "Yes, I will, thank you."

He dragged a coffee table in front of the sofa, elbowed off a year or so's worth of *Peace News*, then snorted the snuff, returned the tin with a flourish, and sat down in an armchair, sniffing like he had a cold. Paulson perched on the arm of the other chair.

"One thing first," said MacIntyre. He fixed a hard stare at Smith. "Tell me, why did the fucking Sorsa have to claim it?"

"Sorsa?" Paulson frowned.

"Scottish Republican Socialist Army," MacIntyre spelled out. "Two dogs and a man. One of Five's pseudo-gangs."

Smith put down her coffee and put up her hands. "I don't know," she said. "Credibility, I imagine. And a pretext to turn over socialists and republicans, if that's where the trail goes."

"As if we need a pretext," said MacIntyre. "Meanwhile, you expect us and the uniforms to waste time pretending to take it seriously."

"No we don't," said Smith. "You're welcome to tell the hacks you're laughing that one off."

"I just wish Five would stop messing us about," MacIntyre said, thumbing a fast message on his phone. He looked up at Paulson when he'd finished. "Anyway. I don't suppose the Agency's interested in our turf wars."

"We encourage them, actually," said Paulson. "But yes, let's get to business. We have the first nuke on the West and no idea who did it. Well, in fact we have lots of ideas, and that's our problem." He sighed and put down his mug. "It's *my* problem." He looked from Smith to MacIntyre and back. "Can we agree that nothing goes beyond this room?"

MacIntyre nodded, predictably and quite unreliably.

"No," said Smith. "Can't promise you that, I'm afraid."

"Oh, well." Paulson put his hands behind his head and leaned against the chairback. "It was worth a try."

"If you suspect blue-on-blue," said Smith, "feel free to spit it out."

Paulson jolted upright. To cover his confusion he segued into a lunge for his coffee mug and knocked it off the table.

"Now that," observed Smith to MacIntyre, "is what is called 'touching a nerve.'"

"You reckon," said MacIntyre, mopping up the spill, "the official line is so much bollocks." He hurled a rag through the open door to the kitchen. "Yes?"

"A weapons accident is the least likely explanation," said Smith. "Not completely ruled out at this stage, I've been assured. But it's a place-holder."

"It's not working," said Paulson. "Your neds are burning out Muslims already."

"Where?" asked MacIntyre, sounding shocked but sceptical.

"Around the corner from here," said Paulson.

"What?"

"That's what it looked like."

They told him about the Spar shop.

"Fucking hell," said MacIntyre. "I liked the Nazirs. Everybody did. Hang on."

He did some more texting then looked up, relieved. "Debt repayment dispute. That's all."

"Glad we've got that cleared up," said Smith. "I hope it's going out on all channels. But go on, Jeff, tell us who you think did it. Or could have done it. Worst case."

"And while you're at it," said MacIntyre, "tell us why it matters to us. I don't know about you, mate, but I have a chief super on my back."

"Okay," said Paulson. "Start with the least worst and the least likely—the terrorists, AQ and its allies. All the indications are that we have that nailed down. There are no known suppliers of nukes to terrorists. Sure, we could be wrong about that, in which case we might as well tear up every bit of intel we have and start over. More to the point, if Al Qaeda had a tactical nuke they wouldn't waste it on a base. They'd go for a city center."

"Could be some kind of gesture," said Smith. "Hitting a legitimate target for a change? If it was some remnant of the defeated regimes, dead-enders rather than jihadists, that might actually fit."

"It would imply that international nuclear-materials accounting is suborned, big time," said Paulson. "Hell of a job."

MacIntyre brandished his phone. "That conspiracy theory's on six websites already."

"That's a given," said Paulson. "No, if it was a nuke it was done by a state, or someone with access to the resources of a state. And a declared nuclear weapons state at that. And it couldn't have been a missile. There are no radar traces. The device was either planted on an incoming plane or lobbed short-range by special forces."

"Spetznatz in Fife!" MacIntyre scoffed.

"Why not?" said Paulson. "Seriously, why not?"

"Risk-reward ratio," said Smith. "As in, not good. Also the question of follow-through." She shrugged. "Not to mention what the point might be. A nuclear warning shot doesn't make sense."

Paulson looked at MacIntyre. "You would agree?"

"Aye, I'd agree. It's fucking ridiculous."

Paulson nodded. "That's my own assessment."

"Hence blue-on-blue," said Smith.

"Certainly not," said Paulson. "That's not even a possibility."

"It must be a possibility," said MacIntyre. "Come on."

Paulson toothed his lower lip for a moment, then realized what he was doing and stopped. It was a tic he was trying to break. He took a deep breath.

"It was war-gamed in the Agency a couple years ago," he said. "Fort Sumter scenario—opening shot in a US civil war. The team that did it got seven kinds of shit kicked out of them. It ended careers. Pentagon, White House, State . . . they all piled on."

He could tell the two Brits were not really getting it. This was something he'd noticed, increasingly, over the past years.

"I know the Agency's political at the top," Smith said, "but aren't the guys like you in the field supposed to be, well, like us? Civil servants? Go and he goeth, sort of thing."

"Exactly," said Paulson.

"Five are not political?" said MacIntyre. "Pull the other one."

"Leave it out," said Smith.

"Yes, indeed leave it out," said Paulson. "We have a clean-up to do."

"Aye," said MacIntyre. "So let's get on wi it, right?" He keyed his phone and the television screen flipped to a display. "Here's what we know."

———

- Susi Abudu; Nigeria; stoning; witchcraft.

- Matthew Holst; Syria; decapitation; invasion.

- Tariq Nazir; Scotland; burning; charge unknown.

3

BOB Cartwright got off the T at Convention Center and walked the couple hundred yards to his office on Newbury. Along the way he bought an americano and a vanilla mocha and a hot beef baguette at the Starbucks stall. Fewer commuters were about than was usual for eight in the morning. Many had the peaky look of a bad night on them. He knew he had it himself. The morning was chill and damp, the sky overcast. Cartwright wore a tweed jacket, blue button-down collar shirt with a tie, and chinos. He was twenty-four years old and a few pounds heavier than he liked. His face was slightly plump and had a black four-day stubble.

The office of Information Management Services was on the second floor of a tenement conversion above a vintage clothes boutique. You could smell the incense and mothballs even when the shop was closed. Cartwright went up the five steps and put his thumb on the plate and his eye to the scanner. The door buzzed. He pushed it open and climbed the flights and used his keycard to let himself in. As usual he was the second to arrive.

Sarah Henk looked up from her desk in reception.

"Good morning, Bob."

"Morning, Sarah."

Henk was a red-haired young woman with pale skin and blue eyes. Usually her smile was as wide as her glasses. Today it was a fleeting twitch.

"Have you seen—?"

"Yeah, I know," Cartwright said. "It's bad."

They talked for a minute about how bad it was.

"At least I won't be fielding many calls today," said Henk. "The market's gonna *tank*."

A small but annoying part of her job consisted of fending off inquiries from people who'd found the company listed in the Yellow Pages as an IT consultancy. Sometimes would-be customers got as far as Henk's desk, and she'd have to turn away from her real work onscreen to fob them off.

"Don't let it stop you enjoying your breakfast," said Cartwright.

He left the vanilla mocha and the baguette on Henk's desk and went into the inner office, leaving the door wide. Three desks with keyboards and screens. A tall window with more protection than the iron bars across it. Four free-standing racks of industrial shelving. Anyone glancing in from the doorway would see only the outward-facing rack, the one that was stacked with software manuals and management scriptures.

The rest were jammed with almanacs and atlases, reference works, military and paramilitary handbooks, war memoirs, and about ten yards of weird shit: conspiracy theories, UFO books, religious and occult texts, science fiction, pseudoscience and real but unorthodox science, journals and books from the political fringes. Cartwright and his colleagues knew that they couldn't rely on online material, because they and hundreds like them spent every working day fucking it up. Contaminating online information was what Information Management Services did. Outsourcing the supply of disinformation to a swarm of freelance contractors had been one of Homeland Security's smarter moves.

Cartwright took the lid off the coffee cup to let it cool for a bit and tabbed to his mailbox. The first item he checked every morning was what was called "the line." Today six line items had stacked up, each of the last five improving upon or contradicting the one before. The final version was two and a half hours old so he reckoned it was definitive.

The official position was that it was an accident with a tactical nuclear weapon.

The semi-official position was that it was an accident with a terrorist nuke captured in Iran.

The unofficial position was to blame AQ, the French, the Russians, and the Chinese, together or severally.

The designated conspiracy theory was to link it with the long-running North Sea UFO cover-up story.

Cartwright sipped his coffee and scanned various sites and thought about his strategy for the day. Peter Hakal came in, said hello, and checked his line. The Lebanese-American was in his thirties, clean-shaven, quiet, and serious. He took care of Arabic and Persian-language outlets. He leaned back and stared at his screen, chuckling.

"Hey, Sarah," he called to the outer office, "guess my line?"

"Blame the Jews?" Henk called back.

"Wrong! The Kurds! PKK!"

"Now that's creative," said Henk.

"What's yours?"

"Nobody," said Henk. "Bad luck, guys, today I get the heavy serious discussions."

"You're welcome," said Cartwright. He hated mainstream. "Have at it."

Anne-Marie Chretien arrived a few minutes later, in a clinging aroma of tobacco smoke and patchouli from her pre-work cigarette on the steps beside the boutique. She wore distressed black lace and a lot of kohl. The boutique was where she shopped for clothes. As she'd once explained, it was the only way she could dress well without looking French. She was twenty-six, slim, very intense, and had worked hard on her accent. Her coffee was from Cafe Noir but that was all right.

She said nothing about her line except, "Oh fuck. This is good."

Bob Cartwright stopped staring at her back, and got to work updating his blogs. He had three ghost soldiers on his string, whose indiscretions and occasional uploaded photographs pinpointed locations where there were no Coalition troops. This was painstaking work, demanding a good deal of fact-checking, Earth-Googling, and cross-referencing to the blogs of real soldiers. His own experience helped, limited though it was to a two-year stint patrolling pipelines in Saudi. Then he moved to the more amusing and relaxing task of posting to his blog called Red Professor, a fictitious Marxist academic and Green Party voter who, today, gloated over the hit on the Brits and speculated that it was the opening shot of what he called an inter-imperialist war with France; and went on to enthuse about the alacrity with which the Chinese were this week covering their eco-cities with geodesic domes, to protect against a giant dust storm; cue invidious comparisons with US disaster management. Finally he cobbled together some .pdf files of USAF documents about hypersonic triangular aircraft being secretly combat-flown out of Lossiemouth and Leuchars and emailed them anonymously to a conspiracy website called Mark Dark.

Two years and three months before it happened James Travis sat down with an espresso at a white enamel table on the pavement outside a cafe near the Jardin du Luxembourg. The Boulevard St-Michel was empty of cars. People ambled down it in ones and twos, at first on the pavements, then in larger groups in the middle of the street. There were no banners or placards. Travis checked the cafe's name over the door and checked his watch. He went back to the counter for another espresso. He fretted that he'd gotten the day wrong, or the place, or the time. Before he sat down again he paused beside two fur-wrapped matrons sipping iced coffee at the next table.

"*Pardon, mesdames.*" He waved his hand at the street, now sparsely crowded. "*C'est la manif?*"

"*Oui, monsieur,*" one of them said, sounding amused. "*C'est la manif.*"

Travis sipped the second espresso more slowly, while the crowd increased by almost imperceptible increments until it filled the boulevard. People on the pavement pressed past, jostling the tables. Others formed a queue in the cafe that soon stretched out of the door, turning the front of the cafe into an eddy in the human flow. A big banner went past: Anglo-Saxons Against Invasion. The two ladies clapped their gloved hands. Travis smiled at the bottom of his cup. More banners and placards. Sans-Papiers de St Denis Contre La Guerre. The ladies' lips pursed.

A hand on his shoulder. "Ah, James, you are here."

Travis looked up at Gauthier. "Hello."

His normally dapper colleague had turned up in Docs, faded jeans, and a puffa jacket with a red sticker and yellow lettering, a miniature of some of the placards sprinkled among the crowd: *LCR 100% A Gauche.* It sounded stronger read out in French: *Cent pour cent.*

But from what he knew of Gauthier, it made no sense. Travis lumbered to his feet and shook hands.

"Good to see you," he said.

Gauthier nodded toward the cafe door. "After me," he said.

Travis shouldered in Gauthier's wake through the crush at the door, past the queue for the counter, through to the back and past the backs of the intent cluster outside the tiny toilet. Up a narrow staircase a couple of floors. Gauthier stopped outside a door and gave five knocks in quick and varied succession. He cocked his ear. The door opened a fraction, then wide. They went in. Overstuffed furniture too big for the room; a mantelpiece with china ornaments and a ticking clock. Smell of cigarette smoke and coffee. The only light came from the window, as did a chill draft and a dull roar interspersed with shouts and chants. A small table in front of the window was spread with sheets of newspaper, on which a tripod camera with a long lens stood peering out. The man standing behind it ignored them. The man who had let them in said nothing and stepped up to join the man at the window, raising a pair of binoculars.

"What's going on?" Travis asked.

"Please, James, take a seat," said Gauthier.

They sat in facing armchairs under the mantelpiece. The electric heater in the old fireplace was off. Gauthier jerked his head back toward the men at the window.

"It is the police surveillance. Quite normal."

A big red balloon with the letters *PCF* in black bobbed past the window. The camera chattered a series of clicks.

"Aren't the Communists in the government?" Travis asked.

Gauthier hunched his puffa closer. "Governments come and go," he said. "The police remain. An expression that originated, I believe, in this city."

"And you have friends in the police?"

"I certainly hope I have friends," said Gauthier.

Travis thought about this. "Ah," he said.

Over the past couple of months he'd made a dozen trips to Paris, liasing with Gauthier on Result's software contract job with EDF. This was the first time he'd decided to stay the weekend in Paris, more because of a bargain flight-and-hotel deal than because he'd had anything specific to do. That Friday, after work, Gauthier had suggested they meet up on the Sunday. He'd named the time and the place, and mentioned in passing that there would be a demo going on. Travis had spent the Saturday browsing the *bouquinistes* of the Left Bank and the Sunday morning roaming Montmartre. He'd emerged from the Metro into empty streets that had surprised him, until he remembered the demo. He'd seen the posters plastered all over the place, *manif* and *dimanche* and *Kazakhstan*, and had failed to make the connection.

There were other dots he hadn't joined, until now.

"And there was me thinking you worked for EDF," he said.

Gauthier scratched behind his ear. "We are in the age of portfolio employment," he said. "In any case—" He sat forward and clamped his hands on his knees. "I have something to ask of you, James. A favor."

Travis found himself quivering, whether from the cold or the coffee or some less explicable excitement he didn't know.

"Go on," he said.

"Result has other contracts in the energy business," said Gauthier. "I would, on occasion, wish to know some details of them."

Travis rocked back and laughed. "Is that all this is about?"

"What?"

"Some energy trading scam? Insider dealing? Helping EDF undercut the competition? You know me better than that."

"And you know me," said Gauthier. He sounded as indignant as Travis felt. "I would not ask you to do that."

"You just did, Alain."

Gauthier nodded backward again. "I thought you had grasped the situation."

"So did I," said Travis. "Until you asked me to spy for EDF."

"If you must put it this way," said Gauthier, "I am asking you to spy for France."

"It'll take more than a couple of guys with a camera to convince me of that," said Travis.

Gauthier sat in silence until Travis realized what he'd just said.

"I think we understand each other," said Gauthier.

———

- Harvey Maclean; Syria; decapitation; espionage.

- Jia Lan Huang; Shanghai; cranial shot; embezzlement.

- Pamela Baker; Ohio; electrocution; infanticide.

4

ROISIN Travis wrestled with the heavy steering wheel and worked the clutch hard as she took the Transit over a bridge whose hump scraped the undercarriage and whose drystone walls almost scraped the sides. The only thing going for the back roads of Fife was that there were no surveillance cameras. Mad Jack had reckoned they had about two hours of daylight before satellite pic and roadside camera processing identified the old white van and started tracking, assuming anyone was looking for them. By then they'd have had time to ditch it.

Ahead was a junction to a wider but still minor road. It probably had cameras but there was no other option.

"Which way?" Roisin asked.

Claire Moyle, in the passenger seat, glanced down at the map on her lap.

"Left, into the town, then right."

Roisin felt reassured as ever by the smile on Claire's calm, serious face. The sturdy, blond young woman from Belfast had been a rock of stability and sense in the sometimes fraught atmosphere of the peace camp, and after her first waverings, as soon as they'd agreed what to do, she'd resumed that reliable role.

"Okay," Roisin said.

She turned and drove the few hundred meters into the small town, turning right on the high street. Gray buildings, closed shops, litter. A burnt car. Not many people on the street.

"Miserable little dump," she said.

"I cursed Lochgelly once," said Mad Jack Armitage, from the back. He stuck his white-maned, white-bearded head between Roisin's and Claire's shoulders and peered about. From the corner of her eye Roisin noticed his look of malicious satisfaction. "'May your men rot on the dole,'" he intoned. "'May your women sell their bodies to strangers, may your children acquire expensive and degrading vices, and may your name be forgotten.'" He dropped the singsong voice and chuckled as he sat back. "Looks like it worked."

"What the hell was that for?" Claire asked.

"For the town's most famous product," said Mad Jack. "The Lochgelly tawse."

"Ah," said Claire, like she understood now.

"The what?" asked Roisin.

"The tawse," said Mad Jack. "The strap. The belt. As used to sting the hands of schoolchildren, including my own hands many a time." He chuckled again. "It was a bad day for that shit-hole when corporal punishment was abolished. And thanks to my curse, it has had many bad days since."

"If you believe that, you really are mad," said Roisin. She said it in an abstracted tone to shut him up. They turned left at Kelty and as they passed under the motorway she noticed that southward traffic was a clogged crawl; traffic heading north on the M90 was flowing freely, and was mostly military: troop trucks, humvees, light armor. She presumed the column would turn west for Leuchars on the A91 a few kilometers up the road. With her and her companions' phones, and the van's radio, out of action since the blast and (she guessed) its electromagnetic pulse, she had no news, but she had a clear idea of what was likely to be going on. Nothing would get in or out of the disaster area except through a military cordon. The survivors would be security-screened even as they were helped. It was standard operating procedure for natural disasters and major accidents as well as mass-casualty attacks.

As they drove on they spotted military roadblocks about fifty meters down every turning to the south.

"Wonder if something's happened at Rosyth," Claire said.

"Again," Roisin added.

"Precaution, I reckon," said Mad Jack. "Naval yards must be high on the lockdown list. That's one reason we were right to avoid the Road Bridge."

They gave the Forth shoreline a wide berth, and followed the roads parallel to the foothills of the Ochils. They crossed the A977—the immediate destination was the Kincardine Bridge, but Mad Jack had predicted a long tailback there—and took more back roads until they hit the main road south into Alloa. A medium-sized town that seemed to have accreted around a rocky outcrop on the ancient floodplain of the Forth, it was a place to pass through rather than a destination. Roisin followed road signs to the town center—most of the traffic this morning was heading across town to the east—and into the broad expanse of a Tesco car park. Even after bypassing the long queue at the fuel-sales area it took her a few minutes of driving around to find a space. Years of asymmetric warfare had done little to dampen the impulse to panic buying.

"Everybody got cash?" said Mad Jack.

They had.

"Right," he said. "One by one. Make sure you take all you want to take. I'll go last."

After their decision he had spent the remaining hours

of darkness making more prints of the most interesting shots. He shuffled them together as Roisin and Claire stuffed their backpacks. Roisin left first.

"See you at the cosmetics shelves," said Mad Jack. Claire laughed.

"I'll remember," said Roisin.

Swinging her pack by one strap, she strolled to the store entrance and grabbed a trolley. The queues at each till were already dozens deep. Faces looked thrawn, anxiety broken by forced levity. Headlines blared from early morning editions, with *The Sun*'s TARTAN TERROR NUKE leading the pack. Roisin swept them all with a glance and walked on. The first item into the trolley was a cheap solar-powered phone with the basics—infrared beam, camera, TV and Internet, no GPS, no diary functions. She went around the back of the aisles, tossing in dried fruit, chocolate, and tins, then headed for the clothing section. She looked at summery racks and realized she had forgotten what normal was. She glanced back at the queues and grabbed a pink hoodie, white plimsolls, and a denim skirt with too much eyelet trim, then stocked up on underwear. The clothes were all made in USA and very cheap. She remembered when cheap stuff came from China.

She circled back and dawdled in the toiletries aisle, picking out shower gel and shampoo, until she saw Claire turn the corner and start searching along the cosmetics shelves. Claire looked up as Roisin drifted her trolley alongside.

"Excuse me," Claire said. "Have you seen Lancôme Nano?"

Roisin pounced on a jar. According to Mad Jack this particular lotion's components mangled certain wavelengths of light, thwarting face-recognition software. It had seemed worth a try.

"That the one?" she asked, handing it over.

"Yes, thanks." Claire peered at it. "I hope it's not tested on animals."

Roisin picked up another jar and pretended to study the small print.

"Contains scales from the wings of sustainably farmed fairies," she said.

Claire chuckled. "Thanks again. Bye."

They left by separate checkout queues. Roisin took her purchases to the women's toilet, where she locked herself in a stall and changed into her new clothes and shoes. She rolled up her jeans and sweater and stuck them in the top of her pack, and put her boots in the now empty plastic shopping bag, stuffed that in and barely closed the drawstring. At the wash stands and mirrors she washed her face, dabbed long streaks of the expensive cream across her nose and cheeks, and scrunched her hair in a ponytail. She walked out of the restroom area and walked across the front of the store to an open-plan cafteria. She took a cup of coffee to an empty table by the window and sat down. She placed her new phone on the table and initialized it while she sipped the black brew.

After a few minutes a woman in a charcoal trouser-suit and white blouse sat down at a nearby table with an espresso. Her blond hair was piled neatly on top of her head; she carried a small suitcase and a folded broadsheet newspaper. She slid the suitcase under the table and laid the newspaper on top, then took out a phone and tapped at it. Moments later a message chimed on Roisin's phone. She read it:

U look like a single mum :-) followed by a string of numbers.

By way of reply, Roisin sent her own phone's number across by infrared beam.

Claire knocked back her espresso, pocketed her phone, picked up her case and left.

Roisin stood up, stepped over to the table, and retrieved the newspaper. As she had expected, a thick envelope was inside it. She read columns on the front page of the *Daily Telegraph* for a few more minutes until her phone chimed again.

Dont look and another number. Roisin tabbed her own number back. Out of the corner of her eye she saw a balding, crop-haired, clean-shaven man in a dark linen suit glance at his watch and hurry out, briefcase in one hand, bagel in the other.

Roisin finished her coffee, picked up her bags, slipped the paper under her elbow, and left the store. She walked across the car park, crossed the main road and another car park, and headed in to the pedestrianized town center. She bought a book of stamps at a newsagent, stuck most of them on the envelope, and posted it at a pillar-box. At the far side of the town center, a couple of minutes' walk farther on, she sat down on a low brick wall and waited for the Edinburgh bus. There wasn't much of a queue. Beside her a young woman, dressed very similarly to herself, sat with arms folded across the handles of a buggy in which a small girl alternated between crying and sucking on a dummy-shaped sweet.

After a few minutes Roisin felt an unfamiliar sting on her calves, and wished she had picked up suncream while she'd had the chance. She dug out the Nano cream, which soothed her skin for a bit. She stood up and shifted to the shade of the bus shelter. The woman and the infant observed her with parallel blank stares. Roisin turned away and scanned the timetable. The next bus for Edinburgh via Kincardine was due in five minutes. She wondered if the others had made it on to their separate transports. The plan was for Claire to head up the covered walkway to the station and take the branch line to Dunfermline. Mad Jack had claimed he would hitch a ride in a delivery truck from the supermarket. Respectably dressed and with a broad repertoire of patter and inside knowledge picked up on his many short-term jobs, he probably could.

Roisin wondered where he had picked up the tradecraft of their disguises and departures. She knew, without really knowing how she knew, that it wouldn't have been enough to fool a dedicated surveillance effort or pursuit, but might be enough to cover their tracks on any trawl through CCTV footage. Her father, in the past couple of years, had made certain arrangements with her. He had been insistent that they should have them, in case she ever found herself on the run. This too now struck her as odd. At the time it had seemed a continuation of the sort of unasked-for information he'd bestowed on her since childhood: a side-of-the-mouth education in obscure macho matters that tended to come up when they were watching television news, about codes and secrecy, weapons and factions, armies and aircraft. Only Mad Jack Armitage, among her acquaintance, knew more about aircraft than her father.

She remembered sitting on the sofa beside her father and his explaining the difference between AK47s and M-16s, and how that was no guide to who had supplied the weapons to whatever gang was waving them about. Complicated tales about Kurds and Shias, MPLA and UNITA, PLO and PFLP and other strings of initials. As far as she could recall, he didn't systematically impart the same arcana to her brother Alec. It was as if her father thought that this was the sort of thing a girl should know, and might not learn from anyone else, whereas a boy could be expected to pick it up for himself.

Now that she thought about it, the knowledge had

been more useful to her at university than it would ever have been to Alec in the Army.

Her mother had taught her other things, less definite but larger. Roisin remembered an excited train journey, from London up to Edinburgh, and walking for miles from a park in a huge crowd, and back to the same park. She had worn a white T-shirt with black lettering, and a big straw hat against the sun. Her mother had worn a long swirly white skirt in the fashion of that summer, and carried a placard. The whole memory of that weekend was confused, the sea of white spattered with red an eerie foreshadowing of television images of a blown-up bus and blood; the throb of music segueing into the sound of sirens and helicopters.

Out of the confusion and fear of that July week long ago, Roisin had sometimes thought, had come her university studies, her activism, all that she now was; a need to understand what was going on in the world, and an urge to make it stop.

———

The bus arrived, about half full. The people on it didn't look as if they were fleeing anywhere. Roisin waited while the woman beside her cajoled the child from the buggy, collapsed the buggy, cajoled the child again, then lost patience and swung child and buggy together on to the bus. Roisin passed over a twenty-euro note for a ticket to Edinburgh. She expected change and didn't get any. She found a seat near the front and sat down with the pack between her feet. The bus lurched off, swayed around a roundabout, and headed along a long street out of town. Another roundabout, then the open road. Roisin dozed. She jolted awake to a buzz of talk among the passengers. The bus idled in a tailback. A sign showed they were entering Kincardine. She listened to the buzz and caught the word "radiation."

It was like water thrown in her face. She pulled out her phone, clipped the bead to her ear, and flicked the screen to Sky News. The picture was a static archive shot of the nuclear power station at Torness, about thirty miles down the coast. The news was that a radiation-leak monitor had been tripped and had put the reactor into automatic shutdown. The explanation was that there was no leak, and that the monitor had responded to airborne radioactivity from Leuchars. Background information scrolled along the bottom of the screen, citing precedents. Roisin saw the words "Chernobyl" and "fall-out" and "plume." She was not much reassured to learn, on closer reading, that almost all of the fallout plume was over the sea and the radiation level was in any case surprisingly low. She guessed that her fellow passengers would be reassured even less. Half of them crowded forward, waited as the bus crawled in the slow traffic, and got off at the next stop, just before the turnoff to the bridge. Roisin glanced back at the remaining passengers and saw the woman with the buggy, who nodded and half-smiled before relapsing into a look of helpless resignation.

Across the long, low Kincardine Bridge over the Forth, and then on to a road where the traffic opened out a bit, and finally to the motorway. As the bus barreled down the on-ramp Roisin looked out of the window at the pipework and tall flues of the oil refinery at Grangemouth, a mile or so to her left. Banners of flame, pale in the sunlight, flickered from the tops of the flues.

Then brighter flames, nearer the ground. Roisin started forward. That wasn't right.

The view was hidden by earthworks at the moment the bus joined the main flow of traffic. As it emerged from behind the grassy berm Roisin saw the entire refinery erupt in a mass of yellow flame. A moment later the flame vanished behind a wall of black. She saw the wall roll across the level ground between the refinery and the motorway.

"Hold on!" she yelled, bracing her knees against the back of the seat in front and grabbing its edge.

Everything went dark. There was a noise like a gigantic clap that made her chest shake. The bus rocked to the right and tilted. Things slid and flew, Roisin clung. The screams of people were louder than those of the tires and brakes. Then the bus banged back onto its nearside wheels and the darkness was replaced by a glare of light. The driver swerved right, past two entangled cars that scraped along the side of the bus, then it was steady again and moving forward slowly.

The middle of the sky to the left was a jet of flame, red at the base and going through yellow to blue. Around it, lazy black clouds rose and roiled into red. It cast shadows across the road. Through the back window Roisin could see no vehicles behind. On the other lane the traffic going the opposite way had come to a complete halt, and not all by choice. She watched three collisions then turned away and looked behind in the bus again. The other passengers were white-faced and shaking, but seemed unharmed. The woman who had gotten on with her was bowed over the child, who was bleeding from the head.

Roisin stood up and went back to try to help. A woman behind the mother beat her to it, checking the child's cheeks and eyes, murmuring concern and advice. She looked up as Roisin approached.

"Wean's got concussion, possible hairline fracture," she said. "Got any cold water?"

"Yes," said Roisin. She fetched out a water bottle. The

helpful woman poured some on folded paper tissues. She already had the child laid out along the seat.

"Got to get her tae a hospital," she said. "Go and tell the driver tae step on it, hen."

Roisin walked to the front of the bus and did so. The driver complied, but after another few minutes the only thing he could step on was the brake. Roisin looked before and behind. All the traffic had come to a complete halt.

"What's going on?" Roisin demanded.

The driver gestured to her ear-bead.

"You tell me," he said.

PART TWO

The Planck Anomalies

5

As James Travis drove north along the M40 toward Birmingham he tried with mixed success to steer his mind from futile worries about his son and his daughter, and from even more profitless concern with his own situation. At the times when he did succeed he found his mind turning, as it often did in moments of mental idleness, to the Planck Anomalies.

These discrepant observations of the fine grain of the universe, still unaccounted for years after an ESA probe had enabled ever-closer inspection of minute fluctuations in the Cosmic Radiation Background, had this spring re-emerged into popular, or at least into informed, awareness. It was because of another probe. The refusal of the US Congress to allocate funds to process the data returned from Pioneer, now beyond the orbit around Pluto, was a standing scandal. It was not one that had much traction; NASA's focus on the manned program and on servicing the USAF's Space Command was too entrenched to protest. What had broadened the topic, spreading it from *Nature* and *Science* to *New Scientist* and *Scientific American* to the serious and then the frivolous press, and beyond that to an expanding penumbra of online debate, was the rumor that data was indeed being processed, and the results suppressed.

Leaks and rumors hinted that the Pioneer results had

revealed new anomalies, both in the data returned from the planet and in the orbital course of the distant machine itself, and that these illuminated the half-forgotten puzzles from Planck. Like many IT professionals, Travis fancied himself a failed scientist—his degree had been in Physics—and he had attended to the ruckus. The official NASA and ESA insistence that some obscure malfunction or miscalculation could account for the anomalies had been widely derided. The least speculative conclusion jumped to was that something was amiss in the small print of Newton. A bolder one was that the Big Bang theory could no longer be patched: one epicycle too many and the whole baroque Ptolemaic orrery of the standard model had gone spinning off into the dark. At the extreme, a cadre of philosophic radicals hailed the anomalies as evidence that the universe was fundamentally different from that envisaged by astronomy.

As to the precise nature of the universe, the extremists divided. Some held that the whole thing was a simulation, created by artificial intelligences in what humanity had conceived of as its future. It had long been argued that the universe known to human consciousness could, in a posthuman future, be simulated many times, but could have happened at most once; and therefore the overwhelming probability was that humanity inhabited one of the simulations. This had reached street level as "the Matrix theory." Another school of thought maintained that the reality of the universe could be confirmed as far as probes had ventured; but that anything beyond the Kuiper Belt could be a colossal construction or illusion. This was known as "the Planetarium possibility."

Travis dismissed the Matrix theory as undisprovable, and the Planetarium possibility as far-fetched. What troubled him was the sincerity and intelligence with which they had been advanced, and their surprising popularity. Not since the Cydonia debacle had there been such a gulf between the established and the believed. It was as if people wanted to doubt the reality of their lives, and the solidity of things.

The container truck a hundred meters ahead of him stopped and slewed across the road. Travis had to brake so hard the seat belt bruised his chest.

———

Jeff Paulson looked at the snarl of arrowed lines that Andrew MacIntyre had light-penned across the screen. Behind it were databases that drew on NSA, Echelon, and GCHQ intercepts, and no doubt others as well. James Travis had been exposed as an agent of the French intelligence service the previous night. That news was what had dragged Maxine Smith away from a routine embassy function. All records of James Travis's work at Result—which included a disturbing number of government contracts—were being frantically turned over at this moment. It was the connection or coincidence of two other names that had brought Smith up from London, and had brought the three operatives together. Paulson's regular job included liaison with Andrew MacIntyre. The Special Branch ran informants in the local antiwar movement, and the phone calls and emails of the peace-camp protesters were regularly monitored. For the first time, the trawl had snagged something of interest.

"Travis, Travis, and Travis," Paulson said. "Jeez. Sounds like a law firm."

"Uh huh," said MacIntyre. "Right little family business."

"That's unusual," said Maxine Smith.

"Not so much in the States," said Paulson. "Post–Cold War. No ideology. Business is the word."

Smith frowned. "Hmm. Let's not prejudge that."

"You think they might be Islamists?"

Smith shot him a look as if he'd made a joke in bad taste.

"Nah, they're in bed with the frigging Chinese." She shared a laugh with MacIntyre. Paulson didn't get it. He let it pass.

"Here's what I suggest," he said. "By the time the regulars pull in the white-van gang you could have asked that they process them separately, let Roisin Travis go as soon as possible, and you could put a tail on her. James Travis did say he was coming for her."

"I don't think she'll lead us straight to her father," said MacIntyre. "She's no that naïve, whatever she is."

"Indeed," said Paulson. "She'll probably go straight to the Stoppers. You could make sure that one of your people is there when she does. It shouldn't be too hard to make her sudden release look suspicious. If she starts casting aspersions about, well"—he circled a finger in the air—"your friend can take it from there."

"Nice one," said MacIntyre, texting fast.

"What about soldier boy?" Smith asked, or wondered aloud.

"Throw the book at him," said Paulson. "See what sticks."

"Oh, I think plenty will stick," said Smith. She thumbed her phone. "Liaison?"

"Of course," said Paulson. He beamed her a number.

"Thanks."

"We'll need to make sure his blog's kept updated after—"

Smith nodded at him, with an impatient glance up

from her phone. "Well, it's your lot who run the key-board commandos. Even for Brits, right?"

"Sure," said Paulson. It was a Homeland Security gig, not Agency, but he didn't feel this was the moment to say so. He swept up Alec Travis's details from the screen, edited out a few irrelevancies, tapped out instructions, and zapped the lot through to the consulate relay. A second or two after sending it, his phone buzzed. The phones of the two Brits buzzed too, one after the other. The message Paulson read struck him like a blow. For a moment he fought for breath. It was the feeling of a second punch.

He waved a frantic hand at the television.

"Clear the screen!" he said. MacIntyre was already doing it. The screen lit with leaping flames.

"Holy fucking shit," said Smith.

They were still gazing at the devastation of Grange-mouth when the news came in of the collapse of a motor-way intersection just outside Birmingham. It was a third punch: explosions had been seen at the pillars. As the first shaky pictures were phoned in Paulson fought down a feeling he hadn't had since he'd watched 9/11 in his teens. It was a deeper insecurity than he had ever experienced in Tehran: the sense of repeated, coordinated blows from an unseen enemy, and of not knowing what was coming next.

He seized on the only thing that could refute his help-lessness.

"We aren't in cleanup mode anymore," he said. "This is a combat operation."

————

Travis got out of the Land Rover and exchanged insurance details with the driver of the car behind, which had rear-ended him and come off worse in the encounter. The details he gave were genuine, up to a point. He used a paper notebook, not his phone, so he had no way of checking those he had received, but all he was looking at was a paint job. There was a risk in giving real information, but less than that of giving false details that might be exposed while the driver of the other car was sitting right behind him. A complaint would put the Land Rover's registration on a police computer somewhere, if it wasn't on one already. Travis had laid preparations for that contingency long before, but he was in no mood to push his luck.

Even if his luck seemed, in a manner of speaking, good.

He looked up and down the motorway. Behind him and the pranged car a long tail of others stretched out of sight around the curve. Ahead, past the jackknifed container lorry which still blocked two of the three lanes, lay the pileup. According to the car radio, which he'd switched on immediately, about a hundred vehicles were mashed together up there. Similar numbers were piled up on the other two approaches to the interchange.

Travis climbed back to his seat, turned his phone from map to news, and looked at the incoming pictures. At least half the vehicles in all three pileups were wrapped around dead or seriously injured people. That wasn't the worst of it. The worst of it, which he could now see in a shot from the Virgin ambulance helicopter hovering up ahead, was the hundreds of other vehicles that had been on the overpasses, underpasses, and bridges when the support pillars had gone down, or whose drivers had been unable to stop when the road in front of them fell away. A chance use of a phone camera had delivered shots of that, too, like a chase-movie stunt.

Every minute or so the news ran a loop of speed-camera footage: flashes, then puffs of smoke or dust coming from a support pillar, followed by that entire section of the pillar showing daylight for a moment before the overpass came down. After a couple of iterations of this, interspersed with phoned-in pictures—some from inside crushed cars, with voiceover screams and pleas—the news cut away.

"And now," said the announcer, "back to Grangemouth, where . . ."

Travis closed his eyes, then opened them. The pictures were still there.

A map came up showing jagged yellow stars at three locations: Leuchars, Grangemouth, Birmingham. A smudged question mark hung over a fourth: the nuclear power station at Torness. It was the first he'd heard about that.

The caption read: BRITAIN UNDER ATTACK.

It seemed a reasonable conclusion. Travis had expected a campaign of systematic, soft-target, mass-casualty attacks for years, and it hadn't happened. The Rosyth naval dockyard bombing, four years earlier, had never been followed up. The mass-transit suicide bombs in London, Manchester, Birmingham, and Glasgow had been bloody gestures, *attentats*, propaganda by deed that had killed hundreds and had achieved nothing else.

Today's events didn't strike him as attention-seeking behavior. They didn't all fit together. The Leuchars nuke was the outlier; the Torness shutdown, a perhaps accidental consequence. He knew from Roisin's heavy hint or slip of the tongue that she had received some warning about Leuchars. That was why he couldn't accept the line that it was a weapons-handling accident. But nor could he accept that it belonged with what had happened right in front of him and what had happened at Grangemouth. It was too far out of proportion.

Unless, unless . . . the Leuchars nuke had been taken

as a signal, and had activated a network that had nothing to do with it. Sleeper cells, instructed to go into action as soon as something big enough happened. Or something bigger looked like it was about to happen. A sabotage network with deep enough cover to enable them to plant explosives in motorway flyover pillars and in an oil refinery. A network with some strategic thought behind it, that could hit at the most vulnerable points of an industrial society, that could sever blood vessel and nerve center and tendon and take it apart limb by limb.

It didn't sound like Al Qaeda. So who else might it be?

"Shit, shit, shit," Travis said.

He hoped he would have a chance to take up the question with Gauthier.

————

His immediate problem, though, was what to do next. In a tool chest in the back of the Land Rover he had a yellow flashing light with a magnetic base. Slapping it on the roof, turning out of the blocked traffic, and going back along the motorway was a tempting possibility. All the lanes behind him were jammed, but the other side of the motorway was clear. There was a gap in the rail of the central reservation just ahead, where the trailer of the skidding lorry had swept it away. The difficulty was that he would draw attention, particularly by posing as an emergency vehicle. Genuine emergency vehicles were, he hoped, already on their way down the empty side of the motorway.

On the other hand, he and everyone else were likely to be stuck here for hours. In that time, it was possible that all the false information and corrupted processing he had long ago laid to cover his and the vehicle's electronic trail would be penetrated. His best chance was to keep moving.

Travis rummaged up the lamp, returned to his seat and clapped the device to the roof, and started up the engine and the flashing light. He eased the Land Rover out of the queue and across the lane to the gap. He stopped before crossing the gap, leaned out of the window, and beckoned to the first few drivers who'd been behind him. They stared at him. He repeated the gesture with more emphasis, then bumped across the central reservation and set off up the other side of the motorway, doing about twenty. One by one, drivers broke away from the tailback and followed. He drove slowly until there were a dozen or so behind him and a continuing flow across the middle of the road, then sped up a little. He kept within the left-hand lane. Nobody tried to overtake. He could see the jam on the other side inching forward, beginning to clear. The flow he had started was continuing. In the rearview mirror the column looked unbroken, with everyone driving along at about forty and leaving a safe space.

As he had expected, within ten minutes ambulances and police cars passed in the opposite direction, lights flashing and sirens howling. A couple of minutes later, to his further lack of surprise, he saw ahead of him a brace of police Jeeps, headlights on and warning lights rippling, straddling the lane a kilometer or so ahead. He braked, cruising to a smooth halt a hundred meters from the roadblock. A black speck lifted from behind the cars and darted forward. As it came closer it resolved into a meter-wide enclosed rotor, fin-stabilized, its rim beady with lenses: a remote-controlled drone. It hovered in front of the windscreen. Travis blinked as the red vertical of a laser scan flickered across his eyes. Then the drone soared straight up and scooted back to the cars. Much farther overhead, a small helicopter drifted from above the other lane and stared down at the scene with dragonfly eyes.

A police officer, burly with Kevlar and bright with fluorescent plastic, marched forward and motioned Travis to get out. Travis complied, keeping his hands in plain sight. He strolled forward to meet the policeman, stopping when he could see his own reflection in the other's shades.

"Yes, officer," Travis said, "what seems to be the trouble?"

The cop gestured at the now stationary column.

"This lot's the trouble," he said. "The motorway's closed."

"I'm sorry, officer, I wasn't aware of that," said Travis. He glanced over his shoulder. "I noticed a gap in the safety rail back there and used my initiative. I'll leave the motorway at the first available exit, and I expect the other drivers will do the same."

"You know it's illegal to cross the central reservation?"

"Of course, officer, but in the circumstances . . ." He was careful not to shrug.

"Let's see your ID."

Travis handed over a card. The cop waved a phone across it, and peered at the card, the phone, and Travis. A speaker in his helmet crackled. Travis could see the tiny sway of his head.

"All right," he said, handing back the card. "There's an exit a mile down the road. Get off there and stay off."

"Thank you," said Travis.

He returned to the Land Rover. The cop, in sudden haste, ran to the cars. The chopper overhead found more interesting sights. The Jeeps joined the rush to the collapsed junction. Travis turned the engine on, stuck his arm out of the window, and brought his open hand forward as he engaged first gear.

"Wagons . . . roll!" he said to no one in particular. As soon as he reached cruising speed he switched the phone back to the Galileo sat-nav map and its moving bead. The last picture he saw before the screen flipped was of the Land Rover and the two cop cars, then a zoom to two figures on the road.

He took the next exit, the column following, and at the first opportunity turned off into the byways and suburban streets. He passed through Dorridge, then over the M42, on which nothing moved. In Solihull he let the sat-nav guide him. He turned a corner into a long street of brick-built houses and small shops and drove straight into a riot.

———

- Larisa Sosnitskaya; Russian Federation; cranial shot; serial murder.

- Ahmed Wazirih; Syria; repeated application of legitmate force culminating in cerebral hemorrhage; terrorism.

- Abraham Irwin; Texas; multiple gunshot; looting.

6

I'll never forget your face
your name, religion and race,
your mother's maiden name
the people you go to see
or who drop by at your place
and whatever it was you said
the last time you spoke to me . . .

The pop song's sentimental sound and sinister words leaked from the young mother's ear-bead. She trudged along the hard shoulder behind the buggy, whose seat had been tilted back so that the injured child lay on her back with her head slightly raised, with a wet folded T-shirt across her forehead. The mother's name was Cara, the child's was Keira. The child's face was white, her eyes open and responding to light, her breathing normal apart from when she moaned. Blood had dried on her scalp, but now and again some mixture of blood and mucus slithered and bubbled from her nostrils. Five ambulances had gone by, weaving through gaps in the stalled traffic or hurtling along the hard shoulder, and had not stopped.

Roisin sweated in the noonday heat, matching her pace to Cara's plod, and wondered how much of her supposed nanoparticle camouflage had dripped away. She and Cara had been walking for about a quarter of an hour. The medically competent woman on the bus, a nurse, had set off on her own in the opposite direction, toward the scene of the refinery explosion and the crashes, and had advised Cara to head for the nearest off-ramp and try to hitchhike to the nearest hospital or GP clinic. Roisin had chosen to accompany them, from sympathy and because she didn't fancy staying too long on the bus. The bus wasn't going anywhere soon, and neither was any other vehicle on that road.

So now she was walking past six lanes of stationary vehicles, along a monotonous stretch of motorway with high grassy banks on either side. Black smoke filled half the sky behind them and had begun to overhang them, pushed forward by the wind from the west that had carried the Leuchars plume out to sea. What Roisin was listening to on her ear-bead was not music but the news. The mobile phone network was down locally, but the phone's radio still worked. All motorway traffic in Britain had been stopped. Five more intersections had gone down. Two more refineries and three fuel-oil depots had gone up. Roisin doubted that she was a priority. The Leuchars Event—as it was now being called—had been relegated by these fresher disasters, which were already being called attacks.

Roisin didn't like their being called attacks. Call them terrorism or sabotage and you had their measure. You knew how to respond: search and rescue, security cordons, manhunts. Attacks incited a different response: defense and retaliation. It had already begun, in street scuffles and petrol bombings against Muslims and Asians. What made her grind her teeth was what these incidents were called: revenge attacks.

Part of her mind reeled off mental drafts of the texts of complaint she might in other circumstances have sent. *How many Muslims and Asians are lying mangled in these crashes and ruins? If Britain's under attack we're all under attack, not just white people! How divisive and irresponsible are you trying to be?* Another part did feel under attack and did feel like hitting back and didn't much care if it hit the right target, because whoever it hit had it coming for *something,* even if only their readiness to defect.

A third part, high above, like the hovering goshawk that inspected the grassy bank to her left, looked down on this *fucking* typical *fucking* liberal *fucking* pacifist dither and scruple and futility.

This was the thing: everybody knew. Everybody knew it was all about oil. Everybody knew the votes weren't counted. Everybody knew who won or lost. Everybody knew the Fix was in. Joining the protest camp had been as quixotic a gesture as Alex's joining the Army.

Her father had disapproved of both. Late the night of the restaurant party to celebrate her graduation, James had sat with his shirtsleeve elbow in spilt masala and sniffed a balloon glass of cognac and said:

"Ah, that's where you're wrong, you see: Armageddon *is* the Rapture."

"What?"

"Millions of stupid Yanks going straight up into the sky."

"Dad, that is *sick.*"

"Thanks, Roisin, I do my best."

Then he'd called for a cigar and grumbled when he had to smoke it outside.

———

Just as they reached the off-ramp, after walking about a kilometer, the traffic began to move again. Roisin could see the traffic cops at the bottom of the ramp checking each car—registration, everyone's ID, glance in the foot-wells, poke in the boot—then waving the cars off one by one. It was another security cordon, though a thin one, this time for Grangemouth. She quickened her pace and waved a hand in front of Cara's face. The woman tapped her ear-bead and the trickle of music ceased.

"What?"

"We can start hitching now," Roisin said. "You get a lift and I'll head back to the bus." It was the only ruse she could think of at that moment.

Cara gazed around as if coming out of a trance.

"Aye, good idea."

They turned and stood on the verge of the off-ramp, thumbs out. A few cars passed. Roisin saw a police Jeep cut across from the motorway's outer lane and into the queue for the ramp. It was that car that stopped.

A WPC leaned out.

"What's the problem, ladies?" she asked.

Cara told her what the problem was. She turned to consult the man in the driver's seat, then turned back.

"There's a clinic in Queensferry," she said. "We're on our way there anyway. Jump in."

She got out and opened the back door. Cara lifted the child out and Roisin folded the buggy, passing it in as Cara slid onto the seat and sat down with the child across her lap.

"Get in," said the WPC, as Roisin hung back. "Plenty of room."

"It's all right," she said. "I'm heading into Edinburgh."

"The buses from the Ferry are still running," the WPC said. "They're the quickest way you'll get into town."

"It's . . ." Roisin hesitated. The WPC's brow was just beginning to cloud.

"Very kind of you," Roisin finished, and got in. The door slammed.

She was still trying to fit the tongue of the seat-belt buckle into the slot when the acceleration pressed her to the back of the seat and the siren's *ee-aw* started. Down the off-ramp, hard left and into the wrong lane, a fast right and a lot of weaving and overtaking. Hedges and trees whipped past. The WPC looked back over her shoulder.

"It's good to be able to do this," she said. "I felt so helpless back there. It's terrible. Burns and everything."

"Where are they taking the casualties?" Roisin asked.

"St. John's, Livingston, even Stirling. A and E will be just about overwhelmed. Lucky for the little girl they haven't piled into the GP's at Tesco. Yet."

"GP's? She needs a hospital," said Cara. "A nurse on the bus told us."

"They have X-ray and ultrasound scan there, don't worry," the driver said. "Anyway, you'll not see the inside of a hospital for that at the moment."

"She could have brain damage," Cara said, sounding tearful and petulant.

"Aye," said the WPC. "She'd still have to wait her turn behind those who definitely have brain damage, and worse."

Roisin leaned across and squeezed Cara's hand. She hoped she would just shut up. A village with a pub and a petrol station flashed past, the siren's complaint echoing off low stone houses. Around a curve and over a crest. The Forth bridges appeared. The sky far to the northeast looked hazy and undisturbed. The car swooped through a long dip.

"How did you two meet?" the WPC asked.

"We were on the same bus," said Cara.

"Which bus was it?"

"The one fae Alloa," said Cara.

"That where you live?"

"Yeah," said Cara. "We were just going to see my mammy in Edinburgh, she was worried." She sniffled again. "About aw this bombing and that."

The WPC turned farther around and gave Roisin a smile. "And yourself?"

"Just visiting a friend. Stayed over." She hoped her expression showed nothing but some slight embarrassment.

"Been in Edinburgh long?"

"A few months," said Roisin. "I came up from London last year."

The WPC turned away with a muttered "Uh-huh."

Roisin was sure that she had given herself away. Her accent didn't fit her clothes. The Jeep cleared two roundabouts and swung into a supermarket car park and juddered to a stop outside the sliding glass doors of an extension with a green cross above it.

"Here we are," said the driver. He grinned over his shoulder. "Seven minutes, thirty seconds. No bad."

"Thanks a million," said Cara. The driver jumped out and opened the door for her. She got out. Roisin hefted the folded buggy after her. The policeman caught it and rattled it into shape. Roisin, dragging her pack from the floor, slid along the seat to follow Cara out.

"Just a moment," said the WPC.

"Yes?"

Roisin turned her head, seeing in the corner of her eye the policeman take Cara's elbow and guide her and wheel the buggy into the walk-in clinic's reception.

"What did you say your name was?"

"I didn't, actually." She said it as lightly as she could.

"Sorry to be a pest," said the WPC, thumbing a phone, "but I need your name and ID to log the incident. Regulations, you know? Especially taking you in the car, it has to be justified."

Roisin ducked to hide the pallor she knew had drained her face and groped down into her pack past the boots and old clothes. She considered jumping out and running. From the glimpses she'd had, the site was surrounded by roads and she didn't know the area anyway. Oh well, fuck, here goes, she thought. Her fingertips closed on her wallet. She tugged it out and passed the ID card over. The WPC waved it in front of the phone and passed it back.

"That's fine," she said. "You can go."

Roisin was sure the tremor of her hand was obvious as she retrieved the card.

"Thanks," she said. "Thanks for everything."

"You're welcome."

Roisin gave a tight smile and backed out. She closed the door and swung her pack to one shoulder and looked around for the bus stop. There it was, a dozen meters away.

The clinic doors hissed open and the policeman hurtled through, straight at her. He had her on the ground and her wrists cuffed before she could draw breath. He squatted back on his heels with one hand pressing down on the side of her head, and one knee on the base of her spine. Roisin stared sideways at tarmac and chewing gum, and then at a pair of brisk black shoes. The WPC's voice came from a great height.

"Roisin Travis, I'm detaining you under the Serious Crimes and Terrorism Act. You do not have to say anything, but . . ."

Roisin listened to her rights and remained silent.

———

She remained silent throughout another fast drive, a longer one, all the way into Edinburgh via a series of back roads and side streets. She tried to keep track of where they were going but became hopelessly lost. They stopped outside a fortified police station on the edge of a housing estate. Twentieth-century identical semis and trampled swing park. Inside it was search, sign for property, scan, photos, dabs, cell. After a quarter of an hour staring at tiles she was taken to an interview room. The WPC who had arrested her sat behind the table. Roisin sat down and faced her across it. A CCTV camera in the ceiling's corner watched them both. The door opened again and another woman came in. She had curly black hair and she looked like she was in her mid-thirties. She wore a black suit that didn't fit as exactly as it should have, over a soft-pleated white blouse that didn't go with it at all. She carried a handbag that didn't go with either, and a legal pad. Roisin thought she was the lawyer and wondered why she wore supermarket.

She went behind the table and sat down beside the WPC. Not a lawyer. She laid her forearms on the table, sleeves going back inches and the suit shoulders riding up, and interlaced her ringless fingers.

"Miss Travis," she said in a kindly tone and London accent as the WPC checked that the CCTV camera was running. "You aren't under arrest. You're being held without charge under the Terrorism Act. Has that been explained to you?"

Roisin nodded.

"And you do understand what that means?"

"Yes."

"I very much doubt that," the woman said. "For one thing, you expected a lawyer." She turned to the WPC and shared a smirk, which on the WPC's part looked forced, then faced Roisin again.

"I'm not a lawyer. I'm not a cop, either. You can call me Smith. No, really, that's my name. I'm a civilian, and although I'm not a lawyer I am here to help you."

Roisin folded her arms. Smith smiled.

"You see, Miss Travis, you do have a choice. You can have a civilized conversation with me and my colleague, WPC Gilliland here. Or, if you say nothing or tell us something we know isn't true, you can have a series of less and less civilized conversations with our colleagues in a series of other places. Oh, I know you and your friends have joked about Gitmo. Your sort always do. Let me assure you, Miss Travis, there are places you can find yourself in where you would wish to God you were in Gitmo. But we don't want that, do we?"

Roisin pressed her knees together to stop them shaking. She unfolded her arms and spread her hands wide and took a deep breath.

"All right," she said. "I've only kept quiet because nobody has asked me anything, and I don't know what it is I'm accused of—"

"You haven't been accused of anything," said WPC Gilliland.

"Oh," said Roisin. "So I can go?"

"That's not how it works," said Smith. "As you know."

"Fine," said Roisin. "Ask me anything you like."

Smith shook her head. "That isn't how it works, either. If you're willing to cooperate, you'll tell us what you know. I would advise you not to waste our time."

"No, that wasn't—"

"People are being murdered as we speak," said Smith.

"If you know anything about why they are dying, or anything that could prevent further murders, it would be as well for you to say so straight away."

That was the closest anyone had come so far to asking a question. Roisin had known why she had been picked up but she hadn't known the angle.

"Of course," Roisin said. "Well, the only thing I know that might be relevant to that—"

"Relevance is our business," said Gilliland. "Yours is to tell us what you know."

"What I was going to say," Roisin went on, "is that I saw the device that exploded at Leuchars."

Smith and Gilliland assumed the same poker face at the same moment.

"Well, to be exact I saw a strange device at the base just before the explosion. It might be just a coincidence. And the other thing I wanted to say is I don't know anything about all the other explosions, apart from being in a bus that got shaken up by the one at Grangemouth."

"I mentioned wasting time," said Smith. "You would be very well advised to tell us *how* you came to see this supposed mysterious device, *what* you saw, and *how* you and your friends happened to be driving away very fast when the explosion happened. Because, you know, that last point doesn't look good. It doesn't look good at all."

"You mean you think we had something to *do* with it?"

"What I said about wasting time," said Smith.

"Well all right," said Roisin. "You know who I am and all the stuff on my ID. I've been staying for six months at the Leuchars peace camp. My brother's in the Army in Kazakhstan. I read his blog. Last night—yesterday evening he said something on it that made me think that maybe there would be something unusual—"

Smith cleared her throat and glanced at the wall clock.

"He said there was a bit of a Flap going on, and that you could hear it all the way to Fife. That's his exact words as far as I remember. And I know when he says 'Flap' he means something to do with flying, with aeroplanes, okay? And 'Fife' had to be Leuchars."

"So he sends you coded messages," said Gilliland.

"No! It's just a joke, lots of soldiers' blogs have ways of referring—"

"I'm aware of such security lapses," said Smith. "Forget about that and go on." She didn't look at Gilliland but Roisin had the impression she would have preferred the WPC to have kept her mouth shut.

"So I went off through the woods, right up to the perimeter, and waited. And sure enough . . ."

She went on to recount everything that had happened, leaving out only the photography, and the names of her companions. At one point she asked for pen and paper, and sketched the device on a page torn from the legal pad. Gilliland frowned over the drawing; Smith, who was, Roisin guessed, some kind of intelligence officer, glanced at it without a twitch, looked up, and nodded to Roisin to go on. She took notes.

When Roisin had finished, Smith closed her eyes, placed her thumb and middle finger across her temples, and massaged them briefly. Then she smoothed her eyebrows and looked up.

"What I don't quite follow," she said, "is why you went to such lengths to evade detection. You say you knew it would look bad that you had received a warning and that you had run away just in time to escape the explosion. Yet you must have known that if we were interested in you, we would pick you up sooner or later. And when we did—as we have—your evasive actions which, I may say, suggest a degree of skill and forethought, would make you look even more suspect—as they do. What do you have to say to that?"

"I suppose we were in a bit of a panic, we weren't thinking very clearly—"

"No!" Smith slapped the table and sprang to her feet. "*Now* you're in a panic! *Now* you're not thinking very clearly! This morning you were thinking very clearly indeed. You disguised yourselves and went your separate ways. The tradecraft was elementary but competent as far as it went. Where did you learn it?"

Roisin stared up at her. "I read a lot of spy novels," she said. "Anyway, if we'd been up to something we'd have had fake IDs."

"Spy novels." Smith inhaled through her teeth. She glared back at Roisin and sat down. "Spy novels." She drummed her fingernails on the table. She rattled out that rhythm a few times.

"Miss Travis," she said at last, "you disappoint me. You said nothing at all about the photographs. Your friends were much more forthcoming."

Roisin said nothing. The mention of photographs might be a bluff.

"Oh yes," Smith went on, "Miss Moyle and Mr. Cunningham alias Armitage have told us everything. They've been very cooperative. Whereas you, I'm afraid, have not. Now, last chance: is there anything else you're holding back?"

"No," said Roisin.

Smith pinched the bridge of her nose, as if spectacles had been resting there uncomfortably. She gathered up her pen, handbag, and pad.

"Fine," she said, standing up. "If that's the way you want to play it."

She walked past without looking at Roisin, paused at

the door, and said, "Take her back to the cells. I'll give the antiterrorism boys a call. Bye."

"Bye, ma'am," said Gilliland.

The door closed.

7

THE trouble with the Execution Channel, Mark Dark had often thought, was that it never showed *really satisfying* justice being meted out. Seeing a few sand nazis getting it in the head in Xingjiang, Khuzestan, or Chechnya was all very well, but it hardly outweighed the depressing parade of terrorist throat-cuttings, and state executions of perverts and retards, that made up the bulk of the channel's output. Not to mention the commie slaughter of various good guys in places like Bolivia and Nepal and the Red parts of China. What Mark wanted to see, and imagined every time he opened his inbox, was *spammers being beaten to death with baseball bats*. Now *that* would be righteous! *That* would be worth watching! Unfortunately there wasn't a jurisdiction in the world that treated spamming as a serious offense, let alone a capital one. To Mark this was a metric of the world's stupidity.

He sighed, sipped a Jolt, and plowed through the server's inbox, his right shoulder aching as he deleted the hundreds of spam messages that had made it past his fierce and constantly updated filters. When he'd finished he rubbed his shoulder, circled his arm a few times, and looked down the headers of the morning's legitimate mail. Fan mail, hate mail, business mail—he dealt with them all with brisk detachment. For most he had boiler-plate replies. He left the serious stuff, the real meat, for last. Today there was a small clutch of emails from people he knew and trusted on the inside, soldiers and civil servants whose addresses, even when masked, retained their .mil or .gov tags. He pondered some neat leads on the Brits' current misfortunes. Finally his cursor settled on the last, a big post that he knew would be significant. It came via an anonymous remailing service that could be trusted, up to a point—it never sent spam, and it had sometimes been a conduit for very hot leaks indeed, but Mark was well aware that even if it wasn't actually run by some spook agency or other it was almost certainly used by them, precisely to plant disinformation on conspiracy theorists like himself. However, in a further twist, that meant that it had to be largely reliable. A honey trap, after all, must contain real honey.

Taking no chances, he moved the document to a fire-walled hard disk segment and ran a first-pass antivirus sniffer program over it. It was clean. It contained six file attachments, each of about a megabyte, labelled AAV-210012.pdf through AAV-210017.pdf. Mark opened the first, drumming his fingers as Acrobat® cartwheeled through its proprietary advertising routines. The screen resolved into the first page. It was stamped with a classification so high that it was illegal for him to be aware that the level existed. Pausing only to verify it in his copy of the current standard illegal download of US Government internal acronyms and classifications, Mark scrolled on the contents page and the introduction, read them slowly, then started skimming. He followed the same procedure with the others.

When he'd finished he tilted his chair back and watched his knee vibrate.

The Advanced Aerial Vehicle 2100 was a triangular

stealth fighter-bomber capable of Mach 7, powered by something called a pulsed plasma fusion engine. Its stealth technology involved physics even more arcane: non-baryonic matter, which could somehow interact with photons to conceal the craft. The implication was that it bent light around itself. The first document, which was evidently not the first in the series, consisted mainly of dry test results from proving flights out of good old Area 51—Groom Lake, Nevada. The next two were about performance in combat missions, several of them flown out of the two big USAF bases on the east coast of Scotland, still called RAF Lossiemouth and RAF Leuchars, and the big base in Gloucestershire, England, just as misleadingly known as RAF Fairford. The fourth document, AAV-210015, dealt with technical problems and glitches, most of them to do with misfires of the engine. The final two documents detailed reports of civilian and hostile sightings of the craft, and with active disinformation measures taken in response: all the way from media censorship to the setting up and running of UFO investigation groups in a dozen countries. Photocopies of press clippings and screen grabs testified to the effectiveness of the campaign: if the craft was seen at all, which its advanced stealth technology made almost impossible, it was almost impossible *not* to see it as a UFO.

Mark checked the news sources. Every reference was authentic. He had expected no less. The North Sea UFO/mystery-aircraft story had been running for decades. He'd run the odd snippet about it himself. The trouble was, he'd never believed it. That advanced black-budget aircraft were tested over the Nevada desert was one thing; that they were secretly flown in combat missions out of bases on the east coast of Scotland or the middle of England was something else. The technology was another giveaway. There was just no way the knowledge and application of anything so advanced could be confined to a military aviation project.

"Pulsed plasma fusion," Mark said aloud. "Non-baryonic fucking matter. This is Majestic fucking Twelve."

This was something worth his best shot. Slowly, almost reverently, he made his way through a dozen encryption envelopes to a piece of software so illegal he had never used it before. It was a verification routine that checked the digital watermark of .pdf files of highly classified military documents, which he'd bought off a man who had worked in the Pentagon and was now running a travel agency in La Paz. Checking the impulse to look over his shoulder as bone-chilling legal boilerplate slithered down his screen, he ran the program over the files.

They passed.

"Good," Mark said. "Very good. Too fucking good to be true."

It was a classic double bubble setup: the intention, Mark did not doubt, was to lure him into publicizing the leak, which would then be discredited at exactly the right moment to make him look very foolish indeed.

There was a thrill in it all the same. To be targeted for such a perfect piece of disinformation, from so deep inside the security state, was just way cool.

"Awesome," Mark said. "Fucking A."

He hid all the documents in a folder of porn files, returned the authentication routine to safe storage, and started looking back over the past day's posts to try and figure out what it was he'd got right.

———

Travis braked hard. The Land Rover juddered to a halt a few meters from a skinhead who was in the act of hurling a brick. His target, to Travis's right, was the window of a corner shop. A second later the brick bounced off the thick metal mesh that covered the window. Another brick thudded against the shop's closed door. The street ahead milled with scores of running men, mostly young, who converged on the shop front. Two or three battered and kicked at the door, others swarmed onto the windows' grilles and began shaking them hard. Above the din Travis could hear a chant: "Mozzies out! Mozzies out!" Somebody with a builder's hammer got to work on the low brick wall around the building. Within seconds others were grabbing the loosened bricks, backing a few paces into the middle of the road and throwing them at the unprotected upstairs windows. The windows crashed in one by one. Shards of glass, and one or two bricks that had fallen short or missed and bounced off the wall, fell on the crowd around the door. By some malign miracle none of the attackers was hurt.

This all took about half a minute, the evident murderous intent rising like a flash flood in a ravine. Travis clung to the steering wheel as if it was a life belt. Farther down the hundred-meter-long street, flames and smoke from a couple of buildings obscured the road. Travis engaged reverse gear, looked over his shoulder, and backed the vehicle slowly toward the road he'd turned in from. He stopped just before the junction and glanced forward to check the wing mirror and saw a man running out of the smoke. The man had very short hair and wore the skinhead uniform of green bomber jacket, jeans, and Docs. He carried a bottle in one hand. He stopped in front of the shop and whirled around to face the doorway. Travis glimpsed a Union Jack patch on the shoulder of the man's jacket as his hands came together. He saw a quick repeated flick of the man's thumb and recognized it as trying to spark a flame from a depleted Zippo.

Travis had the vehicle in first gear and his left foot up and his right foot down just as the lighter finally took and the rag fuse on the bottle flared. Then the man had his arm back and his body half-turned for the throw. As he leaned and swivelled he saw the Land Rover bearing down. He jerked into a leap away about a second too late.

Travis heard the thump as the hood caught the man on the hip and then another thump as his head hit the windscreen. Flash of eyes and teeth then a smear of red down the glass. The man fell off to the side. The brakes squealed as Travis shifted his right foot. At the same moment there was a crash and a pop and the whole view in front bloomed into yellow fire.

Travis slammed the gear to reverse and hit the accelerator again. The vehicle shot backward. Travis twisted halfway over the back of the seat, steering with one hand and looking out of the rear window. He saw the top of a car flash past to the right, then heard a screech of brakes to his left. He looked out of that window and saw a white van still rocking from the stop three meters away. To the front he saw the burning petrol on the road, the man lying half in it, people running or standing and staring. A few flames still licked along the top of the hood. Out of the right window he saw a woman with a small child in tow darting out of a side door of the shop. She reached the edge of the pavement and looked up and down the street. Travis continued into a reverse left turn and then drove forward. He stopped beside where the woman stood, leaned over to the passenger side, and opened the door.

"Get in!" he shouted.

A face framed in a scarf looked back at him, eyes wide. Then a quick sideways glance and she'd grabbed the door handle. She pushed the child inside and jumped in after her and slammed the door. Travis didn't wait for them to fasten seat belts as he checked the wing mirror—nothing behind but the white van, still stationary—put his foot down, and pulled away. He didn't slow until he caught up with the interrupted traffic about a hundred meters farther on. Then he glanced sideways.

The child, on the middle seat, was a girl who looked about four years old. She had tousled black hair and snot-streaked cheeks and wore a long-sleeved T-shirt and jeans with child-size Nikes. The woman wore a blue-green salwar kameez with a gray scarf or shawl covering her head. Travis guessed she was old enough to be the girl's mother.

"Seat belts," he said, looking forward again. In the rearview the junction was still blocked by the van and by the crowd. Some were running after him. The woman buckled in and as she leaned sideways to click the girl's strap she looked up at Travis.

"Thank you," she said.

"Any time," Travis grunted.

"My husband—" she said.

"What?"

"He's still in the shop."

"Oh, Jesus fucking Christ," said Travis. He waved at the phone on the dash. "Call 999."

"We've done that," said the woman, waving her own phone. She had a Brummie accent. "Over and over."

"Jesus fucking Christ," said Travis again. It was on the tip of his tongue to add: *if the Mozzies hadn't blown up the fucking motorway then maybe . . .* How convenient it would be to think like a fascist, he thought, and said something else.

What he said was: "Phone your husband and tell him to stand by the door."

"Okay," the woman said.

"Stay on the call," said Travis. He slowed, waited for a gap in the traffic going the other way, then wrenched the wheel to take the vehicle into a U-turn. Horns blared. Travis ignored them, driving fast back up to the junction and swerving into the empty lane and toward the building on the corner. A small knot of youths were kicking at the side door that the woman and girl had come out of. They saw the Land Rover barrelling down on them and scattered. As he braked, mounting the pavement, Travis saw them regroup a short distance away and rally reinforcements. Travis unclipped his seat belt, leaned over the back of the seat, and raised the lid of a tool chest in the back. He groped inside, barking his knuckles, and his fingers closed around the grip of the Brocock air pistol. He twisted and slid back into the seat, bringing the seat belt across hard to the buckle and laying the pistol between his thighs.

"Now!" he said. The woman repeated it into the phone.

The building's side door flew open and a bearded man rushed out. He ran in front of the Land Rover and piled in to sprawl across his wife's knees. She calmly slammed the door.

"Keep your heads down and hold tight," said Travis.

He demonstrated, forearm crooked over the back of his head, then got both hands on the wheel. He gunned the engine again, released the brake, and shot forward then straight into a handbrake turn. He'd never attempted one before and was mildly surprised that it worked. Flames and smoke roared from the upper floor of the shop; the crowd was spread across the street, watching and yelling. Most scattered in front of the Land Rover, others a bit farther on gathered in the middle of the road. They had sticks and stones and more petrol bombs. As Travis accelerated toward them they let fly. He saw a bottle spinning on the hood right in front of him, trailing a circle of flame like a Catherine wheel. He swerved and the bottle skidded off to the left. The woman flinched and shouted as flame erupted by the passenger window.

None of the burning liquid stuck to the vehicle. Travis marvelled that the thugs didn't know to mix the petrol with liquid soap. But they were brave enough: their line across the road held as he drove at them. When it came to the bit he couldn't drive at a human being in cold blood. His blood wasn't exactly cold but it wasn't as hot as it had been when he'd run down the guy throwing the bomb at the shop.

He braked, elbowed the window switch, and drew the Brocock from his lap. The air pistol was a revolver with compressed-gas cartridges, illegal for years. Travis brandished it out of the window, aiming forward. If he had to pull the trigger his bluff would be called. The men and youths in front of him broke away at the last second. Travis put his foot down and accelerated away. A few sticks and bricks hit the roof and back of the van, and another petrol bomb burst in its wake. Travis weaved among burnt-out cars and through banks of smoke to emerge on a length of the street that looked quite untouched, under a clear sky broken only by columns of smoke between which military and police helicopters beat slow patrols.

The sat-nav on his phone let out a faint *beep*, as if gratified to find him back on his way.

8

THE room was air-conditioned, strip-lit; a little daylight made its way past the windows' steel covers. Rows of desks, racks of screens; a score or so of cops, uniformed and plainclothes. Quiet talk and raised voices, comings and goings. Holding the line against the chaotic traffic, mobbed stores, an implacable antiwar crowd outside the US Consulate, and the occasional flare of torched stores, American or Asian—a Starbucks here, a sari shop there—was the main preoccupation. A grudged handful of uniforms and a couple of Special Branch boys had been assigned to the cleanup team. The uniforms, supervised by Andrew MacIntyre, were searching phone records, scanning CCTV footage from in and around the Alloa supermarket, and trying to track the current locations of the two phones whose numbers were listed on the one confiscated from Roisin Travis. The SBs were out making shifty assignations with their contacts and informants—collaring touts, they'd called it. Jeff Paulson sat at one of the vacant SB desks. Its shelf panel, screen stand, and drawer ends were scaled with enough Scottish CND and Edinburgh Stop the War Coalition stickers to make Paulson wonder just how ironic the display was. The CCTV record of Roisin Travis's interrogation had been fed straight to the hard drive. Paulson was speed-shifting back through it when Maxine Smith walked in, fresh from that particular fray. She pulled up an orange plastic chair and sat down.

Her smile didn't wilt under Paulson's glare. He flicked a thumb at a frozen moment on the screen.

"That was an interrogation?" he said.

"Yup," said Smith. "A light one."

"You don't say. Looked more like an interview."

"Actually, it is an interview. That's what it's called, officially." She took two pinches of snuff, checked the mirror in the lid of the box, and scraped a speck of brown powder from her upper lip with an indelicate fingernail. "I thought it went well."

"Not as well as it could have gone," said Paulson, irritated. "If you'd shaken her to see what fell out."

"I don't do shaking," said Smith. "I leave that to the professionals."

"Well," said Paulson. "Make the call. Like you said."

Smith shook her head. "That was just to put the frighteners on her. She'll be all the more relieved when she's released. Shaken with relief, you might say." She glanced at her watch. "Let her sweat for a few hours."

"You're sticking with that plan?" cried Paulson.

"It's what we agreed."

"That was before the other shoes started dropping. Not to mention, before we knew what she'd seen, and—"

"The *other shoes*," said Smith, "that booted her right into the back of our net. As for what she'd seen—well, *that* was interesting, wasn't it?"

She slid a page from the yellow legal pad across the desk to him. Paulson frowned down at Roisin's sketch. Its labored awkwardness betrayed that she hadn't drawn since childhood; he'd noticed her tongue creep between her compressed lips as she toiled over it. Some kind of cylinder on a gimbal, with a coiled line like a telephone cord leading to a lectern beside which stood a matchstick man.

"That's what she saw? Some guy behind a—"

"The little man is to indicate scale," said Smith.

"Oh, great. If that's to scale then . . ." He looked up, shaking his head. "This could all be bullshit, you know. That doesn't look like anything I've ever seen."

"Looks like a telescope to me," said Smith. "Something astronomical. A big electronic camera, maybe."

"A telescope, yeah, well obviously . . ." He decided to play along, to brainstorm it. "An exploding camera. An exploding telescope. Now what could explode a telescope?"

Sourly, she humored him right back: "Blew its tiny electronic mind looking at the Planck Anomalies."

"The Planck Anomalies . . ." An elusive connection drifted in Paulson's mind. Something about streams of ionized gas, about particles being accelerated . . . He imagined a ray from the sky pointing down to the strange apparatus, and then the sense of the image flipped and he saw the beam pointing the other way, toward the sky.

"Look at it the other way," he said. "Think projector, not camera."

Smith flicked the sheet of paper back and squinted at it, turning it around.

"Like a searchlight?"

"It's a weapon!" he said. "A beam weapon."

"Could be," she said.

"I can see a beam weapon exploding," said Paulson. "Like an overloaded capacitor."

"Well, yes," said Smith. "If an electromagnetic field collapsed, I suppose . . . but a *nuclear* explosion?"

"Hey," said Paulson. "Can we be sure it was nuclear?

Radioactivity in the fallout was minimal. It's already been pegged as an anomaly."

"EMP," she reminded him.

"EMP," he said. "EMP." Something was bothering him. Some other goddamn anomaly. He closed his eyes and raised his finger. "Wait."

He followed the notion back, letting his mind drift, waiting for something to snag. He found himself recalling Roisin Travis's voice. His eyes opened, wide.

"Got it. Something the girl said."

He thumbed the desk screen, reeling back the interview, clocking minutes. It would be near the end. Fast-forwarded voices squealed and jabbered a few times before he caught it. He replayed the snatch:

"Somebody's phone went dead, and then we saw the flash, really bright, you know—like daylight, you could see in color."

Smith shook her head. "Nothing odd about that, you can see colors at night in a lightning flash—"

"Not that bit. The bit before. 'Somebody's phone went dead, and *then* we saw the flash.' Then. The EMP came before the explosion."

"Could be just confused in her memory."

"We can check that. There must be a record somewhere of the exact moments. Compare what the phone companies have, maybe the power companies, see if a spy-sat caught the flash—"

"Are you telling me to do this?" Smith interrupted.

"No, no, just talking to myself. I could ask the NSA."

"More like a job for GCHQ."

Paulson spread his hands. "Well?"

"All right, I can ask." Smith tapped at her phone. "I don't quite see the significance, though."

Paulson reminded himself of the Brit two cultures thing.

"When a nuclear or thermonuclear bomb goes off," he said, "the EMP and the flash happen at the same . . . nanosecond, I guess. So if there was a second's delay, then we're dealing with something that *isn't* a nuclear bomb. It fits with the low radioactivity. That drawing might be accurate after all."

"Hmm," said Smith. "Well, we'll have to wait for the photographs."

"*If* they exist."

"Oh, they exist," said Smith. "I saw the look in Miss Travis's eyes. She's got some basic tradecraft down pat, but she doesn't have the poker face for the job."

That a vanload of scared students from the peace camp had turned themselves in to the police in Dundee had been, along with picking up Roisin Travis, the best stroke of luck in the investigation. It was from them that the local SB had gotten the names of the others at the camp, those who'd left in the other van, and the information that Cunningham or Armitage—or whatever his real name was—was obsessed with photography and that Roisin had been off in the woods. Telling Roisin that Armitage and Claire Moyle had already been picked up had been a bluff.

"Speaking of face," said Paulson. He searched through the interview footage until he found a good shot of Roisin, then turned and tilted his screen so that Smith could see it. "Does she really look that weird?"

Smith stared. "Damn," she said.

She jumped up and hurried across the office to talk to MacIntyre. After a moment Paulson followed. Smith was pointing to the mug shot of Roisin taken downstairs less than an hour earlier. MacIntyre and two WPCs had been using it and the accompanying biometric scan as they checked through the CCTV footage.

"This is how she looks, well-lit and full-face on a high-res camera," Smith said. "And I can assure you, that's how she actually looks." She flipped the picture to the screen-grab Paulson had isolated. "*That*'s how she looks on CCTV."

They all stared at the panda-eyed, hollow-cheeked image. MacIntyre leaned forward and split-screened up the mug shot. No one would have recognized the one from the other. Even the biometrics didn't match: the proportions of cheekbones and chin were out by half a centimeter.

"How on earth did she do that?" a policewoman asked.

"I have no idea," said Smith. "We should check her stuff for anything she might have smeared on her face. Anyway, that's who to look for. Now we know, it should make her a bit easier to spot. Use eyeballs rather than software this time, okay?"

The WPCs, looking glum, went back to the search.

"We've made more progress on the phones," said MacIntyre. "Now that the network's back up."

He led Smith and Paulson to another desk, where a keen-looking young copper was working three screens simultaneously. One showed a blocky sprawl that Paulson recognized as a phone-cell map of Edinburgh. The second was a conventional street map with pinpricks of various colors highlighting locations and addresses of interest. The constable glanced up over his shoulder, overlapped the maps, and touched a key. Two purple blocks started flashing on the street map: one in the city center, the other a bit farther north.

"So the phones are in town," said Smith, not sounding impressed. "And we can track them to within, what? A hundred meters?"

"It's no as bad as that, ma'am," said the constable. He pointed to the third screen, which showed street scenes, one of Princes Street and the other of Leith Walk. "I can pinpoint when the phone moves fae one cell tae another, see? And zoom tae a street camera for whoever's in shot at that point."

Which, in both cases, turned out to be dozens of people. The line between cells was itself blurry.

"Get some cars out there," muttered Paulson.

"Done that," said MacIntyre. "They're cruising nearby." He tapped his ear to indicate that he was in touch.

"Just order a sweep, goddamnit!"

"It's no that simple," said MacIntyre. "Patience, man, patience." He brandished a cell phone that Paulson presumed was Roisin's. "I have a plan."

Over the next half hour Paulson became increasingly tense as the apparent targets shifted farther away from the center: one down Leith Walk—a painfully long street—and the other out of Princes Street toward Haymarket. Time after time, the step between one cell and the next covered too many people to pinpoint anyone. Paulson's jitters weren't improved by the cups of coffee that kept being supplied by an unobtrusive civilian auxiliary. But the young policeman and the system he was working with were more effective than Paulson had at first thought: very gradually, a file of people who appeared in more than one shot was built up and whittled down. A shot from the crossing-camera of a busy junction at the foot of Gorgie and Dalry showed only three figures tabbed, all of them waiting to cross the road. MacIntyre was hunched, poised, thumb on a key on Roisin's phone, murmuring into the mike of his own.

"Now," said MacIntyre. He pressed the key. One of the figures reacted, with an obvious twitch that was almost funny to watch—the reflex of finger to ear, then reaching for an inside pocket.

"Female, dark suit, east side," said MacIntyre. "That's the one."

The woman was still standing on the curb frowning at a phone in her hand when a car on the street U-turned and stopped beside her. The door was open and a hand was on the back of her head before she had time to look up.

"Claire Moyle," said Smith. "Well done. Let's do a zoom."

They were all just pointing out to each other the dark-suited woman's slightly odd-looking features when a cry went up from a WPC on the CCTV archive search job.

"Got one!"

MacIntyre stayed on the job, Paulson and Smith crowded around the other desk. The shot came not from the Tesco car park or the supermarket aisles but from the side of the doorway coverage of another shop, that happened to have caught Roisin—ponytail, hooded top, denim skirt, hollow cheeks, furtive body language, no doubt at all—sticking a packet in a post-office box. Maxine Smith wasted no time on congratulations. She picked up the desk phone and called the station switchboard.

"Get me the nearest sorting office to Alloa," she said. "Now."

Because of the day's traffic disruptions, postal collection in Alloa was running late. It was luck in its nastiest form, a wisp of good blown on the wind of the Grangemouth disaster, but it was something to grab. Smith worked her way up the switchboard tree until she found a senior officer with the authority to order a police collection of all mail from the postboxes within a few hundred meters of the Tesco car park. The day having been what it was, there was not a lot to collect. Meanwhile, MacIntyre's crew managed to pounce on a man in Leith

Walk. A lot of shuttling of police vans and motorcycle couriers followed.

By midnight Roisin, released and followed, had gone to ground in a basement flat in Broughton that belonged to a known antiwar activist and was under discreet surveillance. Smith, Paulson, and MacIntyre were looking at a stack of photographs retrieved from the post, and at a couple of reels of processed film found in the pockets of the man who called himself Mad Jack Armitage.

And Maxine Smith had just learned from MI5's London HQ that all the face-recognition software, all the trawling and tracking and surveillance of the British state, couldn't find a trace of the face, DNA, card transactions, or vehicle registrations of a man who evidently went by many names, only one of which was James Travis.

———

The police hadn't bothered to erase the messages (*mt me @ Wvrly 22:30*) they'd sent to the two numbers stored on her phone before they'd returned it. Roisin concluded from this that Claire and Mad Jack had already been caught—whether lured to the trap so obviously set, or by some other means. The only items of her belongings the police had kept back was her old, EMP-frazzled phone and the pricey pot of Lancôme Nano. From this Roisin concluded that some data still lingered in the phone, and that the trick with the cream worked. She supposed this was useful to know.

———

Just after sunset that evening Travis parked at the crest of a rise on the outskirts of Walsall, looking down the long sweep of the road north. Sparse traffic moved freely on it. Along most of the half-mile downward slope the road was flanked by walls, behind which rose the roofs of villas, hotels, and obscure institutions. Trees dangled their fresh leaves over the long grass verges between the carriageway and the pavements. After the slow, grinding hours he had spent crossing the city, Travis felt the impression of an open road like an open door from a dark room. Most of the center was gridlocked. Through repeated false starts and diversions he had worked his way around it, with an animal-like bristling of multiple senses for any sign of trouble: eyes scanning the near and far distance, nose sniffing the air for smoke, ears cocked to the local radio news and to the sounds of the streets ahead and around him. He'd dropped the Muslim family off with relatives of theirs who lived in a tower-block complex, jointly patrolled as of this afternoon by twitchy gangs of white youths in red T-shirts and Asian lads with green headbands: Maoists and *muj,* they styled themselves. They'd nicknamed the complex Sadr City. Travis pitied them their delusions but it was about as encouraging a thing as he'd seen all day.

Travis munched a banana and gulped water and pondered what to do next. The radio murmured that the motorways, still closed, were now gradually emptying of cars. The Government had announced petrol rationing on the news at three, forestalling panic at the pumps. The allocations were electronic, to be downloaded to all drivers' ID-card chips with their first swipe after the announcement. Travis vaguely recalled the tail end of that project from some years earlier at Result; EDI, Accenture or some such big contractor had made an unholy cock-up of it and Result had been given the lucrative job of clearing up the mess. It was not a project he'd worked on, and it was from before his double life began, so it was not among the systems in which he'd installed back-doors. He wasn't even on to the first reserve tank yet, but fuel would become a consideration in a day or two.

"How do you rob a gas station?" he asked himself, and answered: "With an air pistol!"

He laughed at his own joke and studied the sat-nav map. A couple of hundred meters down the road the map showed a green patch to the left, bordered by black lines, with a clutter of black rectangles and squares in the middle, labelled COLLEGE. Travis decided to check it out. He tossed the peel, stashed the bottle, and drove down, turning left into a long driveway between trees. At the top was a weathered, empty-looking mansion of old stone, its pillared porch overlooking a terraced lawn and an enclosed garden, with a separate three-story block that looked like student accommodation off to one side. Both buildings were dark. Travis drove between them and parked around the back, where sheds and Porta-cabins overlooked a gravelled yard. A light was on in an extension at the back of the big building.

Travis took the Brocock out of his jacket pocket and stuck it in the glove compartment. He unclipped the phone from the dash and put it in an inside pocket. He jumped out and slammed the door, crunched across the gravel, and banged on the door of the extension. The light inside went off, and a halogen floodlight above the yard came on. From inside Travis heard the heavy click of a shotgun breech closing.

"Who's there?" The voice came from a speaker grille on the doorpost.

Travis stepped back and spread his hands, eyeing the lens of a matchbox CCTV on the lintel.

"Name's Travis," he said. "Looking for a place to crash for the night."

"This ain't a hotel."

"I know," said Travis. "They're all full. I can pay cash."

The camera swivelled to the Land Rover and back to Travis.

"How much?"

"Two hundred euros."

"Two fifty."

That would have gotten him a night in a four-star, breakfast included.

"Done."

The door's lock buzzed. Travis pushed and it swung open. He stayed where he was. A light came on. The room in front of him had a wide cooker, a tall fridge, metal sinks, and a row of Formica tables and plastic chairs. Directly across from him was a door open to a hallway dimly illuminated by the windows around the front door. A shadow moved. There was another click. A man stepped into the kitchen and the light. He was young, with a black ponytail and wary eyes. Something in his face was too alert for a caretaker. Travis guessed he was a cook. A double-barrelled shotgun, open at the breech again, hung in the crook of his arm.

"Hi," he said. "My name's Carl." He didn't offer to shake hands. He waved toward the work area. "There's eggs and bread in the fridge, grease in the bottle, tomatoes in tins. Tea. Coffee. Help yourself."

"Is there a microwave?" Travis asked.

"There in the corner."

"Fine," said Travis.

"Well . . ." Carl rubbed thumb and forefinger.

"Just a minute," said Travis.

He went back out and retrieved a soap bag, an MRE, and some euro notes from the Land Rover. He thought about the Brocock and decided to leave it. He locked up and went back. Carl stood in the doorway, watchful, backing into the kitchen as Travis approached. He pointed at a table and Travis laid down the notes and took a few paces back. Carl snatched the notes, fanned them out, then slid them into his jeans pocket.

"Sorry about all this," he said. "Bit edgy, you know?"

"It's been that kind of day," said Travis.

Carl laughed. After that he relaxed a little. He showed Travis to a big old parlor at the front. The place smelled of sun-bubbled varnish and cigarettes. Worn sofas, faded pictures, television, a dead fireplace, and a bay window with shutters and no curtains. "You can crash here."

Travis looked around. On a table in the corner was an old computer with a modem connection. A screen saver cycled fractals.

"Can't I sleep in the accommodation block?"

"More than me job's worth," Carl chuckled.

He went to the inside of the porch and gave Travis the mortice and Yale keys of the front door, and told him to leave and let it lock behind him in the morning.

"You don't live in?"

"Hell, no." He pointed across the garden. "Little lodge with me wife."

"She's sitting there in the dark?"

"That's right." Carl patted the shotgun. "With the twin of this."

"Christ." Travis admired this swift adaptation to new realities.

"Well, I'd best be off," said Carl.

He went out the back and locked the door. Travis heard his steps crunch across the gravel, then saw him heading down the driveway and off behind the garden wall. He didn't look back. Travis moved away from the window and picked up the keys. He unlocked the front door, left it on the snib, and went back to the Land Rover. He returned to the house with a sleeping bag, a Bible, the Brocock, and a Bowie knife, locked the front door, dumped the gear, and went through to the kitchen. The instant coffee was ready to drink about the time the microwave pinged with the MRE. He forked up Thai green curry in the dwindling light, then took another mug of coffee to the front room. He switched on the television and sat on the sofa, sipping the coffee and flicking the remote. The news told him nothing he didn't know, and omitted much that he did. Satellite and Space Station images showed the black plumes of the refinery and depot fires, now hundreds of kilometers long. The speed-camera shots of the collapsing motorway pillars had dropped out of the coverage. More fires were visible from the bay window than onscreen. The focus was clear and narrow, on the rescuers' toil in the motorway catastrophes and at Grangemouth and Leuchars. People who had fled south from Edinburgh and Fife, fearing fallout or further attacks, were urged to return. Parliament was in emergency session; while the emergency lasted, sittings would be from eight in the morning until long past midnight. The Prime Minister and the Home Secretary answered questions that were not the ones asked. Later the news cut away to the war. Truck bomb in Tehran. Civil defense exercise in North Korea. Pyongyang deploys antiaircraft missiles—Japan protests. Travis sighed and flicked to the Execution Channel.

Three Muslim rebels in Xinjiang, kneeling in a row, arms bound behind them, fell to a volley. A US soldier captured in Waziristan screamed, then gurgled blood as a serrated blade sawed through his trachea. His eyes rolled up, pure white, as the blade tilted a little back and forth, then he looked straight at the camera as the edge found the cartilage and sliced with a creak between two cervical vertebrae. The eyes still stared as the severed head was held up. A Nigerian adulteress stumbled under a shower of stones then crumpled in a bloodied heap.

Travis was about to switch off when the episode's cycle returned to the PLA squad taking aim, and this time he watched with his fists clenched, jabbing air as the shots went in and the bodies fell forward and jerked in the dust, and his mouth said *yes*.

He picked up the Bible, sat down in front of the computer, and nudged the mouse. The screen saver gave way to a desktop. Travis clicked to the Web and checked his son's blog. No updates today. He followed the sidebar links to Alec's comrades in the squad and was relieved to see that the day had been uneventful in Kazakhstan. Most of the talk was angry, about the day's events in Britain. One made a passing mention of Alec, who'd been worried sick about someone back home.

Travis tabbed back and re-read Alec's post dated 4th May. A phrase he'd passed over when he'd first read it, a long twenty-four hours ago, jumped out at him:

> Bit of a Flap here, can't say much but I reckon you
> could hear it all the way to Fife.

Travis drummed his fingers. He pictured some enormous bird flapping its wings, flying from Kazakhstan to Scotland, to Fife, to Leuchars. He leaned back in the cracked plastic chair and thumbed his stubble.

He consigned the notion to his brain's background processing and ambled to the kitchen, where he fished the phone from inside his Barbour and checked for incoming messages. None. He returned to the computer and went to a mail website he never connected to from his phone or from work. Its server was located in Bolivia. No doubt the spooks could read the messages, but they couldn't do trackback. After setting up a new ID he emailed Alec: *Rosh is fine and so am I. James.* He didn't know if this was still true—he hadn't heard from

Roisin since last night—but at least it would reassure Alec that she hadn't been killed or injured in the Leuchars Event.

On the same website he checked an account he'd pre-arranged with Roisin as an emergency mail drop. No messages. He left one for her. Then he went to another account that served the same function for Gauthier, from whom he'd gotten the idea—and the information about the website—in the first place. That one had a message. It was in code: a long series of numbers. Travis opened the Bible and followed the references, which weren't to chapter and verse but page, line, and number of letters in that particular Collins edition of King James. The tedious procedure yielded: *Heptonstall from Wednesday.* Heptonstall was a village in Yorkshire. Today was Tuesday. Travis determined to go there tomorrow.

———

The homeward crowds had passed, the air was still warm after a hot day that had burned off the morning damp and chill, and the sun was red enough to cast a warm light on Anne-Marie and not yet low enough to make her shade her eyes. The breeze was from the west too, carrying her cigarette smoke away. Bob Cartwright sat at a pavement table on the corner of Newbury and Fairfield, sipped Harpoon IPA from a bottle, and felt that life was good. On the third side of the table Peter Hakal sipped Coke through a straw and toyed with the remains of a sandwich. Sarah Henk, in keeping with her deep cover as a receptionist, always went home on the dot; the other three creatives almost always worked on into the early evening. They sometimes had a drink together after a particularly hard day. This had been a hard day. Bob still had an odd feeling about drinking outside so close to Ground Zero, but as long as he was sitting down he didn't have to look at the gaps in the skyline where the Hancock and Prudential towers had been. If he didn't look around the corner he couldn't see the rubble in between them either.

Anne-Marie twirled her glass of ABC—her invariable order, anything but Chardonnay—and gazed idly along and across the street, her eyeline drifting upward, stopping and holding for a few seconds, then flicking back down. The eyeballing was so predictable, in Anne-Marie's moments of abstraction, that Cartwright had once replicated the angle, crouching behind the chained-up table early one morning, and figured out that she must be clocking a second-story Vera Wang window display. Did she have wedding-day daydreams, or was it just that she was bored with black? Bob didn't know what it signified for his chances of getting into her bed, but it pleased him inordinately to have got into her mind; that he knew something about her that she didn't know he knew. It made him feel like a stalker, but in a good way.

Any moment now Peter would say something to Anne-Marie. It wasn't that they were rivals—Peter was very definitely married—but he had a tendency to hog conversations. Bob determined to get in first.

"So," he said, "can you tell us your story yet?"

Anne-Marie smiled and flicked her hair. "Is this the place for it?"

Bob could think of another place, but he didn't suggest it. He shrugged one shoulder. There were a couple of other tables occupied and a dozen more civilians standing around, all talking about the day's events more or less nonstop.

"Well," she said, "I . . . came across a story you wouldn't believe."

"Online?"

"Of course online." She stubbed her cigarette and tapped out another from her blue American Spirit pack. "Like all nonsense. But this came from a military discussion board, originally. The local color was good. It looked like an authentic piece by a middle-ranking army officer, naturally pseudonymous. It claimed that what exploded in Scotland wasn't a nuke but an experimental fusion reactor, captured in a cross-border raid into China. It was being developed by a French-Chinese-Russian consortium. French agents triggered the explosion or sabotaged the device, because it is also usable as a particle-beam weapon that the French leftist government and their ex-commie and neo-commie friends intend to use for antimissile defense in a future nuclear showdown with the Coalition." She lit and inhaled. "Don't look at me like that, Bob."

"That's a very dangerous idea to be floating around," Cartwright said, hoping she'd catch the ambiguity.

"Certainly," said Anne-Marie. "But the story continues. It further claimed that this was being covered up by the Pentagon and DC because if there's one thing the heartland is afraid of, it's nuclear war—after all, that could affect them and not just the coasts! The threat of it could be the tipping point for heartland isolationism, maybe even mutinies. That post was immediately countered by the suggestion that the explosion was an American black op. As a warning to the Brits not to go wobbly, and as a provocation to stir up anger against the Muslims."

"That's insane," said Bob. "Nobody would believe that."

"Exactly," said Anne-Marie. "It was immediately torn apart. Leaving the first theory looking better by comparison. Quite neat."

"Anger has been stirred up," said Peter Hakal. He

grimaced. "Talk about provocations is very provocative in itself."

"That's true," said Anne-Marie. "I myself was a little disturbed by that."

Bob looked from Peter to Anne-Marie, alarmed. He leaned forward and spoke quietly.

"We don't know what the strategy is," he said. "Our clients do. They know what they're doing. Let's not get bent out of shape over details, you know what I'm saying?"

"Ah," said Anne-Marie. She scratched her ear; her trailing cuff masked her mouth as she spoke. "Either story could be bait, for example."

Bob nodded firmly, and glanced sidelong at Peter. "The clients are very serious about . . . prejudices, okay?"

"So I've noticed," Peter said. "Serious, no question about that." He drained his Coke and stood up. Bob picked up the tab and dropped a fifty. As he returned his wallet to his pocket his PDA buzzed. He took it out and looked at the message. It was an urgent action request to take over the blog of an English soldier called Alec Travis. The appended list of URLs scrolled way down.

"New one on the string," he said. "Starting now. Damn. I'll have to go back and research it."

"Can't do it from home?" Anne-Marie asked.

"No, definitely not. It's a Brit."

"I'll stay and give you a hand," said Anne-Marie.

Bob Cartwright hoped his ears hadn't gone bright red.

"Thanks," he said. "That's—that's very good of you."

"Any time," said Anne-Marie. She stood up and glanced across the road, at street level this time. "Let's get some decent coffee at DeLuca's. We could be working half the night."

———

Back at the office Bob Cartwright knew he wouldn't get any work done until the coffee was ready. He needed a caffeine rush to clear the beer from his brain. While he was waiting he checked Mark Dark. The forged documents he'd passed to it not only hadn't appeared, there wasn't a hint or a teaser about them. Instead, on the site's blog page:

> We're living through a very odd moment, folks. Until we know who or what was behind the Leuchars explosion, we won't know what world we're in. Somebody knows. It could be a handful of people, or maybe just one. They've already opened the box and seen if the cat's alive or dead. The rest of us don't know, and until we do the wave-function hasn't collapsed. Whoever knows the truth and exposes it—and it could be just one person—will change the world and the future for us all.

> Scary thought. We're used to the decisions of presidents and generals making a difference. Because we think of them as having been put there by something bigger—will of the people, will of God, forces of history, whatever. We don't like to think that one random joe or jane off the street could make that kind of difference. But they can, sometimes without even knowing it.

> Here's an example, and I swear it isn't a stretch. Everybody agrees the 2000 election—or the November Coup, if you like—made a huge difference

to America and the world. What nobody knows is who
decided it. It wasn't Bush or Gore or even the Florida
Electoral Commission. It was some guy or gal in
Florida who said no to a bunch of commies trying to
get on the ballot. I've checked this out, and it turns out
that the Workers World Party—that's the commies—
fell short of their ballot-access requirements by just
one signature. Boo hoo. But think about it. In any state
there's always a few hundred pissed-off losers who'll
vote commie if they can, and Democrat if they can't. If
the WWP had run in Florida they'd have pulled
hundreds of votes from Gore—just enough to swing it
for Bush.

OK, so imagine Bush wins. In August 2001 Bush is in
the White House. On August 6 he gets a President's
Daily Brief across his desk headed "Bin Laden
determined to strike in US." (I know, I know—there's
serious doubts over the reality of that memo, but let's
leave that aside for now.) Would he have turned
around and ordered a cruise-missile attack on
Afghanistan? Like hell he would. He's like his daddy, an
oil man and a spook man. He would've worked through
the FBI, CIA, and the mukhabarats—the Arab secret
police forces, nasty pieces of work but basically
on-side against radical Islamists—to track down Al
Queda. He could've gotten the oil majors to lean on
the Taliban, say with the Unocal pipeline deal, to turn
over Osama Bin Laden. Whatever. There's just no
fucking way he'd have followed in Clinton's footsteps.

But Gore did. His cruise-missile strike killed Bin
Laden, dozens of other AQ sand nazis, and hundreds
of innocent Afghans. Whatever Bin Laden was
planning, it wouldn't have been anything like as crazy

and over the top as what was provoked by the sheer
fucking outrage Gore's assault on Afghanistan
aroused. It was a gift to the sand nazis—suddenly
they've got a martyr, a Che Guevara figure,
and they've got a huge base among ordinary Muslims.
Can you imagine the 9/11 attacks happening without
that? Out of a clear blue September sky? I can't.

Without 9/11, Gore couldn't have attacked Afghanistan
again, then invaded Iraq, then taken out the Iranian
nuke program. Without the Iran attack: no oil spike, no
world slump, no Chinese export crisis, no worker-
peasant upheaval, no Two Necessary Corrections in
Beijing, no Straits Incident, no PRC slo-mo breakup,
no . . . and so it goes on, right on down to the totally
fucked-up mess we're in today. And there you have it,
a whole chain of consequences from a tiny decision.
For want of a nail . . . jeez, it's like chaos theory. Talk
about a sensitive dependence on initial conditions!
Some unknown dude in Florida who said no to a
commie with a clipboard changed the course of
history.

If you're that dude and you're reading this, thanks
a bunch.

———

What the hell was all that about? Cartwright wondered.
Mark Dark—whoever he, she, they, or it was—had never
before harked back to 9/11. The site had a page of links
to the standard revisionist histories—but then, no self-
respecting conspiracy site could do without one. The
page itself was skeptical of the 9/11 skeptics. So was
Cartwright. He knew all the stories and rumors, and not

even in a job that had paranoia as an occupational hazard had he ever been impressed by any of them.

There were people who still swore they'd seen planes
hitting the towers. There were even photographs of
planes heading for the towers. There were engineers who
claimed that the towers could *only* have been brought
down by fuel-laden jetliners slamming into them. There
were calculations that purported to show that no amount
of explosives that could feasibly have been in the underground car parks could have brought down the towers.
There were even documents floating around that claimed
to be the raw turnstile records of the car-park companies, showing that the number and size of vehicles in the
car parks just didn't add up.

It was all rubbish. Two of the airliners that took off
from Logan Airport on the morning of September 11,
2001, had been turned around by their hijackers within
minutes and aimed directly at the Massachussets State
House and Faneuil Hall. They had flown *past* the towers, there was no doubt about that; and in a last-moment
glimpse, or a cleverly framed photograph, they could
look as if the Hancock Tower and the Prudential Tower
were the targets. Add the fact that the towers had top-
pled toward each other at almost the same moment as
the aircrafts' impact, and you could see how the oddly
persistent tale arose. It was given superficial plausibil-
ity by apparently genuine traces of an alternative plan,
to fly airliners all the way from Logan to NYC and into
the World Trade Center—rejected by the terrorists, no
doubt, because there was no way they could have done
that without being shot down long before they reached
their targets.

The factoid about the explosives was nonsense too.
A dozen or so carefully parked SUVs packed with
THX—an explosive so intense that it was used to trig-

ger nuclear bombs—would without doubt have been enough to demolish the towers' foundation pillars. Just a few years earlier, a much less sophisticated attempt had almost brought down the World Trade Center in New York.

Apart from the whole paranoid shtick about Gore—the standard right-wing rant was that he'd planned all along to invade the Middle East and drive up the price of oil as a desperate measure against global warming—the 9/11 sceptics were, Bob had often thought, being driven by denial, an inability to accept the sheer demonic *elegance* of the attacks. Using airliners, products of America's highest technology, to destroy its oldest national symbols—the State House with its golden, mosque-like dome, taking with it the monument to the Union dead and setting half of Boston Common ablaze; and Faneuil Hall, its aerial destruction synchronized with another round of underground car-park demolitions that had taken down Government Center and the Old State House; and in Philadelphia, the target of the third airliner, Independence Hall with the Liberty Bell—all this had shown a deep semiotic sophistication. So, in its way, had using SUVs to bring down skyscrapers. In its economy of means it was like a haiku from hell. It was an appalling grace note, a signature flourish, that the toppling skyscrapers had between them crushed the mall that lay at their feet. If the terrorists had wanted to ram home a point about the country's oil dependency, its profligacy, the fragility of its foundations, they couldn't have picked a better way.

———

"Coffee," said Anne-Marie.

"Thanks," said Cartwright. He inhaled and sipped.

The smell had an earthy undernote that amplified the slight grittiness on the tongue. "Very good. I can get on with the job now."

"What have you been doing, while I have been busy?"

"Oh." Cartwright wasn't sure if it was shyness or absentmindedness that had kept him looking at the screen as she approached and handed him the mug. He glanced up at her and pointed to the screen. "This guy, I dumped a load of fake USAF documents—the old North Sea hypersonic bomber angle—on him, and he hasn't taken the bait."

Anne-Marie took in the page at a glance.

"I think he is saying something to you. He is teasing you. He is the one fishing—for more evidence."

"Maybe. These conspiracy types, they're professional paranoids. If you can get something past them, they really run with it, but . . ." He shrugged. "Nothing for it at the moment. I'd better get on with the job."

"What do you need, Bob?"

"I'll have to get the books myself, actually—"

"No, I will get them."

"Oh well. Thanks. British Army stuff. Regimental names. Ranks. Weapons and tactics. War memoirs, SAS memoirs."

"I know the sort of thing."

She turned in a black flurry and vanished between shelving. Cartwright could see her arched feet and high heels, and the occasional flicker of a hem. He sighed and looked back at the screen, sipping coffee and right-clicking through a string of Brit soldier blogs from the Khazakhstan deployment, and trying to get the situation straight in his mind. Alec Travis was *in* the Royal Corps of Signals, and *with* the Royal Regiment of Scotland. They were stationed in foothills of the Tianshan Moun-

tains, near the point where Kazakhstan, Kyrgyzstan, and
Xinjiang met. The fight they were in had more corners
than the borders. Uighurs, Kazakhs, Maoists, Muslims,
Chinese: these were only the crudest of dividing lines,
enclosing sectors that overlay each other and encom-
passed narrower and deeper divisions. There, your enemy's enemy was not your friend. The Brit strategy, if
there was one, seemed to be to hunker down, let everyone else fight each other, and occasionally make a sortie
to tip the balance according to some calculus of advantage whose rationale was impenetrable from outside
and (Cartwright began to suspect) from within.

Anne-Marie returned with a stack of books. This time
Cartwright looked up at the sound of her steps. She put
the books on the desk and dragged up a seat.

"What have we got, Bob?"

He showed her. She scrolled through Alec Travis's
blog, which was titled *Flash in the 'shan*. The latest entry was for the previous day. The blog's sidebar had a
long list of links, almost all to other soldiers. Anne-Marie
brought them onscreen one by one, reading recent posts
and tabbing about from one to the other, then back to
Flash. She read very fast.

"This kid's been arrested?" she asked.

"Seems so."

"Why?"

Bob pointed to an entry. "He mentions a Flap. That
might have been indiscreet. Or coded."

"'Loose lips sink ships,'" Anne-Marie quoted. "Still,
it would need some devious mind to read much detail
into it."

"I think that's the point." Bob shifted in his chair. He
could feel her breath with the small hairs of the side of
his neck. "I don't know the details, obviously, but the

channel the request came by was via counterintelligence. So he's in deep shit."

"But all we have to do is keep the updates going? Nothing more than that?"

"Yeah." Bob skimmed the blocks of text. "It's not like he has a hard style to fake, put it that way. It's just keeping the details convincing without, you know, blowing any ops ourselves."

Anne-Marie enlarged a blog icon and pointed a precise oval black-laquered fingernail on a line. "Look at this."

The blog was called *Stan Boots* and the guy signed himself *size12*. The line read: "Chinks **moaning** about the Usu job, fuck em." The link led to an official PRC protest about an alleged Special Forces ("helicopter-borne mercenary bandit") air assault action in or near the small town of Usu, on the edge of the Junggar Pendi plain.

"That could have been the Flap he mentioned," she said. "The date and time fits."

"Uh-huh." Cartwright looked again at the line about the Flap: *all the way to Fife*. He banged his fist on the table, making the empty mug rattle and Anne-Marie jump.

"What?"

"*I* know what this is all about! I know why I got this assignment! It's part of the same thing we've been working on all day!"

Anne-Marie's black eyebrows arched. "Yes?"

"Leuchars. Fife. Scotland."

"Ah. I see." She sounded doubtful, then smiled. "Well, if there is a connection, I have noticed something else you might be interested in. From a few days ago, in several blogs." She leaned past him, her shoulder brushing his. Her fingers flicked over the keyboard. On screen, she patched up extracts from various blogs, highlighting phrases and drawing lines between them:

don't laugh, we spotted UFOs last night. Unifucking-dentified fucking flying objects

lights over the 'shan again

Not One Of Ours. Should be a new acronym: NOOO.
went over so fast it left a green streak

On clear nights, sky as black as a coal cellar, you see meteors and satellites. No mystery.

That last was an officer.

"This all smells of disinfo," Bob said. He leaned back and laughed. "Jeez, how many of these blogs *are* genuine?"

Anne-Marie joined in his laugh.

"But Bob, don't you see?" she said. "We can tie this in with Alec Travis's blog, and as well as keeping it updated use it to strengthen the cover story. The hypersonic bomber cover story, I mean."

"Make it a crash recovery story, link it to the Usu raid, which is in the public domain anyway, whatever it was . . . hmm." He kept smiling at her, just to see her smile back. "It's creative, yeah, but it's deviating a bit from the line. What if it's . . . well, too close to whatever it is we *are* covering up?"

"Like, the UFOs are HTS?"

"HTS?"

"Heim-Theory Ships." She wrote it out for him.

"Oh," he said. "*Heim*. Gerhard Heim."

He vaguely recollected having seen the story, somewhere on the weird-science shelves. Gerhard Heim had been a German rocket enthusiast, then engineer, in World War II. After maiming himself in a laboratory explosion he'd dictated an immense body of arcane quantum physics to his wife. Decades later, it had been discovered that Heim's equations were the most accurate model available of particle interactions. This discovery had revived interest in an implication of his theory that was more difficult to test: that a sufficiently powerful electrical circuit could generate antigravity, even—and here it got very hairy indeed—a faster-than-light hyperspace drive.

"That's the one," said Anne-Marie.

Bob shook his head. "The Heim drive tests never came to anything."

"If they had," said Anne-Marie, "would we know? There are of course those who claim that the test we know of was rigged to fail, and that the real test was a success. There are rumors about secret work on the Heim drive, HTS, the spindizzy as some call it—after a science fiction story—all over the net."

"On the usual dubious sites?"

"The usual suspects, yes. Which is why I think these stories too are disinfo, and we would not be cutting too close to the truth if we threw this in. Think, Bob, what we have already. We have one story that Leuchars was a recovered nuke from Central Asia—Iran, anyway—and one story that it was a mystery aircraft. And, as I said, I had the one about an experimental reactor recovered on a cross-border raid into China! If any of these were too close to the truth I doubt that we would be told to spin them. Would you not doubt it?"

Bob sighed. "I need another coffee."

This time it was he who got up and poured, Anne-Marie who thanked. He sat back down beside her. "You're right, of course," he went on. "I mean, if they're even playing with the Fort Sumter scenario, or a French attack, or one of our own black ops—God, if all these are part of the cover-up, what the hell is the truth? How could it be worse?"

"Oh, Bob," she said. She laid a hand on his wrist, startling him. "You have been in this job how long? And you are still naive. The truth is probably some miserable piece of nonsense, some ridiculous incompetence that will only be revealed under the FOIA when we are all old, if we live that long. I was disturbed, I will say offended, by the blaming it on France, but you were right, it does not matter. It does not matter how dangerous the stories we put out seem to us, because the people they influence are not those who make the real decisions, but those people whose attention must constantly be diverted from the real decisions and the people who make them."

"Good God." He grinned at her. "What are you? A commie? *French?*"

She laughed. "*Je ne suis pas marxiste,* to quote the words of Marx. I am a realist." She took her hand off his wrist and placed it on the pile of reference books. "Now, let us compile a suitably realistic blog entry for the unfortunate Private Alexander James Travis. Just an update for now, with perhaps a mention of a rumor about Jenggar Pendi as a hint of more to come. And then let us ever so subtly draw that to the attention of your friend Mark Dark, and call it a day."

"Call it a night, you mean."

She looked straight at him. "No, Bob, I do not mean call it a night."

———

Anne-Marie had a flat above a Latino twenty-four-hour store on a street of low-rise wooden buildings in Somerville. She bought a pack of American Spirit cigarettes and Cartwright bought a bottle of Chilean Cabernet. The stairs squeaked and the door creaked. A tiny lobby was half filled by hanging coats, most of them made from pelts and hides. The air smelled of incense that masked the stale tobacco smoke. There was a door to his right that he guessed was the bathroom. Two doors opened from the end of the lobby. One was occupied by a bed, a wardrobe, and a dressing table, all too big for the room. Anne-Marie led him into the other, equally crammed with a table, a gas cooker and sink, bookshelves, and a sofa. Lights hung at awkward heights or poked up from cluttered corners like hands from graves. He placed the bottle on a low pokerwork table in front of the sofa and glanced over the bookshelves while Anne-Marie lit a joss stick and rattled about for a corkscrew and glasses. No surprises, really: Friedman *père* and *fils*, Galbraiths likewise, Norton anthologies, American Studies textbooks, Gore's *Earth in the Balance* and *Democracy Arms,* George W. Bush's *Out of Iraq: The Folly of Nation-Building*—the ghost-written manifesto for his second failed presidential bid; a slip-cased Shirer on the Reich, Overy on the War, Service's *Stalin,* yards of American history and English-language science fiction and meters of French novels and polemic.

She rested her chin on his shoulder. "James Blish," she said, stretching an arm past him and fingering a thick paperback from the shelves. "That is where the 'spindizzy' word comes from."

He took in the title and imagined Manhattan aloft, an urban starship with the Twin Towers its proud bridge, the Statue of Liberty its bowsprit. "*Cities in flight.* Jeez. Does the Heim-Theory drive promise that?"

Her chin rubbed behind his collarbone. "Not that I know. And not the meteor screen." She traced an airy dome. "You know, the force field? Just antigravity and the hyperdrive."

"Just the stars, then."

"*Seulement les étoiles,* yes." She sighed. "It is science fiction, but I wish . . ."

He turned, slipped an arm around her waist, but she disengaged.

"A glass," she said. The corkscrew folded out from the slender back of a Laguiole knife handle. Her tug was practiced and decisive. She snuggled up to him as they sat. He poured the wine left-handed and passed her the glass. She took two sips and lit up.

"What a waste," he said. "Might as well have gotten Thunderbird."

She replied to this sophistication with a smoke ring. They drank some more.

"We keep looking at each other and looking away," she said.

"It's good to look at you," he said.

She closed her eyes and made a sinuous movement with her neck and shoulders. "You're kind."

"No, no," he said. "You really are beautiful."

"That's not what I meant." She opened her eyes. "I have no insecurity about my appearance. I meant, you are kind."

He covered himself with a laugh. "Not, I hope, nice."

"Never that."

"Good."

She stubbed the cigarette. "Let's take the bottle to bed."

He took the bottle and glasses and she took the cigarettes and ashtray. He was going to comment on how smoking in bed was a really bad idea, but thought better of it. In an awkward interstitial moment, like those cut from between shots in a movie, they put all the stuff down on a bedside table, beside the alarm clock and the reading light. They stood facing each other. He put his arms around her waist and she put her arms around his neck. She pulled his head toward her and their mouths met, open. Their tongues investigated each other. She had an uneven tooth that snagged the inside of his lower lip. He found himself lying beside her on the bed without quite recalling how they had fallen on it. The lace of her dress felt scratchy on the inner sides of his arms. He lay facing her, stroking her flank, and staring into her eyes. She looked down. Thing about chinos, they could hide a passing excitement but not an ongoing one. She slid her hand to his crotch and smiled, then rolled back and sat up. He tried to take her dress off but the hook-and-eye fastenings were too many and too small for a guy used to Velcro and zips. She laughed and finished the exit while he gracelessly scrambled out of his clothes and shoes. Along the way he retrieved a condom from his pocket. He tore open the packet with his teeth as he turned to face her, naked. She had left on her bra, suspender belt, and stockings and she was waving a condom packet at him. He made to roll on the condom but she took it and rolled it onto his cock with her mouth while he thought hard about something else.

"That's a good French letter," he said, when she looked up.

"Fucking Yank," she replied, grinning. Her hair was tousled and her face was flushed. He slid his hips into the smoky embrace of her stockinged thighs.

"On or over?"

"On," she said. "Elbows."

She rolled on her back. He groped, found her hot wet cleft and guided his cock in with his fingers then covered his face with his wet hand as he thrust. He tried to go slow but he came far too fast. She forgave him. He had the rest of the night to make sure her forgiveness was earned.

9

IT was the light that woke him. Travis had set the alarm on his phone but he slept through it. Daylight from the half-shuttered window disturbed his eyelids and his sleep. He struggled out of the sleeping bag, pissed and washed in a poky lavatory under the stairs, and made himself a breakfast of toast and omelette. The tinned tomatoes turned out to be a metallic-smelling sludge, which he threw under a bush. Rain hissed on the yard and dripped from the trees. From the porch the view of the city was hazy, and not with smoke. The air throbbed like a headache with the thump of helicopter rotors. Before leaving, Travis checked the news. The motorways were still closed. The underpass explosions were referred to as suicide bombings; flicking channels, he caught a passing mention of car bombs. The Leuchars rescue operation, increasingly forlorn, was one focus. Another was the international response: NATO summit, UN Security Council, the President of the United States. Travis heard the Home Secretary promise "Firm measures to protect our Muslim citizens." A clip of armored cars, soldiers, and riot police.

Travis watched, sucking at his lower lip, clenching and unclenching his hands. He picked up his phone and considered browsing for news more detailed and less censored. His heart wasn't in it. He checked his son's blog, and was immensely relieved to see that it had been updated. He pocketed the phone, cleared his stuff out to the van, rinsed the crockery, and left it on the grimy steel channels of the draining board. After a last look around—he found he'd forgotten the Bible, which alarmed him—he let the lock snick behind him, dropped the keys through the door, and walked around the back to the Land Rover. Setting the sat-nav to avoid motorways, he drove down the drive and turned to the left and the north. He found the A515 and followed it to the Peak District and the Pennines. Bypassing Manchester he followed the Galileo trace through a tangle of moorland back roads and reached Hebden Bridge at about noon.

The rain had passed over about an hour earlier. Travis parked the Land Rover behind a dry-stone wall just outside the town. He slid the Brocock into his pocket and walked along a lane between hedges that had no leaves or buds. The fields seemed filled with weeds until he recognized the shoots of oilseed rape. At the junction with the main road he hung back as an armored personnel carrier lumbered by, still in its desert dun and pink. Behind it came four long coaches. From their windows excited children peered out from under the gloomy eye lines of bearded men and head-scarved women. A humvee brought up the rear, the soldiers wary behind mirror shades and bristling with rifles. Travis crossed to the other side of the road and watched the column vanish around a bend, then set out again.

The town was small amid the hills. Stone houses, a stone bridge, a cobbled market bordered by bakeries and craft shops on one side and the river on the other. Across the way was a car park. It was packed with coaches, double-decker municipal buses from Leeds and Bradford, and cars overloaded with belongings stashed inside or lashed to their roofs. Children ran about; adults stood in watchful knots, or queued at stalls from which smoke and steam drifted. Travis caught smells of rice and spice. Behind the car park, on the fields and beyond the edge of the moor, soldiers moved briskly to erect tents and shelters and to dig latrines. The fence posts and rolls of barbed wire in the back of one of the trucks would go up later.

Taking care not to look, Travis walked past the nascent refugee camp and on up the hill.

———

Heptonstall was a hilltop village with streets of tarmac at the summit and sloped cobbles at the sides. It had been the site of some skirmish in the Revolution; as he toiled up, Travis imagined the clang of Roundhead armor and Cavalier hooves. The High Street was the usual post-slump dump; decayed tourist-trap pubs, charity shops with the estate-agent signs still above the doors, a dismal Asda and Tesco competing their special offers. Turning his collar against a wind that blew from unexpected directions, Travis skulked along one side of the street then the other, ducking into and out of pubs, loitering in front of windows full of dusty lampshades, cracked ornaments, and scuffed baby shoes. He found Gauthier under the awning of the smokers' shelter at the back of a greasy-spoon cafe just before the petrol station at the end. A baseball cap and two days' growth of dark stubble made him recognizable only on a second look. Travis shelled out two euros for a cup of bitter instant and took a different table. He meditated on whether the mild buzz he felt came from the coffee or the second-hand smoke. Gauthier never met his eyes. Travis ambled out, heading past the petrol-station queue and downhill toward the tree-choked ruins of a textile mill he'd noticed on the way up.

"We must stop meeting like this," Gauthier remarked, catching up after fifty meters. "Like homosexuals in the dark ages."

"Now there's a cover," said Travis.

"Should we hold hands?"

Travis laughed. "Perhaps not in sight of that lot down there."

"Ah yes, your fortunate Muslim citizens, being firmly protected." Gauthier paused on the road and lit a cigarette. It was not a habit Travis had noticed in him before. He remarked on it.

"I am preparing a cover," said Gauthier. He exhaled smoke and a sigh. He nodded down toward the camp. "What do you think of . . . all that?"

"I'm appalled," said Travis.

Gauthier resumed walking. "At a certain point it becomes rational," he said.

"What? Ethnic cleansing?"

"Yes," said Gauthier. "When there is no longer any basis for trust, separation is better for all concerned."

Travis hunched in his Barbour, jamming his hands in the pockets, feeling a chill that wasn't from the wind.

"I'm disturbed to hear you say that," he said.

"It's your country," Gauthier said. He sucked hard on the cigarette, and waved the cherry-red cone of the tip as if scribbling on air. "Tell me how much more it can take, from a community that sends out such saboteurs as we have seen over the past days?"

"A good question," said Travis. It was one he intended to repeat.

"Europe may be defined," said Gauthier, in a lecturing tone, "as the lands where the Muslim conquests did not reach, or were stopped, or were reversed. Europe is not like the United States, where Muslim immigrants become Arab-Americans overnight. If Europe is to define itself again, the Muslim question must be addressed along with the American question. The tensions in the United Kingdom must be seen in such a light. For that reason, the government of the French Republic is intending within the next days to make an offer to take in any British Muslims who wish to leave."

"That's . . . generous," said Travis. "Considering the problems it has already."

"The problems it has, yes," said Gauthier. "It is not envisaged that the settlement would be permanent."

Travis decoded this. "You'd send them on? Deport them?"

"Yes," said Gauthier. "Along with the unassimilables in the French Muslim population."

"Where to, for heaven's sake?"

"Their countries of origin."

"And if these don't take them?"

Gauthier shrugged. "Eastern Europe? Madagascar? The possibilities are many."

This had to be a provocation.

"I see," said Travis. "Or if you prefer a more . . . *Allied* genocide, Central Asia, where Stalin sent the Chechens . . ."

"*What* genocide?" cried Gauthier. "The Chechens were then deported for collaboration with the Nazis. Some perished, yes, but there were enough left to come back. They're still here and they're still Nazis. These are the same people who gave us Beslan. They need expect no soft measures from us."

"The Americans would never stand for it," said Travis. It was not the strongest objection he could think of.

"To hell with the Americans," said Gauthier. "They

continually prate to us of how we are appeasing the Muslims, becoming 'Eurabia.' They constantly talk as if to tell us that Muslims have no place in Europe. Very well. What do they want from us? Racist attacks? We can do racist attacks. Mosque burnings? We can do mosque burnings. Ethnic cleansing? We can do ethnic cleansing. Deportation? We can do deportation. Concentration camps? We can do concentration camps. Genocide? We can do—"

"Enough," said Travis. "At some point along that scale, the US would intervene."

"Precisely," said Gauthier. "The ceaseless meddling of America on behalf of their favored Muslims—in Chechnya, Kosovo, and Xinjiang, for instance—while oppressing and maligning other Muslims not currently in America's favor, is a very sore point with certain powers. A realignment of French policy toward the unassimilables would be an unmistakable indication of its commitments."

"Hang on," said Travis. "If France offers to take in British Muslims, there'll be an even bigger incentive to push them out. It could destabilize the whole situation, it could . . ."

"Yes, yes," said Gauthier. "Nationalist reaction against the Americans has been very limited. A few cases such as your own, with all respect, are not enough. But against the Americans plus the Muslims? The reaction then could be massive."

"That's diabolical," said Travis.

"Yes, it is," said Gauthier, as if he'd heard a compliment.

They reached a path that led away from the road toward the ruined mill. Travis glanced along it.

"That might be a good place to talk," he said.

Gauthier indicated his acceptance by flicking down his

cigarette butt, and making his treading on it his first step off the road.

They walked along the path, between low stone walls that became obscured by ever taller trees as they approached the ruin. Two of the mill's walls, a gable end, and a tall chimney were still erect. Beech and silver birch grew high within the walls' shelter. Ivy twined around rusting chains and great toothed wheels. Moss covered the lower stones, seeping.

Gauthier kicked his way through long grass and weeds to a corner. He lit another cigarette.

"Well," he said. "You got my message."

"Yes," said Travis. He kept his hands in his pockets. "Picked it up yesterday."

"And, I presume, the warning?"

Travis smiled. "'Sell apples, buy oranges'?"

"That one." Gauthier nodded. "I received it too."

Travis's knees shook. It had never crossed his mind that Gauthier might also be on the run.

"What? How did—"

"I was on a business visit to Sellafield. All very legitimate, all EDF. I was not even doing anything on the side. The message woke me in my hotel room. I suspect I got out shortly before the SB boys arrived. This godforsaken hole seemed a good place to lie low. I contacted you because, frankly, I hoped you could help me get away."

"So that's why you're here," said Travis. "I thought you were going to debrief me or something."

"Debrief you?" Gauthier coughed a laugh and some smoke. He looked at the half-smoked cigarette with distaste and dropped it fizzing into the moss. "The Result operation is over. Rolled up. Do you *have* anything new to report?"

"No," said Travis.

"Well, then."

"Well, indeed. Fuck. I keep wondering what mistake we made." He shook his head. "I thought I'd covered my ass, I didn't talk to anyone, obviously, and you—you're a fucking professional operative, I'll give you that. Do you have any idea, as to how . . . ?"

"I suspect we have both been burned, James."

"That's what the message—"

But Gauthier was shaking his head.

"Not only exposed. Burned. From within the service."

Travis closed his eyes and took a deep breath.

"Do you mean by a traitor—or a mole—or by the top? If it was from the top, why did we get a warning?"

"It is not a question of moles," said Gauthier. "It is possible, yes, but I suspect something more subtle. Our service has cooperated closely with the Allied services, notably the CIA, for decades. We do have interests in common, James! And opponents in common: the Islamists, of course, also the FSB—the Russians still try to penetrate the French state, they have agents of influence in the political parties, and not only the Communists—it is very complex. There are divisions over whether to confront or appease the Coalition. It is not even a question of factions—there are tendencies and inclinations that sway each one, and in a sudden emergency, who is to say which will come out in front? There are the usual politics of bureaucracies. There are procedures that are autonomous and almost automatic. So it is quite possible that one hand could have betrayed us, and another hand warned us. It is possible of course that the British or the Americans have discovered you and me at the very moment of the present crisis, but I rather suspect we were deliberately exposed."

"Hung out to dry. Fuck. Oh well. It's a rough business."

"You could say that. We are pawns who have been

sacrificed." Gauthier shrugged. "If of course I make my own way home, or otherwise escape, nothing more will be said. But the intention, for now, at some level, I think, is that I should be caught. You also."

Travis stared at him, his mouth dry. He summoned spittle and swallowed. "Why?"

"Panic," said Gauthier. "It is thought necessary to throw something to the wolves, and we are to hand."

Travis frowned. "Panic over what, exactly?"

"The device that exploded at Leuchars."

"The warning I got came through within minutes of the explosion," said Travis. "That's hardly enough time for someone to decide to burn us, and somebody else to decide to warn us."

"The explosion was not the cause of the panic," said Gauthier. "The cause would have been the capture of the device, some hours earlier."

"The device was *French*?"

"Not precisely, but . . . let us say there were French technicians involved in its design and construction."

Travis was not at all sure where he stood. He decided on a gambit.

"It was flown in from Kazakhstan," he said, as though that was an objection to what Gauthier had just told him.

Gauthier's eyes narrowed. "Very good, James. And how do you know that?"

Travis told him about his son's cryptic online remark.

"Shit," said Gauthier, "that's interesting." He cupped an elbow and knuckled his face. "And your daughter, Roisin, she was outside Leuchars, was she not? I take it she got away."

"She did," said Travis. "I suspect Alec may have warned her. She said something that suggested—"

"Said?"

Travis filled him in on that too.

Gauthier looked sympathetic, almost ashamed. "Whoever burned us chose well," he said. "You realize, James, that the British services must regard you as far more important than you are? Because you are connected not only with me, but with your children, and thus Leuchars and Kazakhstan and . . . the device and where it was captured."

"And where was that?" Travis didn't want to think about the other questions he could ask.

"China. Xinjiang, to be precise."

Travis had been a bit vague since the Straits Incident on which provinces it would be precise to refer to as Chinese, but he knew that Xinjiang was contested. He let that pass.

"How do you know?"

"I know it, ironically enough, because of my work at EDF. The project is secret. Very secret. But I have to know something about it, in my other capacity, so that I do not, ah, find myself investigating the wrong people— discovering a secret network within EDF that is in fact the secret project." He ran his thumbnail along his lower lip. "If we are caught we will tell everything, James. Everybody does, eventually, and in our situation . . . well. We have little motivation to hold out, no?"

Travis could only agree.

"I am offering to tell you what I know," said Gauthier. "Not so that you can corroborate my account, if I am caught, because you will of course tell them that I told you, and that is no corroboration at all. But so that you understand what is involved. Do you wish to know that?"

"Wait a minute," said Travis. "Suppose I'm picked up, and you aren't?"

Gauthier shrugged. "Then you will tell them, and I will not."

"I'm wondering if that isn't the idea," said Travis. "No offense."

"There are better conduits for information than you," said Gauthier. He rubbed his stubble. "Or me. It is of course possible that we are both being so used. I don't know. No, my friend, the only reason I wish to tell you this is that the information is crucial in understanding the gravity of the situation, and if you are caught it would satisfy your interrogators. It is important always to have something to tell them."

"Okay," said Travis. "Go ahead."

"Very well," said Gauthier. He shifted his feet apart and propped an elbow on the wall and fiddled with the pack of Camels, tapping a tab and not getting around to lighting it, as if he was trying to quit rather than start. "The Leuchars device was almost certainly a prototype fusion power plant of revolutionary design. A new development in plasma focus fusion, inspired, rumor has it, by some deduction from the Planck Anomalies. It—"

"The *Planck Anomalies?* Fusion? How?"

Travis suspected Gauthier of spinning him a line. He was almost amused.

"It was not direct, of course," Gauthier said. "By calling into question the Big Bang model, the Anomalies revived interest in minority theories, particularly the Alfvén plasma cosmology, and in certain observations that had been held to support it, which turned out to have practical relevance to fusion research." He waved his hands in interweaving arcs. "It is to do with how plasma streams interact in certain complex stellar environments. The Pioneer data confirmed it with observations on the boundary layer of the solar system—the shockwave of the solar magnetosphere and the interstellar medium. That is the real origin of the secrecy and controversy around the Pioneer results, and not at all the metaphysical rubbish about the true occult nature of the universe. However, even before the Pioneer data, the Russians and Chinese had made the necessary deductions from the Planck data, designed a machine, and were developing the hardware in collaboration with ourselves, with EDF." He sighed. "For reasons that seemed good at the time—remoteness, access to certain mineral resources, and so forth—the project was sited in Xingjiang. That was before the Muslim rebellion in that province, and the Coalition cross-border hot pursuit raids from Kazakhstan. Now, I know for a fact that there was such a cross-border raid, probably by special forces, immediately prior to this unfortunate sequence of events, and I have reason to suspect—suspect—that it targeted the Xingjiang experimental power facility. The entire fusion device, which is relatively compact, may have been captured. Its strategic significance is obvious. With reliable, cheap, clean fusion power, the nations in question could be independent of Middle East oil, indeed of many strategic resources. The whole purpose of the US conquest of the area would become irrelevant—as would, of course, our attempts to counter it. We could simply withdraw from the competition. You see?"

Travis shook his head. "Why the secrecy? Why not share it with the Americans? It would get them off the hook too."

"Ah," said Gauthier. "That, I'm afraid, is a question I have sometimes asked myself. I have not asked anyone else, because the answer is too obvious. Plasma focus fusion produces a narrow, tight beam of ionized gas which can be used to generate electricity directly. It can also, with some small modification, be used to produce a much more powerful beam. A particle beam. It is a weapon."

"Even so," said Travis, "if everyone had it—deterrence and all that—"

"It's not a deterrent," said Gauthier. "It's the ultimate missile defense. The whole question then, you see, becomes who gets it first. After it is deployed, it might be safe to share. Not before."

"And not with the Yanks and the Brits," said Travis. "Christ Almighty, if these bastards get it first—!"

Gauthier laughed, sounding relieved. "James, you do not disappoint!"

Travis winced. "My patriotism died at Isfahan," he said. "And got buried in the pandemic. But . . ."

"But what?" Gauthier had stopped leaning on the wall, and stood poised.

"The sabotage, the motorway bombs—"

Gauthier flapped a hand toward the camp far below. "Their doing." He frowned. "You suspected us of *that*?"

"Yes, I did," Travis admitted. "Thought it was a bit too clever for the Mozzies, to be honest."

"Unfortunately not," said Gauthier. "It was an AQ operation, for sure. No doubt the French and other services have sabotage networks in the UK, but I know nothing about them, and I doubt very much they would be activated for anything short of all-out war." He got around to lighting his cigarette. "I thought you were having qualms about Leuchars."

Travis stared. "What? The explosion wasn't an accident?"

"I don't know," said Gauthier. "Perhaps the device is unstable and the scientists or military were too impatient. Or the flight itself destabilized it, who knows? But the possibility must have occurred to you that those from whom the device was captured might have sabotaged it, or triggered the explosion remotely. For that matter, who is to say that a technician or scientist was not captured along with it, and committed suicide to stop it falling into enemy hands?"

"Holy fuck," said Travis. He badly wanted to sit down. He leaned back against the wall instead, looking away to the side and not at Gauthier.

"Would the morality of that disturb you?" asked Gauthier. His voice was too casual.

The sky was blue with white clouds. Travis wanted that to be his last sight, if it came to that; if Gauthier decided that he was unreliable and chose to end it. He closed his eyes, but that just made him see what he'd seen on television, from the ruins of Leuchars. He opened his eyes again and looked over at Gauthier, and measured his answer.

"Of course it would," he said. "But that doesn't change anything. Do you think I haven't thought things through? To where this could end?"

"And how do you see it ending, if I may ask?"

"World war," said Travis. "What else?"

"There is that possibility," Gauthier allowed. "In the long run, it is impossible to live in peace on the same planet as a rogue superpower. However, war is not the preferred or indeed expected endgame. World war, aside from some quite unpredictable breakthrough, still means mutual destruction. No doubt the Chinese could ride it out in the sense that their national survival would not be in question. For Russia, let alone for France, that is not at all probable." He inspected the tip of his cigarette and took another draw, then stubbed it against the wall with an inch left. "No, my friend, there is a much more desirable endgame. That is to win without a war. And for that, the plasma fusion device must be in our hands, and most definitely not in the hands of the Yanks and the Brits, as you so eloquently put it."

"Okay," said Travis. "That's desirable all right, but you haven't told me how anyone expects to get there."

Gauthier scratched the side of his head and smiled. "That I don't know, James. I'm just a soldier. A spy, to be precise. As are you."

"Yeah, spies who've been burned."

"We are that," agreed Gauthier. "Still, we should not let petty resentments cloud our resolve. It's possible that a panic over the capture of the device has given the tendency toward appeasement the upper hand among our political masters, and that is why we have been burned. It's also possible that we are being used for some other purpose entirely. None of that, really, is any concern of ours. My task is to return to France. Yours is to avoid capture. Both are in our personal interests. Let us see to them."

———

There was a small Travel Lodge at the end of the village street. Apart from the chambermaids it had no staff. Gauthier used a credit card to let himself in the main door, the lift, and the bedroom. The room had been cleaned but still stank of cigarettes. It had a wardrobe, a bed, a chair, a table, and a tiny en-suite bathroom. There was about two feet of clearance everywhere. The window, as Travis soon discovered, didn't open. He turned away from it to see Gauthier taking a thin, steel-cased laptop computer from a briefcase and laying it on the table. Beside it he placed a neat stack of passports, driving licenses, ID cards, and bank or credit cards. Gauthier spun the chair toward Travis, and sat down on the edge of the bed. Travis slung the Barbour over the seat back and sat and adjusted the height. It was an office chair, and not very good. His back was going to hurt after a while.

"Have you tidied the room?" Travis asked, waving a hand at the walls and ceiling.

"Swept thoroughly," said Gauthier. "It's clean."

"Good," said Travis. He peered at the wall sockets behind the reading lamp, half-liter kettle, and token pad of hotel stationery. "No Wifi sticker and no modem port either."

"They do have wireless here, believe it or not," Gauthier said.

Travis opened the shell and waited as Microsoft waved its flag and sang its little song.

"You want me to hack?" he said.

"I want you to make me invisible," said Gauthier. "As you have done for yourself."

Travis rubbed the back of his neck. "Well, there's a problem there," he said. "Aside from my access being revoked, I expect every line of code I ever wrote is being crawled over right now."

"I'm aware of that," said Gauthier. "And how many lines have you written?"

"Thousands," said Travis. "But on the relevant projects, a handful. The cops and spooks will know where to look, especially with the help of the suits at Result."

"I presume," said Gauthier, "that you made allowances for that possibility."

"Oh, sure," said Travis. "I mean, I knew it would come into play in awkward circumstances. It's not like I did it to dodge speeding tickets. So it's all buried in tangles of C and Perl and Java applets and—"

"Yes, yes," said Gauthier. "And anyway, I'm not asking you to repeat that. I just need a quick-and-dirty hack on a few databases. Police National Computer, DVLA, Passports, HM Customs and Excise."

"Is that all?" said Travis.

The sarcasm passed Gauthier by. "Yes," he said, after a moment's thought. "Yes, I think that's it."

Travis tilted the chair back. "Fuck me," he said. He thought back over various scams and security holes he'd had to deal with, or had heard of. "This'll have to start with social engineering. Do you happen to have a clean phone?"

Gauthier rummaged in his briefcase and handed over a carton.

"Virgin," he said.

"No, it's Orange," Travis said, opening the box.

"I meant—" Gauthier began, then caught on and laughed.

Travis reached into the table's drawer and found a local telephone directory. He propped it in front of him, open at the listing of police stations, then went online. He Googled up police stations until he found one in Kendal that had a helpful website listing all its personnel. He used the View Source option to reveal the Web page's raw code, and checked that the last update to it was recent enough to be current. It was last modified a couple of months ago. He cut to a black software website, searched carefully, and downloaded a couple of pieces of illegal code. He rebooted the computer in command mode, found the programs he'd just acquired, and made them live. One of them could be used to disguise the computer's IP address and trackbacks. The other hacked the phone. He parked the new phone right in front of the computer's infrared port and ran the program to spoof the SIM card to falsify caller ID. He started it off with the desk number of a detective inspector whose age was close enough to his own for his voice to

sound convincing and whose duties included fighting
identity fraud. He took out his own phone and scrolled
through its directory for the numbers of the technical
help desks of the institutions Gauthier had listed. He
made particular note of the techies he knew by name but
who didn't know him by voice.

"Right," he said. "Ready to roll."

"Anything I can do to help?"

Travis waved a distracted finger at the kettle. "Coffee," he said. "This'll take a while."

It took most of the afternoon. Travis almost went
hoarse with fake accents, and weary with variations on
"Sorry, old chap, this is very embarrassing, but I seem
to have forgotten . . ." After a while it all became easier:
once inside any particular government system, a lot
could be done online in other systems. Within three
hours Gauthier's stack of cards and passports had become a sheaf of false identities that could be confirmed
and cross-referenced as long as no one checked for a paper trail or otherwise dug too deep. Some of the identities
perplexed Travis, but he knew better than to query them.

Gauthier boiled a fresh kettle and they finished the
last of the instant drinks. They were down to decaf and
herbal tea. Gauthier flatly refused the decaf. Travis sipped
it and tried to fool his brain with the smell. The coffee
smell also served to mask the herbal tea's fruity odors,
which Travis vaguely associated with illness. Thinking
about it, he remembered that Deborah had drunk a lot
of Ribena when she didn't know she was dying.

"Well," said Gauthier. He riffled the stack and put it
all in the briefcase. "That should get me to France, one
way or another."

"It's not good enough for a plane," Travis warned.
"Sorry I couldn't do better."

"You did well," said Gauthier. "What are your own plans?"

Once again, Travis heard something forced in the lightness of Gauthier's tone. He didn't know what was in the briefcase, still open across Gauthier's lap. He let his right arm relax down the side of the chair. He could feel the weight of the Brocock in the swing of his jacket. He didn't know what good that would do. He turned the chair around so that the right-hand side was parallel to the table, and pushed it back a bit so that Gauthier could see the screen. Travis toggled to news and tabbed through a succession of images: a halal butcher's shop and a pub, burning in Southall; a reporter in front of the White House, and another in the lobby of the UN building, while a crowd shouted outside; a British Army patrol in Almaty; a flight of B2 stealth bombers taking off from RAF Fairford.

"Plans?" He shrugged. "When nobody knows what's going to happen today, let alone tomorrow?"

"Yes, yes," said Gauthier. "A nuclear war can ruin your whole morning. But seriously, James."

"Oh, I've planned for nuclear war," Travis said. "In fact, that's more or less the plan I'm working on now. War or civil breakdown. I have a vanload of emergency kit and a place to go to up north."

"Flee to the Highlands?" Gauthier smiled.

Travis snorted. "Too many targets in the Highlands. No, the Borders, actually. A small cottage."

"You and half of Scotland, from what I hear."

"There is that," said Travis.

"And your daughter?"

"Why my daughter?"

"She is the only person in this country that you care about."

"I suppose that's true." He hadn't thought about it that way.

"So what about her?"

"We have an arrangement," Travis said. "A place to meet, in an emergency."

Gauthier frowned. "That's a risk."

"Don't worry, it's all prearranged." Travis half-turned, spreading his hands. "Come on, man, I know about secure channels."

"That is not the problem," said Gauthier. "Think. Roisin got away from the vicinity of the explosion shortly before it happened. The authorities will want to speak to her, especially given that she is your daughter and they know about you. She has almost certainly been arrested. If not, she is on the run. If she has been arrested, it would be an obvious move to release her and follow her in the hope that she would lead them to you."

"She knows how to shake off a tail."

Gauthier's eyelids drooped. "Really, James? That is an advanced skill. Who has taught it to her? You?"

"As it happens, yes," Travis said. He closed the lid of the computer and leaned back and turned a little farther to face Gauthier directly. He kept his right hand resting on the computer and held his cup in the left. He sipped. The coffee was tepid. "I taught her lots of things, from when she was quite small. I always knew, you know? That something like this could happen. Ever since 9/11, I guess, but it was the Iran bombing that clinched it. This fucking country's going down."

"So you taught your daughter tradecraft?" Gauthier placed his cup carefully down on the bedspread. His left hand held the briefcase on his lap, his other hand settled behind the lid.

"Survival skills," said Travis. "Elementary stuff."

Gauthier's eyes didn't flicker, and the briefcase lid concealed his hand, but Travis caught a movement of his right shoulder as he reached for something inside it. Travis threw the coffee at his face and in the same moment clutched the computer and swung it around in a slicing motion whose trajectory ended just above Gauthier's left ear. Gauthier ducked, perhaps as a reflex reaction to the splash in his eyes or because he saw the blow coming. The laptop weighed a kilogram and was a centimeter thick. It would have cracked his skull and probably killed him. As it was it sliced across the top of the back of his head, cutting the scalp, and the flat side delivered a glancing blow to the side of his head. He fell sideways and slid off the corner of the bed. His hand dragged the briefcase after him and it fell open on top of him. Travis dropped the laptop and lunged for the case. Cards and passports scattered across the floor. The half cup of herbal tea had splashed across them.

Travis flipped the case up—his feet were still at the base of the chair, his stomach was across the corner of the bed—and found a small black automatic pistol. He grabbed it—Gauthier's hand hadn't reached it. Then he was holding it in both hands, and was back on his feet, looking down. Gauthier sprawled and rolled, hands to his head. Travis grabbed the jacket off the back of the chair, kicked the chair in Gauthier's direction, and backed off farther. He retrieved the Brocock and slung the jacket aside on the floor.

Gauthier sat up and leaned back against the wall. He looked dazed. Blood poured down the side of his head. His face streamed with tears that mingled with the coffee dripping from his hair.

"What the hell was that for?" Gauthier demanded.

Travis waved the automatic.

"I was only going to threaten you," said Gauthier. "It's not loaded."

Travis brandished the Brocock in his other hand. "Well, this fucking is."

"You tried to kill me," Gauthier accused.

"You were going for a gun! What do you expect me to do?"

"Not that," admitted Gauthier.

"And why were you going to threaten me anyway?"

"I became suspicious," said Gauthier.

They glared at each other.

"Oh for fuck sake," said Travis. "Let me get you something for your head."

———

Later that evening, Travis accompanied Gauthier down the road to Hebden Bridge. The Frenchman carried a small valise. Just outside the village he paused beside a high, crumbling drystone wall. "Excuse me," he said, and disappeared behind it. Travis vaguely assumed he'd been caught short. Five minutes later Gauthier reappeared. He wore a white collarless cotton shirt, a long jacket, and baggy trousers. A small round blue cap on his head emphasized the bandage on his brow. His visible skin had browned a little. Grime darkened every line in his face, and accentuated his weary, wary expression, quite unlike his normal bright alertness.

He handed Travis the valise.

"Wait here," he said. "Burn these when you can." The accent was flawless; someone familiar with Bradford could have narrowed its origin to a few streets.

Travis nodded. *"Bonne chance,"* he said.

Gauthier looked at him blankly for a moment, then

gave an uncertain grin. "Dunno what you're saying, mate, but the same to you."

Travis watched as Gauthier walked away, his gait heavy, his gaze downcast; across the cobbles and toward the camp, merging with the still-growing crowd, becoming invisible.

PART THREE

The Scottish Regiment

10

ROISIN woke late Wednesday morning in a twisted sleeping bag on a camp bed in a room that smelled of cat. At first she wasn't sure where she was. She looked at clothes slung on a chair and remembered they were hers and not somebody else's. With that it all came back. She wanted to bury her head again. Once straightened, the sleeping bag was comfortable but her bladder wouldn't let her stay. She struggled out, rummaged clean knickers from her pack, and found the bathroom. The clothes she'd changed out of in the Tesco loo yesterday were piled in a reeking heap beside the laundry basket, still with their police tags. When she'd washed and dressed she went through to the kitchen and found Evangeline Groves sitting by the table, with a cat and sunshine on her lap, a cup of coffee in her hand, and the day's *Morning Star* under her elbows. A retired teacher and still-active Communist, which in Roisin's eyes made her older and more eccentric than Mad Jack, Evangeline had long white hair and expressions too young for her face. Whether the news was good or bad it was as if she had learned something new and not seen it all before, which in most cases she had.

"Morning, Roisin," she said. "Sleep well?"

"Like a dog," said Roisin.

"Better than sleeping like a cat," said Evangeline.

"Which is what I had to do. As always." She slid a clean cup across the table, followed by the cafetiere. "There's some left."

"Thanks." Roisin drank it gratefully.

"You're not a vegan or anything, are you?"

"No."

"Oh good. I think of these things as eating disorders, you know. Let me get you some breakfast."

"No, no, I can—"

Evangeline stood up, ignoring protests from the cat and Roisin, and got busy with bacon and eggs and toast and fresh coffee. Roisin, embarrassed by her own ungraciousness, which stemmed from being unused to being looked after, and suddenly aching with hunger pangs, read the paper. USAF BLAMED FOR LEUCHARS HORROR. It turned out that this blame was being laid by spokesfolk for the Stop the War Coalition, the Muslim Association of Britain, and the Communist Party; but—as the article pointed out—the government and the USAF itself, by attributing the disaster to a weapons-handling accident, seemed to agree. Far more contentious was the next lead article, below the fold. *Grangemouth, M-way Blasts— Communists Accuse!* It was awesomely typical of the *Star*'s sub-editing that at first glance Roisin read it as "Communists Accused." That wouldn't have surprised her. The actual accusation did.

In a sensational development, Britain's Communists attributed yesterday's terror attacks on oil refineries and motorway junctions to a clandestine US sabotage network. Speaking for the Executive Committee, Party General Secretary Madeleine Murray cited "credible US security sources" for her claim that a Gladio-style terror network is operating in the United Kingdom. The aim of this network, she said, is to pave the way

for transforming the longstanding "special relationship" into a full-scale US military takeover of Britain.
In the buildup to a Third World War, US strategic
planners see this as the only way to ensure the stability of the alliance. "We can't go to war while the Brits
are one no-confidence vote away from neutrality, or
indeed the other side," one source said. "And if the
Brits can't secure their own infrastructure, and protect
their own Muslim population, we would have a solid
pretext for intervention." The plan is backed, the source
continued, by the pro-US wing of the British establishment.

Of particularly sinister significance, Murray added,
is that this plan was to be implemented in the opening
days of a global war. Whether Wednesday's explosions
indicate that the war has begun, or that the operation
was triggered prematurely by the Leuchars nuclear-
weapon accident, remains to be seen. In either case,
urgent action is called for.

At this point Evangeline returned with breakfast. After
the plates were emptied and the second coffees poured,
Roisin stabbed a finger at the article.

"Do you really believe that?" she asked.

"That the Yanks were behind it?" Evangeline shrugged.
"I wouldn't put it past them."

"Okay," said Roisin. "Let's get this clear. The *Communist Party* has a source inside the CIA or whatever. This
Deep Throat coughs up that the US has a plan to take
over Britain in the run-up to World War Three, despite
the fact that it has free run of the place as it is, and that
this takeover would be resisted by British forces. And this
plan includes blowing up oil refineries and motorway
junctions that would be far more useful left intact, besides killing hundreds of people on their own side. *And*

it includes making sure it gets blamed on the Muslims, so that the US can be seen as *protecting* Muslims. And on top of all that, the whole thing may have gone off half-cocked!"

"Yes, dear," said Evangeline. "That's more or less what Madeleine's saying."

"And you don't find any of that incredible?"

Evangeline ran a fingertip across a bleary eyelid. "No, as it happens I don't, Roisin."

"Is this because the Party's always right, or something?"

"Oh, come on," said Evangeline. "You know me better than that, dear."

"All right," said Roisin. "Sorry."

"Never mind," said Evangeline. "Now, I have to say, I know Madeleine Murray, and she wouldn't say something like that without good evidence. As for the improbability of it all, and the Communists having a Deep Throat—well! What would you say to a story that back in the nineteen-forties the British and the Americans were *literally* parachuting *literal* Nazis—Waffen SS men, who were hidden right here in Edinburgh—into the Soviet Union? And that the man they put in charge of the whole operation was a Soviet agent, Kim Philby, who of course betrayed it to the Russians? Or that sections of the British military seriously considered a coup, *twice,* because the head of the CIA had convinced himself, and went on to convince various British spooks, that a right-wing Labour Prime Minister was a KGB agent?"

"These things happened?" Roisin hadn't heard this even at SOAS.

"Yes, they happened." Evangeline waved a hand at the stacks of books around the walls. "There are respectable books about these plots, and plenty more like them. Google up Operation Gladio sometime, and what that led to. There's no idea too crazy in conception and too cocked up in execution to be unbelieveable, coming from these people. But the point is, Roisin, that it makes political sense. I know it doesn't feel like this with the antiwar movement being so feeble, but Britain really is unreliable. If the antiwar MPs in all the parties got together they could bring down the government. If they agreed to stick together they could even replace it with an antiwar government, maybe even without a new election—"

"Yeah, yeah, the Popular Front." Roisin had heard this Left-Right alliance stuff from Evangeline before.

"Why not? It works in France."

"'Works' is putting it kindly. And even if it did, it would just put us on the opposite side of the war, it wouldn't stop the war."

"That's as may be," said Evengeline. "The point is, if it did put us on the opposite side or just neutral, it's a realistic enough prospect for the CIA to have at least a contingency plan for it."

"But it's such a crazy plan!"

Evangeline just looked at her until she laughed.

"All right," she said. "We'll see. Maybe. Anyway, the *Star*'s wrong about one thing, I'm sure of that—what the explosion actually was."

Evangeline nodded soberly. Roisin had told her most of the story the previous night.

"We should get that to the *Star*, then."

"Will they print it?"

"They'll quote you, at least, I'm pretty sure of that. But they won't run with it unless you have evidence."

Roisin sighed. "We sent photos to some papers, maybe including the *Star,* but we didn't have much hope they'd get through."

"I suppose it depends how clever Mad Jack really is," said Evangeline.

"He's clever," said Roisin.

"But caught?"

"I think so. Otherwise I really would have heard from him." She looked at her phone and considered looking for news. She couldn't face it, so she had to ask. "Have there been any more attacks?"

Evangeline shook her head. "Nothing new. Lots of high-level meetings. Chiefs of Defence Staff and so on. And troops have been deployed overnight to protect Muslims in England. Apart from that—well, the Stop the War sit-down outside the consulate got broken up. There's an emergency meeting at twelve-thirty in the Peace and Justice."

"I'd better go," said Roisin.

"Oh, you must," said Evangeline. "People will be so glad to see you."

———

People weren't glad to see her. Sitting at the table in the cafe of the Peace and Justice Centre below St. John's Church, Roisin sipped Fair Trade coffee and nibbled organic carrot cake and looked at a dozen closed faces among the fifteen around the table. The majority's expressions only concentrated the mood she'd sensed as she'd walked up Leith Walk and along Princes Street with Evangeline, who'd caught it too.

"The panic's over," she'd said. "Now people are *really* scared."

The Asian-owned shops along the upper stretch of Leith Walk were closed, some shuttered or boarded up. One broken, scorched window of an electronics and junk shop had among all the melted mobile-phone cases a small piece of charred cardboard still legible, reading:

computer's sword's gun's DVD's. The guns, Roisin
guessed, would have been the target. Little more than
toys—air pistols, replicas, blank-firers, or deactivated,
and all illegal to carry out of the shop, though not, by a
quirk of the law, to sell—they would have been useless
for the shop's protection but useful to have on the street.
Smoke from Grangemouth hazed the sky and gave the
breath a gritty aftertaste. Small children wore surgical
masks, in pandemic-retro fashion. Older Asian men and
all Asian women, even if quite evidently Sikhs or Hindus,
always had the company of at least one young Asian
man. Only white people walked on the street alone, intent on their thoughts or the murmur of their phones
in their ears. The races and religions were ecumenical in
their faces, all with the same withdrawn, watchful look.
In Princes Street some shops were closed and others had
queues, quiet and intent, not jostling.

It was as if, with the fear of, and flight from, fallout
over, and quite other dangers emerging, people had sobered up—or sobered down; hardened somehow; ceased
to be susceptible to displacement activities like driving
south in the car or attacking random Muslims. They
were waiting for proposals and explanations that made
sense. That was a lot to read into the thrawn features of
the folk on the streets, but it was what was being said
out loud around the table.

"Seems tae me this stuff about a strange device is a
diversion," said Malkey, the Scottish Socialist Party guy.
"I'm no saying you didnae see something, right, but
what can we dae about it anyway? The focus has got tae
be on building the fight for a nuclear-free Scotland. Tae
make a big issue out of what exactly it was that exploded
is tae wander ontae the territory o conspiracy theorists,
and we're no going there."

"Well, there's definitely some kind of conspiracy going on," said Roisin. "What about the refineries and motorways?"

"We condemn the attacks, and we defend Muslims against backlash. What else is there for us tae dae?"

The man from the local mosque's peace group nodded firmly. "Aye, that's the way."

"Now wait a minute," said Evangeline, brandishing her *Morning Star*. "If that was a false flag operation, then it has to be exposed. Surely that contributes to defending the Muslims, who're getting blamed for it quite unjustly."

"With all due respect," said Joe Watson, another SSP guy but English, "that's a matter for investigation, not agitation. I mean, we'd look pretty silly if we ran with this CIA plot theory and some AQ cell was turned up in Clackmannanshire with a stash of recently fired mortar tubes or whatever."

"There's already been a claim that Leuchars was a Scottish Republican terrorist attack," Jacqueline Thomas said. She was the CND branch chair and another old CP stalwart. "That could be used against the Left, obviously."

"All the more reason for us not to touch it with a barge pole!" said Joe.

"That's not the point," said Roisin. "The point is that there's all kinds of wild theories flying around about the Leuchars explosion, even in the papers. Suppose tomorrow or the next day the government drops the accident line and claims it was a Russian attack? Talk about looking silly then. Because that weapons-accident line *is* a cover-up, and if we don't challenge it, we're colluding in it—and maybe playing into the hands of the authorities, when that line doesn't hold, which it won't. The truth will out, and it's much better that we should be the ones who *get* it out." She looked around, and felt she was talking to a wall. "Mad Jack and Claire and I took a lot of risks to get it out, and even if that hasn't worked, I'm going to go on trying to get it out."

"The truth is out there, is that what you're saying?" Malkey asked, raising an uneasy laugh that was followed by an awkward silence.

Peter Dalgleish, the local Stop the War Coalition membership secretary, cleared his throat and shifted his chair.

"That kind of brings us to another question," he said. He glanced across at Malkey; Roisin caught or perhaps imagined a small nod in reponse. "It's serious, and I wanted Roisin to have her say first. Mad Jack and Claire are being held at Wester Hailes Police Station. Same place as you were at, right, Roisin?"

"Yes, I said I thought they'd been arrested—"

"Aye, well, I checked. They're being held there without charge under the Act. Now, it happens Jennie Mulgrave—that's the campaign lawyer, she can't be here—was told they were arrested in Edinburgh yesterday around six. They weren't caught up in the Grangemouth cordon or anything. Now, Roisin's told us she was arrested early yesterday afternoon, told the coppers about everything except names and the photos, and then was released without charge. So what have the filth got on Mad Jack and Claire that they don't have on Roisin?"

"I don't know," Roisin protested. "You know what they're like! For all I know, they might be tailing me to see if I go to—the Russian Consulate or something!"

This wasn't getting her anywhere. The only sympathetic looks she got were from Evangeline, Jacqueline, and a young guy with a CND badge, who she just knew had to be another CP peacenik.

"I think," said Malkey, "the question is, what dae they have on Roisin? Sorry, Roisin, but you have tae admit, it does look a wee bit odd, you getting released like that. Is there something you're no telling us?"

"No, there is not!"

Dalgleish scrolled a page on his PDA. "You were at the peace camp right through the winter, you've known all of us for months, and you never saw fit to mention that your old man's a computer security consultant who's done a lot of work for the government. He isn't returning calls, by the way. Nor did you mention you have a brother who's in the army."

"So what! It's nobody else's business. How did you find that out anyway?"

Dalgleish spread his hands. "You have an online trail like everybody else, Roisin."

"Exactly! Like everybody else! Anyone can find out anything they want about me." She looked him in the eye. "Or you."

"Sure, go right ahead. The rest of us . . ." He glanced around the table.

"What are you driving at, Peter?" demanded Evangeline.

Dalgleish leaned back. "Nothing. I'm not casting aspersions on Roisin. It's quite possible she's being used inadvertently."

"Which means it's possible I'm not," said Roisin. "I call that an aspersion all right."

The consequent hubbub went on for a minute or two before Evangeline banged on the table with an empty mug.

"Listen! Everybody!" she said. "This is getting completely out of hand. Here's what I suggest. The meeting should just get on with organizing the demo, and in keeping up the pressure to have Claire and Mad Jack released. Anyone who is interested in what Roisin saw can just contact her—through me, if you have to—and we can organize some investigation. Perhaps the Scottish CND comrades could look into it."

This won a few nods and a moment of relaxation. Then Malkey spoke up again:

"I'm sorry, but that isnae good enough by a long shot. It cuts right across our efforts tae get Claire and Mad Jack out. Petitions and legal representations and that. Because what they'll be accused of is spying on the base. And what Roisin is saying, and wants us tae publicly admit, is that they *did* spy on the base."

"Oh come on," said Roisin. "Everybody knows we base-watch."

Malkey scratched his head. "Aye, but Stop the War disnae officially endorse aw that goes on at the peace camp. What went on, I should say. And if some of us continue tae discuss and investigate this story, it just piles up the evidence, because we're aw watched and phone-tapped and that. Specially Scottish CND, because of . . ." He hesitated, looking a bit shamefaced. "Aw that old Cold War stuff."

Jacqueline's and Evangline's lips compressed at the same moment; the young CND guy looked baffled.

"Let me get this clear," said Roisin. "You're saying that anyone who talks to me on the phone or in any other in-secure way is playing into the hands of the cops by making it look like we were spying for the Russians. Thanks a lot, comrade!"

"This is becoming divisive," said Jacqueline. "I suggest we drop the matter and move on."

Everyone hurried to agree. Roisin stood up.

"Fine," she said. "Good luck with the demo and petition. And a street stall, don't forget that."

She walked out, shaking at the knees. The long patio behind the church's basement was below street level, bordered by old gravestones and overlooking the tree-shaded ancient graveyard from which the slabs had come. The air held a smell of cake and coffee and poster inks. She had sat on this patio many times. In breaks from the peace camp it had come to seem almost home, at least a refuge. The smell of it sent her back. By the time Evangeline caught up with her, at the top of the steps, Roisin was in tears.

Evangeline put an arm around her.

"Bloody Trots," she said. "Don't let them get to you."

Roisin shrugged the arm away. "You weren't much help."

"Now, that's—"

She stepped ahead of Evangeline and turned around to face her. She screwed up her eyes and sniffed hard and wiped the back of her wrist across her nose. Bloody skirt didn't even have pockets.

"Fucking cops!" she said. "That's what they are! Touts, not Trots."

"Who?" demanded Evangeline.

"Peter or Malkey. Maybe both."

"You can't be serious, Roisin. You can't say that."

"Yes I fucking can. Didn't you see what they did back there? They smeared me and froze me out of the movement. They implied I was a police agent. That's a *classic* police-agent trick." She found her fists at her forehead. "But I can't say that, because then it looks like *I'm* the one doing it. Oh, fuck, it's all so—"

"We have to be so careful," Evangeline said.

"Yes, *you* have to be careful," Roisin said. "Malkey there just managed to slip across not to talk to CND people because they're CP and therefore might be spies for Russia or China or—oh God, it's too absurd. And you didn't notice or you just rolled over."

"He didn't *say* that. He said—"

"I know what he said. And I know what he didn't say."

"Don't teach your grandmother to suck eggs!"

The cliched admonition came at Roisin sideways and knocked her out of the frame. It was the image of Evangeline as her grandmother that did it. She saw the two of them standing there on the pavement spitting tacks and they didn't look like a grandmother and granddaughter. They looked like lovers having a spat. *Cat fight! Cat fight!*—the playground cry came back and it made her laugh. A shudder went through her, as if she'd been out of herself for a long time and had just been shaken back into place. And with that, the puzzle pieces shook into place too. She had not been released to disrupt the antiwar movement, nor to be tailed back to some nonexistent foreign handler. She was not being frozen out of the movement to cover up anything, but to reveal something. It was nothing to do with the politics. It was all about her; her real life; her real self.

This is me, this is my life, this is not all happening in my head.

She was standing at the corner of Lothian Road beside a church under a smoke-reddened noonday sun with light traffic on the carriageway and people pushing past her on the pavement and looking at her with curiosity, and in front of her a woman with long white hair was laughing in a friendly and relieved manner.

This isn't about ideas anymore.

Evangeline's place in Roisin's mind click-click-clicked like slides in a juddery projector, from not-grandmother to not-lover to not-mother.

Roisin stepped forward and hugged Evangeline. The older woman's shoulders felt warm under her thin old-fashioned cheesecloth smock. Her hair smelled like grass.

Her clothes smelled of fabric conditioner. Roisin stepped back.

"It's all right," she said. "I'm all right."

Later she added, "I was in a bad place."

She was in a good place now. She knew what to do. It was all simple when you got back into yourself. When you stopped worrying, stopped fretting, stopped the dither, and the yammer of ideas, and just saw.

Evangeline wouldn't see it, and Roisin didn't try to make her see it. On the way back she bought yet another new phone, used it to check her father's dead-letter-drop, left an urgent reply, then chucked the phone under the front wheel of a passing bus. Evangeline raised her eyebrows at that, but made no objection. After they got back to Evangeline's place, Roisin just sat in the basement flat that smelled of cats and books and newspapers and listened to the washing machine and then to the tumble dryer as it vented warm air into the now shaded back garden. She listened to Evangeline too, and she nodded and smiled and said things now and again but she didn't argue because she had stopped arguing with herself. She accepted the laundering and the conversation and the dinner and the television, and the book of MacDiarmid and the dram that she carried with her to the warmth of the sleeping bag. She knew that Evangeline would be appalled by what she was thinking, and she nevertheless took Evangeline's hospitality as sensually and guiltlessly as the cat did. This wasn't about ideas anymore. It was about bodies in motion and hers among them, even in the slow motion of sleep.

11

JEFF Paulson parked his car in the Greensides multi-story and walked briskly up the sloping curve to the top of Leith Walk and made a sharp left into Waterloo Terrace. He glanced at morning-edition headlines that were almost all the same number: 1,319, the confirmed fatalities to date. He observed the diminished rush-hour traffic and bus-stop queues and pedestrian huddles at crossings, and averted his eyes from certain window displays. The corner sustained a bunch—a whole goddamn bouquet—of bridal shops and every time he walked past them he had a flashback to a minor but iconic 9/11 image. The news channels didn't show corpses back then, and a shot of a roomful of mangled mannequins and white veils and dresses covered with gray dust, from the wrecked Priscilla of Boston store on Roylston, had stood in for massacred innocence and sullied hope. They'd stopped re-running it after the first wedding-party friendly-fire slaughters in Iraq.

The litter of trampled placards, scrawled-on sheets, satirical masks, left-wing newspapers and tear-gas cartridges began at the corner and thickened as he approached the consulate. It stood on a one-sided street on the side of Calton Hill, overlooking an old graveyard and the railway lines below it to Arthur's Seat, on whose steep grassy slope below the cliff-face TROOPS HOME

YANKS OUT had long ago been spelled out in giant letters with some evil concoction of weed killer and fertilizer that made them ineradicable. They even appeared through snow.

Past the Brit cop barrier at the entrance to Regent Terrace, then the buzzer and ID scan at the gate box, then the Marines at the door, the blast door, the metal detector, more Marines, the sniffing dogs, the puffing chamber, the shoes handed back. The Marine who handed them back had seen Paulson three hundred and twenty-seven times and had yet to betray a flicker of recognition. Paulson wore slip-ons—the hassle and humiliation of stooping or getting down on one knee then the other to retie shoelaces had long since become too much.

Hayworth was Cultural Relations. Paulson did the rap above the brass plate, paused, and went in. Hayworth looked up from a desk and under eyebrows.

"Sit," he said, waving a paw.

Hayworth sucked on an empty pipe and scanned a flat screen and looked down at sheets of paper for a minute or two. Paulson sat out the performance. He recognized his own report from the previous night, and the photos. Hayworth eventually patted and tapped the papers together and laid them aside.

"Good work," he said.

"Thank you, sir."

Hayworth rattled his pipe stem between his teeth. "Still happy with SCRAP?"

SCRAP was Andrew MacIntyre. Scotland Station had long since run out of dignified cryptonyms like SCEPTRE and SCIENCE for its agents. It was an exhausted running joke that they would soon have to draw the line at SCUM.

"Yes, sir. He'll keep it quiet. Smith insisted on Five's retaining the film spools, of course."

"I meant in terms of boxing in the Travis woman."

"Oh yes," said Paulson. "I have that triangulated. The two agents on his string assigned to that job are SCRUB and SCROTE. Unknown to him and each other, of course."

Hayworth affected a disillusioned expression, then chuckled.

"Venal little shits, aren't they?"

"I prefer to think of them as patriotic and entrepreneurial, sir," Paulson said, a little stiffly.

"Well, yes. Speaking of which. The Brits are not at all happy about all this, as you can imagine. They know as well as we do that it wasn't a straightforward tactical-nuke accident—if they didn't know it before they certainly know it now, having seen the pics—and they also know that sticking with that story is sinking HMG's media credibility faster than a Chinese junk bond. And the fact that the accident or sabotage happened on our watch, quite literally under our guns, doesn't make even the truth much of a fallback. It still looks like carelessness on our part, which it wasn't. At least half the one thousand, three hundred and nineteen dead so far are *ours*. As for the disinformation campaign . . ." The end of his pipe stem vanished into an eyebrow like a duck into reeds. "I sometimes wish Homeland Security's fighting keyboarders were a little *less* creative in covering all the bases, not to mention covering their ass." The reeds quivered for a bit, then the pipe stem soared. "The front desk here—here!—has had to field a dozen calls so far this morning about Russian secret weapons, French perfidy, imminent counterstrikes, heartland isolationist coup plots, and flying fucking saucers."

"Flying saucers? Sir?"

Hayworth flourished the pipe. "The top-secret triangular hypersonic bomber standby."

"That one."

"Yes. Getting a bit long in the tooth for my liking, but

it seems it can still be trotted out and fools can be found to ride it."

Paulson had seen plenty of evidence that such a bomber existed, most memorably and directly one night under the stars in the mountains above Tabriz, but he knew better than to say so.

"Uh . . . sir, if it's not presumptuous to ask . . . I mean, it might help in maintaining the cover story if I actually knew—what *is* that thing in the photos?"

Hayworth frowned down at the prints.

"It *is* out of place to ask," he said. "But, as it happens, I honestly don't know, myself. I couldn't tell you if I did, of course, but I don't." He looked up, meeting Paulson's eyes with a frankness that had him almost persuaded. "I don't. I'm sure the brass know, but that's by the by, because what they *don't* know, and what is quite frankly driving them frantic upstairs, is *why* the damn thing blew up on us. You understand, there's a world of difference between its being down to some fumble-fingered grunt or overeager physics nerd, on the one hand, and on the other somebody's malign intent. Because believe you me, if turns out to be malign intent *from any quarter* it is going to be treated as an act of war, a WMD attack, with all the consequences that follow. I have that right from the top." He looked at the ceiling, as if the top was located there, like God.

"The White House?" Paulson was impressed.

"From POTUS, in person, on the direct line an hour ago."

"Oh."

"Oh, yes. Among other things, she had a message for you."

"For me? Sir?"

"Functionally, not personally. Her exact words were:

'Get after that fucking Frog spy-ring family and squeeze every last fucking drop out of them.' "

"I trust you told her that's exactly what we're doing, sir."

"I did, but she seemed less than impressed, particularly as so much of it is being handled through the Brits." Hayworth held the bowl of his pipe under his nose and inhaled, then seemed to realize what he was doing and put the pipe down. "She was frankly surprised that, given the proximity of"—he glanced at the paper—"Roisin Travis to the Grangemouth explosion *as well as* the Leuchars event, there's no mention of any attempt to locate *James* Travis in the vicinity of any of yesterday's *other* explosions. She also found the aforesaid proximity very suspicious in itself. She mentioned the possibility of, for example, a mobile-phone detonation."

"I think we can rule that last out, sir. We found no record of any use of her phone other than exchanging numbers with the other two. And on the face of it, to rely on detonating such a major and time-critical explosion from a passing bus seems a remarkably failure-prone procedure. Leaving aside the point that it was as a result of that explosion that we intercepted her in the first place. However, the point about James Travis is well taken. I have to admit, sir, we didn't think of it that way." He felt like kicking himself as he remembered his own voice saying, *This is a combat operation.* "We almost did, but when one is thinking in terms of tracking a spy on the run one doesn't . . ."

"Indeed," said Hayworth. "I think it's a slim chance, myself, but worth following up."

"We still have a few cops at Wester Hailes assigned to us, sir. They can check all footage of all the explosions. I'll get them onto it."

"You do that," said Hayworth. "And I'll start moving heaven and earth to get more than 'a few cops at Wester Hailes' assigned to this operation. Meanwhile, there's the third member of the Travis family to work on."

"The soldier."

"Private Alec Travis. He's under arrest. I'd like you to interrogate him."

Paulson swallowed. "Yes, *sir*. But that would mean—"

"You don't have to fly to Somefuckedupistan. Private Travis is being flown to RAF Lossiemouth. He's due to arrive in two hours. You'll be there to meet him." Hayworth smiled. "He won't know he's in Scotland, and I'm sure you won't tell him."

A disorientation job. That should make things quicker.

"Very good, sir. I assume the trains are—"

"Drive to Edinburgh Airport, park, head for the military area. There'll be a Chinook on the pad." Hayworth glanced at his watch. "Move."

Paulson moved.

———

There wasn't, as it turned out, a CH-47F just for him. Chinooks and other choppers were taking off and landing at Turnhouse—the military insisted on the airport's official name, like there might be some other airport in Edinburgh—all the time. Most of them were going to Leuchars with rescue/recovery crews and equipment, or returning with casualties, but enough were shuttling to and from other bases for Paulson not to have more than a half-hour wait before the dispatcher pinged him for a Lossiemouth flight. He used the time to call Maxine Smith and pass on what Hayworth had urged.

The aircraft was only half full, with a dozen RAF Regiment soldiers and a couple of officers, and Paulson bagged a right-hand window seat without difficulty. The Brits ignored him, to his relief. The chopper took off fast and steep, and flew low under a high cloud ceiling. Everyone was told to stay strapped in throughout the flight. The seats faced inward, but Paulson was able to twist around and look out just after they crossed the Firth of Forth and leveled out. He followed the Fife coastline with his eye and thought he could just see Leuchars in the far distance, with the faintest hint of helicopters above it like gnats, but that was all. The oil rigs in the North Sea were more apparent. After that he glanced out now and again, as the landscape changed from the green of farms to the brown of moors, then to the sides of mountains, but most of the time he sat and gazed inward, meeting the likewise abstracted gaze of the soldiers. There was nothing of the banter he remembered from his own stint.

The journey took just over an hour. As the helicopter descended he glimpsed another Firth, bluer than the Forth's, white-topped, and a northward-facing shore fringed with sand. As he deplaned behind the soldiers the civilian reflex to duck as he walked beneath the rotors almost caught him, but he corrected it. The soldiers trotted away and Paulson headed for the nearest office. It was no shame to duck under the stiff breeze from the sea, or to cringe a little from the noise. The airfield was far busier than Turnhouse. Tornados and F-16s screeched off every few minutes, usually to return escorting transport aircraft and the occasional bomber, sometimes to loiter over the horizon.

"I'm here to meet a prisoner," Paulson told the desk sergeant, handing over his cards.

The sergeant examined and scanned the cards, iris-scanned Paulson, peered at a reading, and then looked right back at him with some disdain.

"Enjoy your stay," the sergeant said. He leaned back and called over his shoulder: "Another one for the facility, Private!"

Paulson hadn't known Lossiemouth had what the Agency called a facility, though it didn't surprise him that it had. Nor did it surprise him that, when the private escorted him past a row of identical concrete blockhouses, he was able to identify the facility by smell. A heat shimmer above the flat roof was another clue.

The private took him around to the side of the building, to a plain door, and knocked. It was dark inside. A face looked out, nodded, and beckoned. Paulson turned to thank the soldier, but he'd turned on his heel and walked off without a word. Just before Paulson stepped inside, he heard a heavy growl from the sky and looked up to see the familiar silhouette of a C17 Globemaster, coming in over the Moray Firth. If his prisoner was on board he had arrived just in time.

The door closed behind him. Paulson stood for a moment until his eyes adjusted to the dim light. The air was sub-zero and stank of shit. He could smell his breath going in and see it going out. He was in a wide vestibule in front of a soundproofed door on which red-on-white lettering extended in a strip from top to bottom, from the huge NO UNAUTHORIZED ENTRY through to the small-print legal boilerplate at the foot. Beside the door was a large poster, black print on white, with the UK Government crest, spelling out the relevant provisions of the Health and Safety at Work Act; and a small one, red and white on black, from the Scottish Executive doing the same for the Smoking and Health (Scotland) Act. From all of this Paulson gathered that only herbal cigarettes could be stubbed out on prisoners.

The man who'd opened and closed the door was the

only other human presence in the room. He was slim and dark and wore a white coat.

"Good morning, Mr. Paulson," he said, extending a hand. The grip was firm, the accent Californian. "Dr. Walker."

"Good morning, Dr. Walker."

"Have you been in a facility before?"

Paulson shook his head.

"You'll have had interogation training?"

"Army and Agency." Paulson cracked a thin smile. "In resistance only, I'm afraid, not application."

"Don't worry," said Walker. "You will have professionals. All you need to do is feed them the questions. No, I only asked because otherwise you might find the procedures disturbing. Do you feel you require orientation beforehand, or that you may require counseling afterward?"

"No, thank you." Paulson found the thought of counseling by the likes of Walker more disturbing than that of participating in stress interrogation.

"Your choice." Walker shrugged. "Before we go in, though, I must impress upon you not to say anything that could compromise the location. Having a facility *over here* rather than *over there*—and Britain is, for the present, very much *over here*—puts limits on what we can do. The trick is not to let the prisoner suspect for a moment that he isn't *over there*."

"I understand."

Walker opened the door. Paulson flinched back. The stench became almost overpowering: shit, piss, vomit, unwashed bodies, the iron whiff of blood. He had expected the noise to be as bad as the smell, but it wasn't: quiet voices, moans, weeping, the growling of dogs. He took a grip of himself and walked forward. The floor and walls were bare concrete that seeped condensation. There was one row of ten cages, of which eight were occupied. There was plenty of room to pass the outstretched arms. The light fixtures were wire-covered bulbs.

The door at the end of the prison row was not sound-proofed. It was of thin wood, splintered here and there as if it had been kicked through. No sound came from behind it, from which Paulson inferred that nobody was being interrogated. Walker gestured for him to go first.

The interrogation room had stone walls, also damp. There was a scatter of chairs, an iron bedstead, a long trough with a battered board propped at the end. Hooks on the ceiling and rusty iron loops screwed into the walls, from some of which hung chains and shackles. A blunt hook held a coiled hose. The floor looked as if it was hosed and scrubbed regularly, but it still had stains. Duct tape, paper towels, and clingfilm were racked neatly on rollers under a shelf, on which lay an assortment of power tools. Two doors stood open at the far end, one to a corridor and the other to a cage in which a pair of Alsatians stood, gazing intently out. Their ears pricked and their growls became louder when they noticed Paulson. Walker stared them down and slashed the air with his index finger. The dogs' ears drooped and they flattened their forelegs, wagged their tails and whined.

Walker pointed to a camera in the corner of the walls and ceiling.

"You can observe by CCTV, if you prefer," he said.

Paulson shook his head. Walker pressed a switch on the wall. A door at the other end of the corridor opened and a man, shackled and jumpsuited, blindfolded but not earmuffed, shambled forward between two soldiers who gripped each of his elbows. His arms were behind his back. The jumpsuit was soiled at the crotch and—as soon became apparent—at the seat. As the trio approached Walker slipped a catch on the cage door. The two dogs hurtled forward, banged open the door to the prison row, left it swinging, and pelted down to the far end and back, barking all the while. Yells and screams from the prisoners added to the cacophony. The man in the jumpsuit pulled back, and was dragged forward. The dogs leapt back into their cage. Walker clanged the door shut behind them, then strolled across the room and kicked shut the door to the prisoners' row. The barks stopped, the shrieks persisted. The two soldiers pushed the man down onto a chair, his plastic-tied wrists behind his back and his arms around the chair back. One soldier grabbed duct tape and ripped off long strips of it, with which he secured the prisoner's ankles and shins to the chair legs.

Paulson asked the questions. Walker indicated the stress methods. The soldiers applied them. Afterward they stripped the prisoner naked. One of the soldiers washed him down and bathed his cuts and bruises with a high-pressure hose. They placed him in one of the two unoccupied cells and left him there. As was required under some of the laws referred to in the small print on the facility's outer door, the CCTV camera recorded the whole procedure.

———

Like most CCTV and mobile-phone cameras, the one in the facility had been manufactured in the United States, where debt-bondage and environmental refugees ensured a steady supply of cheap labor and the devalued dollar kept the products competitive. As was the case with almost all such cameras made in the US, its firmware had been designed in India. Like most such designs, the high-level concept work had been done in Bombay, and the low-level programming grunt work had been farmed out to Guangzhou, which under what was officially known as Socialism With Even More Chinese Characteristics had become what was officially known as a Skilled Socialist Labour Export Zone, or, less respectfully, as the cubicle-farm of the world. Certain particularly skilled socialist laborers of Guangzhou had incorporated some undocumented features in the machine-code level of the programs. The most notable, and quite unnoticed, of these features was one that selected, copied, encrypted, and transmitted data at random intervals and by diverse routes to a secret annex of the Department of Artificial Intelligence of Beijing University. The data's selection criteria were set and continuously refined by a natural neural network cultured from the cortical cells of a long-deceased cat, genetically predisposed and behaviorally conditioned to recognize images of death and pain. The only human intervention required, when the images reached Beijing, was to select those most appropriate to upload to other parasitic programs, distributed across dozens of quite unrelated communications and surveillance satellites, which generated the phantom presence in near-Earth orbit of a so-called virtual satellite, whose principal output was the Execution Channel. Over time, the network learned to anticipate the selection criteria applied by its operators, and to offer ever-more useful images, requiring less and less human intervention to select. The operators, who were themselves carefully selected members of the International Department of the Central Committee of the Communist Party of China, recognized and recorded this as a further achievement of socialist labor.

The neural network also made other and subtler connections that its operators did not recognize at all.

Paulson knew nothing of any of this, and like almost everyone else took for granted that the Execution Channel was an ingenious and perverse American black op.

12

Roisin felt cleaner than she had for months. Her jeans, T-shirt, and denim jacket felt as soft as a summer frock. Their laundering and her showering gave her the impression she was walking around in a waft of perfume. It was almost glamorous. Heavy rain overnight had washed the sky, leaving a chill blue morning. She strolled down the ramp from Waverley Bridge, holding her breath through the knot of last-gasp smokers at the boundary, and stood on the concourse of Waverley Station and read the departure boards. The East Coast line was still cut at Leuchars—the rubble of the station blocked the track—so the London trains were starting from Waverley rather than Aberdeen. They were crowded, not with refugees but with people who would normally have driven or flown. Downed flyovers and closed airports had done what the $200 barrel couldn't. The timetables were unreliable. Roisin bought a ticket for Berwick-upon-Tweed at the machine and at 10:15 boarded the delayed 10:05 GNER train to King's Cross. Her Leatherman Squirt, in a deep pocket of her rucksack, made it through the metal detector at the platform gate. The four-centimeter blade was street legal but she was relieved not to have to argue the point. There were no seats left but you could stand. Roisin placed her rucksack between her feet, wedged herself between other people's stacked luggage near the doors, and glowered herself a foot of personal space. The fresh-washed feeling didn't outlast the further twenty-minute delay before the train lurched forward.

The sandstone tenements of respect and of neglect, the floodlights of a football ground, the shorefront suburbs, the new estates. The widening Firth. Somewhere on the other side of it was where she had been for the past half year. She knew too little of this side, of Edinburgh, of Scotland. It was not her country and in her stay here she'd been ever and again reminded of it, in this attitude or that expression that suddenly revealed a gulf in comprehension or premise. In long winter nights around the campfire Mad Jack had told her—and anyone else who would listen—what little she knew of the geology and history of the area. Prestonpans slid past—there had been a battle there, one that the Jacobites had won. One of the SSP guys who'd visited the camp had called the anti-feudal reforms in the bloody aftermath of the Jacobites' defeat "the Scottish Revolution": a revolution from above, liberating but repressive at the same time. Maybe that cold-blooded, self-imposed regime change was at the back of the strangeness of the Scots, what Claire Moyle had called their statism—"their inbred focking statolatry" was how she'd put it. Being an anarchist in Belfast couldn't have been easy, especially for someone from a Protestant and Unionist background, but it had equipped Claire with exactly what the Scots didn't have, a fock-youse attitude to authority and a bone-deep hostility to nationalism and the state. Roisin wished it had been Claire and not her who'd been at that meeting yesterday—she'd have cut through the crafty maneuvers like a laser.

The train passed a small castle, in good shape, and a coal-fired power station in ruins, its demolished smoke-stacks two neat parallels in brick. Beyond the low hills of the present horizon, out over the sea, three jet fighters banked in a chevron of vees.

Roisin wasn't worried about Claire; she was too tough to intimidate and had nothing to hide. If she confessed about the photographs they might throw the book at her, but she'd get off the standard scare charges ("in possession of materials that might be useful to," etc.) in court. She'd be all right unless the Brits tossed her to the Yanks, which in the circumstances seemed like an empty threat. (Roisin was not as sure about that as she'd have liked.)

Mad Jack was a different story. Claire could plausibly plead that she didn't know the addresses of the media contacts and—no doubt—conspiracy sites to which the photographs had been sent, but Mad Jack couldn't, because he'd written them, and probably from memory at that. His memory was phenomenal; it went with his peculiarities like the random gifts nature threw to autistic savants. His personality disorders were in part a pose, Roisin was sure, but it was the part that wasn't a pose that worried her. Mad Jack would crack, under nicotine deprivation if nothing else. She could just see him, ruefully accepting a cigarette after at most two hours of evasive rambling and fidgeting.

Out on the water the Bass Rock loomed, and far beyond it a skyline row of cliffs. Volcanic plug, sedimentary rock: somewhere farther along the ragged curve of this coast was Siccar Point, in whose folded strata James Hutton had discovered the depth of time, the first unconformity between science and the Bible. The same Bible had been the solid ground, the rock, for the Covenanter preachers condemned to that basalt pyramid—Scotland's

Alcatraz, its Robben Island—the Book whose savory verses they had screamed while James the Second and Seventh had supervised, with an interest perhaps more than forensic, the crushing of their thumbs and the splitting of their shins.

Tears sprang to her eyes, as they always did when the thought struck her that that particular prerogative was back: the right of the sovereign to condemn, to put to the question, without due process and for reasons of state; that on that sore point all the Revolutions in Britain and America had been for nothing. That *America* had been for nothing; that dismayed her.

She was glad Alec was all right, that so far he hadn't been caught up in this. She'd checked his blog before she'd left Evangeline's place, it had recently been updated and he sounded fine, and dropping odd hints that the Flap had been all about some kind of unidentified flying objects over mountains. She guessed that he was trying to step away from the indiscreet allusion to Fife.

Past Dunbar; then a raw quarry, a white lighthouse, an old chimney standing on its own among trees, then the stacked sugar cubes of Torness. From outside there was no way of telling whether it was back in operation, after yesterday's shutdown. She'd seen a freshly spray-bombed slogan on the wall at Waverley Bridge: IT ISN'T RAIN, IT'S FALLOUT. She despised that sort of thing; she was glad it wasn't true. The newborn lambs in the fields would live to be eaten. She stared out of the window at the cliffs of another headland and at another sea-skimming flight of fighters and wondered how long she could be confident about that.

But the final war was too big a worry, too remote no matter how close it might be. The insight that had struck her outside the Peace and Justice came back. It was all about her. She hadn't been released to act as a traced isotope in the antiwar movement. The security services already had that covered, from within as well as from without. No. It wasn't even Claire and Mad Jack, really, who'd be the focus of attention in this case. It was her, specifically and personally. She glanced, without stopping to think, at the faces around her in the crammed vestibule. The fleshy concentration of the man with the suit and ponytail, engrossed in his phone screen; the blank outward gaze of the mother with a kid hugging each knee; the lowered eyes of the young guy with a new backpack at his feet and an old paperback under his nose. It could be any of them, but it was probably not. It could be somebody in the carriage, not even looking her way: the woman with the compact, the man with the laptop. Or perhaps not on the train at all, but monitoring the feed from the cameras that poked from every ceiling corner. At the station someone would fold a newspaper, someone else would fall into casual stride, and would be looking somewhere else whenever she looked back.

That was how it would work, a Five tail as her father had called it. The business with the new phone yesterday had been the last piece of tradecraft she'd done, and ever intended to do. She'd taken no precautions today. No doubled-back bus routes, no alleyway dashes, no side-street sprints, no department-store saunters then up the service lift and down the stairs and out the back. None of that. Just a straight stroll to the station, stopping only to download more cash to her card at the NatWest hotspot. The account was partly funded by her father, and had kept her in frugal supply for the past few months. She'd been a bit tense, just before the screen indicated that the transfer was complete: she'd worried that the account had been frozen. But that sort of harassment wouldn't be what she was up against now. The security services wanted her on the move.

If it was her the security services were following, then their real interest had to be in her father. She was not at all certain that this was all a terrible mistake.

A hillside of gorse and firs flicked past; a clump of Scots pine marked the entrance to a glen that opened out after a few minutes to green rolling hills as the train cut across a corner of the coast through farmland and past a grand old sandstone house with decorative turrets and sloped and terraced lawns. Then back to the edge of the sea, along a cliff-top route past narrow coves and jutting promontories of the same sandstone as the house, with the sea stretching to a horizon soon interrupted by the distant spit that stretched out like a long arm shielding Berwick upon Tweed from the south.

The train slowed, sending her swaying. It stopped in the station and she shouldered and elbowed her way out. She waited on the platform, gazing at a ruined remnant of city wall, until the train creaked off again and the other passengers who had alighted had departed. Then she shouldered her pack, and not looking around strode off into Berwick, town of cobbles and towers, earthworks and gates, bridges and beaches; feeling light on her feet and no weight on her back, feeling as always the relief of being back in England and out of Scotland, south of the Border, back in the free world.

———

Mark Dark sometimes dozed in the daytime after a late night, and slept outright after pulling an all-nighter, but he never let his mother know this. Whatever happened, he was always up and about before she was, busy before she left for work, and awake when she came home. Coming in from the strip mall at seven in the morning with fresh waffles, hot coffee, and a couple of early editions in time for her breakfast burnished this image, and he did it when he could.

Sandra licked maple syrup off the crook of a finger, put down the sticky bottle, and stared across the table long enough for Mark to notice and look up.

"Your friends in England. Are they all right?"

"I don't know, Mom. Most of the guys I met were from London."

"That's in England."

"Yeah, Mom, but it's a long way from Scotland. There are no Libertarians in Scotland. Well, there's one in Edinburgh. I'll email him."

"You do that." Her gaze became reminiscent. "I was so proud when you gave a paper at that conference."

"So was I, Mom. It was great." Mark felt slightly guilty about this subject. He'd talked up the Libertarian Alliance conference, where two years and six months or so ago he'd given a talk on Internet conspiracy theories, so much that he'd left Sandra with the abiding impression that he had been a star speaker at a major scholarly symposium, whose proceedings were eagerly awaited and closely studied by government advisers and intelligence experts around the globe. He'd long since paid back the three hundred dollars he'd thus wheedled from her toward his airline ticket, but the white lies still made him blush.

"All those lawmakers and professors you met. You should write to them. Ask what we can do to help."

Sandra had the impression—not in this instance at Mark's insinuation—that Members of Parliament were enormously important and powerful figures. A Tory backbencher had been on a panel about Europe, another had delivered a witty after-dinner speech. Having had a beer with one, applauded the other, and shaken hands with both was evidence as far as Sandra was concerned that her son had a hotline to the nerve center of the British Establishment.

"I'll do that if I have time. But I don't think the Brits need any help."

"With all those terrorist attacks and Muslim riots? Sure they do. Everyone was talking about it at the church last night. We could send care packages for the refugees."

"Last I heard, it was the Muslims who're being displaced."

"I know that, Mark. And last I heard, Christians are supposed to help anyone who needs help."

Mark tackled a piece of bacon and a gulp of coffee before replying. He didn't trust himself to sound reasonable straight away.

"You're totally right, Mom," he said. "And I will ask, okay? But . . . well, I kind of think it's up to the Brits, you know? I mean, it's the Brits—well, some of the whites, anyway—who're pushing out the Muslims. It's their responsibility. And we got millions of DPs in our own country, and you're helping them."

"It isn't millions," Sandra objected, pro forma. "It's a couple hundred thousand. You shouldn't believe everything you see on the Net."

Jeez, Mark thought. He knew better than to argue with that one. Having once totted up, personally, all the figures from every local paper he could find online in the US, he had come up with a million in FEMA camps and another million fending for themselves one way or another, on the streets or in the debt-bondage *maquiladoras*. The official figure, invariably used by Administration droids and mainstream media talking heads, was a tenth of that. Mark had actually posted his own total not to dispute the official figure, which most well-informed people regarded as risible, but to deflate the much higher figures that he'd seen bandied around—some respected bloggers and websites claimed five million in the camps alone, and three million missing presumed dead as a result of first the pandemic and then the various droughts, hurricanes, tornadoes, and infrastructure breakdowns that had caused the displacements. But when he'd raised it with Sandra she'd yelled at him and then cried for an hour. She gave three evenings a week to the church's work at Evansville's FEMA camp, with its two thousand four hundred and twenty-six DPs, and the thought that this wasn't one of the largest of about fifty camps, as she'd always believed, but one of the smaller islets in a far vaster archipelago than was officially acknowledged was for her not to be borne.

It had taken Mark a lot of painful late-night thought before he'd figured what that was all about. It wasn't just that the figure he'd given made the task seem overwhelming. It wasn't, even, that it undermined Sandra's faith—there was no other word for it—in the President's grip on global warming. It was that it struck at her secret hope that Mark's father, Jack Dark, would someday turn up. All the evidence—remaining photographs, emails, CCTV captures from local stores and the gas station—was that Jack had fallen for some DP chick from New Orleans and run off with her. Sandra had divorced him for abandonment long ago, and resumed her maiden surname, Hope. But, Mark reckoned, she still clung to the comforting notion that the whole thing had been some bizarre amnesiac episode, and that Jack would find his way back through the DP system to the Evansville camp. Or something. Such things had happened. Heartwarming stories of missing folks with missing memories returning after years were a Fox News staple. Mark had never believed any of them—at least as presented—and he didn't have Jack lined up as a likely candidate to come back even with a fake memory loss. As a boy he had loved his father and he still missed him now and again, but his cold and adult assessment of the man was that for all his kindness and energy he'd been a feckless, impulsive, immoral shit.

Mark had written up the whole story on his blog, certain that his mother wouldn't read it and hoping, still, somehow, that his father would. Rather to his surprise, even with all the names and details, this hadn't made his connection with the Mark Dark website any more obvious than it already was. Lots of readers of blogs like his just skipped anything personal, or followed the site and ignored the blog. Some of the people he met in the mall or in the neighborhood who knew of the blog still just thought it was funny or even cool that he had the same name as this weird conspiracy site.

"Okay, Mom," Mark said. "Whatever. Point is, we have enough to do here, and the Brits are well off enough to look after their own."

Sandra wadded her empty plate and cup, and stood up. "That's what worries me. I don't think the Brits think of the Muslims as their own anymore."

"It's not that bad."

She slipped a linen jacket on over her light dress and peered in a wall mirror to apply her lipstick.

"Not yet, maybe, but we've all seen how these things start."

"Yeah," said Mark. It kind of burned him that he hadn't thought of that. He'd been too intrigued by the questions about what had blown up and whose hand was behind it to think about the other angles. Ethnic cleansing in England—that would be something to see. He didn't say that.

Sandra picked up her purse. "Bye," she said.

"Have a good day, Mom."

She blew him a kiss and went out. Mark waited until her heels had clicked out of earshot then closed the main door as well as the screen door against the hundred-degree heat outside. He turned the air-conditioning up full and went down to the basement, figuring on earning just enough over the odds to pay for that particular addition to the household bills.

But first, he had to look at the world. He checked his television split screens and trawled websites. The dust storm in China had abated. The fast-built Fuller domes over China's vaunted eco-cities had performed to spec; North Korea had just taken delivery of a dozen. Mark fired off a comment that this was probably for fallout protection, turned to his email, and worked his way down his inbox. One email header amid spam, dross, and routine comments caught his attention: *Leuchars object Kazakhstan origin?* The sender was *ans3lm,* an occasional anonymous correspondent who had sometimes tipped him off to interesting stuff in the past.

Hi Mark Dark

Thought you might be interested to know that some Brit troops in Kazakhstan have been speculating on just what it was that blew up in Leuchars. Check these out:

A list of links followed. Mark zapped through them. Brit soldier blogs, all of which mentioned UFOs, lights in the sky, strange aerial phenomena. The strongest stuff was on two: *Stan Boots, Flash in the 'shan.*

Stan Boots had:

Rumor: SAS guy in the bar. Swears he was on the
<u>cross-border raid</u> and knows the cause of the Flap,
and that it's connected to the lights over the 'shan.
Clammed up when pressed, and you don't press
snake eaters too hard. Conclusion: wait for the memoir.

The latest entry in the latter, by a guy called Alec Travis, was astounding. It linked to that entry and added:

No need to wait. I saw it being loaded on to the C17
for Leuchars. Big fucking triangular object, looked
like a stubby jet. New model MiG? I don't know, but
I reckon that's what blew up.

Mark scrolled up and down the blog. He followed a trail of embedded links. He stared at the latest entry for a while. It was either disinformation or one hell of a security lapse. On a sudden suspicion, he toggled to View Source on his screen toolbar, to reveal the raw code underlying the blog post. Nothing odd there. Then he looked at the blog header code. The list of keywords, not shown on screen but there to be picked up by search engines such as Google, contained a surprise:

Alec Travis, soldier, Brit, British Army, Kazakhstan, Signals, soldier blogs, war, football, soccer, UFO, HTS

Mark whooped. He called up Google cache and found a version of the blog as it had existed a day or two earlier, then viewed the source. The list of keywords had everything except the last two.

"I know what UFO is," said Mark, "but WTF is HTS?"

It took another moment with Google to find out.

"Heim Theory Ships," he said. "Holy fuck."

The blog entry he'd just been looking at was close to the top of the first Google page returned. Some clever hack elsewhere had to be driving it so near the top of any search on "HTS." Anyone Googling "HTS" was likely to notice the blog entry, even though the abbreviation didn't appear in the entry iself, but was buried behind it where few would look. What most readers would see was a mention of a mysterious triangular object, linked to speculation about a cross-border raid, the object that exploded at Leuchars, and UFOs over the Tianshan mountains.

Mark repeated the exercise with "AAV-2100," the name of the alleged secret craft in the alleged secret documents he'd been sent, and found—after a longer search, this time—that it was cropping up in the hidden keywords of several of the Brit soldier blogs he'd just been looking at—though not, as it happened, in that of Alec Travis. Another check on Google's cache of earlier versions revealed that it too had been added within the past few days—the irregularity of posting made it hard to pin down more precisely. It could have been in the past twenty-four hours.

Mark stood up and walked about, then ran up the stairs to grab a Jolt from the kitchen fridge. He walked back down more slowly, settled in front of his screens, and sipped while he pondered.

Someone was trying very hard to convince him that a secret aircraft—whether a commie knockoff captured from the Chinese or a US original retrieved from Chinese territory—had been transported to Leuchars and (presumably) had blown up there. It didn't seem unduly paranoid to connect *ans31m* with the anonymous source of the supposed USAF documents. Whether *ans31m* was a witting or unwitting conduit of disinformation was irrelevant—from now on, Mark would have to treat with suspicion any material he or she sent. Mark wondered if any other conspiracy or parapolitics sites had received anything similar. A little further Googling showed nothing of the kind. The usual nutball sites carried UFO speculation about Leuchars, but they needed no cleverly planted documents to make them do that sort of thing. The relatively sober and serious sites did, and Mark could easily imagine how some of them would fall for it. Too many bloggers were more politically sharp than they were computer literate—even website developers had become so reliant on software tools that they seldom looked at the underlying code. Mark did boring HTML coding for a living. Clicking on View Source was second nature.

If anyone else in the conspiracy community had received the same disinformation, quite a few of them were likely to publish it. Indeed, any halfway assiduous searching on Leuchars, or on UFOs, or HTS, was likely to begin turning up the soldier blogs and all their spurious connections. And after they'd gone out on a limb with this juicy story, they'd have the limb sawn off, discrediting it and them at the same time—keeping the true cause of the Leuchars explosion as obscure as ever, which no doubt was the intention. The good old double bubble.

Now he had a story. He even had a title: *UFO Disinfo Circles Leuchars*. He grinned to himself, drained the Jolt, and hit the keyboard running.

———

The Cobblestone was a small old-fashioned hotel with a cobbled yard behind it and a tiny public bar just off reception. The bar had three tables and a games machine. An elderly couple and a young man were sitting there when Roisin put her head around the door. Roisin glanced around to make it clear she was looking for somebody, then smiled vaguely and backed out. She went over to the reception desk, checked in, took her key, and went up to the room. It had just been serviced; the hotel had had an overnight inflow and then outflow of over-hasty refugees fleeing nonexistent fallout.

Apart from the trouser press and the fire notice the room seemed like a guest bedroom in a house. Three walls were hung with reproduction paintings of young ladies in long white dresses, picnicking and punting under wide hats and lacy parasols amid trees and flowers in a gauzy period haze. Roisin dumped her rucksack and shrugged her jacket and flung herself backward on the bed. She gazed at the paintings for a while, imagining herself in the scenes, a fantasy that was partly erotic and partly anguished. What was seducing her was the thought of being somewhere like that, being someone like that, serene and safe and protected and above all somewhere else, away from all this. There were men in the pictures, shadowy attentive figures who pushed poles or hefted hampers. You could look at the men and let the imagination give them features beyond a beard or a black hat. Claire had surprised her once by pinning up a small photograph of Che Guevara in the shelter, and even more by transferring a kiss to it by fingertip in a moment when she'd thought herself unobserved.

"There's politics," Claire had said, "and there's hormones. The difference is, you can argue with politics."

After that Roisin had stopped hiding her monthly charity-shop haul of historical romances behind the stack of spy novels and serious books under her camp bed.

She clutched her crotch, rolled, sighed, rolled again, and sat up on the side of the bed. The wall that didn't have a painting had a flat screen hanging on it. She picked up the remote from the bedside table and flipped through news channels, then flicked to Internet access and checked her brother's blog. Updated: she was pleased to see that. It was the content that surprised her. The object that Alec had seen being loaded on the C17 was certainly not the one she'd seen being unloaded.

She drummed her fingers on the bedside table, and turned over possibilities in her mind. Alec could be lying. His blog might have been hacked. He might have been arrested and his blog ghostwritten. The possibilities were all disturbing and she dared not email Alec to check—if he was in trouble, further contact with her wouldn't help his case.

There had to be some other way to check, but she needed to think. For that, she needed to get outside. She unpacked her rucksack, stuck the little multitool in the smallest pocket of her jeans, and slipped the phone—the one the police had taken and returned, and therefore presumably still tracked—in the inside of her jacket. She stuck her key card in the top pocket, picked up a brace of cellophane-wrapped biscuits from beside the kettle, and went out.

The corner shop in the next street had a boarded-up window and a scorched door. The shop was still open, with a bill on the newspaper board outside displaying today's headline: PROTECT OUR MUSLIMS, SAYS PM. Roisin bought a bottle of water. The man and woman who ran the shop moved as though they hadn't slept. Behind them, under the cigarette shelves, a young man with a lock-on gaze sat, right arm draped behind the back of the chair, holding something heavy in the shadow. It might have been a stick.

A couple of turns took her to the path up to the town's earthworks. Brown signs with white lettering and the

Heritage portcullis. Atop the earth wall she walked northward, buttoning her jacket against the chill wind off the North Sea. Long grass, gulls, a golf course. Breakers rolled to the beach, bearing dry-suited surfers. Small long-beaked dun birds moved across the beach like a vapor, their brisk thin shanks invisible, and took off meeping whenever a surfboard ploughed the sand. The flock circled, returned, repeated the process, like they had short-term memory loss. The surfers trudged then paddled back out and rode the waves in again. Oil tankers marred the horizon's line, jet fighters ruled new parallels above it.

From the Leuchars shore she'd seen many a similar scene. She'd sometimes thought it would make the perfect snapshot of imperialism: the resource hauled, the force projected, the way of life protected, innocent in its enjoyment, guilty in its ignorance. Surfers, tankers, jet fighters: she could have made a postcard of it, and sent a copy to every one of the billions on the other side of the equation. Having a lovely time. Wish you were here. Most of the recipients *would* wish they were here; none more, perhaps, than some of the millions mobilized in the states that had broken away, to claw themselves collectively upward in a painful high-acceleration burn to what they hoped was a different orbit.

Now she saw it differently.

On a headland she skipped down some perfunctorily hacked stone steps to the beach, and walked along the seaward side of the strandline. The tide was halfway out. She left steep-sided footprints in the stiff sand. She rounded the next promontory and found herself in a small cove with a cave in the cleft and a boulder as big as a car about ten meters from the cliff. She waited there for an hour. Now and again she chugged water from the bottle and checked the time on her phone's screen. At

14:00 she stood up and headed back. She found the steps to the sea-facing wall in a back street, climbed them and walked along the wall, peering through gun emplacements and exploring munition stores. On to the beach again, and then along the wall along the side of the river. At the end of that she went up the sloping High Street, over white drifts of cherry-blossom petals dislodged by the past night's downpour. She stopped off at a pub called the Reiver's Rest. A steak pie and a pint occupied her until 15:00. Out she went again, and down to the long narrow bridge. In the middle of that she stopped and watched the still-infrequent trains on the viaduct for a while, then walked on, and back to a different pub, one decorated with antique posters and furnished with mismatched chairs, one of which might have been a barber's, or a dentist's. The pub's TV was tuned to Sky News, not sport. Conversation was low and raw. Roisin drank a half pint of the local brew, used the Ladies', and walked back to the High Street at 17:00. She took a Chinese takeaway to the beach and ate it slowly, sitting on the end of the harbor wall; threw the remains to a gull and the cartons to a bin, and returned to the hotel. She showered, jilled off, dried off, pulled her clothes back on, set three alarms on her phone, and then crashed on the bed and slept off the dinner and the drinks for an hour. A full stomach and a little alcohol had become unfamiliar in the months at the peace camp.

She woke with a plan. When you couldn't work *in* to a problem, her father had told her, the trick was to work *out* from it: if the center was hidden, you had to search along the periphery. The spy novels called it taking back-bearings.

She brewed up a sachet of instant, switched on the screen, swung out the remote's keyboard wings, and went online. Alec's blog remained the same, with the weird crap about a triangular aerial vehicle being loaded up for Leuchars. Roisin saved the link to that latest post and copied it into a blog search engine. The search took several seconds longer than she'd expected.

Two hundred and fifty-seven sites linked to the post. That struck her as a lot. But then, some people did obsessively track soldier blogs.

She opened a new window and repeated the process, this time with a post from a few days earlier, a routine one about daily Army life. Eleven, all war nerds. She did it several times, and always got a dozen or so results. She smiled. Poor guy didn't even have groupies.

Okay, so his latest one had been a big hit. She returned to its page of results, scanned it, paged on. A predictable clutter of UFO nutter natter. She flipped the search ordering from *View by Time* to *View by Significance*. This ordered the links to Alec's post by how many other sites in turn linked to them. At the top of the list was an item on a website called Mark Dark. Roisin recognized the name—it was one of Mad Jack's favorite sources of information. She clicked through.

UFO Disinfo Circles Leuchars

Documents pointed out to this and other sites (and rogue-state-offshored here, here, and here, and a number of blog pieces and other items appearing on the Web, strongly suggest a serious campaign of disinformation around 5/5, aiming to set investigators chasing after the familiar UFO will-o'-the-wisp. Yes, folks, it's time for the good old North Sea triangular mystery aircraft to be rolled out of the hangar again! This one's got faked "leaked" USAF documents and "eyewitness accounts" in soldier blogs of funny lights in the sky and (a nice touch) a mystery aircraft—

captured or recovered by a Special Forces raid into
Xingjiang, China—being loaded onto a Globemaster,
destination RAF Leuchars, just hours before the
explosion. What clinches that one as a black op, as far
as I'm concerned, is that the blog's hidden keywords
have been changed to include "UFO" and "HTS" in
the past couple of days—check for yourself on the
Google cache. "HTS", in case you don't know, stands
for "Heim Theory Ships", which is the latest version of
the super-advanced black tech storyline. For earlier
versions see Nazi flying saucers, Roswell, Area 51
alien tech, Majestic 12, chemtrails, HAARP—all
comprehensively discredited as black propaganda
ops. I don't expect HTS to turn out any different, if and
when we ever get FOIA on its ass. So, folks, what
gives?

Roisin skimmed the documents, archived at three different sites in La Paz, Caracas, and Havana, and opened the
blog links. One of them, as expected, was to Alec's blog,
but it intrigued her that the other links appeared to confirm what Alec's implied. Seeing Alec's blog held up to
the world made her uneasy, as if her family affairs were
being pried into.

She returned to Mark Dark:

Analysis: This disinfo campaign shows the, ah,
watermarks of secret state activity at a very high level.
Documents of this quality are not faked and leaked
lightly. Likewise, meddling with actual soldier blogs
(as distinct from running "ghost soldier" blogs) requires
the express permission of superior officers and the
cooperation or coercion of the blogging grunts. It may
be that Alec Travis, frex, is a loyal Brit who is happy to
run disinfo when asked. But most soldiers are very

reluctant, for the good reason that putting disinfo
in their blogs (as distinct from self-censorship of
operational matters etc) undermines confidence
in their blogs among the folks back home, whose
reassurance that Their Boys are OK is for most grunts
the object of the exercise. So if I were one of Pte
Travis's friends and family, I might be a little worried
about the lad.

Onward. Where was I? Oh yes—the significance of this.
I've said all along that whatever blew up on 5/5 came
from the state resources of a declared nuclear power,
and was unlikely to have been an accident, at least not
the tac-nuke handling accident that is still the official
line. Speculation is, of course, rife on teh Interwebs: an
attack by a hostile power; a US government attack
simulating such (i.e. a false flag operation); a strike from
within the US military, portending a coup or civil war;
sabotage of a captured device (sekrit weapon, sekrit
aircraft, power plant, alien spaceship) by whoever it was
captured from. That last seems to fit in with the UFO
disinfo campaign. Some or all of these may be (and to
my certain knowledge, at least one is) disinfo put out by
US Govt agencies. But the curious thing is, one of them
must be true OR the truth is even more unsettling than
anything we've imagined.

My own take is that the US and/or UK Govts, or key
elements thereof, know damn well what happened and
are terrified of its implications. World war or civil war,
that's what the choices are, realistically; and throwing
out as much chaff as possible is the only way to keep
this under wraps until they have got their shit together
and decide WTF to do next.

*What do the rest of us do next? Stock up on those
bags of pasta, tins of tuna, and bottles of water.*

Oh, very droll, Roisin thought. The analysis made
sense, as far as it went. The thing she'd seen looked more
like a secret weapon than anything else. She hoped that
Mad Jack had indeed sent the photographs to Mark
Dark, among all the others, but she doubted that they'd
ever get to him now that Mad Jack and Claire had been
arrested. Still, it would be nice . . .

She caught herself at that thought. Would it be nice?
What if the truth, whatever it was, would be enough to
start a war?

Her phone chimed a reminder she'd set herself, for
21:00. Time to go downstairs.

———

She went outside first, partly with the thought of antici-
pating the expected encounter and partly she needed the
air. She circled upwind of the smokers' patio adjacent to
the bar and stood in the gateway of the hotel's cobbled
car park, dark within its high walls but watched over by
infrared CCTV. The lemon sky shaded to a dim pale blue
at the zenith, pricked with more stars than she'd see at
this time from Edinburgh but fewer by far than she'd
seen from Fife. A moving point of light emerged from
nowhere, climbed, flared for a few seconds brighter than
anything else in the sky, then faded to nothing again, like
the universe in the standard model. The International
Space Station, still going around and around, still crewed
by astronauts and cosmonauts from the contending
powers and their client states. A world in miniature—
Roisin felt a sudden fierce wish that it was just that,

self-sufficient, something that could survive whatever happened here below. But that, she knew, was a futile fancy: the Station would burn like a moth in the first seconds of a world war, too tempting a piece of high ground to be left to fall into enemy hands. But still, the wish wouldn't go away.

She looked up and down the street, saw nobody she recognized, and went into the hotel bar. Two elderly couples and two young men—the place had livened up. Roisin idly wondered which, if any, of them was on the Five tail. She bought a pint of dilute orange and sat in a corner. The television was tuned to Sky Sport, showing a late-season UEFA cup qualifier. Roisin sipped her drink and focused on her phone. Its screen was as cramped as the bar; it seemed appropriate. She scrolled through websites and flipped TV channels, more or less at random.

Ten o'clock. She looked at the door. One of the young men nipped out for a smoke, one of the old men returned with an empty pipe in his mouth. Roisin ordered a vodka and lime, picked up a discarded *Scottish Daily Mirror* from a table, and settled in her corner to read. The headline fatality count had reached 1,687. On a spread of seven inside pages she saw more pictures of the burned and the blinded than she'd seen in ten years of one-sided tactical nuclear strikes. Editorials and letters seethed with demands for explanation and retaliation. Other pages dealt with the usual preoccupations of diet and debt, fashion and fame. Roisin was reminded of something Mad Jack had once said, no doubt stolen from someone else: that a daily newspaper was as bizarre in its juxtapositions as any work of the Surrealists or Dadaists or William Burroughs.

More surfing and another drink, with a packet of peanuts this time. Twenty to eleven. You could smell the stale smoke off people's clothes as they came and went.

Roisin checked the Edinburgh Stop the War website. It had just been updated. Legal action on behalf of Armitage and Claire, petitions, a street stall. She smiled. The phone chimed again. Eleven. She looked up.

Maxine Smith walked through the door.

13

THE first thing that struck Roisin about Maxine Smith was the flicker of anxious scrutiny in her gaze. This was followed by relief, and then composure, all in such swift succession that Roisin might have imagined it. Smith fixed Roisin with a tight-lipped smile, ordered a gin and tonic while keeping an eye on her, and clicked over and sat down. She laid a phone on the table, a few inches from Roisin's. She wore a light summer dress, glossy and floral, with pink slingbacks and a matching handbag with a slender shoulder strap. Just a thirty-something woman out on the town. Her scent matched it, mumsy but desperate.

"He isn't coming, you know," said Smith.

Roisin couldn't keep the gloat from her voice. "No," she said. "But you have."

Smith raised her glass, smiled, sipped, then put the glass down and poked about with the cocktail stick in the slice of lime.

"Ah," she said. She took a deep breath. She opened her handbag and took two pinches of snuff from a small round tin. Then she checked in the mirrored lid and dabbed her upper lip and nostrils with a Kleenex. Sniffed again. Roisin observed the entire procedure with distaste.

"Take that look off your face, young lady," said Smith.

Roisin shrugged and edged farther back into the corner.

"So," said Smith, her nostrils contracting briefly, "it was me you were waiting for."

Roisin nodded.

"Thought so," said Smith.

"No, you didn't," said Roisin. "You thought I was waiting for a man. You said so yourself."

"All right," Smith conceded. "But you'll allow that your coming here without covering your tracks suggested you might be up to something else."

"Such as?"

"A diversion. But then, of course, you'd have made more of an effort to look like you didn't want to be followed." Smith smiled, and twirled a hand. "Such complicated games we play, in the secret world, don't we?"

The television was still loud with talking heads. The young men and one couple had gone; the remaining old man and woman were deep in drink and recriminatory reminiscence. The barman was watching the box. No one was listening. Roisin leaned forward nonetheless.

"I'm not *in* the secret world! That's my whole fucking *point!*"

Smith recoiled, clutching her glass as if Roisin had spluttered droplets of spittle in the drink. "Explain."

"Give me a minute," said Roisin. She stepped up to the bar and distracted the barman away from the matchpoints table on the screen and into pouring her a double vodka and lime. After sitting down and taking a hearty slug of it she glared across the little round table at Smith.

"Fuck you," she said. "I know who you are. You're from the security services, and you think I'm a spy. You think my father is involved, and you have grave suspicions about my brother."

Smith blinked, too hard. "Your *father*? What makes

you think that? It's your friend Norman Cunningham whom we were most suspicious of."

"Mad Jack?" Roisin laughed loud enough to turn heads. She lowered her voice. "He doesn't have that nickname for nothing."

"It's a pose," said Smith. "He's highly professional. It was he, and not your 'spy novels'"—her voice dripped sarcasm—"who taught you tradecraft. Photography, of course not digital; aircraft identification; evasion and escape." She reached a hand forward; for an alarming moment it seemed that she was about to lay it on Roisin's wrist. "Of course, I can well accept that you didn't realize what he was doing—what *you* were doing."

Roisin leaned back, folding her arms. "You don't catch me like that."

"How *do* I catch you?" Smith's smile was wholly kind. "I'm sorry, Roisin. That was unfair. I don't want to catch you out." Her hand went to her hair; a finger twirled a curl. Roisin watched, cold and detached; the gesture left her with the same mild disgust as the woman's snuffing. "I know you didn't know about the microfilms."

"What microfilms?"

"We got the number on CCTV of the white van you abandoned in the Tesco car park in Alloa. Last night it was spotted in Glasgow. The little scrote who stole it didn't get rid of it—or out of it—fast enough. There was nothing inside. Now, we *knew* there had been photographic equipment in the van, because we have the photographs. So the Glasgow police turned over the ned's flat, and found the gear. He'd been trying to flog it on eBay." Smith sniggered. "That's the trouble with the criminal mind, you see. There isn't one. Anyway, among the haul there's one piece of equipment none of us have seen in a long time: a microfilm camera. The good old-fashioned kind that can shrink a page down to the size of a full stop. Now, Mr. Cunningham aka Armitage hadn't said anything about *that*. So at his next scheduled wake-up in Wester Hailes—every hour on the hour, by the way, quite effective—I personally introduced this line of questioning. And he eventually admitted that yes, as well as sending the prints that he and you and Ms. Moyle put in the post, he'd mailed a dozen or so more prints as microfilm strips to the media, to the French, Russian, and Chinese embassies, and to various unsavory and usually American websites whose snail-mail addresses he happened to have."

"Good for him, in a way," said Roisin. "To be honest, though, I've been kind of worrying that getting the photos out may not have been such a good idea as it seemed at the time."

Smith gave her another tight-lipped smile. "They'll all be intercepted before they reach their destinations, I can assure you of that. I needn't spell out our own routine arrangements. As for the conspiracy sites, the US Postal Service has been alerted. Nothing posted to them from anywhere Mad Jack could have passed a letterbox will get past the nearest sorting office, if it gets that far."

Roisin shrugged. "Why are you telling me this?"

"Well," said Smith, clearly enjoying herself, "that was when we realized that Mad Jack Armitage was, you might say, beneath suspicion. He's clearly a lot more competent and together than he pretends, but he isn't an agent of any intelligence service." She paused, scrutinizing Roisin's face for any reaction. "At least," she went on, in a judicious tone, "not any intelligence service connected to the Leuchars explosion."

"Why not?"

"Because," said Smith, "that particular service *would know already* what had really happened, and would *not* be interested in telling the world about it, as Armitage so clearly is. Unless there is some very complex double bluff going on, which is a question I'm only too happy to leave to, ah, higher levels. Besides, Armitage genuinely is too flaky to be recruited by any intelligence service worth its salt."

"Glad you've figured that out," said Roisin. "So that's him off the hook. Good."

"Off that particular hook, of espionage, yes. And you very firmly on it."

"Oh, yeah, that," said Roisin. She did her best to remain calm. She knocked back some more vodka and lime, set the glass down, and looked Smith in the eye. "I can explain that."

"I'm listening," said Smith.

"You're suspicious of my family," Roisin said. "Me, my father, and my brother, yes?"

Smith's face betrayed a flicker of a bleak expression, then returned to diligent, amused attention. "Yes."

"The messages, the photos, the phone call, and then my dad disappearing . . . it must have looked suspicious."

"Why do you think your father has disappeared?"

"Hasn't he?"

"Answer the question."

"He said he was going to come for me. I told him not to, but I didn't expect him to listen. And I got a message from him saying he was on his way."

"You did, huh?" Smith took another pinch of snuff, more delicately this time.

"I replied that he shouldn't." Roisin looked around, as if searching, then grinned. "And he hasn't."

"You had a prior arrangement to meet here."

"Yes," said Roisin.

"And you conduct clandestine communications?"

"You could call them that, I suppose," said Roisin.

"You were going to explain," said Smith, "why all this isn't as suspicious as it looks."

"My father's a survivalist," said Roisin. "That's all. He's been expecting a nuclear war or a . . . big attack for years. When I told him about the nuke on Leuchars he went straight into activating his plan to hole up somewhere. Meeting me was part of it."

"Meeting you here? In Berwick?"

"Berwick, yes, and some other places, depending where we both were at the time. That was the plan." Roisin laid her open hands on the table. "Really. That was it."

Smith sniffled and took a sip of G&T. "'Really. That was it.'" She fidgeted with her hair again. "So why were you so anxious that he shouldn't make the rendezvous?"

"Because I worked out that you suspected him—us— and I didn't want him dragged off. I mean, I knew it had to be about us because you didn't need to release me to lead you to anyone in the antiwar movement."

"Oh? Why not?"

"Because you have that sewn up," said Roisin. "You have agents in it already."

Smith made a show of letting her gaze wander. The television had switched to MTV. "I didn't hear that, so I can neither confirm nor deny it."

Roisin laughed, and Smith joined in. Roisin relaxed a little.

"So . . ." she said. "Have I cleared it up for you?"

"Just two little problems," said Smith. "First of all, what's a girl with a good degree from SOAS been doing at a peace camp for six months of her precious first year after graduation?"

"Oh!" Roisin nodded. "I agree with you. It was futile. I'm finished with all that."

"And when did you decide that?"

"Yesterday."

"Quite the sudden conversion," said Smith. "Road *from* Damascus, you might say. So what are you now?"

"I don't know," said Roisin. She shrugged. "What's the use? It's like my father once said: 'This fucking country is going down.' I just don't want to go down with it."

This was not quite true, she realized. She didn't want to see it go down. But that was not something she could discuss with Smith.

"Your father said that? 'This fucking country is going down'?"

"Yeah."

"What an interesting choice of words. Not 'This fucking country is going down the tubes,' or 'down the drain,' but 'going down,' period."

"I don't get it."

"Well," said Smith, "if you heard a criminal say about somebody, 'That fucking bastard is going down,' you'd know what he meant—a threat."

"It could be just a prediction." Roisin felt she'd said the wrong thing and wished she could backtrack. "Anyway, my father isn't in any position to make threats."

"He certainly isn't," said Smith. "Which brings us to the other little problem with your story. He's on the run, and he's on the run because his cover has been blown."

"His *cover?*" Roisin felt cold all over. "Cover for what?"

"His work for a foreign intelligence service. We know that right from the top. He's a spy all right. And a saboteur."

The room swayed for a moment. Roisin pressed her hands on the table and breathed hard. She had known this. At some level she had known this. The rage—the hatred, even—for the Americans and the British alliance with them that he'd now and then let slip over the years since she'd clung to his elbow on the sofa and watched the news of the first nuclear attacks on Iran—all that had vanished a couple of years ago, around about the time of the invasion of Kazakhstan. She had at first ascribed it to his rage's being overshadowed by concern about Alec, but Alec had been in greater danger on his earlier deployment, in Iranian Kurdistan. Something else had changed, some subtle shift in her father's stance, that she had recognized as very similar to the change in herself when she had stopped raging and got active in the antiwar movement—the relief of actually doing something. But his disdain for the antiwar movement hadn't moderated a jot. James Travis was no longer raging, he was *doing something,* for which she could see no evidence but in his untoward calm, his straighter back, and brisker step. Her next thought was that he'd found someone, but he wouldn't have kept that a secret, and his dismal round of old girlfriends, office flings, and mercy fucks had not let up. Then she had suspected another kind of clandestinity, and wondered if he had become a secret Communist; in retrospect it was the absurdity of that speculation that had enabled her to laugh it off and not probe deeper, for fear—she now saw—of what she well knew she might find. He no longer worried about the war because he had changed sides.

She kept her head. She stared right back at Smith and said, "I said I knew you thought he was a spy. But a saboteur? That's insane! What's he supposed to be sabotaging?"

"He's been corrupting government databases for at least two years," said Smith. "We know that for a fact. We suspect he's been supplying false ID to operatives and agents of the service he works for, as well as undermining the effectiveness of major IT projects—although that, well"—she rolled her eyes upward—"how could anyone tell? Along the way he's managed to mess up his own ID records, car registrations, bank accounts, everything. We had to eyeball a *lot* of video to find a trace of him. And do you know where we found it? In a news report from the Birmingham motorway junction collapse. The thing is, we *expected* to find him there. I won't say why, just that we had reason to suspect he knew something about the explosions, and bingo, there he was."

"Along with hundreds of others," said Roisin. "He was driving north and got caught in the tailback. So?"

"Another coincidence," said Smith. "Like you at Grangemouth, huh? Maybe. But what happened two days ago was a series of attacks that killed thousands. You were on the scene of two of them, and your father on the scene of one. We *know* he's an agent. That isn't something we can ignore, now is it? Would you think?"

"No," said Roisin. An implication caught up with her, like a slap on the back of the head. "Are you saying the explosions might have been the work of—the same intelligence service?"

"That's exactly what I'm saying."

"Good God," said Roisin. Her knees were shaking under the table. "That's . . . beyond disgusting. I can't believe my father would be involved in that."

"I'm not saying he was. But we need to know what he knows."

"I . . . I can see that."

"So will you tell us where he could be found?" Smith leaned forward again, head tilted. "You can think of it as giving him a chance to clear himself, if that makes it easier. He won't be tortured. We don't torture agents of intelligence services."

Roisin didn't believe that, but that wasn't why she shook her head. "I can't tell you, because I don't know. If he'd told me, we wouldn't have made the arrangement to meet here. I could just have gone straight there."

Smith seemed to accept the logic of this. She sat back and nodded slowly.

"All right," she said. "All right. I believe you. I also believe, for what it's worth, that if you've been used by anyone it's been unwitting on your part. I know"—she held up a hand as Roisin made to interrupt—"that's not very flattering, but just take it, okay? You don't want me to develop a high opinion of you, believe you me."

Roisin clenched her teeth and nodded.

"So I'm telling you something in advance, just so that you don't do anything reckless. We are releasing pictures of your father as a man wanted in connection with the attacks. To the police and to the media. They'll be on the news sometime tonight, and in tomorrow's papers. Front page, I expect. Now, we've made no mention of you, but I wouldn't put it past some enterprising reporter to track you down. So . . . if you value your privacy, not to mention your safety, I'd advise you to keep out of sight." Smith drained her glass and smiled. "Not out of *our* sight, but then, I don't think that's a possibility. And if you so much as try to contact your father, we'll know about it, and all bets will be off. Understood?"

There was something in Maxine Smith's expression that made Roisin think she was not as confident as she sounded—as if Roisin still held some card she didn't know about, or had forgotten, and Smith was anxious that she shouldn't realize what it was. She straightened her back.

"Yes," she said. "I understand."

"Good." Smith glanced down at the empty glasses. "Another?"

"Vodka and lime, thanks."

They were alone in the bar. MTV played low. Behind the counter the barman was washing glasses and listening on his ear-beads to some other music entirely. Roisin could see it from how his shoulders moved. Her phone showed the time as 11:27. It seemed a lot longer than half an hour since Smith had come into the room. Smith returned with the drinks. She placed them on the table and waved to the barman.

"Could we catch the news, please?"

"Aye, sure."

Smith sat down, slinging her handbag on the chair back, and gave Roisin a sympathetic smile. Roisin looked at the screen with dread, waiting for the mug shots and the talking heads. The countdown to the half-hour on BBC News 24 started, then the signature tune stopped. The screen flickered to another channel. Roisin was taking a first sip and saw the barman frowning at the remote and thumbing it without effect. On the screen a naked man was curled on the floor of a cell. One side of the cell was barred, the others concrete. The view was from above and a bit off, as from a corner of the ceiling. The man had short hair and stubble, and bruises down his sides and on his arms and thighs. The floor around him reflected light as if wet. The man convulsed several times and then lay still. Limbs splayed, eyes wide, face to camera. A caption appeared at the foot of the screen.

Smith's chair clattered over and her glass crashed as she lunged for the bar counter. She grabbed the remote from the barman, and jabbed the buttons to no avail. She pushed up the flap, shoved past the barman, and reached for the wall socket. The barman yelled and grabbed at her arm. A moment later he was doubled over the counter, and the screen was blank.

The face and the words stayed in Roisin's eyes.

———

- Alec Travis; Scotland; repeated application of legitimate force; suspicion of espionage.

14

Roisin watched Maxine Smith's frantic mouthings and realized that she had a moment in which to choose, before her own denial gave way. In the cold nausea of shock she stood up, pocketed her phone, and walked out. There was no point in running; Smith almost certainly had backup, maybe only the local cops on standby, probably more. Roisin saw no one lurking in shadows as she pushed through the big swing doors and on to the street. But then, that wasn't how it would be. It would be the car a block away, someone behind a first-floor window, that couple in a clinch at the corner. The thought came to her that all this could be a paranoid delusion, or a simple mistake on her part—that she wasn't worth all the attention she imagined. If she thought too much about that she would giggle, and then she would break down. So she stopped thinking about it; for a moment, even, she stopped thinking. Her father was a spy and her brother was dead because of it. That thought remained, held above her head with an effort, but not yet crashing down. That would come.

She set off in the direction of the station, her neck and shoulders rigid, her back straight. Her Kicker boots whispered on the flagstones. Behind her, within a minute of leaving, she heard the swift ticking of high heels. Smith was, very likely, armed; trained in unarmed combat, certainly. The tiny Leatherman blade could in theory slit her throat, but the hand clutching it would never reach the neck.

Roisin was passing through the town gate when the quick steps caught up. They echoed in the deep archway. On the far side of it Roisin stopped, stepped aside, and put her back to the wall. Smith walked out from under the arch right on the curb, and stood facing Roisin in the pool of light under a streetlamp. A couple of cars went by, then an Army jeep.

"Roisin, I'm so, so sorry," Smith said. She opened her arms. "I didn't know anything of this, I swear."

Roisin found her knuckles pressing hard on her lips. She lowered her fist, and found herself hitting the side of her thigh, over and over. She let that be.

"You must have known."

"I knew—" Smith stopped, and looked from side to side, or perhaps shook her head slowly. It was hard to tell, under the yellow sodium light. "I knew he had been arrested, and would be interrogated. But I swear to God I had no idea it would be that kind of—"

Now Smith's fists too were clenched, and moving toward and suddenly away from each other as if trying to push together the like poles of two strong magnets.

"I never expected him to—" Her voice choked off.

"You never expected him to *die,* is that it?"

"No, no, that's not what I meant! I never expected that *bastard* to—" She looked away. "This has all gone . . . shit, shit, shit."

The numbness of denial was giving way to anger. Hold it there. She had a clear sight of a pit she could fall into. Not yet.

"Don't wash your hands of it, you Brit cow. You're just as capable of it as the Yanks. Don't think I don't know what goes on—what's always gone on."

Christ, at this point she was having flashbacks to lectures about Kenya and Malaysia and Iraq and to Claire talking about Northern Ireland. It was pathetic how predictable it all was in her head, like indignant letters to the editor. She had thought she was past all that.

"I'm not washing my hands of it," said Smith. "Yes, of course I know what goes on. But this wasn't—oh, God, that poor kid." She took a deep breath. "Yes, I'm responsible."

For some reason she couldn't fathom, this admission instantly turned Roisin's anger against herself.

"No, it's my fault, all that stupid self-indulgent wank, it was like a game, you know, it was like playing soldiers, it was just another way of not taking it seriously, like changing the channel, it was fucking therapy, and suddenly it's all live and real bullets and my brother is *dead*."

Smith stood very still. A train rumbled through the station, not stopping. Another car went past. A jet screamed in the sky.

It all came down, then. Roisin felt her knees give way, and then she was sitting on her haunches with her knees at her chin, and her knuckles grinding the hair on the sides of her head, and her mouth opening to a thin howl that echoed between the walls and under the arch. She felt Smith's arms around her shoulders. After a while Smith steadied her steps back to the hotel.

PART FOUR

The Burning Summer

15

THE air rifle coughed and kicked. Warning scuts flashed white across the field, too late for the target. The *spang* of the shot rang in Travis's ear as the rabbit jumped and flopped. He strolled over to pick it up. It lay in the long damp grass, blood oozing from a nostril, welling in the watery ruin of one eye. A clean head shot, to his satisfaction; a pregnant doe, to his momentary shame. He picked it up by the hind legs. The pads of the feet were warm, the claws cold.

The pleasure of the kill stayed with him until the moment when he pushed down on the barbed top wire of the roadside fence to swing his legs over it, and the thought came back to him that he had been hammered an inch farther into the ground. That was how it felt. He straddled the fence for a minute, for two minutes, leaning hard down on the wire. Then he swung his other leg over it, stiff and heavy as a log, and trudged up the single-track road as if the rabbit had the weight of a stag and was for someone else to eat.

He pushed open the gate, closed it behind him with a loop of wire over the post, and walked under dripping birches to the back of the house. Under the slated lean-to roof by the back door he hooked the rabbit head down with the previous three, and looked at them all without appetite though he knew he'd eat the oldest of them, killed the day before yesterday, tonight. It had been like that every other day. He considered the possibility that this could be the day hunger wouldn't return, and dismissed it. If he were to waste away it would have already happened. The thought was a comfort nonetheless, like the folded Laguiole knife cached on his belt and the Toollogic knife clipped to his shirt pocket, and the memory of the technique for slitting the wrists: down, not across.

In its copse within the square of drystone wall the house stood at the top of a low hill among lower hills. The Land Rover was inside the old tractor shed. He had scuffed the tracks, methodically, the night he'd arrived. He took no other care to conceal his presence, but the truth was he had not gone more than half a kilometer away in the six days he'd been here, nor seen another soul. From the side away from the road he could look across the hilltops and see, on the tops of a higher range, a row of tall windmills whose limbs turned languidly or spun to a blur, their movements equally useless in the vagaries of the climate change that had called the windmills into being and almost at once rendered them quixotic. Their only function now was as phone masts. The low moan of the shifting wind in their vanes was carried by the same gusts that stirred them, and that rattled the slates on the roof through the brisk, unpredictable squalls. At this moment they were silent, the early morning air still. The sun's heat was already uncomfortable on the skin of his head, recently shaved.

Travis opened the back door and stepped out of his wellingtons, propped the air rifle at the side of the dresser, and padded over to the kitchen range, where he lit the gas under the kettle for some tea. The kitchen, with its deep Shanks sink and wooden draining board, the cracked, dusty Coronation plate on the wall beside the battery-powered Ninja Turtles clock, the ivory-handled Sheffield cutlery in the squeaky drawer, its net curtain and the dead, dessicated flies on the bubbled paint of the sill, comforted him in an obscure way in its very gloom. The ritual and routine of spooning dry leaf from a grease-sticky chinoiserie tin into a warmed china pot with a cracked mahogany-brown glaze, pouring on the water and waiting, further calmed him. Just when his guard was down the grief took him again and shook him. He slumped over the table, pushed his forehead against the smooth, uneven wood, and let tears and snot drip.

In time it passed, like a squall. When he stood up, he had the feeling that this time he was over the worst. He had mourned his son, and was ready to avenge him. He mistrusted this feeling. He had had it, to his certain recollection, five times in the past three days.

He poured tea into a mug, tipped a rough measure of sugar straight from the packet after it, stirred, chucked the teaspoon into the sink just to hear the clatter, and took the mug through to the front room. South-facing, the room was brighter than the kitchen, dominated by a wear-fuzzed brown leather sofa, a blank television, and a cold fireplace. He sat by the small table at the window, facing west, in the shadow that lay across that side of the table. On the table was a Nescafé jar containing a bunch of dried flowers and crusted with dead green algae, the Bible that Travis used for coding and decoding messages to and from Gauthier, and the laptop that Gauthier had abandoned with the rest of his gear in the Heptonstall hotel. Travis put the mug down and watched the rainbow curlicues of steam in the slanting sunlight a cubit away from him, and eyed the brushed-steel fascia of the computer lid.

This was the test. If he could open the computer, he

was ready. He'd checked a few sites on his phone. He
had watched the news on television, over several days in
which he had gone from being the lead item to a now
routine reminder that he was still at large. He had spent
a long cold Sunday in front of the Execution Channel,
on what he had known would be the last day it repeat-
edly screened the cycle that included the clip of Alec's
death, partly to lacerate himself into feeling anything at
all, for at that time he was still numb and unbelieving,
and partly to indulge the delusion that he could burn
through time and causality to give that last empty gaze a
gaze to meet. Hard as all that had been, it was different
from going online. Online was action, it would put him
back in the fight with no turning back. It was like an
oath.

He drank the strong sweet tea and thought about it.
When he put the mug down he found that his fingers
were sticky with sugar. Irritated, he jumped up. He was
already rinsing his hands under the kitchen cold tap
when he realized what the intensity of his unease at the
stickiness meant. He had always hated keyboarding with
sticky fingers. He smiled, rinsed the mug, poured more
tea and sugar into it, and went back to the front room.

The clamshell lid opened at a touch, to a tedious setup
screen. Not to Travis's surprise, Gauthier's last use of the
machine had been to restore it to the factory settings,
and to eliminate all obvious trace of Travis's activities.
The traces would still be there on the hard drive, for any
serious police or security inspection to discover, but the
gesture was appreciated. The data was certainly beyond
Travis's reach—but he remembered some of the pass-
words (they were pathetically, culpably memorable)
that had given him access to government databases. He
tabbed through defaults on autopilot, welcoming the
mindless minutes it gave him to think.

The suspicion he'd had, in his conversation with Gauthier, had hardened to a conclusion on his drive that night from Hebden Bridge to here. It was that in somebody's plans, perhaps but not necessarily Gauthier's, he had a role. That role was to be caught and to confess. He could see it now. It would be very civilized. No cage, no cell, just a room in a country house deep in the green machine of England, and a persistent patience that in his case would be redundant, because he would tell everything at the first opportunity—including that his handler had expected, almost urged him, to do just that. It was not a role he had the smallest intention of playing.

The computer was ready. Travis hot-linked it to an outdated but unused and unregistered satellite phone, uplinked the phone to the Galileo network, and accessed the internet through an anonymous gateway. He began with a search on "James Travis." It returned at the top of the page: "Private Alec James Travis—Death Faked!"

Travis closed the lid and cursed conspiracy theorists. When tears stopped leaking down his face he went online again.

————

Tuesday, May 12. 5/12. A week on from 5/5, and still no answers. Mark Dark knew what the mainstream media headlines would be before he'd so much as dislodged the screen saver. The Leuchars fatality count would be up—now over two thousand—and the news from Britain would be bad: a riot here, a car bomb there, a new protection camp opened somewhere else, a baying crowd somewhere jeering and stoning a thinly protected convoy of refugees heading south or east for the refuge offered across the Channel. Reception camps had been opened in French ports. The only new information that

had come out had been the release of pictures of a
wanted man, in the British media late last Thursday evening: James Travis, wanted in connection with the motorway bombings and oil-industry explosions. A couple
of reports in the London press had identified him as
the father of Alec Travis. They even mentioned that there
was an Alec Travis whose death had been shown on the
Execution Channel, and an Alec Travis whose blog posts
still appeared regularly. The conspiracy sites had gone
apeshit about that connection. In the mainstream media
it was all but ignored. As far as they were concerned,
Private Alec James Travis was still deployed in Kazakhstan, and the Execution Channel was unreliable, as well
as being war porn, distasteful to admit to even looking
at. The conspiracy buffs and antiwar sites had recorded
the clip, but that just made it one more piece of internet
flotsam. Mark had recorded it himself, but he hadn't
made a big deal of it. He was genuinely unsure that it
too wasn't disinfo, yet another double bubble for the un-
wary. There were plenty of sites—mostly UFO cranks,
to be fair—who claimed it was just that. There was no
evidence at all that the names weren't a coincidence.

Details on James Travis were sparse: he had worked
on some Government IT projects, and was suspected of
enabling or even conducting the sabotage of at least the
oil refineries, and of ID tampering to provide cover for
the terrorists who'd carried them out. There was no official hint of a connection with the Leuchars event, which
was still being attributed to a tactical nuke accident.
Some quite plausible pieces by reliable sources—
mainstream and blogger—had speculated that the
anomalously low level of radioactivity was because the
weapon that had exploded had been a new-generation
black-budget nuke with a "clean," non-fission trigger:
the long-awaited laser-fusion warhead, a battlefield-

transforming tactical innovation because it could be adapted to every scale from city-buster down to rocket-propelled grenade. Now that was the kind of device that could be just about believed to be capable of accidental discharge from mishandling, particularly if it had been, well, *beta-tested* on some god-ridden hole in the bandit badlands of Tienshan.

And if *that* was what had happened, *no wonder* the authorities were so cagey about it! No wonder they were flooding out the disinfo like squid ink! Mark had the post ruefully admitting this already written in his head, but on this too he'd hung back. Part of the reason was that the disinformation he'd been sent was just too good for even something as important as this; and partly it was because something nagged at him about Travis. But perhaps the major part of his reluctance was the anxiety of success: his exposure of the UFO disinfo operation, and his early reference to Pte Travis, had sent the Mark Dark site's credibility and hit rate soaring to a degree that he hesitated to jeopardize with speculation.

There had been one attempt—it seemed rather desperate—to launch the Heim-Theory connection. Once again, *ans31m* had drawn Mark's attention to it, this time more cunningly. The anonymous source had congratulated him on blowing the UFO disinfo, and jeered at a cluster of mutually linking far-left sites that were running with an even wilder version of the story. Mark recognized at once that this was intended to send him down yet another false trail; with that in mind, he followed it nonetheless. The sites—most of which had snide, self-mocking monikers like "Gonzalo Dog," "Red Professor," "China Doll"—all cited reports and video clips of the Fuller domes over Chinese eco-cities, and of the Pyongyang antimissile deployment. All this, it was claimed, was a cover for the encirclement of these cities with "Heim-field antigravity generators" or "spindizzies," which would send entire towns of socialist pioneers soaring into space. One such spindizzy, of course, was the device that had exploded at Leuchars. . . . Mark had hesitated to respond to this, suspecting that to do so would only draw attention to it; he'd eventually posted a short piece pointing out the silliness of it all and linking to as many debunkings of the Heim Theory as he could find—not a hard task, as it turned out, but he still felt the episode had wasted an hour of his life.

He was about to make an early start on his day's work when his mother called from upstairs. He trudged up the steps. Sandra stood by the door ready to go out. He'd already said goodbye to her a couple of minutes ago.

"Yes, Mom?"

She held out an airmail envelope, slit open. "This was addressed to me, care of the church, but it's for you. I forgot to give it to you last night, I was so tired."

"That's okay, Mom, thanks."

"It's from England." She gave him a pointed look. "Have you contacted anyone in England, like you said you would?"

Mark looked down at the colorful stamps, the blue *Par Avion* sticker, the Edinburgh postmark. "No, Mom, sorry, I just haven't gotten around to it."

"Well, you should. Today. Folks at the church are real keen."

"Yeah, okay, Mom. Have a good day."

"You too." She smiled and went out. Mark let her heels click away, turned up the air-conditioning and went back downstairs. The screen saver had kicked in again. He let it be and looked at the envelope. His mother's name, Sandra Hope, and the church's address were written in large flowing letters and a mannered script, somehow feminine, somehow foreign: a handwriting that looked like an Indian call-center accent sounded; and in red ink. The letter, addressed to *My Dearest Nearest Mark,* was written in the same hand and color on several crinkly blue sheets of airmail bond. It read like Nigerian-scam spam: fruity with flattery, larded with God and trust and loyalty to the Queen of England— the phrase "truth" (or "law" or "freedom") "under the Queen" recurred several times. On the second page a phrase made Mark almost splutter Jolt on the keyboard: "Help me, Obi-Wan Kenobe—you're my only hope." Mark read it more carefully from there on, but it was just more of the same obscure drivel, asking for some unspecified help and understanding, and about this and that "under the Queen." To round it all off, it was signed: *My Royal Highness, Princess Leia Organa.*

Mark had received plenty of lunatic snail-mail, as well as email, but heretofore nothing that simultaneously advertised and undermined the writer's apparent lunacy like this. The two *Star Wars* references were like a nudge and a wink, that signified a hidden message. Like Princess Leia had hidden the plans of the Death Star in the robot.

Invisible ink? Mark rummaged in a desk drawer for a UV lamp. Nothing showed up. He tried heating each page with a carefully brandished lighter flame. Nothing.

A code within the writing, which had necessitated the artificial, repetitive style? Mark re-read it with dyslexic concentration on non-syntactic pattern, looking for a recurrent grouping, a numeric reference, a hint, a clue. Nothing stood out. Perhap it was verbal—was the royal signature a pointer? He counted the occurrences of "under the Queen" and found thirteen—a prime, a possibility! Transcribed every thirteenth letter and got gibberish. Multiplied it by the number of letters in the phrase, tried again. More gibberish.

Mark laid out the pages across his keyboard and let

his eyes unfocus and his mind drift. *Star Wars.* Princess Leia. Death Star. Hidden plans. Under the Queen. My Dearest Nearest Mark. My only hope. Hope . . .

Sandra Hope! That was written *only* on the *envelope*!

He rocked forward and snatched up the envelope. Time didn't seem to pass as he repeated on the envelope the whole process of the UV, the warming, the counting. It crashed to a halt as he found that too was hopeless. Hopeless! Wait a minute . . . *Hopeless?* Maybe if he removed the letters in "Hope" . . . nah. Too complicated for a cipher that was intended for him to crack. He laid the envelope in front of him and let it all go blurry again. The British stamps. The Scottish postmark. Under the Queen. My Nearest Dearest Mark. My Royal Highness . . .

He shouted out and jumped to his feet. His hands were shaking a little as he carried the envelope to the kettle, and steamed off the stamps, each one with its profile of Elizabeth II. Under the stamp nearest the postmark, he found a black strip a centimeter long and a millimeter wide. It slid at a fingertip touch in the slick of diluted glue. Mark looked at it for a minute. Now he was shaking all over.

He placed his empty Jolt can on the opposite corner of the envelope and went over to the woodchip table along the side of the basement. It had bowed under the clutter from earlier times in his life: a few souvenirs from his own stint—a trophy 9mm Nirinco, a tile from Babylon, a chunk of Kevlar that had saved his life; stuff from grade school and high school and boyhood hobbies—a baseball bat, a thin introductory stamp album, a whole stack of football albums and sticker sheets with empty rectangles, a football helmet, a mound of obsolete electronics and racks of format-locked DVDs; garage tools from when they'd still had a car, an abandoned carpentry project, a stack of kit from when he'd shown some promise at biology, before all the Intelligent Design crap had come in and ruined it for him. The microscope was under a plastic cover thick with greasy dust. He eased it off, searched further for the expanded-polystyrene tray of instruments. The microscope's batteries had leaked green and white goo like inorganic mold. He used a Gerber's pliers to tug them out and dispose of them, the same multitool's file to burnish the contacts. Dug replacement batteries out of a drawer, then a replacement bulb. The microscope light lit when he switched it on. He lugged the instrument over to the desk table, then took the tweezers, a glass slide, and an eyedropper from their shaped compartments. All kiddie kit, but it worked.

He washed the tiny strip in drops of water, picked it up with the tweezers, laid it on a slide, and placed a delicate square leaf of glass over it to hold it in place. Just as he had done years ago with eyelashes, the legs and wings of flies, razor-blade shavings of plant stem, drops of puddle water and (secretly) samples of his own semen. He clipped the slide to the window above the light and peered down the eyepiece at 30X magnification. He made several overshoots and undershoots before his thumb and finger remembered the sensitivity of the knurled focusing knob.

Ten frames of microfilm. They'd been reshot from prints but looked as if further maginfication would show up even more detail. The first frame had a caption in silvery ink: *Leuchars device 5/5*. Mark moved the slide, under its retaining clips, lost all sight of it for a moment—that overshoot problem again—and again gradually got the hang. He swallowed hard, his mouth dry. The gimbal, the podium-like control panel, and the circular, gear-toothed base all struck him instantly as resembling those of an antiaircraft missile battery from a ship. The cylindrical device itself was no missile pod, nor any projectile weapon. It looked exactly like he'd always imagined a particle-beam weapon, except that—going by the scale provided by the human figures in view—it was far smaller.

He sat back, blinking. He switched off the light, mindful of the danger to the film from the bulb's heat.

"Thank you, Princess Leia," he murmured. "You're beautiful."

For the first time since 5/5, he felt certain he knew what this was all about.

Star Wars.

———

A new message had appeared on the dead-letter site. Travis decoded the string of numbers to "Home safe." So Gauthier had made it back to France, and was apparently still in the service's good books, just as he'd expected. Unless . . . well, there was always an "unless." Travis leaned back, pushed away the laptop and the Bible and the scrap of paper with the decrypt, and drummed his fingers on the table. He gazed out of the window, part of his mind attending to the sparrows that flew back and forth on their way to the eaves, from where hungry chirps sounded all day long. He felt relieved that Gauthier had gotten back, and receiving the message gave him the sense for the first time since 5/5 that he was in contact with the service. In the days and nights since he'd seen Alec's death on the Execution Channel, his mind had been roiled with doubts and self-questionings and self-recrimination. This renewed contact—tenuous and questionable as it might be—made it possible to think more calmly now, to think it through.

Uncertainty is information. Travis didn't know if he'd

picked up or made up this maxim. It held as well for systems analysis and high-level project work as it did for intelligence. He had the feeling he'd known it for a long time. Work your way in from the periphery, the penumbra, to whatever's in the black box. What *must* be in it.

So start from the top, and from what you're most reluctant to think about.

The most painful uncertainty was about Alec. At some level, Travis was not completely convinced that his son was dead. The conspiracy theorists could be right. It was perfectly possible that what had been shown on the Execution Channel had really happened, and was not a death but some delayed-action, drug-induced spasm and rigor. This wasn't a hope Travis clung to; it was more an obsessive thought that gnawed at the validity of his grief and thus kept the pain alive.

It seemed to Travis inconceivable that the Execution Channel showed material at random. It wasn't mere war porn; something about its selection of images was willed, as if to drive anyone who watched it into despair, or extremism on one side or another. It was a driver of emotional swings, an engine of mutual hatreds. Nobody knew who was behind it, but the likeliest explanation was that it was a US psywar operation. Psych up our side *and* the enemy—smoke 'em out, bring it on!

In that case, then, the same forces that had seized Alec—Travis had no doubt about the fact of Alec's arrest, given that Alec was his son and had dropped a heavy hint in clear text to Roisin—wanted Travis and everyone else to think it very probable that Alec was dead, and to think it possible—just barely possible—that he was alive. And clearly, the person on whom this would work most powerfully was Travis himself. He was the intended recipient of that image, the target of the ploy.

As for the intended consequence—why, that was

exactly what he had most wanted to do: to break cover, whether by turning himself in or going on a rampage that would have the same result. Anything, anything, to end the uncertainty. His adversary most wanted him to do what he himself most wanted to do.

He hadn't. Count that as a victory, and move on to the next uncertainty.

Roisin. Last Wednesday, the afternoon he'd spent with Gauthier, she'd left a message at her dead-drop letter site warning him not to meet her at their designated rendezvous in Berwick-upon-Tweed. He'd seen a brief report in a Scottish newspaper that Roisin had been arrested and released. Score one for her perceptiveness, and Gauthier's: she evidently believed she was being tracked, just as Gauthier had predicted. But why should that make her warn him off? She wouldn't have known, at that point, that he was a wanted man: *that* news hadn't been released until just before midnight, in fact just after the pictures of . . .

Travis shook his head. About Alec, he had already done all the cold thinking he could bear. He had to concentrate on Roisin.

Roisin, Roisin. Travis drummed his fingers again. Had he ever given her grounds to suspect that his preparations, and his arrangements with her, were for anything more than survival in an emergency? He paced through to the kitchen, made himself an instant coffee, took it back to the table. It was possible. It was possible that he'd given himself away. He couldn't see it. He couldn't see it. But that didn't mean she couldn't. Women were better than men at picking up that sort of thing.

A thought struck him that made him thump the table and almost spill the coffee.

Shit! Was it possible that Roisin had been recruited to

British intelligence at SOAS? That her ill-judged sojourn at the peace camp was best explained as an intelligence-gathering operation?

No. She was too good, too educated, too much of a catch to waste on something like that. No matter how stupid MI5 and the rest could be, they wouldn't waste someone who knew about the Middle East on a job that could be done by someone far less qualified. A young SB operative could grow dreads and go crustie. A disillusioned or compromised activist could be turned. British intelligence had turned top men in the IRA. Compared with that, the antiwar movement was the softest of targets; its left-wing core a little less so, but not much.

So, no. Not that. She was not an agent. But she had known, or suspected, that whoever was tracking her would be interested in him.

And on Sunday she had left a new message, mourning Alec, swearing vengeance, and asking Travis to meet her at one of their alternate rendezvous, in Carlisle. Now *this* time, she *did* know that he was on the run. Which implied that she was very confident she wasn't being tracked, or that she didn't mind anymore being tracked to him.

He couldn't see her being confident of not being tracked. Roisin had been turned, or was otherwise compromised. If she had been convinced that the accusations against him were true, or at least that he had a case to answer—which she might have been, if she already suspected him of some clandestine affilation that would interest the security sevices—he could see why she would have been turned. He was very glad that every time he'd mentioned the location of his hideout to Roisin he had, just as he had to Gauthier, referred vaguely to "the Borders." The thought of the police checking every isolated cottage between Carlisle and Berwick-upon-Tweed made him smile.

Travis banged the table again, as if counting coup. Score two for him. He had turned uncertainty into information, again.

His next uncertainty—and, now that he came to it, the most painful to deal with—was about himself. He stared out of the window again for a while, and then went online again.

———

As he compiled and launched his queries and tabulated their results, another part of Travis's mind, that floated above and around the Boolean logic like a wisp of cloud drifting between tower blocks, processed a darker and vaguer query. A fuzzy logic, a calculation whose terms were moods and hints, stray thoughts; evaluations and intuitions. What was he? What had he really been doing, these past two years?

Treason, for sure. That had never been in question. About that he had never fooled himself for a minute. He was working against the interests of his country, not just the government or the state. Roisin, now, *she* had worked against the government, against the state, perhaps she'd even thought she was working against the ruling class; but she would never have thought her enemy was England, or even Britain. (And for that reason, perhaps, she could have been turned, if she had been persuaded that the state's interest and England's were, in some matters at least, the same.) She had believed that people could be persuaded to oppose the war.

Travis hadn't. He couldn't explain, even now, even to himself, how he'd acquired this conviction.

Companies, UK, construction, infrastructure, recruit-

ment, Result, IT . . . Travis sifted pages of returned links into spreadsheets, refined his queries, went on.

Motorway, Birmingham, project completion dates . . . He ran it again with a lot more exclusion terms, then burrowed into a Department of the Environment billing system for subcontractors, the password for which was "padd13s" - somebody should have been sacked for that, Travis thought.

It wasn't that he hated England, or even the Americans. Somewhere in the back of his mind was a core of regard for an ill-defined England, something that combined his childhood memories of the 1970s with the sort of things he'd been taught in school about England; and with something else he could have sworn he had sensed, once, years ago, standing one night in the dark outside a Victorian replica of an ancient manor house, a plutocrat's indulgence long since converted into a conference center, and he'd left the loud and drunk conversation of his colleagues and crunched across gravel and then across a wet lawn and between trees to stand out of sight of the lights on the edge of a field. The smell of grass, of turned earth, of cow dung; and a sound made up of a multitude of quieter sounds, as the sound of a factory is made up of the sound of all its machines, and the roar of traffic from the sound of many vehicles; this sound of deep England was made up of the small animal noises of the night: rabbit patter, hedgehog snuffle, bat echolocation, the mincing tread of a fox; and the white noise of the wind in the grass and the branches and in the field of no doubt EC-subsidized oilseed rape; a sort of rising and falling sigh, the breathing of a gigantic sleeping man, and beneath it all a subliminal hum that was, he fancied, the engine noise of the machinery of plant cells, the molecular whir of the Krebs cycle going about its business.

He couldn't say he had been loyal to this England, nor

that he had betrayed it. In that matter there was no
choice, nor sentiment. That England was; you were part
of it regardless; it was a machine that had made you and
would one day break you down.

*Grangemouth   maintenance   contractors   Result
personnel* . . . Now he was getting somewhere.

But the more superficial England, the England he'd
imagined when he was growing up in it—it had been
connected to that deeper England, like instinct to the
conscious mind, in a way that the England around him
now no longer was. Because it no longer resonated with
his sense of himself, it seemed to him that it was no longer itself.

And for this he'd spied for France?

Yes. That was about the size of it. He had no special
regard for France. The thing he liked about France was
that it was French. The thing he hated about England
was that it wasn't English. This had nothing to do with
race or religion or nation or politics, as far as he could
see. The blacks and the Muslims weren't the problem.
At some point England had simply failed itself. In his
own mind he had connected it with the times it had
failed him: the incompetence and lack of preparation for
the pandemic that had killed his wife and half a million
others; the hollow justifications for the attack on Iran
which he'd been so sure the Commons would see
through. But they hadn't, and the war vote had been
bounced through on a snap division. And the people
who hadn't filled the streets in consequence. But the failure went further back than that, and he had no idea, really, of when it had happened. There was no moment he
could put a finger on. It was like that annoying cliche of
Roisin's, about boiling a frog. There had been a time
in his life when he had known, without thinking about
it, without noticing, that he was living in daylight; there

had been moments when that daylight had diminished almost imperceptibly, like when another thin slat is nailed across a window, moments he associated with the deaths of certain public men, from suicides or heart attacks; and after a dusk too gradual to alarm him, he had found himself in the dark.

In the dark. That was it. Being in the dark about what was going on; being kept in the dark—that was his grievance. It was what, ultimately, had been behind his decision to make his own use of the dark. You keep me in the dark? Very well. I will walk in darkness and strike in darkness.

refugee labour EU Balkan trial acquital gangmaster . . . Cross-reference, correlate, run some more queries.

He looked at the results of all his queries. He turned them over in his mind and ran them through yet more programs, probed into a few more government databases, and when he was finished the rest of the morning and the whole afternoon had passed. He could see the picture clearly, right there on the screen. It appalled him, still, that he'd been able to do what he'd just done. The incompetence, the insecurity of the systems—as a professional it shocked him. It was as if for his whole working life he had been writing in water.

Someone else was striking in darkness, and it wasn't him and it wasn't France. He licked the tip of his finger and made a stroke in the air: score one for me, again. That made three.

Three strikes and you're out.

He considered sending the whole thing to Gauthier, and to Roisin. But the risk was too great that the wrong people would read it. He'd have to set up a meeting, face to face. Where? Out of the country, obviously. There had to be some country where he wouldn't be expected to go. Some place where he knew someone who would take him in, without question or demur, knowing who he was. He didn't want to check into a hotel, where his passport data would go straight to the police. He had a false passport, yes, but any slip along the way could link his false passport to him, and that would be that.

He stood up, his straightened back creaking, and recovered a battered Moleskine notebook from the inside pocket of his Barbour. Years of cryptic notes and scribbled addresses, some of which he'd followed up. Johanna Halvorsen, Stockholm. He smiled, remembering, and shook his head. He turned a few more pages, rejected some more addresses. Then he came across one that stood out. Hannu Katainen, Oslo. Project manager, fiftyish. Said goodbye in the beer garden of an old pub near the cathedral, the evening after they'd production-run that KPMG contract job, or was it Norsk Data? Five years ago. Long time. Whatever. Hannu the Finn. Big tall guy who'd given his address in careful capitals then shaken hands. "Any time, my friend, any time. I mean that, man." Eyes bright from too many akvavits, but still. The thing was, his Norwegian colleagues didn't call him Hannu the Finn. They called him Hannu the Red. He hadn't been a Red since 1989, but he retained certain reflexes, as Travis had discovered when conversation turned to the war. There had been a hardness there that the past five years would have done nothing to diminish.

Travis snapped his fingers, deciding, then walked out to the lean-to for this night's rabbit. Tonight he would leave his messages for Roisin and for Gauthier. Tomorrow he would move.

———

Mark Dark spent the next few hours experimenting with digital cameras, lenses, strips of duct tape, cardboard cylinders, all in an attempt to make digital pictures from the microfilm. It was a frustrating, finicky job: light leaked into the cylinders, he couldn't get the timing right, the focus would be off, pressing the camera shutter jiggled the microscope tube and blurred the result. But it absorbed him, like any hack did, and the sense of triumph when he finally got the result—with an obsolete phone camera braced in position and triggered remotely, each shot having to be set up again as he moved the camera aside, peered down the tube, and shifted the slide millimeter by millimeter—was enough payoff to make him dizzy.

As soon as he had the pictures uploaded from the phone camera to the desk computer he uploaded them further, to the same offshore warehouse sites he'd sent the USAF fakes to. He wasn't planning on publicizing them until he had time to write a full analysis, but at least they were now safe from a Homeland Security raid. When that was done he sat back with a sigh of relief, and noticed the time. Shit, his mother would be home in an hour! And there was something he'd promised her to do. Now what was it?

Oh yes. Contact that English lawmaker. Justin Deedes, that was his name (and his nature, as he'd tediously chuckled—just in deeds, *fnar-fnar*). Mark had been procrastinating that contact out of embarrassment at the thought of offering the Brits help from a church charity. He'd have to phrase the suggestion quite carefully, maybe as an aside in an email about something else, some excuse to email this guy out of the blue. Mark was sure the MP was unlikely even to remember him. They'd chatted for a while in the Red Lion before the evening sessions.

Deedes was a bit of a conspiracy buff himself, but his interest was in a conspiracy theory so convoluted and improbable that Mark had never had any time for it: the old Golitsyn tale that the entire Soviet meltdown had been a crafty Communist maneuver to retain power while reviving the stalled economy with market forces and Western capital—a gigantic rerun of Lenin's New Economic Policy—while the Party cadre bided their time for a new socialist offensive . . . Mark smiled. Come to think of it, it didn't sound so crazy these days, with commies in the Kremlin's Unity Coalition, and the "Two Necessary Corrections"—anti-capitalist and anti-Western—hardliners ascendant in the Forbidden City. Maybe he'd just mention that . . . no, it wasn't enough. What small favor could he reasonably ask a Member of Parliament to do for him, to sweeten the offer of charity?

Mark smacked his forehead. One thing MPs could do was ask questions in the House—heck, they could even question the Prime Minister! And Mark knew just what question he'd like to have someone ask. Travis, that was it. Private Alec Travis. He could ask Justin Deedes to ask in the House of Commons whether there was any truth in the report of the young man's death. Or if not to ask the question himself, to pass the request to whatever MP represented the area where Travis came from . . . the MP's—what was the word?—*constituency* had to be fairly close to where Travis came from, it was a Home Counties Tory marginal. Maybe it was even the same constituency.

Mark called up a few web pages he'd looked at about the case, and found himself looking at the "Wanted" picture of James Travis. Something had been bugging him about that picture for days. He scratched the side of his jaw, frowned, and then went to the web page of Justin Deedes, MP, from which a portrait gazed back at him. It flattered the man's looks, but it brought back sharply a vivid memory of his actual appearance—suit a little shabby, features a little ratty—as he sat in the Red Lion in Westminster and bent Mark's ear about the Soviets and the bloody French, and—

Wham. The rest of the memory came back as if triggered by a smell. In the course of the rant Mark's attention had wandered, overhearing—or eavesdropping on—scraps of another conversation a few feet away, between an Englishman and a guy with a French accent. And just as he'd stood up, he'd heard the Englishman say, "Nah, I just hate the Yanks"; and he'd glared at him.

The man whose gaze had for a couple of seconds locked with his had been James Travis. At least, his face had been the same. Of that Mark was sure. He put his elbows on the table and his head in his hands and closed his eyes, shaking with the shock of that recognition and thinking back. The trick was not to try. Instead he tried to recall the conversation with Deedes, and to see if anything from the overheard conversation drifted back. Deedes had been going on about the Russians, drug money, Islamists—fuck, the French guy had called him and Deedes liberals! And he'd used the "C" word! What was that about! Then the other two had talked about the war, their families—"son in the Army," that phrase had made Mark's ears prick up. The Brits didn't have the draft, so having a son in the Army was a little unusual, especially in the middle classes, and this guy had been very middle class. Mark's knowledge of Brit accents wasn't, he knew, comprehensive, but the way he figured it, if he could follow what they were saying they were probably middle class. This guy had been upper middle class, in American terms: someone with a good job, professional, not just *a job*. So far, so fitting the profile. Then something about a daughter, and Islamists and Zionists—another flag had gone up. He hadn't caught the details, and in particular not her name. Or rather, he had caught it and had had a mental glitch processing it. It hadn't fitted, it had sounded like some kind of raghead name. It hadn't passed from the short-term memory buffer to long-term storage.

But something else had. Travis, or the man who'd looked like Travis, had said something about "antiwar." Now that was a word that Mark always noticed. He checked Antiwar.com every day.

He sat up and Googled. *"James Travis" daughter antiwar* didn't return anything remotely relevant. He tried *Travis antiwar Leuchars* and got a brief article in *The Scotsman,* titled "Peace camp activist freed."

A name jumped out: Roisin Travis. He knew it was pronounced "Rosheen." Was that the name he'd heard? It wouldn't take him long to check for occurrences of it in conjunction with that of her possible father: school yearbooks, local news items, something would be out there.

Two others, not named, still held under ". . . suspicion of having material that could be used in the commission or preparation of an act of terrorism—a catchall charge often used by the authorities against base-watching activities, such as plane spotting, note taking, or photography."

Mark's gaze flicked to a corner of the screen with the thumbnails of the photographs he'd received, and to the mugshot of James Travis. He thought back to the conversation between Travis and the French guy, and recalled what Travis was now being sought for. His uncertainty was over. The wave-function had collapsed.

He also knew *exactly* how he could help the displaced British Muslims.

16

Disguise was, Travis knew, like magic, in that its essence was misdirection. In the past week of misery he had not neglected its preparation. Even when sitting staring at nothing, he had sat in the sun. When he had needed distraction he had hacked back overgrown hedges, weeded plots, sanded and painted window facings. He had lost his office-worker's indoor pallor. His shaved scalp had reddened, then begun to tan. The hair on his face looked more like beard and less like stubble.

On the morning of Wednesday, the thirteenth of May, he stood in front of the bathroom mirror. The Celtic thorn fake tattoo on the side of his neck still looked real, if a little faded. In the passport, one of several he'd prepared over the past couple of years, his bald and bearded face looked younger, matching the passport's date. The tattoo was recorded in it as a distinguishing mark. His bushy salt-and-pepper eyebrows were trimmed and dyed black. The changes to his normal appearance were small, but they made him hard to recognize. Nothing that could fool biometrics, but that he had fixed well in advance, at source. He could only hope that this particular corruption of the national ID system had not yet been traced to him.

He wore a red and white nylon sports jacket he'd bought a year earlier, deliberately sized a little tight around the shoulders, with light khaki chinos, an open-necked pink shirt, and brown Timberland shoes. A Leeds baseball cap covered his head; designer reflecting shades covered his eyes. The rest of his clothes—likewise unworn casuals, but less solecistic—were packed in an overnight foldover shoulder bag along with underwear and toiletries, all of which had been bought on a credit card in the same name as the one on his passport. In his wallet were crumpled receipts going back a long way and ten identical minicab business cards, nine of them crisp in a translucent plastic case but with their gloss slightly scuffed, one of them creased and mouse-eared at the corners.

He prowled the house, checking and rechecking that he'd turned off the gas and water at the mains, that the fridge was empty, that nothing had been left to rot. He recognized it as displacement activity but did it all the same. The only decision he had to make was whether to take the laptop. He'd checked all the sites and placed all the messages he needed to. He'd saved the searches and results and spreadsheets to a memory stick on his key ring, and to another on a pocket clip. The computer had been reset once more to purge all trace of yesterday's online activity, then used only to buy his airline ticket to Oslo, book his seat, and print off his boarding pass. This cleaning would pass scrutiny no more, or less, than the one Gauthier had carried out earlier; but then, if the laptop's hard drive was being investigated, his whole plan would have failed. Gauthier was safe in France; his security, at least, wouldn't be imperiled by any failure of Travis's. On balance, swayed a little by discomfort at the thought of having only phone access to the net, Travis packed the laptop. He stuck his thumb under the shoulder strap and lifted. Still well within the carry-on allowance. For a moment, as his gaze fell on the two folding

knives high on a shelf, he considered taking them and
checking the luggage. The Laguiole had been a present
from Deborah, the Toollogic from Alec. But no. Checking the bag would conflict with his already processed
check-in. He could put the knives in the post to the hotel, but then, what if . . . ?

He shook his head. "You never know," he said to himself. "You might come back."

With a wan smile at this hope, he hefted the bag,
glanced around one more time, patted his pockets for
passport, money and boarding pass, and went out, lock-
ing the door behind him. He strode down the path without a backward glance and turned in to the road, heading
up and over the hill, in the direction opposite to that for
the nearest bus stop. His big bevelled watch, worn only
long enough to circle his tanned wrist with a conspicuous pale mark in its shape, showed 8:12 A.M. His flight
was at 15:55. Plenty of time.

———

The bus to Newcastle arrived on time, at 9:45. Travis
had reached the stop twenty minutes earlier and had
spent some of the time wiping dust from his boots and
applying polish from a sachet he'd once found in a hotel. An elderly lady sat at the front, two young men at
the back. Travis handed over his ten-euro fare, slung his
bag on the luggage platform, and sat near the middle of
the bus, close to the emergency exit. On the way he
picked up a *Metro* from the stack and, when he'd settled
in, took off his cap and shades and pretended to read it
from the back.

The bus made its way between hedgerows and drystone walls, past the farms, clusters of houses, and the
occasional isolated cottage. A man with a wheeled suit-

case got on at one stop, two girls going in for a day's shopping at another. The bus turned left onto the main road, and picked up speed. The next stop was in a small satellite town, Ponteland; a dozen or so people got on there, by which time Travis had stopped keeping track. The luggage rack had become crammed.

The next stop, a few miles down the road, was for the airport. Several people, Travis guessed, would be getting off there. He considered joining them, but decided against it. He had planned to arrive at the airport via the fast link from Newcastle. His cover address, and supposed business, were both in Leeds. Arriving directly from the countryside might have been awkward to explain. He didn't want one tongue-tied moment in front of any plexiglass window or visored face, nor to leave any obvious trail back to the house.

The bus swung onto an exit ramp, around a section of roundabout, and off toward the airport's terminal. Travis noted hands gripping the sides and backs of seats as the bus crossed a flyover. The motorway system had been reopened within three days of the attacks, with traffic being routed around the damage. There had been no short-term alternative, if the country wasn't to starve, but fear remained. Five people stood up and pressed toward the front, awkwardly maneuvering their luggage. The bus halted a hundred meters from a terminal entrance. Up ahead was a tailback of cars and taxis, cop cars, armored cars, a thick crowd around the glass doorways under the DEPARTURES sign. After a minute's queuing, the driver's radio crackled and he said something into it. A pause. The bus door sighed open. The five airport passengers debarked, grumbling as they hauled their luggage between fenders toward the sidewalk. Travis's bag now lay alone behind the rail. He noticed the driver glance back at him. Travis hesitated, then shook his head and smiled. The driver responded with a twitch of an eyebrow and a shrug. The doors thudded shut and the bus moved forward again, elbowing its way into the slow outward flow through a barrage of horns and flashed headlights.

The crowd at the Departures entrance had grown, and was now being added to from inside the building. As the bus headed for the exit, Travis was glad he hadn't joined it. It looked like he wouldn't even have saved time. Probably a security scare—some idiot leaving a bag unattended in the foyer.

Through the side window Travis saw an airliner on final approach, coming in low across the semi-rural, semi-urban landscape. As it passed in front Travis recognized it as an Airbus. It was very low, and too fast, flashing past tens of meters in front of the bus's windshield. Travis could hear the engines, still loud, and had time to notice that the flaps weren't down. His head whipped around just in time to see the plane slice through the top floor of the terminal building and disappear in an eruption of black smoke.

"Jesus!" Travis screamed. "Did you see—?"

Every head but the driver's had turned too. The driver gave one glance in the rearview mirror and put his foot down and a hand on the horn. A hubbub of shock and speculation filled the bus, and curdled in seconds to cries of "Mozzies" and "terrorists." Travis had twisted around to peer behind him, as had everyone else. As the bus drove fast down the on-ramp to the dual carriageway, the terminal passed out of view, leaving only the rising smoke. Travis, still staring out the back, found everyone turning to stare at him. He'd gone for a look that fitted the name and occupation on his business cards. It now occurred to him that, with a beard and shaved head and tattoo on darkened skin, he might look like something else entirely.

"Fucking Mozzies," he announced. "Christ, I hope that was just an accident, but, I mean, fuck."

This seemed to reassure everyone. Travis settled back in his seat and took out his phone and tuned it to the news. Its lead was still "Airport Security Crackdown"; the details, which Travis scrolled impatiently through, were of a new threat: suicide terrorists using laptops or phones to interfere with the controls of fly-by-wire airliners.

Travis made a conscious effort not to look at his bag.

Within seconds, the news caught up with what he'd just seen. "Breaking News—Newcastle Airbus Crash." No speculation yet. Small mercy—the two stories would soon be as linked in the news as they now were in minds. God, how many had died in that crash? Travis found his gaze blurring. He put the phone away and folded his arms across the seat back in front of him and pressed the bridge of his nose into his forearms, and braced his shoulders to stop their shaking. Then he wiped his sleeve across his eyes and sat back, breathing deeply. He should stop kidding himself. His grief wasn't for anyone else's losses; but then, at some level, it was. He remembered Deborah, years back, looking away from the first confused television coverage of the July seventh bombings, three days after she'd come back from the Make Poverty History march.

"We'll be in this shit till we die," she'd said.

For her, it had been true. Travis was not sure it would be true for him. Maybe, maybe he could . . .

It was only then that it struck him that he was unlikely to be flying anywhere that evening. Air traffic would almost certainly be grounded. He'd have to take the ferry.

He took the phone out again to search for timetables. When he unlocked the keys the news was still on. The screen had split between the Newcastle crash and a new Breaking News segment:

"Terror suspect French agent, says MP."

Below that was a now familiar picture of his face.

———

"What do you think of this?" said Bob Cartwright, pointing to a block of text at the foot of the screen. He and Anne-Marie had just come in to work. The line hadn't come down yet. While waiting, Bob had made a start on the fake Red Professor blog. He knew he'd have to update Alec Travis's blog, *Flash in the 'shan,* but he felt bad about it. He suspected that the Execution Channel clips in circulation were genuine, and that the young soldier was dead. All the clever disinfo he'd added to the blog over the past week now seemed ghoulish.

Anne-Marie Chretien, on her way back from the coffee percolator, stood beside him and looked over his shoulder, taking the chance to press her hip to his side.

It is precisely because the lagging countries accelerate their development and tend to become level with the foremost countries that the struggle between countries to outstrip one another becomes more acute; it is precisely this that *creates the possibility* for some countries to outstrip others and oust them from the markets, thereby creating the preconditions for military conflicts,

"Scroll down," she said.

"Wait," said Bob. "Tell me what you think of it first."

"It's . . . perceptive," she said. "Topical, if arguable. A

bit too sharp for your imaginary professor, though. Who wrote it?"

"Hah," said Bob. "Gotcha."

He scrolled down to reveal the rest of the quote:

for the weakening of the capitalist world front and for the breaching of this front by the proletarians of different capitalist countries.

J. V. Stalin, 1926

Anne-Marie laughed. "You got me. But your professor wouldn't quote Stalin."

"Shit," said Bob. "Not even for the 'inter-imperialist contradictions' trash he keeps banging out?"

He felt a little resentful—it was, after all, one of Anne-Marie's stories he was trying to strengthen. Some days ago, after Mark Dark had blown the UFO/HTS story as disinfo, she'd suggested spinning a line about spindizzies around Chinese cities. That one hadn't, so to speak, taken off—Mark Dark, for sure, hadn't fallen for the ruse—but it was amusing and worthwhile to let the Red Professor and his imaginary comrades run with it. Bob had enjoyed concocting solemn dialectical justifications for scientific great leaps forward. And this morning it had taken him, oh, minutes and minutes of research to find a suitable quote, and he had stumbled across it on a site called "marx2mao." He knew it was an authentic site because certain documents on it had been recommended reading on his stint, for any conscripts interested in a military career. Some officers quoted Mao's military writings so much that they sounded like Red Guards.

"No," said Anne-Marie.

"Why the hell not?"

"Kiss of death for his credibility."

"Um, that was the point," said Bob.

"No," Anne-Marie repeated. "I mean the credibility of the persona. You'd do better having him quote Mao."

"Mao was worse," said Bob.

"No doubt," said Anne-Marie. "But that is not the point. Americans hate a dead Russian tyrant more than a dead Chinese one. Trust me on this."

"Uh . . . who's the American here?"

Anne-Marie sauntered to her desk, then spun the chair around to face him. "You have studied business, science, and military affairs, Bob," she said. "I have studied *America*."

"Okay," Bob said. "So tell me why my professor—"

"Look, Bob," said Anne-Marie, sounding annoyingly patient, "to this day, what rival power is considered the most dangerous? China? Or Russia?"

"France," said Bob.

Anne-Marie laughed. "Yes, but because France always has an inclination to ally with Russia. And Russia is still the only power that could rival America for the top place." She shrugged. "Basic geopolitics."

"Or maybe 'inter-imperialist contradictions.' "

Again she smiled and again she took it seriously. "That too, yes."

She held his gaze for a moment, in a way not at all like she had a few hours before, in the night; and then, as if not finding something, turned away to her screen. Cartwright returned to the blog. He deleted the Stalin quote, frowned at the hole this left in the argument, then decided to paraphrase the quote without attribution. That left open the option of setting up a nice little bit of Red-baiting from another real or false blog later, maybe even some contrived dust-up about plagiarism. Neat. He pasted the text back in and started editing. *It's precisely **because** the less advanced countries . . .*

The desktop's speaker chimed. The line was in. Cartwright saved and minimized the blog and looked at the line. His indrawn breath coincided with Anne-Marie's, and with Peter Hakal's arrival in the office.

"What's with you two?" Hakal asked, sitting down. "Bad news?"

"Yeah, you could say that," said Cartwright. "Check the new line on who's to blame for 5/5. The President's about to announce it officially."

Hakal rattled some keys and looked up from his screen.

"Shit," he said. "France."

Sarah Henk had abandoned the reception desk and rushed in.

"Have you *seen* this?" she said. "Have you *seen* it?" She pushed her fingernails up the sides of her head and into her hair. "Oh, God, it makes me want to get out of town."

"It's not that bad, Sarah." Anne-Marie stood up and put an arm around her shoulder.

"Like, yeah, how bad can it get?" Sarah shrugged away and sat down heavily on the side of a table.

"Let's wait and hear what the President has to say," said Bob.

It wasn't necessary, and nothing was said, but they ended up gathered around Anne-Marie's screen, huddled together; Bob with his hands on her stiff shoulders, Hakal's elbow just touching his, Sarah Henk on the other side clutching his upper arm so hard it would mark the skin. Anne-Marie had flipped to CNN, which was in a holding pattern, showing the President's Seal with no voice-over.

The President appeared at her Oval Office desk. Bob Cartwright, as ever when he saw her, felt a slight thrill that he knew was an uneasy mix of personal, political, and patriotic admiration with an erotic twist that was perhaps inevitable on looking at The Most Powerful Woman In The World™.

"My fellow Americans," she began, "early this morning I took the grave decision to put our nation's strategic nuclear forces on Level One alert. Shortly afterward, I summoned the French ambassador, and requested he deliver a note to his government. In that note, I respectfully but urgently requested the president of France to clarify the position of his country in relation to ours. The government of the United States has received incontrovertible evidence that recent tragic and terrible events on the territory of our closest ally, Great Britain, including the nuclear explosion at one of our own bases, were deliberate acts carried out by persons ostensibly acting on behalf of the French Republic. Our shock and dismay at these evil and appalling deeds is matched only by our resolve that they shall not go unpunished. There is a small but real possibility that they were carried out by some rogue element, or as a provocation, by forces only pretending to act for France. In the interests of peace and security, therefore, and in order to make clear to the world that we seek no quarrel that is not forced upon us, I have offered the French president the opportunity to dissociate his government from these atrocities, and to identify, repudiate, and extradite those responsible. I have impressed upon him that time is of the essence, and that our patience is short."

She took a deep breath and a sip of water. For a hysterical moment, Bob wondered if there was a clear plastic bottle in the Oval Office trash can, and if its label was Evian.

"I regret to say that this matter, serious though it is, is not the gravest of the concerns I have had to raise in my note. My fellow Americans, many of you will be aware that the nuclear detonation at RAF Leuchars, in which over a thousand of our servicemen and -women—and indeed their children—and almost a thousand British civilians were blasted without warning into eternity, has been the subject of much speculation, some of it ridiculous, some of it malicious. It has also, I assure you, been the subject of the most urgent investigation by the agencies of our government and those of our friends. Secrecy and misinformation have for too long been the parents of conspiracy theories, many of them"—a phantom, fleeting smile— "vast. It is time, my fellow Americans, it is long past time for your government to level with you, as one group of Americans, your servants, to a much larger group, yourselves."

At this the President leaned forward, put her elbows on the desk, and opened her hands in front of her, in full soccer-mom kaffeeklatsch mode. The artifice was evident in the way the camera smoothly tracked downward and angled a little upward, keeping her eyes center screen. When she spoke again she'd discarded the diplomatic, almost forensic tone for a colloquial, confidential delivery.

"Very briefly, my friends, the truth is this. We've known for a long time that the French have been carrying out secret research and development on Chinese territory. Last week, our Special Forces carried out a daring mission to prevent the site of some of these secret developments from falling into the hands of Al-Qaeda terrorists. The device they recovered, which exploded at Leuchars due—we now know—to a deliberate command signal sent from French territory, was an antimissile particle beam weapon of revolutionary design. We have reason to believe that this device wasn't a prototype. Devices with a similar radar signature have been deployed in great numbers around certain cities and industrial sites in Communist China and North Korea. There are unconfirmed reports that smaller numbers of them have been detected in Russia—and in France. Given that an antimissile shield could allow an aggressor to think, falsely, that they could get away with a nuclear first strike, our concern over this entirely unprovoked and sinister deployment is grave indeed."

She straightened up, and rested her hands, fingers interlaced, in front of her.

"We can be proud that our country has never sought war, never provoked war, never resorted to aggressive war. I have instructed our ambassador to the United Nations to bring this matter to the urgent attention of the Security Council. In that venue, I am certain, the French Republic and the Russian Federation will wish to show the world that they are civilized powers, *great* powers in the true sense of the word, and that they stand ready to disengage themselves from any entanglement with radical rogue regimes such as those of China and North Korea. Until that time, the strategic forces of the United States remain on alert. Be strong, and God bless America."

Fade to black.

Anne-Marie flicked off the CNN feed as soon as the talking heads' babble began, and turned around as though surprised to find the others behind her.

"Well," she said. She stood up and got herself another cup of coffee, and marched to her desk with a directness that made clear she expected the others to be back at theirs. Peter and Bob hastened to their screens; Sarah Henk hung around, sitting on the edge of Anne-Marie's desk. Anne-Marie swiveled her chair and stared at Bob and Peter. Out in reception, a phone rang unanswered. There was a click as the answering machine cut in, then silence.

"What caused this?" Anne-Marie asked.

It struck Bob as a strange way to put the question, but he knew what she meant. He'd been following links as fast as he could read. He looked up, looked straight at Anne-Marie.

"We did," he said.

17

THE ferry from Newcastle to Bergen sailed from the Royal Quays at 1:30. The bus to the Royal Quays from Newcastle Central Station departed at 11:10. The bus Travis was on was due to arrive at Newcastle Central at 10:40. At 10:35 Travis, after having read the news about himself, finished the painfully slow business of making an online ferry booking from his phone. He could have done it a lot faster from the laptop, but he didn't want to take the computer out of the bag. Not while the news kept worrying away at suicide terrorists with laptops. Not while he had an airline e-ticket receipt and boarding card in his pocket. Not while he looked like a Muslim trying to look like a non-Muslim.

As he slid the phone back into the inside pocket of his jacket he realized that the bus hadn't moved for five minutes. They had come off the A167 and were in a narrow street of office buildings overshadowed by some municipal edifice to the right. The engine idled; the driver sat with his elbows on the steering wheel. As Travis made his way to the front of the bus he noticed police cars coming and going, very fast, up ahead, and saw that there was a police station on that corner. The road immediately ahead was blocked by a policeman who stood on the center line beside a motorcycle.

"What's going on?" Travis asked the driver.

"Trouble at the Central," said the driver. "At the bus terminus."

"Any idea what?"

The driver shrugged. "Riot or something."

"Bugger," said Travis. "I have a bus to catch in half an hour."

"Buses aren't going anywhere," said the driver. "Not until the trouble's sorted."

"Wouldn't like to count on that," said Travis.

The driver looked straight ahead, making clear that this was not his problem. Travis sighed.

"Excuse me, mate, would you mind letting me off here?"

The driver shook his head. "I can't let anyone off except at a stop."

"Well, we're stopped now," said Travis, trying to make light of it. "Traffic's not moving."

He reached for his bag, hauled it onto his shoulder, and glanced from the driver to the big double door with a twitch of his face that could have been a half-smile or a wink.

"Go on, I'll just nip out."

"Didn't you hear me?" the driver said. "I—can't—let—anyone—off. Security regulation." He tapped out every syllable on the spine of a thick blue book on the dash. "Reg-u-la-shun."

"Oh, good grief," Travis said, his accent slipping too far south for a moment, then recovering. "Okay, okay."

Fuming, he returned to his seat, and sat down with the bag across his knees. Several scenarios of threatening, cajoling, or bribing the driver fast-forwarded through his mind. They all had the same ending, with him explaining himself to a policeman. He looked out and saw car drivers with their elbows propped on their rolled-down windows. At least they had fresh air. Now there was an idea. He leaned forward, stretched up, and opened a small ventilation window in front of him, and was about to do the same for the window beside him when he saw again a small handle with a red notice above it: EMERGENCY EXIT. The handle was behind a thin sheet of glass, on which the fine for uncalled-for use had had a zero added to it in marker ink.

Travis read the notice. He put on his cap and shades, eased his hand into his jacket sleeve, tugged the cuff in after it and clenched his fist around the fabric, then punched the glass. He pulled the handle down. Thudding sounds from the window's rim were followed by the sharp, shrill ringing of an alarm.

"Hey!" shouted the driver.

Travis shoved at the window. It resisted for a moment, then clattered to the street. Travis swung his legs through the vacant space, clutched the edge, and jumped out. He landed on top of the plexiglass sheet, which skidded under him. Unbalanced by the bag on his shoulder, Travis fell awkwardly, grazing the heel of his hand on the gravelly tarmac, jarring his pelvic bone on the flat window and wrenching his right shoulder. Yelping with pain, he stood up. The driver was in the window space now, reaching out. His fingers grasped for Travis's head and missed by a centimeter. Travis ducked, snarled, and jumped away. He transferred the bag to his left shoulder, and loped off between fenders and exhaust pipes to the near side of the street. A backward glance showed no pursuit—the driver wasn't in the window. Travis guessed he'd be back in his cab, and probably on the radio.

Travis brushed small black stones from the heel of his hand, licked at grime and a few drops of blood, and tugged out his phone, wincing and gasping at the pain in his shoulder. He tugged down the brim of his cap and ambled forward, thumbing the phone to GPS and tapping on the Central Station symbol on the map. The station was only a few hundred meters away. A circuitous route of more than a kilometer lit up, bewildering him until he noticed the one-way arrows on streets. The phone's default was for driving. Irritated, he changed it to walking. A new route zigzagged across the screen, starting a few steps behind him with a passageway through an office block into the next street. He retraced his steps and ducked into the passageway. One side of it was spray-bombed: YANK'S OUT MOZZIE'S OUT. Travis remembered a slogan he'd once seen, neatly painted on a pedestrian bridge over the railway at Hayes and Harlington station: *Only the less clever are racially prejudiced.* He thought of Gauthier and wished it was true. The time was 10:47. The route turned sharply right when he reached the end of the passageway. He glanced over his shoulder, saw no one, and started to run.

———

Sandra was crying on the phone. Mark distanced himself from it by setting the phone to speaker and putting it down on the desk. He picked it up again when the sobbing stopped.

"Mom," he said.

He got a sniffle for an answer.

"Mom, it's not as bad as it sounds. It's not war."

"Not yet, you mean. I know that's what you mean. I can hear it in your voice."

"That's not what I mean, Mom. The President is in control—"

"*God* is in control."

"Yeah, yeah, I know, Mom. What I mean is, the President knows what she's doing."

"I *know* she does. It's the Russians and the French I'm

worried about. Do they know what they're doing? And that crazy asshole Kim Jong Il."

"Mom, we've been deterring them since forever."

"And now they've got secret weapons—"

"Mom, listen, please. We have Space Command. We have nukes in orbit. *We* have secret weapons. I know that for a fact, Mom."

"No you don't. It's just stuff you got off the Internet."

"Mom, there are *books* about this. It was in the *Washington Post*. We have black-budget projects that nobody knows about outside the military. The stuff on the Internet is to hide what we *really* have."

"It's easy for you to say that. Saying things like that is *what you do*."

Mark took a deep breath. "Mom, I've never said this before, not to anyone, and I don't want you to repeat it to anyone. Okay? Promise?"

"Okay," said Sandra. She sounded doubtful, but intrigued.

"Well, when I was on my, uh, tour, I saw things you wouldn't believe. Heck, I didn't believe them. Weapons that can take out a tank or a missile battery or a hardened bunker from, like, nowhere. They just leave a red-hot metal splash. Aircraft that go so fast they're over the horizon before the sonic boom reaches you. And that's with them flying low. You know, treetop height? And then they can go straight up to orbit. I've seen one of them do that, saw it with my own eyes. And we've got snooper mikes that can hear whispers miles away, and translate them, and pinpoint their location. So we do have stuff that if we had to use in a big way, the enemy *literally* wouldn't know what hit them."

Sandra said nothing.

"Mom?"

"I know we'd win a war," Sandra said. "I don't see

how all of that would stop it happening in the first place. If it's all so secret, it isn't even a deterrent. And now we know the Chinese have something more advanced than we ever thought—"

Mark forced a laugh. "Mom, the Chinese are still flying knockoffs of *Soviet* planes. Maybe they do have some new beam weapon, but they can't attack us with it. And we don't need missiles to take it out. That weapon I told you about, there's no defense against it. None."

At this point Sandra started crying again. Mark mumbled whatever soothing nonmilitary nonsense came into his head until she put the phone down.

Jesus! he thought. You'd think with her faith she'd at least have more goddamn courage, acceptance, whatever. Wasn't that the whole *point*? She didn't seem to be any better off than he was. And she didn't have his awful suspicion that it was he himself who had brought about the crisis. Mark wondered if this notion wasn't just the sort of delusion of influence that for bloggers, and in particular conspiracy-minded bloggers, was an occupational hazard.

Early yesterday evening, he'd written a long email to Justin Deedes. He'd attached his digital pics of the microfilm photos. Shortly afterward, he'd posted the same pictures to his site, along with an explanation of why he thought they were authentic. He hadn't said anything about James Travis, or why he'd guessed he was working for the French—he'd put that in the email to the MP. He wasn't going to say anything unless Justin Deedes raised the matter.

It might have been because he'd gained attention and credibility by exposing the UFO disinfo, or it might have been because other people had been holding back and waiting for someone else to make a move, but whatever it was it was like he'd pulled his finger out of a dam. The post with the pictures was more linked to than anything else he'd ever done; a couple of mainstream Brit papers—the *Telegraph* in England, the *Herald* in Scotland—had picked up the story in their noon editions, with hints that other copies of the microfilms existed and were known to them.

Another dam had now broken: this morning, a few hours earlier in England, Justin Deedes had stood up in Parliament and asked some very direct questions. To his own surprise, he had gotten direct answers. Just before the President's speech had come on, Mark had been looking on his screen at the MP's exchange with the Home Secretary, the British government official whose gig was the equivalent of Homeland Security.

Justin Deedes (Weatherington North) (Con.): Mr. Speaker, I would like to raise some matters with the Home Secretary. First, could my Right Honourable friend comment on allegations that Private Alec James Travis, of the Royal Corps of Signals, has died in custody, in a secret facility run by United States security services on British soil? Can he explain whether this is connected with the fact that Private Travis's father, Mr. James Travis, is being sought in connection with the recent terrorist outrages? Could he, while he is on the subject, perhaps throw some light on the recent arrest of Private Travis's sister, Miss Roisin Travis? Finally—

[interruptions]

Deedes: Finally, without compromising national security, could my Right Honourable friend comment on two related matters which have just reached the public domain, namely: that James

Travis is also suspected of being an agent of the French security service, DGSE—

[interruptions]

Speaker: The House will come to order.

Deedes: I am about to finish. The remaining matter is that of the photographs, now in the public domain, alleged to be of the device that was the immediate cause of the Leuchars tragedy. Does my Right Honourable friend have any information as to the authenticity of these photographs?

Home Secretary: Mr. Speaker, the honourable Member has raised a large number of questions, five by my count. Let me express my regret that my honourable friend did not see fit to inquire beforehand with my office as to the suitability of raising them in this place and at this time. It shows, I believe, the reckless opportunism of the party opposite, which demonstrates once more their unfitness—

[interruptions]

Speaker: Order! Order!

Home Secretary: Thank you, Mr. Speaker. I will now answer the questions. Questions regarding the reported deaths of service personnel should be put to the Ministry of Defence, and due care should be taken not to name or otherwise identify individuals before the notification of their next of kin. However, in this instance, and in view of the fact that the next of kin is at present a fugitive from justice, I feel able to answer. It is with great regret that I have to announce that the young man in question did in fact die from a previously undiagnosed cardiac condition following a routine investigation. This investigation was in connection with the illegal activities of his father and his sister, though I must stress that to the best of my information Private Travis had no knowledge of his father's activities, had only the most exiguous knowledge of the illegal aspects of his sister's activities, and was innocent of anything but carelessness, and was a loyal soldier to the end. The Ministry of Defence will conduct a full internal inquiry.

With regard to Mr. James Travis, I can confirm that he is under suspicion of espionage as well as sabotage. With regard to the precise intelligence service for which he is thought to have operated, I cannot comment beyond noting that a protest has been lodged by the Foreign Secretary at the embassy of the French Republic.

[interruptions]

Speaker: The House will be cleared unless it comes to order.

Home Secretary: Finally—yes, I see we have reached the final question. I have made no investigation into the authenticity of the photographs, and I shall refer the question to the Ministry of Defence, from which an answer is expected shortly.

Justin Deedes (Weatherington North)(Con.): Mr. Speaker, I thank my Right Honourable friend, but I must point out that his account of the death of Private Travis is partial. It is notorious that Private Travis died after suffering extreme physical and mental stress tantamount to torture. The details of his death were shown on the Execution Channel.

Home Secretary: My honourable friend is on record as supporting the right of free speech for purveyors of extreme pornography, advertisers of addictive and poisonous drugs, and preachers of racial hatred. I must say that I am disappointed but, sadly, not surprised that he has chosen to legitimise also the publishers of slanderous defamation and what can only be described as a pornography of violence. To mention this disgraceful disinformation outlet in this place, let alone to cite it as evidence in support of a controversial contention, is to stoop beneath even . . .

And so on, and on. Mark reckoned that Deedes had been so taken aback by getting straight, if long-winded, answers that he'd failed to follow through. He shouldn't have gone for the peripheral issue of Alec Travis.

What Deedes would have done if he'd had his wits about him was to have asked what the Government intended to do about France.

———

Travis ran past a church, across a junction between more stationary vehicles, and on to Neville Street. The front of the station filled the other side of the street, behind a clutter of covered walkways, access ramps, bus stops, and taxi ranks. Between him and the ferry bus stop, which according to the map was in front of the station and down the street to his right, a dense crowd filled half the roadway. A dozen or so police cars and vans, lights flashing, formed a gappy cordon around the fluctuating perimeter of the crowd, as if pushing them back. Some of the gaps were partially filled by thin lines of police in riot gear, also moving forward. Above the heads Travis saw the white drift of tear gas, the black distant flecks of hurled impromptu missiles.

Staying on the side where he was, he turned right and

hurried along the pavement, body-swerving past by-standers and onlookers, of which there were as usual plenty. A newsstand had been knocked over, its contents strewn across the road. Boys snatched up colorful pictures of improbably endowed women. Travis saw a grainy photo of his face under the headline FROG SCUM on the front page of *The Sun*. North of England noon edition, just out. He stared at it for a moment, then grabbed it up, folded it, and stuck it under his left arm.

He passed by the edge of the crowd and looked across the road for the ferry bus stops. It was then that he realized that the crowd's focus *was* the ferry bus stops. Several coaches were lined up in front of the station. Around two of them the crowd was clustered thick and pressing hard. The tops of the coaches swayed as they were rocked back and forth. The din of fists, boots, and missiles hitting the buses was continuous. There was no shouting or chanting. The crowd was quiet and determined. The cops' long batons rose and fell, and now and then someone was dragged away and slung in a van, but there weren't enough cops to break up the mob. Travis couldn't understand it, until he realized that most of the available cops would be out at the airport dealing with the crash.

Travis crossed the road and walked up beside a WPC in a fluorescent coat and striped round hat who stood behind a van, holding a loud-hailer.

"Excuse me, officer," he said.

She turned, looking harassed. "Yes, what?"

"Could I borrow your loud-hailer for a couple of minutes?"

"What?"

"I have some information to impart to the crowd which may serve to dispel their misconceptions. Ma'am."

"Who the heck do you think you are, mister?"

Without a beat Travis handed her his business card. "Kevin Levin, officer. Minicab driver. And hoping to be a passenger on one of these coaches."

She glanced down at the card. "So?"

"The loud-hailer, for a moment, if you don't mind." He gave her the most innocent grin he could muster. "If I do or say anything wrong, please feel free to arrest me." He held up his hands, very painfully, wrists together.

"Oh, God." She looked around as if to check that no one was looking. "Just take it."

"Thank you, officer."

Willing his knees not to shake, Travis jumped up onto the hood of the nearest abandoned car. He had about two meters of clear space in front of him and could see, across twenty-odd meters of seething heads, the terrified or furious and mostly dark faces behind the windows of the buses. Fucking Mozzies, he thought, psyching himself into character. He took the newspaper from under his left arm and held it up, again painfully, in his right hand. With his left he grasped the loud-hailer and pressed the trigger switch.

"Oi!" he shouted. The loud-hailer howled with feedback. He did it again with the same result. A few heads turned.

"Oi!" he shouted again, getting it right this time. "Listen up! Everyone! Lay off for a minute!"

More heads turned, including some in visored helmets. Travis glanced down with a smile and a confident nod to the cops, then faced across the crowd again. People were looking at him out of sheer curiosity.

"Look at this!" he shouted, flourishing his copy of *The Sun* with its front page held outward. "This is who blew up the junctions! It wasn't the fucking Mozzies! It was the fucking French!"

"Who says?" someone yelled. The cry was taken up, in a jeering tone. Good. He had their attention now.

"*The Sun* says! That's who! The Prime Minister says! That's who!"

"Fuck the Prime Minister!"

"Yeah, fuck the Prime Minister. I don't like him and I don't like the Mozzies either. But it wasn't them! It was this bastard"—he turned the paper around as if to check it—"Travis, that's his name. A French spy! That's who's behind it!"

With that he threw the paper as far forward as he could. Pages flew everywhere. Hands reached up and grabbed for them—all but one getting the wrong sheet, but that didn't matter. Travis hopped back off the car, ducked behind the police van, and handed the loud-hailer back to the WPC.

"Is there a French consulate in Newcastle?" he asked.

"I don't know."

"Well," said Travis, "you might want to check, see what I mean?"

She was looking at him as if she'd just watched a three-card trick. Another officer, this one in riot gear, stepped around the side of the van.

"Best be off," said Travis. "Bus to catch."

He walked right past the riot cop and around the van and around the backs of the police. They'd stopped pressing against the crowd. People were looking about and arguing. Some were drifting away, through the police line. Others were listening to their phones—to the news, Travis hoped. He circled around the edge of the crowd as fast as he could. He kept an eye out for the little enamel British or English flag badges favored by the fascists, but he didn't spot any. The people in the crowd were an odd mix, young men and slightly older women. They didn't seem to be organized. As the crowd thinned, a wedge of

four cops cut through it, toward the oblivious or unbelieving remnant who were still hammering on the buses.
Travis reached the sidewalk and turned along the rank,
checking bus stop notices until he found the one for the
Bergen ferry. It wasn't one of those that had been attacked.

He paid a twenty-euro fare and sat next to the emergency exit, and he kept his cap and shades on until the
bus pulled out at 11:18. Eight minutes late. Not bad.
Travis looked out at the Tyne, the bridges and boats,
the showy arc of the Millennium Bridge, and then the
docks. He made it to the ferry without trouble, found
that there were enough vacant seats belowdecks that
he'd have enough room to stretch out and sleep overnight if he couldn't get a last-minute cabin berth, wandered around the ship for a while, and went to the bar.
At 2:00 the news came on the big screen behind the
bar, and he watched the US President's speech, live from
Washington. He reached into his jacket pocket, found his
key ring and closed his fingers around the USB memory
stick. In his half-hour ramble around the ferry before
its departure, Travis had noted that it had air-sealable
hatches, meter-wide circles of gear-toothed polished
brass on parts of the upper decks, and an operating the-
ater; and had deduced the existence of several fairly large
spaces behind bulkheads to which there was no obvious
access. He expected this voyage to be its last passenger
run for a while.

He wished he'd thought to take the ferry in the first
place. He could have kept the knives in his pocket. His
shoulder still hurt. He swallowed a brace of paracetamol
and ordered another drink. His mouth was still sour from
the bitter pills. Behind him the lounge was in an uproar.

"Cheer up," said the bar steward. "It may never
happen."

"You're right there," said Travis. "Make that a double."

———

"We didn't cause it, Bob," said Anne-Marie, after Cartwright had explained his theory. "There's no way all this happened in response to Mark Dark's photographs."

"We built up his credibility," Cartwright repeated. "We gave him all that disinfo and he didn't run with it. He blew that op wide open. And that meant that last night, when he did get—"

"Yes, yes," Peter Hakal interrupted. "And as soon as the pictures were out, the already existing story line about the captured device and its French connection hardened up. That is all very well, but I still think there must have been more going on already. The most that this conspiracy site will have affected is the timing of the conflict's becoming public."

Cartwright stared at him bleakly. "Timing is everything."

18

In the evening of Thursday, May 14, Roisin sat in the living room of the safe house in Wood Green, North London, and waited for a phone to ring. The phone was the mobile she'd bought in the Tesco store at Alloa on the morning of 5/5. It lay on a coffee table in front of her, beside empty mugs, disheveled newspapers, a television remote control, and a tin of snuff. She had sent the phone's number and nothing else in an email to her dead-letter site the previous evening, in response to a request from her father. The phone hadn't been out of her reach in twenty hours.

The phone rang. Maxine Smith's hand twitched toward it, then withdrew. Roisin snatched it up. The number shown on screen didn't look like any kind of phone number. She accepted the call and put the phone to her ear.

"Hello?"

For a second or so, nothing.

"Roisin?"

"Yes! Dad!"

"Hi, Roisin. Good to hear you. Are you with someone?"

"Yes."

"Your sponsor?"

She thumbed the privacy key. "He's asking if—"

Maxine Smith, who was speed-thumbing her own phone, looked up and nodded. "Tell him yes."

Roisin put voice back on.

"Yes."

"Thought so. Does your phone have a speaker option?"

"Hang on." Roisin tabbed through menus. "Yes."

"Excellent. Put it on."

Roisin selected the option and placed the phone on the table.

"Can you hear me okay?" Her father's voice boomed tinnily.

"Yes, that's fine."

"Good. Okay. Shit, if you are where I think you are, the room's probably bugged and in any case I'm sure this call is being monitored. Fine. Don't bother trying to trace the call, by the way—it's routed through a rogue-state cutout."

Maxine Smith smiled tightly and continued to jab at her phone, like someone knitting through a quarrel.

"Though by all means persist," James Travis went on, sounding amused. "As long as you pay attention at the back. Roisin, I have some urgent information of great interest to your sponsor's company, and to the competition. I intend to hand it over simultaneously to your sponsor and to a representative of the competition, in your presence. If there's the slightest—"

Maxine Smith was shaking her head.

"Dad," Roisin interrupted.

"—funny business—what?"

"I've just been told that's not acceptable."

"*What*'s not acceptable?"

Maxine Smith pointed toward herself, then held her forefinger straight up and moved it toward and away from Roisin.

"Uh, it's got to go to my sponsor only, I think."

Maxine nodded.

"Confirmed that," Roisin added.

"Fuck that," said Travis. "It goes to both companies, or it goes to the competition only. I'd prefer both companies to have it, but if I'm forced to choose, the competition gets priority. There's a very good reason for this, which is intrinsic to the information and will be understood on sight of it. As well as, uh, a more personal and sordid reason which I needn't spell out. Do we have a deal?"

Maxine Smith shook her head and made the yap-yap sign with fingers and thumb.

"Uh, my sponsor says keep talking."

Travis's laugh cackled from the tiny speaker. "Still trying to trace the call? Okay, I'll keep talking. Like I was saying, if there's the slightest sign of funny business during the handover, the information is destroyed irrevocably. This very much includes information I have in my head. You know me, Roisin, and if your sponsor has any lingering misconceptions about me I'm sure you can correct them. You can confirm that whatever else I am, I'm devious, resourceful, expert, and all things considered I don't have a lot to lose. Uh-huh?"

"Oh, yes," said Roisin. She felt wrenched. The circuitous transmission was losing nuances, but anguish wasn't one of them.

"Right," said Travis, sounding firmer. "While we're on the personal aspect. I'm hoping that when your sponsor sees the information, they'll know that it's in their own interest that the representative of the competition gets home safely. If that happens, and if *I* get to walk away afterward, I'll be willing to cooperate in, ah, an audit trail of previous bad practice. It's in the nature of the business that time is of the essence, and you know you'll get information faster with my cooperation than by . . . than without. Are we of one mind on this point?"

"Uh, let me check that."

Roisin pressed the privacy key again and raised eyebrows to Maxine.

"Hmm," said Maxine. "If he's offering to redefect and confess in exchange for freedom, he might need a new identity to avoid getting stiffed by the long arm of the DGSE. Not sure we can offer that. I'd have to run that past my superiors. It would take time. And I can't just go ahead and offer it anyway, because double-crosses on that particular guarantee are a no-no. Word gets around. See if that's what he wants."

Transmission on again.

"Hi," said Roisin. "Are you asking for the whole life insurance package? Because my sponsor isn't sure it's company policy or affordable at this moment—"

"I'm not asking for protection from the competition," said Travis. "And I'm not sure life insurance is exactly relevant at the moment. Besides, I have reasons to think the competition wouldn't be at all averse to my cooperating in an audit on your side. After all, it was the competition who terminated my contract in the first place. And the state of play in the market has moved on. There are hostile third parties involved. That's what my information is about, and that's why I can't give it to you now— because, believe me, if I could I would. So—bottom line: I give you this information, I walk away, and when I hear from my friend I get in touch again and we'll take it from there. Do we have a deal?"

Roisin looked at Maxine, who nodded slowly.

"Yes."

The sound of a deep breath came over. "All right. Roisin, have you given details of our letter-drop site to anyone but your immediate sponsor?"

"No."

"And has your sponsor given the details to anyone else?"

Maxine shook her head.

"No, Dad, it's clean."

"Then—shit, wait a minute. That isn't good enough. Hang on. Roisin, do you still remember the details of the alternate site?"

Her father had given her a mnemonic for another Web address, but that had been a long time ago. Some kind of hymn . . .

"Uh—"

"'There . . . ,'" he prompted.

"Sorry, it isn't—"

"Think gory surreal image of redemption."

There is a fountain filled with blood, without a city wall.

"Got it."

"Good for you. Consult with your sponsor about ways to access it without anyone, including anyone from your sponsor's company, looking over your shoulder. Then go there, and you'll find your instructions. They're quite simple, but you must follow them exactly. Otherwise the deal is off."

"Okay, got that."

"See you soon, I hope. Bye."

"Bye, Dad."

The call ended.

Maxine Smith blew a long breath past her teeth and reached for the snuff tin. She took two pinches and another deep breath.

"Fu-uh-uck," she said.

"What?"

"You know what he's telling us?"

"I'm not sure."

"I'll tell you later. We have to go out." Smith stood up. "Now."

———

The sky was pink, with black clouds. The pavements of Wood Green's main streets seemed to reflect the colors: pink with cherry blossom, black with ash. Roisin and Maxine crunched over broken glass and past boarded-up houses. Several days of an unnatural alliance between white and Afro-Caribbean mobs had left most of the Asian-owned shops trashed. Only the sudden shift of blame to France had stopped the violence. A few logical-minded knuckleheads had moved on to smashing the windows of Prêt à Manger, Plaisir du Chocolat, and La Perla outlets, but their hearts hadn't been in it.

Maxine stopped at a 7-Eleven to buy a new phone and a wad of phone cards, then guided Roisin swiftly around a corner to the least welcoming pub Roisin had ever been in, and she'd been in a few. It was clean and re-spectable and not rough, that wasn't the problem—it was dark and smelled only of male pheromones and deodorants, and everyone stared as they came in, then turned away. Maxine was served drinks at the bar as if under protest, or coercion by the Equality Acts. She steered Roisin by the elbow to a booth in the darkest corner.

To Roisin's surprise, Maxine, sitting with her back to the wall, surveyed the joint with amused nostalgia.

"Takes me back," she said. "Student days, oh my. Mind you, back then they were cool with dykes."

"Oh," said Roisin. "I see."

"The penny drops," said Maxine, eyes glittering. "Re-lax. It's me who looks like the closet. At least you're wearing Hawkshead."

"Oh, fuck off." Maxine's baiting could get old fast. Had it been only a week?

"Anyway," said Maxine, not at all contrite but getting back to business, "the good thing about this place is that I'm fairly sure it isn't bugged. Plus, any cops here are off duty. Call it progress. So let's fire up this phone and go online."

"You were going to tell me what this was about."

"Did we listen to the same conversation? Your old man was letting us know that he thought *my* company might be compromised."

"He's messing with your head," said Roisin.

"That thought had crossed my mind. However . . ." Maxine scraped at a thumbnail with an incisor and inspected the result without satisfaction. "So had that stuff about hostile third parties. And it's not like, you know, my company has such a sterling record in that regard. As our cousins delight in reminding us. Not that they have anything to crow about."

Cousins, ah. Roisin winced and took a slug of vodka and orange.

"Let's get on with it," said Maxine. She shoved the phone across.

Roisin initialized it and accessed tiaffwbwacw.org.cu. The site had been created in the past hour. It contained a screenful of gibberish. She saved the page to the phone's memory and tried to recall the mnemonic of the matching site where the PGP Plus signature file was stashed. Oh yes: the hymn's second line. *Where our dear Lord was crucified who died to save us all.* And indeed, wod! wcwdtsua.org.cu had the goods. She downloaded it and ran the decrypt. The plaintext was almost an anticlimax. She slid the phone across to Maxine.

"Like he said," said Maxine. "Simple."

"Do you want to go for it?"

"Oh yes. I think now I can make the deal stick, too." She glanced at her watch. "We have a lot to do. We'd better get moving."

Roisin remained seated. "Before I go anywhere," she said, "I want to know if *our* deal still stands."

Smith looked surprised for a moment, as if caught a little off balance.

"Why ever not? Of course it does. Now let's drink up. Remember to hold hands on the way out."

"In your dreams," said Roisin idly, and was taken aback to see Maxine blush and look away.

19

THE sky to the north was already bright when Jeff Paulson climbed aboard the 4:40 A.M. BA Oslo flight from Aberdeen. He picked up an early edition *FT* from the freebie rack in the airbridge and in the hatch repaid with a genuine smile the company-policy one the flight attendant bestowed. As he trailed his rolling case down the aisle to Economy and wedged it into the overhead locker among the Samsonites and overcoats of red-eyed oilco execs he experienced a small rush that he hadn't felt since 5/5: the joy of being ahead of the game.

Window seat, over the wing. Paulson snicked his seat belt and unfolded the newspaper as far as he could without getting in the face of the guy in the aisle seat. The front page headline was FRENCH DENIAL IRKS US. Oil was up, after a paradoxical downward blip when for a few hours a fusion-speculation feeding frenzy had outweighed the war scare. The war scare was definitely predominant now.

French denial—hah! The consulate scuttlebut was that the President had been characteristically precise when she'd said that the Leuchars detonation signal had come from "French territory"—a coded transmission from the French consulate in Edinburgh milliseconds before the blast was in the NSA bag. Paulson took this rumor with a heavy discount, but he guessed that something like it was true. Whatever it was, it could hardly be as convincing as rounding up a French operative and one definite and one possible French agent, all linked to the scenes of the crimes. Paulson's enthusiasm for pulling this off was tempered by the knowledge that the cross-hairs of his country's wrath were already drifting east: China and North Korea had been warned to come clean on their antimissile deployments or face unspecified consequences; Moscow's Foreign Minister had urged the other SCO members not to aggravate the situation in the Pacific region, which looked very like an attempt to dissociate Russia from the commie bad boys and had as such earned an instant rebuff from Beijing, delivered in the backhanded form of a fulsome declaration of Shanghai Cooperation Organization solidarity issued by the Kazakhstan government-in-exile. But France was still in the frame, and if Paulson could nail them in it he would. Smith's message last night had put him ahead of the game, that was what counted, even if the game had moved on.

The door closed, the plane taxied, the cabin crew went through their safety-information calisthenics. Paulson spared them one glance more than most of the passengers did when he checked where the nearest emergency exit was. One row in front. Fine. Despite the Newcastle crash, the subsequent day-long grounding of British flights, and the immediate total ban on phones, laptops, and PDAs from cabin seats—though not, as yet, from carry-on luggage, thanks to frantic backdoor last-minute lobbying by, well, red-eyed oilco execs—Paulson felt no more nervous than usual. The flight was in the hands of God and of His more enthusiastic believers, as ever since 9/11. Something about taxiing was so tedious and soporific that, as usual, Paulson nodded off, and awoke with a dribble of drool from the side of his mouth as the plane banked out over the North Sea. He furled the paper, wiped his chin, and looked out of the glass ellipse at oil tankers, broad-nib ink-black inches on swells like ripples.

The breakfast trolley rattled, an outstretched arm and a stretched smile delivered black coffee, cold water, and a dick-shaped doughy trick fruitcake that stuck to his molars and was booby-trapped with blueberries microwaved to scalding heat. Paulson abandoned it, accepted a second coffee, wiped sticky fingertips on scented tissue, returned the tray, and dozed again. He woke with a forehead pressed on breath-fogged glass, to look down on a choppy landscape of forests and farms.

He swallowed hard to relieve the pressure in his ears and turned his watch forward an hour. The time didn't feel like 7:35. Deplaning was uneventful, the passport check nominal, the currency exchange painful. The terminal was an airy space of blond wood, black iron, and high glass, giving him the impression of walking along a section of upended balsa-model wing. Paulson bought a plastic liter bottle of Teacher's at the supermarket-scale duty-free and a train ticket at a machine. His suitcase wheels roared over slats in the revolving door. The platform was open air. Smokers sucked hard and discarded several centimeters of stub as the train doors opened. Inside it was like being back on a plane. The television screens cycled through safety announcements in Norwegian and business news in English. Oil up, shares down. Paulson woke at Central, invoked Lonely Planet on his phone, strolled smugly past the taxis, and caught a tram to his hotel.

The bed tempted him, but he had work to do first. He called the embassy and checked that the technical boys had done their work, the physical team was ready to roll, and that the OP—the observation point—was secure

and expecting him. Everything was in order. He hung a
DO NOT DISTURB sign on the door, set up an alarm call
for 11 A.M. and set another alarm on his phone, and hit
the sack. It wasn't yet 9 o'clock. Maxine Smith and Roisin Travis wouldn't arrive at the airport for another hour.
Their rendezvous with Travis was set for 1 P.M. Paulson
fell asleep confident he was still ahead of the game.

———

Travis sat on the balcony of Hannu Katainen's fifth-story
apartment and munched his way through slices of bread
with ham and cheese, sinking a cup of coffee along the
way. While eating he browsed a stack of leaflets and a
tear-off street map from tourist information. He needed
to refresh his memory. As he pushed the plate away,
Hannu ducked through the french window to the
balcony, put a fresh Kona pot on the table, and sat
down, tugging awkwardly at his jacket wrists and trouser knees. The Finn was decades and promotions beyond
his beard-and-T-shirt programmer days but still wore
his suit and tie like a disguise. He poured coffee in silence and lit a cigarette.

"Well," said Travis, "today I'm—"

Hannu raised a palm.

"Don't tell me what you're going to do," he said.

"I wasn't," said Travis. He shuffled the leaflets. "I was
going to say, I'm going sightseeing."

"Of course. And I don't read the newspapers. Bombs
in England? I saw the headlines, of course. Terrible, terrible."

Travis didn't laugh.

"I can stonewall very stubbornly," Hannu added.
"One advantage of being an old Stallie."

"I was wondering," Travis said, "if another advantage

might be, I don't know, some political or administrative contacts?"

Hannu frowned, shaking his head. "Of course I know people who know people. It's a big business and a small country. But in terms of favors to call, personal contacts—no." One shoulder of his jacket rode up. "If you're thinking of asylum—Norway is not neutral, but it is pulled in both directions, and that's reflected in the officialdom. Depending on whose office sees you first, you might get asylum, or an extradition hearing. Luck of the draw, I'm afraid."

"Better an extradition hearing than—" Travis planed a hand upward.

Hannu fizzed out his cigarette in a slopped saucer and lit another.

"There have been some extraordinary renditions," he said. "Not many, but some."

"I'll stick to crowded places," said Travis.

"Yes, do that." Hannu stuck out his lower lip and blew smoke past his nostrils. From the park between blocks, the cries of kindergarten kids playing soccer echoed up. "To save you the further embarrassment of asking—no, I have no strings to pull on the other side. In case you were wondering." He grinned. "Every fucking Komsomol I knew—back, you know, *then*—became very rich very fast in the nineties, and I imagine is now wondering where it all went wrong. So, no help to you."

"Never crossed my mind to ask," said Travis, quite truthfully. Russia was the last place on his mind to flee to, and he had known very well that Hannu's "old Stallie" ex-commie reflexes didn't include any lingering loyalties to Russia. It was on Hannu's hard-earned, bone-deep hostility to big-power arrogance that he'd counted—or rather, gambled, and with more success than he probably deserved.

Hannu looked at his watch, stubbed his cigarette, and stood up.

"I have a late start today," he said, "but it is a start. Will we see you this evening?"

"I don't know," said Travis.

"Drop the key through the door when you leave," said Hannu. He stuck out his hand. "Just in case."

Travis grasped his hand. "Thank you for everything. You and Elina."

"Ah, forget it," said Hannu. He chuckled. "I'll do my best to forget it myself."

Travis waited for the door to close, then carried the crockery through to the kitchen, washed up, and went to the spare bedroom. He packed the laptop in a small black backpack he'd bought in Bergen, padded two folded garments, a few small items, and a slim plastic wallet around it, and pocketed a Swiss Army knife he'd bought at the same sports shop. The big shoulder bag and the clothes he'd worn on his trip he left behind. He placed the two memory sticks in separate button-down pockets of his shirt, stuffed the map and leaflets in an outer pocket of his jacket, checked that his phone was in the inside pocket, and left the house. As he dropped the keys through the door he wondered if he would indeed be back, and chose not to dwell on the thought. He clattered down a stairwell of parquet and wrought iron, put on his cap and shades, and stepped out into hot sunlight. He walked past the bike sheds and bins and turned right along a residential street of apartment blocks and gardens dripping with lilac and lobelia to the nearest main drag, Bogstadveien, where he walked down the road for a couple of minutes then caught the next tram back up.

He bought an Oslo Card block ticket and after a few hundred meters hopped off at the terminus, Majorstuen, crossed to the metro station, and took the next train going north and uphill. The slope got steep after a few stops. He watched who was on and who got off. When they reached a station where the train stopped and only one man on the carriage, lugging a bike, rose to leave, Travis exited by the other door in time to see a total of three others get out. Vettakollen was a quiet suburban halt, with painted wooden houses among trees on one side, the view over Oslo on the other, and a lot of graffiti on the fittings. He dawdled down the platform, made sure that all who'd gotten off had left, and crossed to the other side. Within ten minutes a return train glided downhill. No one else was on the platform. Travis waited until the last second and jumped between the closing doors.

He stayed on the train as it went underground after Majorstuen and got off two stops later, at Stortinget. He emerged into terraced plazas of sculptures, fountains, and trees to find a protest going on in front of the parliament, the Storting. Not to his surprise it was about peace, and very noisy. There was no agreed platform, just competing loudhailers from the Storting's steps. Parliamentarians and civil servants watched from upstairs windows. Pacifists preached, revolutionaries ranted, humanists urged, and, from behind a thin police cordon, conservatives barracked. Travis plunged in joyfully and zigzagged in an overall diagonal direction across the crowd, accepting leaflets without demur and turning around often. By the time he emerged at the northern corner he was confident that if he was being followed at all it was by a far larger operation than anything he could hope to shake off.

He walked down Karl Johans Gate and turned left at Stortorvet, the square facing the cathedral, in front of which another, much larger and quieter crowd prayed or silently witnessed for peace. No cops and few placards here, and no noise: just the drone of the dominie, behind whose voice organ music drifted from the church's open doors. Going through this congregation would make his path obvious rather than obscure, but that wasn't the only reason he felt reluctant to repeat the maneuver. The sight and sounds disquieted him in a way the other protest hadn't. These people weren't political activists. They were normal folk who were deeply afraid of what was happening; and who, unlike their nonreligious fellows, had a way to express their concern that connected it with something primal.

He continued along the back of the square, crossing a street and tramlines, past the pub where five years earlier he'd gotten drunk with Hannu and his team. For a central part of town there was a lot of broken glass on the streets. Every bus and tram stop was littered with pale brown rectangles like quarter-sized tea bags. Wet snuff: the product and the habit were Swedish, the littering wasn't; like the graffiti, it was one of the ways that Norway seemed grottier, more anarchic and alienated than the rest of Scandinavia. For some reason he couldn't articulate to himself, this made Travis feel more confident that he'd made the right choice of country for the fraught encounter ahead.

A couple of hundred meters along Torggata brought him to a wide plaza. The last time he'd seen Youngstorget was on a weekend, when it was a flea market; today there was only a row of sunshaded stalls along the side, selling handbags and hammocks, sunglasses and software. All, probably, pirated: the brand names were Chinese but the prices were American. Travis strolled to the far side of the square, a row of shopfronts in a granite wall beneath a colonnaded gallery. On a bench an old man sat, leaning forward, explaining something at length to pecking pigeons. Close by was an iron sculpture of a little space-man standing atop a complicated metal egg, looking up. Travis smiled at the cheery figure and walked to the cafe in the far corner. Scores of tables, some under awnings, some open, and mostly vacant, stood on the cobbles and flagstones around it. A waitress in blue jeans and black T-shirt and apron looked up from wiping the table nearest the door. Travis nodded and smiled, raised a finger, and stepped inside. After he took his shades off and his eyes had adjusted he saw that the Politiker'n Cafe Bar's interior hadn't changed. Framed black-and-white photographs of politicians still covered the walls: Gorbachev, Annan, Hirohito, Mao, Brezhnev, Brandt, Nixon, Ford, Carter, Bush, Clinton, Gore, Clinton, Blair, Honecker, Havel, Botha, Mandela . . . all as they would have wished to be seen, at the height of their power or fame. The cumulative impression of transience was overwhelming.

Travis used the gents', washed his hands, and returned to the table just outside the door. He ordered a coffee and put his bag on the chair beside his and the laptop on the table, claiming territory. The time was 11:47. He didn't mind the wait. He had a lot to think about, and writing to finish. He gazed along the perspective of the wall and colonnade, and scanned the square slowly, until when he faced directly left he could see the high red-brick office block of the *Arbeiderpartiet* with its red rose logo. The plaza's proximity to the social-democratic headquarters had been one factor in his choice of rendezvous. Like the expanse of now-busier tables around him, and his position in the inner corner of the plaza, it helped to ensure that anything that happened to him wouldn't go unnoticed. Despite all his precautions, he had no way of knowing that Gauthier and the Brit would be the only intelligence-service representatives to turn up. He eyed other diners and drinkers, and realized it was futile. The possibilities were too many: stall keepers, waiters, the old man with the pigeons . . .

The waitress returned with the coffee.

"Eighty kroner," she said.

He gave her a hundred and told her to keep the change.

She looked surprised. "Thank you."

Travis smiled. Just for the certainty that he now had all the time he needed at the table, twenty kroner was cheap. The time was 11:53. He left the coffee to cool, and opened the laptop.

20

JEFF Paulson entered the red fortress of the Workers' Party at noon. He gave a name to the receptionist, waited while he buzzed and murmured, signed the clipboard when the nod came, and clipped a visitor's pass to his lapel.

"Fifth floor, room five-ten."

"Thanks."

He stepped from the elevator into a red-carpeted corridor on whose beige walls were hung framed socialistic-looking posters of women workers and African kids, and portrait photographs among whose subjects Paulson recognized only JFK, Brandt, Blair, and, rather to his surprise, the President of the United States. This did little to make him feel on friendly ground, no more than had the assurances from Oslo Station that despite its alarming name the *Arbeiderpartiet* was solidly pro-NATO and pro-market, staunch in the War for Democracy—and in favor of motherhood and apple strudel as well, no doubt. That put them just about where the Chinese commies had been ten years ago.

A young man with red-framed glasses and a trimmed beard stood in the doorway of room 510. He stuck out a hand.

"Johan Hansen."

"Jeff Paulson."

He followed Hansen into the neat, uncluttered office. Binoculars on the windowsill, headphones and mike beside the computer on the desk. Hansen beckoned him to the leather swivel chair.

"Cameras feed to the monitor," he said. "You can split screen, so"—he moved and clicked the mouse—"and speak to your team, so. Separate channel for audio feed from the bugs."

"Excellent work," said Paulson, trying things out. "Thank you."

Hansen stepped back. "Do you wish me to leave?"

"You're very welcome to stay," Paulson said. "How discreet do you have to be?"

"I have authorization for this," said Hansen, reflexively glancing upward. "My relationship with the embassy is quite open. However, shall we say it would be simpler if I were here working and you were, perhaps, dealing with a network fault, if someone without clearance should drop in. Naturally I have had all incoming calls diverted, so as not to disturb you. If you prefer—"

"No, no," said Paulson. "Stick around." He looked up. "If there's a coffee going, I'd be grateful."

"There is a machine in the corridor," said Hansen. "But it is much better from the cafe across the square."

"Machine's good," said Paulson.

———

It was Gauthier who arrived first, on the dot of 12:45. Travis had wanted Gauthier's presence to be a *fait accompli* when the others arrived. He closed the laptop, pocketed his phone, and stood up and shook hands. Gauthier pulled out the seat opposite, caught the waitress's eye, and sat down in one fluid sequence.

"Good trip?" Travis asked.

"Naturally," said Gauthier. He smiled at the waitress. *"Au lait, s'il vous plaît."*

"Black for me," said Travis.

She went away.

"I was sorry to hear," said Gauthier.

Travis nodded. "It's been hard, but—" He opened and closed a fist.

"Perhaps this is not the time."

"There will come another," said Travis.

"We may discuss it."

They looked at each other, then away.

"I'm glad you came," said Travis.

"I should say I disapprove strongly of the arrangement," said Gauthier. "As does the service. But in the circumstances . . . well. We had little choice in the matter. Is there no chance to persuade you to leave with me? Now?"

"Nope."

Gauthier seemed to accept this. A silence dragged until Travis broke it. "How are things back home?"

"My wife was relieved to see me," said Gauthier. "Once she recognized me. There was what you might call a double take." He brushed his hand on his now clean-shaven cheek. His fingers stroked the scar under his hair. "I see you have learned well yourself."

Travis touched his cap. "Thank you. But you recognized me."

"Again, the double take. Ah, thank you." The waitress had returned. Gauthier paid, Travis waved away the change.

"I'll have to account for that," Gauthier grumbled, pocketing the chit and fumbling out a cigarette packet.

"Easier to start than stop," Travis observed.

"So I have found."

"Try the local vice," said Travis, sticking a finger to his mouth. "It's safer."

"But more disgusting."

They talked idly for another few minutes, during which Travis became increasingly distracted. The tables behind Gauthier had filled up and Travis kept having to shift and lean to see past heads and shoulders to the little spaceman statue. At 1:00 he stood, stretching and craning, and rubbed his back as if it hurt.

A young woman in a slippy summer dress and a straw hat and swinging a small black backpack from a crooked finger walked up to the statue, placed the hat on it, and stepped back and took a photograph. She put the hat back on her head, and took another photograph. Then she turned around and walked in his direction. Travis sat back down, shaking a little at the sight of Roisin. As she approached she slowed down, and just before she reached their table hesitated, with a slight frown. Travis took off his cap, put the bag on the ground, and rose to meet her. As he edged out from behind the table she flew at him.

"Dad!" she said into his shoulder.

"Oh God, oh God," said Travis. He was crying himself. "We have to be—"

"I know." She pulled away a little. Her hat had fallen off. "Everything's okay, Dad, I mean about now."

"Good." He hugged her closer, brought his mouth between her hair and her ear. "Listen. If you want to get away at any point—I have a black bag like yours. I'll put it under the table. Take it to the ladies'. It has everything you'll need. Okay?"

She stepped back and blinked at him. "Dad, that's a big—"

"Let's sit."

He sidled back. Roisin sat beside him, on the seat where the bag had been.

"Your hat," said Gauthier, handing it across.

"Thanks." Roisin put it back on and fumbled in her own bag, took out a tissue and blew her nose. "Sorry. I'm a mess." She placed a purse and phone on the table and slid the bag to her feet.

Travis made the introductions.

"Delighted," said Gauthier. "Roisin. I wish it had been in other circumstances."

"Don't talk to me about the fucking circumstances. Just don't."

Gauthier clammed up.

"It's not his fault," said Travis.

"I know," said Roisin, with a sidelong glare.

"Ah, *there* you are!" said a voice. A woman in a business suit stepped up to the table and swung herself confidently into the seat beside Gauthier. Travis had a moment to form an impression of her—bright, smiling, professional, quite attractive—before she introduced herself.

Another awkward silence.

"Well," said Smith. "Here we all are. Shall we go through the motions of doing lunch?"

"I'm not hungry," said Roisin.

Travis and Gauthier looked at each other and shrugged.

"Drinks, then," said Smith. She asked around and waved thousand-kroner notes at a passing waiter. "Two white wines and two beers. Aren't we predictable?"

"Professional hazard," said Gauthier, lighting up again.

"While we're waiting," said Smith, after placing the order. "You have something to show us, Mr. Travis."

She took a small tin from her handbag and snorted snuff. Gauthier watched her, eyebrows raised.

Travis's mouth was dry. He swallowed tepid coffee. All his talk about destroying the information had been a bluff. He had only one fallback action to take if anything went wrong: a preset call on his phone. The impulse to look over his shoulder was like gravity. He resisted it. He opened the laptop, opened the file, and spun the device around on the table.

"All yours," he said, pushing it across.

For a couple of minutes Smith and Gauthier scanned and scrolled, with awkward mutual deference, like two people going through the same revolving door. Travis clicked out one by one the blades and tools on his new Victorinox, folded it up again, and slid it sideways to Roisin. She palmed it without question or thanks. When the drinks arrived a moment later the knife wasn't on the table.

Smith closed the computer, kept her left hand on the lid and with her right raised an ironic glass. "Cheers."

"Absent friends," said Travis.

Roisin ground a heel on his foot.

Gauthier glanced at the computer.

"Perhaps you can explain to us the significance," he said.

"Uh-huh," added Smith. "Companies, people, numbers, countries, dates. Bit of a dog's breakfast."

"That's the raw data," said Travis. He scratched his ear. It was his professional conscience that itched. "Well, not entirely raw, I mean, it's spreadsheeted and so on. The sources and searches—"

"Yes, we had reached the appendices," said Smith. She drummed a thumb on the case.

"I just wanted to prove to you I wasn't bullshitting," said Travis. "I mean, it's evidence."

"No doubt," said Gauthier. "Evidence for what?"

Travis wondered if he'd gone about this the wrong way. Never start a presentation from the raw data. But no, maybe it would have been harder to convince them from the top down.

"If you open it again and drop down the—" Shit, he couldn't remember the menu; it was all reflex now. "Pass it back a minute."

He opened the narrative document, with the diagrams, and all the links and highlights in.

"There. The *Private Eye* version."

They resumed their study. Gauthier's frown deepened. Smith breathed in sharply a couple of times, took snuff without looking anywhere but at the screen. Roisin people-watched. Travis sank half his half liter.

Gauthier leaned back, then Smith. They looked at each other. Gauthier rolled out a hand. "You first."

"Doesn't prove anything," said Smith.

"It's not a fucking indictment," said Travis. "It's an in-vestigation. A *prima facie* case."

"I wouldn't pass it to the Met," said Smith. "Even they would laugh at it."

Travis was certain this was a lie. For a moment he couldn't think why she should do this, and then he thought about delay. She was spinning things out, tem-porizing. He turned to Roisin. "She's taking the *piss*."

"What have you shown them?"

Travis looked across at Smith, then Gauthier.

"Roisin's a civilian," he said. "Do you want me to tell her, or should she . . . piss off?"

"Don't underestimate her," said Smith, with a warm tone Travis didn't expect. "She's welcome to listen."

Gauthier waved a languid hand and lit a cigarette.

"Okay, *ladies* and gentlemen," said Travis, wishing Roisin would take the hint, "if you insist on me spelling it out. It shows a network of companies and subcontractors using mainly immigrant labor, much of it illegal and coming in via people-smuggling routes that go through the Balkans and Central Asia as far as Afghanistan. Some of the laborers, and even some engineers, are former—or supposedly former—mujahedin from Bosnia, Kosovo, and Chechnya. All the companies are linked to each other by contracts or directors or key personnel, and all of them have in the past five years done maintenance work on the motorway junctions and oil industry sites that were sabotaged. There are other networks in that line of business, but none that so much as overlap this one when it comes to work on these particular sites in that particular time frame. And if you look at who's giving them the contracts, you'll see it passes through the company I worked for, Result, and on into Private Finance Initiative arrangements that can be traced further back to, guess who, officials who were at one time or another in companies at the top levels of the network."

"Network?" said Smith. "More like a cat's cradle of false positives. If you've found evidence of anything it's of backhanders, backdoor deals, corruption. Construction industry's riddled with it. PFI scandals? Send it to *Private Eye,* yes, that's the place for it."

"Jesus," said Travis. He turned to Gauthier. "What do you think?"

"I would think it worth investigating. The question, James, is what do *you* think? Whose network have you uncovered?"

Travis stared at him. "Isn't it obvious? It's AQ."

"And the Result connection?"

Travis had been so thrown by Smith's stonewalling that he'd missed making that point—the main point! He leaned across the table and lowered his voice.

"I think it overlaps with the operation we were involved in. I think it's been compromised, and not just by AQ. They're patsies for someone else."

"You have evidence for this?"

Travis shook his head. "That's why you have to take it back. Take this back." He fished in his shirt pocket and handed Gauthier a memory stick. "I think the whole thing, not just the sabotage but the Leuchars detonation, may have been your ostensible allies setting you up. The Russians or the Chinese, maybe both."

Gauthier started. Smith guffawed. Travis jolted back.

"This is no joke," he said. "Shit, the terrorist attacks alone are a *casus belli*. If I'm right we're all sleepwalking into *the wrong war*."

"All this," sneered Smith, "to get you off the hook—and to get the French off the hook? I'd expected better."

Gauthier stubbed out his cigarette and turned to her.

"I did not expect it," he said. "But I did recognize some names, and some connections. Parts of the network that James has identified are known. It is not AQ, though some involved may think they are AQ. I repeat: it is known, in part. Known to us. It is run by the—by an American agency."

"Oh, come off it," said Smith. "Why the hell would they do a thing like that?" She drained her wineglass. "We seem to have reached an impasse."

Travis, for the first time, found himself sharing Smith's incredulity. He couldn't believe Gauthier believed the CIA was behind the terrorist attacks. He couldn't believe Smith believed that all he'd uncovered was a tangle of coincidences.

"Take the data, anyway," he said. He handed the other memory stick to Smith, who looked down at it and twiddled it between finger and thumb.

"Excuse me," said Roisin. She reached down to pick

up a bag, unzipped it, and dropped her purse and phone in. "Back in a mo."

———

Roisin sat on the toilet seat and poked about in the bag. Inside were a pair of blue jeans and a black T-shirt, on top of which lay a slim belt, snazzy wraparound sunglasses and a scrunchy, as well as the purse, phone, and pocketknife she'd dropped in the bag herself. Under the clothes she could feel a pair of sneakers. Down the side was an A4 pink translucent plastic wallet. She snapped it open and found a throwaway Oslo street map, thousands of kroner, hundreds of euros, a passport with her photo and another name, and a cash card in the same name wrapped in the chit giving the PIN. Her legitimate passport was in the side pocket of her purse. She had a choice.

Gee, thanks, Dad. The clothes puzzled her for a moment until she connected them with the cafe's staff dress code, and with her father's insistence in his message on exactly what she should wear and carry. This was a one-off opportunity to get away. She had maybe a minute to decide. As soon as she thought that she realized she'd already decided. It had become obvious that the meeting wasn't going according to plan, and that Maxine might very well have no intention of honoring her deal with James. This struck Roisin as a reason to suspect she might have no intention of honoring her deal with Roisin. Unlike her father, Roisin had nothing left to bargain with. But what really decided her was the thought of getting away—from the Brit intelligence services, from the whole mess, from Maxine.

She slid out of the dress, hung it on the door hook under the hat, and scrambled into the T-shirt and jeans, stepping out of and into one shoe at a time to keep her bare feet from the floor. The jeans were too wide in the waist—maybe James had remembered her size from before her months in the peace camp. She cinched the belt and stuck the knife in her jeans pocket. The sneakers had black socks inside. She pulled her hair straight up and scrunchied it to a pile on top of her head. She put on the glasses, wedged her purse, switched the phone off to avoid at least that easy tracking and put it and the glasses case in the plastic wallet. She placed the empty backpack and the strappy shoes on the cistern. Then she thought of bomb scares, and in a moment of inspiration lifted the lid off the cistern. She rolled the bag up tightly and jammed it behind the inlet pipe and sank the shoes to the bottom. It wouldn't interfere with the ballcock, and the reduction of the flush might be slight enough not to be noticed. Speaking of which . . . she flushed the toilet and left the stall. She had a reflex impulse to wash her already wet hands, but instead walked straight out. The cafe was dimmer than the loo. She peered over the shades. Around the back of the bar was a brighter-lit kitchen area. Waiters and waitresses hurried back and forth with lunches and dirty plates. Just outside the kitchen was a row of hooks with long black aprons hanging from it. She grabbed an apron and put it on, picked up a tray with an empty glass on it from the bar, and laid the plastic wallet on top.

She nudged the shades up and walked out the door and straight along the aisle between tables. At the last empty table before the open plaza she put down the tray, picked up the wallet, and walked on, all the time looking straight ahead. Facing her was a row of shops which formed the street level of a redbrick office block across whose upper floors was a sign saying ARBEIDERPARTIET and a red rose symbol. For a moment she imagined walking in, introducing herself as a persecuted peace activist and throwing herself on the mercy of the Norwegian socialists.

She smiled, then almost stumbled as the thought ceased to be a fancy.

Why not? She wasn't a fugitive and didn't want to act like one. In her father's account she had a story, a story that Maxine didn't seem to believe but that she did, and that could stop the war if it reached someone with political influence and access to publicity.

She crossed the street, found the party office entrance among the shop fronts, and walked in.

21

"Why don't we just do a runner right now?"

The moment Maxine Smith had gone inside the cafe, the two spies had put their heads together. Paulson could see them both in a single close-up.

"No," said Gauthier. "Smith will have backup. The only way out is to complete the negotiation."

"Well, it's not going very fucking well," said Travis. He leaned back out of shot. The hidden camera, on the corner of a nearby awning's support rods, pulled away to bring him back in. "I think Smith is trying to spin this out. She's waiting for something. If she has backup, I don't think it's all in place. Hence my suggestion."

Gauthier shook his head. "She is trying to pump us for information. For admissions."

"You think this is being recorded?"

"Oh yes. Naturally."

"I fucking hope so," said Travis. "At least some other spook might take my information seriously."

"Oh, Smith takes it seriously—"

A phone rang in Paulson's ear and Maxine Smith's code flashed up on the screen. He toggled.

"Yes?"

"Roisin's disappeared. Can you—"

"What the fuck do you mean, disappeared?"

"She went to the toilet, remember? Ten minutes ago.

I got worried. She's not inside here and when I described her the bar staff said someone had found a dress and hat in the loo. *Her* dress and hat."

Paulson had a momentary vision of Roisin Travis walking around in her underwear. He had a feeling he would have noticed that. "She must have gotten changed."

"Nice to see you're on the ball, Sherlock. Now, can you run the last ten minutes of the doorway back? Patch it to my phone—no, hell, that'll take too long. Get someone in the team on it, right away."

"Yeah, sure, but—" Paulson relayed the request, then patched Smith on again. "What's the urgency?"

"What?" Smith sounded distracted.

"I mean, is she that important? Now we've got Travis?"

"Listen," said Smith. "It's Travis who must have set this up. Stashed clothes for her or whatever. So he's up to something we don't—"

"He wants his daughter out of it. You insisted you think she wasn't—"

"Fuck, fuck, fuck," said Smith. A few deep breaths.

"What?" said Paulson. The two spies were still talking. He wanted to listen to them, not this distraction.

"I told her about you," said Smith. "About you and . . . her brother."

Paulson felt a cold chill down his back.

"*What* did you tell her?"

"I showed her your file. Five's file on you, I mean. She intends to kill you."

Paulson felt as if the floor had given way under his chair. He made a choking sound that caused Hansen, sitting in an office armchair and tapping away on his PDA, to look around sharply.

"What in hell possessed you to—"

"Look," said Smith, sounding desperate, "I'm *sorry*. I

had to make a *deal*. Travis for you. I was going to re-
nege on it, of course, I was going to warn you, but now
I don't know what—"

Another voice cut in. "OP Alpha, we have positive ID.
On your screen now."

"They've spotted her," said Paulson, looking at the image. "Six minutes ago. Hair up, shades, long skirt—no,
an apron. But I think that's her."

"Thank God. Where'd she go?"

"Straight across, this way—hold on." A tram had
passed across the image, and she'd disappeared from the
next shot. The viewpoint had cut, to jerky CCTV capture
from this side of the road, then from a doorway. Paulson
peered at the white-lettered caption of the feed.

"'AP ingang'?" he read aloud.

"That's your street-level entrance, OP Alpha," said the
voice from the surveillance team.

"Shit!" Paulson yelled. "She's in the building!"

Hansen jumped out of his chair and came around the
desk and looked over Paulson's shoulder. Paulson
pointed frantically at the picture of the girl. Hansen
snatched up a desk phone.

"Oh—my—God," said Smith. Paulson heard a noise
that made him think of wheels turning in her head, but
was probably just her teeth grinding. When she spoke
again, her voice was calm and businesslike.

"I don't know how she found you were in there. Or *if*
she did. Maybe she's going for political asylum or something—"

"I'm not betting on that!"

"Don't. Do you have a sidearm?"

"Hell, no. Christ, do you think she has? She was carrying something pressed to her chest."

"Call the cops. Call security. And pull back the physical team. You need protection, fast. Travis stashed clothes

for her—he could have stashed a gun. And Gauthier—he might—Jesus, what are we *in*?"

"Christ Almighty," said Paulson. Duty took precedence over self-preservation, not to mention recrimination. "We gotta grab these two. We don't have enough people for both jobs."

"I'll call the cops on them," Smith said. "I'll try to keep them talking. You look after yourself."

"Got you. Out."

He got the message to the physical team—a squad of three, all armed and posted at various places in the square—in seconds. He split the screen and saw them sprint, chairs and table toppling as they jumped up. Hansen was still jabbering away in Norwegian. Paulson wished he knew the language. The intrigue that Travis had described and the sudden outflanking of this whole op, apparently by its three subjects acting in concert and with God knew what backup, and above all Smith's betrayal, had put him in a paranoid frame of mind. If he let it go on for another minute he'd be doing a James Jesus Angleton skydive onto Torggata.

Hansen put the phone down.

"I've called the police," he said. "And the building security, of course."

The phone rang.

"Yes, let them in!" Hansen snapped, and slammed it down. "Your men are here," he added.

"Where's the girl gone?"

"She asked to see our press officer, Tor Gudmundsen. He agreed. She was given a visitor card and directed to his office."

"Where—?"

"Fourth floor."

"Well call Mister fucking Gudmundsen and ask—"

"I have already done that," Hansen said, as if through clenched teeth.

"Sorry," said Paulson. "I'm a tad nervous right now. She's coming after *me.*"

"What, she is some kind of assassin?" Hansen glanced at the door, as if expecting it to burst open.

"She's a crazy bitch with a personal grudge," Paulson said. "That doesn't mean she's not—"

The door banged open. Hansen jumped.

"OP location secured *sir*!" the physical team leader said, over his shoulder from the doorway, which he quite adequately filled.

"Thank you," said Paulson.

"PT One and Two are here. Subject is being traced by PT Three, sir."

"Good. Good work."

"Request to clarify rules of engagement, sir."

"Subject may be armed," said Paulson, "but is high-value if captured. She's not to be shot except in immediate self-defense."

"Shoot if she reaches, sir? I'll pass that to—"

"No, wait," said Paulson, as Hansen looked at him with open-mouthed horror. "Shoot if she *draws,* got that?"

"Yes sir!"

Hansen still looked shocked. *Sorry if we have to stain the carpets of your cozy Euro socialist offices,* Paulson wanted to say. He looked back at the surveillance from the cafe, to see if the cops had arrived. Smith had sat down again and Travis was talking to her, waving his hands. Paulson put one earphone to his ear and keyed the sound feed, and got a ghastly feedback howl. For a relieved second or two he thought it was the police sirens. Then an alarm sounded through the building, a repeated rising and falling note that set his teeth on edge and resonated with the earphone's cacophony. Before he could say a word another sound began, close up and distant, audible through partition walls, through the window, from his own pocket. It was the sound of ringing phones.

"What a fucking time to have a fire," he said, half smiling at Hansen until he saw the color leeching from the man's face.

"That is not a fire alarm," said Hansen. "It is a nuclear attack warning."

————

Behind Maxine Smith, and elsewhere off to Travis's left, chairs clattered and glassware shattered. Travis looked around in time to glimpse three men in white shirts haring away across the plaza and vanishing behind the row of stalls.

"I *thought* the prices here were a bit steep," said Smith. Travis glared down her forced laugh.

"From three different tables?" He turned his head this way and that, a thumb on his phone's keypad. "Something's up, don't try to tell me it isn't."

At least Roisin had gotten clean away. Smith had returned, after a delay of her own, and immediately accused him of arranging it. He hadn't bothered to deny it. The conversation had gone downhill from there, despite his and Gauthier's repeated attempts to drag it back to agreeing to the deal.

"Roisin is in that building," said Smith, pointing. "She's in grave danger. Phone her. Now."

"Oh, don't give me that," said Travis. "You just want to track her phone."

"Fuck you, I'll do it myself." Smith speed-dialed on her own phone and held it to her ear for half a minute.

"Roisin," she said, and Travis felt his heart jump like a trout, and then sink as he realized she was leaving a message, "if you get this, please, please stop right there. Don't do anything stupid. Stay right where you are and drop the phone and move your hands slowly away from your body and up."

She put the phone down. "Voicemail. Fuck."

Travis was shaken by the distress in her face and voice. Her complexion had gone blotchy. He doubted that could be faked.

"What? What's going on?"

Smith looked from him to Gauthier, and back.

"You set her up," she said. "You sent her in there. You fucking ruthless bastards."

"I don't know what you're talking about!" cried Travis. "I helped her get away from you, that's all. I had no idea she was going in there—to do what?" He shook his head. "Why is she in danger?"

Smith stared at him. Her tongue went to her lips, then her lips compressed.

"Fuck this," Travis said. This was getting too weird for him. Whether Smith was still playing some mind game or Roisin was genuinely in danger, he didn't know. The dismayed thought that she was in danger made him want to jump up and run into that building—for all the good that would do. He didn't know what to expect next, but he didn't think his future was good or long. He didn't look at his phone as he pressed in one second the sequence of keys that sent the data and the report he'd compiled to every newspaper, news channel, and muckraking website he'd been able to find in a long session the previous night. He glanced down at the screen, to see that the message had been sent. It had. He looked up again at Smith, who was gazing at his phone like it was a swaying cobra.

"Fuck you," he said.

"What did you just do?"

"That report you didn't think was important," he said. "Send it to *Private Eye,* you said. Well, I just did, and to *Pravda,* the *Telegraph, The Times*, the *Johannesburg Post, Haaretz,* the BBC, Al Jazeera, CNN, *The Guardian*, and *Le Monde* and Antiwar-dot-com, and—"

Gauthier and Smith faced his gloat with masks of identical dismay.

"You fool," said Smith. "You utter, stupid fool."

Gauthier put his head in his hands.

Travis's question was lost in the klaxon's bray.

————

There was no panic. One minute people were sitting or strolling in the sun, the next they were standing still, phones pressed to their ears. And then they began to walk, not running, not pushing, toward the nearest doorway. Some around Travis headed for the cafe entrance, others across the square to the shops or offices. Traffic came to a standstill on the streets. Cars, buses, and trams emptied into buildings. Travis saw the crowds vanish like mercury down a plughole.

Somebody tugged at his sleeve. He turned.

"Get indoors!" Smith said. Gauthier, beside her, was poised as if frozen in stride.

"What's the fucking point?"

"We're not at a ground zero," said Smith, looking at her phone. "The airport might be, and ships in the fjords. There might be flash and falling debris and fallout. We think."

"Is that all?"

"Counter-force strike from Russia. That's what the news says might be on its way. Get inside."

Travis shook her hand from his arm and stepped back. "A Russian first strike? That's crazy."

"I didn't say a *first* strike. There have been—oh fuck, just look!"

She stuck her phone screen under his face.

Blasts rock Shanghai, Moscow, Pyongyang. Reports are coming in . . .

"Oh fuck," said Travis.

He turned and ran across the fast-emptying square.

22

WHAT a way to die, Roisin thought. Standing in a cluttered office with her wrists painfully zip-tied at her back, the final war beginning on flat screens on the walls around her, a smart-suited social democrat guilty and petrified behind a desk, and an American holding a gun to her head. It was like fate, condensing and underlining for her a lesson that was no longer any use.

"Nobody comes in here," the Yank said.

"Please understand," said Tor Gudmundsen, from behind his desk, "people may come in, this room is in the supposed solid core of the building, with no windows, and therefore a designated emergency gathering point—"

"Shut the fuck up," said the Yank. "Move to the door, stand in the doorway, and tell your people to keep the fuck out."

Gudmundsen complied, edging around the desk and avoiding Roisin's gaze as carefully as he did the filing cabinets and back-issue stacks. As well he should: he'd taken a phone call in Norwegian just after she'd arrived, then quite deliberately kept her sitting talking while the Yank came in; Gudmundsen had calmly nodded hello to him over her shoulder and resumed the conversation as the Yank strolled up behind her to grab her arms, tie her wrists, and lift her out of the seat by her hair. Gudmundsen had cooperated promptly with the Yank, frisking her in a clumsy embarrassed way and taking the knife from her pocket and placing it on his desk beside Roisin's plastic wallet, which he was ordered to empty.

"Subject disarmed and secured," the Yank had said, into the air. "Weapon appears to be a folding knife, sir. No firearm found."

Roisin had got as far as "Bu—" when the muzzle was pressed harder to her temple and the request "SHUT THE FUCK UP OR I'LL BLOW YOUR FUCKING HEAD OFF DO YOU UNDERSTAND" was shouted at her from a few inches away. Her ears had still been ringing from it when the ringing of phones started, the alarm had sounded, and the first news flashes began to appear on the silent screens.

One channel was now showing a live shot from outside Dongtan, China, alongside an archive picture taken from the same location, the top floor of a Shanghai skyscraper. The earlier picture showed the eco-suburb, all green wooded parks and glittering faceted domes and sweeping concrete curves and early evening lights. The live shot showed the same evening skyline with a flat gap and drifting smoke where Dongtan had been. Dongtan had been one of the places where the US had claimed that the new anti-missile weapons had been deployed. As far as Roisin could see from the spatter of dots coming up on a map shown on another channel, the same was true of a swathe of cities and industrial zones along China's east and south and into North Korea, as well as a few Moscow suburbs and Siberian towns.

Whatever had hit Dongtan wasn't a nuke. No mushroom cloud, no heat flash, and very little blast damage. It looked all the more terrifying for that—death from above, against which anti-missile missiles or the claimed new particle beams offered no protection. It didn't even seem to be a kinetic energy weapon: one big enough to

destroy a small city would have had effects at first indistinguishable from a nuke. Roisin guessed it was some
space-based beam weapon, far more powerful than anything yet imagined. If what she'd seen at Leuchars was a
beam weapon, as she now supposed had to be the case
because the US President had said as much, America
must already have weapons that made it look like a
laser pointer. No wonder the alarm had sounded: one
rational strategy for the Russians right now was to
launch everything they had before it was destroyed on
the ground.

All of this went through her mind in about a minute,
along with the thought that maybe, just maybe, if she
hadn't taken those photographs and sent them out
none of this would be happening, or at least not happening yet.

She felt oddly calm. The prospect of the final war was
still too big to grasp. Even the thought that if she wasn't
dead in the next few minutes, then within a few hours
or days she would surely be wishing she was, couldn't
become real. If it had become real she would right now
be doing all she could to get herself shot in the head. Instead she stood with her knees knocking, watching the
end of the world on television. She supposed the final
news flash would be the screens going blank. After that
there would be nothing to hope for but that for her the
final flash would be close. As the old CND leaflets had
cheerfully pointed out, the brain was annihilated before
the pain had time to reach it. More likely, unless Oslo
was itself a target, there would be a ground tremor, falling masonry, flying glass, fire, fallout, and any number
of ways and days to a slow death.

The American, whom she could see out of the corner
of her eye, now stood a meter or so away with his pistol
in both hands, aimed straight at her head. He was pay-

ing the apocalyptic news screens no more attention than he'd have given a fish tank. He was looking straight at her, and past her to the door. Tor Gudmundsen was arguing with someone outside in the corridor.

"Let him in," said the American. Gudmundsen stepped aside and a man walked in. Roisin glanced toward him and immediately flinched away. She recognized him from the file Maxine had shown her: Jeff Paulson. The shock of seeing the man who had tortured her brother to death contended with cold thinking. Maxine had said nothing about Paulson's being here. That was bad enough, but how had he known she was here? Roisin suspected at once that Maxine had warned him. The new betrayal didn't come as a shock.

Another man walked in behind Paulson. White shirt, earpiece, gun aimed upward and then at once trained on her.

Paulson walked behind her, sat on the desk and leaned over to the back of it. There was the sound of drawers being pulled out.

"Sit her down," he said.

The first Yank caught her shoulder and pushed her into the swivel chair he'd earlier hauled her out of. He pushed her arms behind the seat back and stood up. Paulson tossed him a reel of parcel tape. He taped her ankles together behind the chair's pillar. After that everyone in the room relaxed, except Roisin. The cracking sounds of the meters and meters of tape being ripped from the reel had echoed the sounds from her joints and back.

Paulson picked up the Swiss Army knife James had given her, from the desk where Gudmundsen had tossed it. He toyed with the blades for few seconds, then looked up at Gudmundsen.

"Get out," he said.

Gudmundsen gave Roisin a stricken look, for which she felt no gratitude whatsoever, and got out. His place in the doorway had been taken by a third white-shirted Yank. Paulson pushed Roisin's knee with his foot, turning her to face him in the swivel chair. The position of her body was already beginning to hurt.

"Who sent you?" he asked.

Roisin glanced sidelong at the guy who'd tied her up. He was still pointing the gun at her. Paulson seemed to understand.

"You can talk now," he said, quite pleasantly. "Who sent you?"

"Nobody sent me," said Roisin. "I came in here to discuss something with the man you just sent out."

"You intended to kill me," said Paulson.

So Maxine had told him that too.

"I still intend to kill you," said Roisin.

Paulson laughed.

"I expect we'll both be dead soon enough," said Roisin. "But I didn't come here to kill you. I had no idea you were here. I wouldn't have come here if I had. Not without a better weapon than that, anyway."

Paulson clicked out the smaller of the knife's blades and pretended to test its edge on his thumb.

"You can do a lot of damage with a knife," he said. He waved the blade in front of her eyes.

"If you use that on me," said Roisin, "you'll prove you're nothing but a sadist. The position I'm in is already painful. In ten minutes, it'll be excruciating. With very little force you can make my knee and elbow joints hurt like hell. If you think pain leads to truth you need only wait a little. But as I said, we'll both soon be dead anyway."

She had no idea where this defiance was coming from. It wasn't courage, she was sure of that.

"Well, the matter is pressing," said Paulson. "I'm sorry, but I really do have to know who sent you. I don't believe you, you see. And I'm not too worried about incoming missiles. Put that right out of your mind. Think about this instead."

As if following her suggestion, he placed a foot on the inside of each of her knees and pushed outward. The pain nearly made her black out. It died to a dull ache when he stopped pressing, though not at once. Just before she opened her eyes again it occurred to Roisin that Paulson really did need to know who had sent her. He must think he was still in immediate danger. Maxine would have been very unlikely to have told Paulson of her deal with Roisin until she had no alternative. It must have come as a shock. Which meant that the danger that would seem most plausible to him wouldn't involve her father, or Gauthier, or Russian agents inside the Norwegian Workers' Party, but—

Yank Number One grabbed her hair again and jerked her head back. This was good from her point of view because it filled her eyes with tears and made her voice shake when she spoke.

"I'll tell you!" she said. "I'll tell you everything! Just don't hurt me again, please!"

"Who sent you?" Paulson repeated.

"It was Maxine," Roisin sniveled. "She told me you were holed up in this building before we arrived at the square. She said she would let me go to find you and try to kill you if my father and the Frenchman confirmed something that MI5 already suspected. She didn't tell me what it was, but when she heard what they had to say, she gave me the nod, and I went. She said I would have maybe ten minutes to find you before she had to warn you, in case you noticed I was gone, and got suspicious. But even if that happened, she said, it didn't matter to her, because the warning would disrupt the surveillance and let her and my father and the Frenchman get away."

It sounded plausible to Roisin because it was what she wished had been true. It would have made everything so much more bearable if it had been.

"Who hid the clothes you changed into?"

"Hid them?"

"In the women's restroom? Who hid them?"

"Nobody," said Roisin. "The jeans and T-shirt and the other stuff were in my bag all the time. That was the plan. I grabbed the apron myself. I left it at reception, because it's the cafe's property."

Paulson's face betrayed a flicker of a small puzzle solved. Then his expression changed.

"What was it that MI5 suspected and the spies confirmed?"

"About the AQ network," Roisin said.

Paulson pushed her knees again. This time the pain made her scream.

"If you scream again," said Paulson, "I'll tape your mouth and ask you to nod or shake your head. Imagine how much more time that would take. I'd also have to apply stress between questions, not just when you don't answer truthfully."

Roisin nodded. Snot had gathered on her upper lip, more than she could sniff away. The ache in her back was now worse than the throbbing pain in her knees.

"What was it that MI5 suspected and the spies confirmed?"

"Uh, before I answer that are you sure you want me to talk with these other guys here?"

Paulson looked surprised. "Why should that worry you?"

"I don't want you to get angry."

"No," said Paulson, "you don't. Now answer the question."

"All right," said Roisin. "The ostensible AQ network that carried out the attacks in Britain is recruited through the CIA's mujahedin pipeline. And the Russians have compromised some French intelligence ops in the UK, including the one my father was involved in, and maybe it was they who actually triggered the Leuchars event. There might be some crossover between these two, meaning that the Russians managed to get a grip on the CIA's muj network via their infiltration of the French operations." She thought for a moment, and found herself speaking with some animation. "Hey, that makes sense, doesn't it? I didn't *think* the CIA would have activated that plan just then!"

Paulson was looking at her very oddly.

"What plan?"

"I read a story last week in a British, uh, left-wing newspaper that the attacks were part of a CIA contingency plan to create the conditions to impose a US occupation on Britain. But it seemed to me a bit premature, whereas if the CIA plan existed and it was the Russians who activated it, it all makes sense."

"If you read that in the newspaper I think you mean," said Paulson, "you can be pretty damned sure it's Russian-planted disinformation. FSB active measures."

"Maybe it is," Roisin admitted, "but they seemed to have solid sources for at least the existence of the plan."

"There is no such plan," said Paulson. "And there's no CIA muj pipeline."

"Maxine Smith believes there is," Roisin lied hastily, "and as soon as she heard the spies confirming it, she gave me the nod to go after you."

"Why?"

"She's very . . . what you would call patriotic. She was outraged about the plan. And she was furious at what you . . . what you . . . what you did to my brother." The last words came out in a rush.

"Oh, she was, was she?" said Paulson. "As I recall, her exact words were: 'Throw the book at him. See what sticks.' You think you're smart, Ms. Travis, but that bitch is a lot smarter than you."

"I know that," said Roisin.

Paulson closed the knife and slid it across the desk to within reach of the man behind Roisin. He stood up and looked across at him above Roisin's head.

"We're finished here," he said.

23

Mark Dark's first thought as the news broke was that he was very glad he was already *in* a basement. His second was that he was very glad that Evansville, Indiana, was a long way from any nuclear targets. His third was that even if these notions were incompatible they still made sense, because what he was seeing just took the whole nuclear war survival handbook and tore it up and threw it away. It was like seeing the aftermath of an alien attack.

Maybe it *was* an alien attack. There was nothing left of these cities but *smoking holes in the ground*. The jingo cliche had been made literal, right there on CNN and Al Jazeera, right before his eyes. The first satellite pictures appeared, live: Pyongyang looked as if someone had removed it from the map with a hole-punch.

"We are deep in WTF territory," Mark mused, and that was it, he had his headline. He was good to go.

Deep In WTF Territory:

Breaking: North Korean capital Pyongyang and at least ten cities in southeast China, mostly satellite eco-cities and/or Special Industrial Zones, two sites near Moscow and one in Siberia have been reduced to smoking holes in the ground within minutes of each other around 08.00 PST (20.00 local time) in what

Libyan Defense Minister Sa'ad Al-Bari has just described on Al Jazeera as quote "a coordinated imperialist-Zionist sneak attack" unquote and is elsewhere being default-attributed to US Space Command's unleashing of a hitherto unknown weapon of tremendous power and unknown operating principles. Estimated fatalities to date based on declared populations of destroyed cities run to > 10 megadeaths. Nuclear-attack warning sirens are reported from several European capitals including London, Paris, Stockholm, Oslo, Berlin (updates here) as fears spike of a massive Russian and/or Chinese nuclear response. No such warnings so far reported from anywhere in US. No official statement from US Government and no unofficial statement from sources. US nuclear forces alert level remains at One, Homeland Security General Threat Level remains Orange as of this moment.

First-cut analysis: holy fucking shit.

Considered analysis: We are deep in "WTF?" territory. The list of cities struck matches closely the unofficial US Govt list of anti-missile beam weapon deployment alleged in POTUS speech yesterday Thursday, May 14, with the conspicuous absence of Paris. (Note also its overlap with the list of cities in PRC and NK where the fast-build Fuller domes were erected last week. Was this a cover for the anti-missile deployment?)

Two possibilities:

the new anti-missile weapons have blown up (or been blown up, cf Leuchars Event (wiki here));

the US has just demonstrated that it has weapons against which the new anti-missile weapons are no defense at all.

I incline to the latter because:-

The aforementioned Leuchars Event was at first indistinguishable from a tactical nuke. What we've seen from China and NK is not. (Just in: broken windows < 1 km from Dongtan crater perimeter. Broken windows!) This is something new. It's so new that there aren't even rumors on teh Interwebs about it. It's not a nuke. It's not a KE weapon. It's not a beam weapon, at least not as we know it, Jim. It's something radical, like non-baryonic matter or a string-theory tech application or space-time manipulation or something even wilder. Like I say, deep in WTF territory.

Lack of immediate US threat-upgrade/alert-level response, and target distribution, suggests US strategic thinking includes peeling off France from Russia and Russia from bad-actor SCO bloc partners PRC and NK (cracks are already showing at diplomatic level) and tactical thinking that any Russian and/or Chinese overwhelming counterforce or countervalue strikes can be taken down at will.

Short form: We are now Battlestar America. Watch the skies.

————

Mark paused with his virtual finger on the Post icon. Had he really written that the US had just killed upwards of ten million people? Had he gloried in it? He had. He could understand himself. Shock at what had happened and dread of what might be about to happen made the idea of an invincible America almost irresistibly reassuring. But in the cold light of a calmer day, if that ever came, he would look back at this part of his post with shame.

So he added a few more lines:

This leaves open the question of whether the US first strike, if that's what it was, is justified. If it was not to preempt an imminent threat that could be dealt with in no other way, then it's mass murder, plain and simple. But we all know that. So I'm certain there was an imminent threat. It's not like the US has ever proclaimed a doctrine of preventive war, or used a new and immensely destructive weapon on an Asian country just to send a warning message to the Russians.

With his conscience thus salved, he posted the update and went back to watching the news. NORAD had scrambled fighter jets over the major cities. Homeland Security was pulling out all the stops: clips came in from Washington, D.C., of the National Guard on the streets, the Capitol sealed off, a column of tanks on Pennsylvania Avenue. . . .

"Wait a fucking minute," said Mark.

———

Jeff Paulson waited until the last member of the physical team had backed out of the room, then closed the door. He wished he could lock it behind him.

"All done?" he said.

"Yes, sir."

"Let's get the fuck out of here."

"Sir, do you mean get out of the building?"

"Yes, I do." Paulson set off briskly down the now empty corridor.

"Sir, in the event of expected or actual nuclear explosions in the near vicinity our advice on best practice is to remain indoors and when possible underground or otherwise as close to the ground as possible consistent with subsequent unimpeded egress, sir."

Paulson walked faster. The three physical security men stepped up their pace.

"Look, are you guys from Oslo Station?"

"No, sir. We're from the embassy guard."

"And seconded to Oslo Station?"

"Seconded to your command, sir."

"Good," said Paulson. "Well, let me bring you up to speed. I kept half an eye on the news screens, and I can tell you America has some kind of weapon that can eat nukes for breakfast. We don't need to worry about fallout. We need to get back to the embassy. We're in the offices of a Euro socialist and no doubt commie-infiltrated party. We've committed serious crimes on its premises. The cops have been called, as it happens to protect me from our recent acquaintance, but the Brit operative may by now have sicced them on to us. I appreciate that you have diplomatic immunity. Well, I don't, not here. Not in this country."

They'd reached a stairwell. Paulson looked down it, cocked an ear, decided all was clear and was about to head down when one of the guys leapt ahead of him to the first landing, another pressed close to his shoulder, and the third dropped to one knee and faced down the corridor. All had their weapons drawn.

"Stop," said Paulson.

"Sir?"

"Let me finish." His voice echoed in the stairwell. He lowered it. "The only armed force we're likely to meet are the Norwegian police. Our best chance of getting out without being noticed is to stay calm, conceal your weapons, stop calling me sir—'Jeff' or 'Mr. Paulson' will do, thank you—and above all stop talking to me like you've swallowed the fucking book. Got that?"

"Sir! Yes sir!"

Paulson glared. "Jesus fucking wept," he said.

"Mr. Paulson," said the guard beside him, "you don't ought to talk like that, it's a goddamn breach of the fourth commandment."

"That's better," said Paulson.

As he went on down the stairs Paulson found himself unsteady at the knees. He was shaking all over, and not just with relief. He hadn't enjoyed stressing Rosin Travis. That was the mistake the Administration's critics always made. They assumed you did this stuff for fun. Paulson guessed this was because most of them were conservatives.

They reached the foot of the stairwell without incident, passing offices in which people huddled in packs and wall screens babbled, made their way along a service corridor to reception, and found it deserted. They exited to a silent street. Looking up and down the sidewalk, Paulson saw no one around. He led the team between abandoned vehicles, and through the row of stalls, where racks of mirror shades reflected the sun. The only living things on the square were pigeons, and an old man talking while he fed them crumbs from vacated tables. Glancing back, Paulson could see in the shop fronts the ranked backs of people facing away from the windows. As they had no doubt been told by the authorities to do.

Eurotrash, disciplined and terrified to the end.

He cut diagonally across the square and broke into a fast jog, the team behind him. The embassy was only a mile or so away, up past the big park. An easy run. The one thing that troubled him was the memory of the implacable hatred in Roisin Travis's eyes after the tape went over her mouth. He should have killed her when he had the chance, he thought. He could have gotten away with it. Then he shook his head: nah, it just wasn't worth it. It would have been hard to justify in the report.

———

Travis found the receptionist in the middle of the third crowded ground-floor office he struggled through. Just about everyone had an elbow out, as they held phones to their ears and made repeated attempts to get through on overloaded networks. Nobody looked anywhere but at the nearest news screen, on the wall or a desk or in their hand.

"I can't tell you that," the man said. "It's a security matter. The police are on their way."

Travis took a deep breath.

"That young woman is my daughter," he said. "The security men you let in are armed and think she's a menace. She isn't. I must find her and them before something terrible happens. If the police are on their way it's on foot."

The receptionist shook his head. He wasn't paying much attention.

"I'm not armed," said Travis. He spread his arms as far as he could in the crush. "Frisk me if you like."

"No," said the receptionist. "This is a matter for the US embassy."

"Do you think the US embassy gives a flying fuck about this right now?"

"We are in a war situation," said the receptionist. "It may be even more important than I know."

The temptation to head-butt, to grab bollocks, was hard to resist.

"Fuck you," Travis said.

He pushed his way out and stood looking along the corridor. Think, man, think. Roisin had not gone into this building on some wild mission, as Smith had suspected but had refused to explain—he presumed she thought it had something to do with an outer ring of surveillance, which he and/or Gauthier had sent her to disrupt. Well, they hadn't done that, so Roisin must have had some other reason, if he could only figure it out.

He ran back to reception and looked at the switchboard. Somewhere there would be a "last ten calls" list, but the equipment was ancient and he didn't have time to hack. He looked up at the notice board above the desk, showing the various offices and their occupants. Long Norwegian names, and that was just for the jobs. He imagined Roisin coming in here, in a hurry, impulsive as usual, reacting to the situation she'd just walked away from, looking up at the board and wondering whom to speak to if she wanted—

Press. That was it. Tor Gudmundsen, Room 413.

Travis jabbed a lift button a couple of times, saw a red light winking, and took the stairs at a run. He raced along the fourth-floor corridor clocking numbers and slowed down as he reached 407. The offices had windows to halfway down the walls, as did the doors. Travis ducked, crept forward, and raised his head cautiously. He couldn't see anyone in 413. He took another couple of steps forward and pressed his ear to the door. He heard a faint sound like a dog whining.

He stood up, opened the door, and stepped into the office. The first thing he saw was the pink document case on the desk, then the knife, open. No sounds. Every wall was hung with flat screens, even beside the windows. Maps and talking heads, silent above scrolling captions.

"Roisin!"

The whine came again, much louder, almost a grunt. He moved his head this way and that, trying to locate the sound. A row of filing cabinets near the desk stood a yard clear from the wall. He looked behind it and found Roisin, eyes red and wide, mouth taped up, her body bowed outward around the seat of the desk chair, which had been jammed in there with her on it. He pulled her and the chair forward, cut the plastic ties at her wrists, and hacked through the tape around her ankles. She slid forward on to her knees, the chair toppling behind her. As her knees took her weight she screamed through her nose, and rolled on her side. She ripped the tape from her face and screamed again with her mouth. He sat on the floor and caught her in his arms. She sobbed into his shoulder. After a minute she pulled away, and touched the reddened rectangle across the lower part of her face, wiped her nose on her arm and rubbed at her knees, wincing.

"What did they do to you?"

"Only this," said Roisin.

"Who?"

"Jeff Paulson. The same CIA man who tortured Alec."

"Christ! Where is he?"

"He left, with his three heavies. About five minutes ago."

Travis hammered the floor with his fist.

"Did you really come here to get him?"

"No," said Roisin. "It was all an accident. But I will."

Travis sighed. All this, all this, because he . . .

"Revenge can eat you up inside," he said. "And we'll never catch him."

"I can try. And that bitch Maxine, she—"

She stopped.

"What?"

"Paulson said she was involved too. But why should I believe him? But then again, why should I trust her?"

"Do you have to?"

Roisin looked at him. Her face—marked, blotched, tear-streaked—looked quite different when she smiled.

"Not anymore," she said.

He smiled back. Roisin's face clouded again.

"If revenge eats you up," she said, "what do we have instead?"

"I don't know," said Travis. It was not a question that had occurred to him before. "Justice?"

"Justice." Roisin looked as if she was struggling with a complicated calculation. "Yeah. I suppose."

"You know," Travis said, "if it wasn't so goddamn futile, you know the bastard I'd go after? Gauthier. I'd just call up the DGSE, and tell them straight. Fuck, I'd tell the world. If there was still a world."

"Tell them what?" Roisin caught the top of the desk, tried to heave herself up, waved him away when she failed, and tried again. She stood up, leaning heavily on the desk, and turned around and half sat on it, legs straight to the floor.

"The Russian cut in," Travis said. "On the French job on Result, yeah? How they hacked a command link to the CIA's British muj?"

"Yeah, Dad, I did follow that conversation." Roisin sounded like herself again.

"It was Gauthier. Had to be. When the Result operation was burned, nobody else but him and me fell out. And I *know* it wasn't me."

"Very interesting, but so what?"

"I think some huge Russian diversionary operation matters now the Yanks have attacked China! I think the

French should know their supposed allies tried to get the Yanks and Brits to attack *them,* and still could."

The fact caught up with him that there was more than revenge to exposing Gauthier. It was something that had to be done. He reached past Roisin for the landline phone. "You know, I should call the DGSE from here."

Roisin was laughing.

"Dad," she said, "do that if you like. But it doesn't matter anymore. None of it matters."

His hand recoiled and his body jolted as if he'd touched a live wire.

"What? Have the Russians—"

"Haven't you seen the news?" She pointed to the nearest screen. "I had five minutes with nothing but the news to take my mind off the pain."

The screen was filled with a sharp, enlarged picture, clearly from space, of the waxing crescent moon. Dozens of lights pricked the dark side. Roisin spoke her own voice-over.

"The cities weren't destroyed, Dad," she said. "They went into space. They went to the fucking moon."

24

The Government of the Russian Federation is pleased to confirm the successful launch earlier today of several experimental space platforms applying plasma focus fusion technology and Heim Theory antigravity propulsion. The Defense Ministry apologizes to any citizens inconvenienced or alarmed by the necessary secrecy surrounding the preparations, and assures all citizens that the platforms are expected to make a safe and early return to their places of origin. The Foreign Ministry looks forward to a relaxation of international tensions, and to fruitful international cooperation in the application of this new technology for peaceful purposes on a sound commercial basis. It notes with admiration the bold steps already taken by fellow members of the SCO in the application of this technology and assures them of its continuing close attention to their progress.

———

The Praesidium of the National Assembly of the People's Republic of China is proud to announce that today the Chinese people have recorded another triumph in deepening and heightening the advance of the socialist market economy and the construction of Socialism With Even More Chinese Characteristics. Led by the Communist Party of China, guided by the imperishable principles of Marxism-Leninism, Mao Zedong Thought, and Deng Xiaoping Theory, holding fast to the Four Modernizations, Three Represents, and Two Necessary Corrections, and applying the profound dialectical materialist principle of seeking truth from facts, the workers, peasants, scientific intelligentsia, patriotic bourgeoisie and advanced artificial intelligences of the PRC, working behind the great steel wall of the people's armed forces, have constructed truly revolutionary systems of breakthrough propulsion and defense that have enabled ten cities, three Special Industrial Zones, and an undisclosed but assuredly large number of defensive military bases, to be transported safely, securely, and swiftly to near-Earth space and to the lunar surface.

While stressing the purely peaceful and experimental nature of this astounding triumph of the freely associated producers, the Praesidium permits itself to indulge the hope that it will prove a stinging rebuff to the schemes of imperialism, hegemonism, revisionism, dogmatism, and great-power chauvinism, and deliver a severe and serious setback to the criminal manipulation of legitimate popular discontent by these and other dark forces using the spiritual poisoned daggers of backward superstition, reactionary fundamentalism, and national separatism

to drive deep and painful wounds into the
suffering and bleeding body of our beloved
socialist motherland.

Eternal glory to the People's Republic of China,
homeland of ten million taikonauts!
Lasting glory to the CPC!
Long live proletarian internationalism!

———

The Central Committee of the Workers' Party of
Korea, in the name of the Eternal President and
Great Leader Kim Il Sung and of the Dear Leader
Kim Jong Il, today joyfully hails the heroic working
people of the DPRK's glorious capital Pyongyang
in their world-shattering application of the juche
idea and the mastery of man over nature in
transporting themselves forever beyond the reach
of the imperialist aggressors and their neo-colonial
lackeys by embarking on an epic journey into the
cosmos. Resolutely smashing the decadent-
capitalist and modern-revisionist anti-human
self-limiting interpretation of the great scientist
Albert Einstein's Theory of Relativity and firmly
grasping the revolutionary implications of self-reliant
scientific thinking, they have overcome the supposed
barrier of the speed of light and expect within days
to reach Alpha Centauri. On the undoubted
successful completion of that journey they fully
intend to further explore deeper into the cosmos
paying special attention to the search for habitable
extra-solar planets. In this endeavor they have the
inestimable advantage of the on-the-spot advice
and counsel of the Dear Leader Kim Jong Il. In his

bitterly regretted though heroically borne physical absence the Central Committee is unbreakably united in its determination to strive to continue on the path of self-reliance, retaining as all its members do in their hearts many vivid and imperishable memories of his incomparable personality and a thorough acquaintance with the unparallelled literary legacy enshrined in his collected and now thankfully completed writings which will undoubtedly preserve for all posterity the true and lasting significance of his profoundest thoughts.

The Central Committee notes that in accordance with the army-first policy, the leading cadres of the People's Army and many other senior officers have enthusiastically volunteered to stand firmly shoulder to shoulder with the working people of Pyongyang and with the Dear Leader and the great steeled cohort of veteran Party cadres in their outstanding and unprecedented mission. The Central Committee assures the government of the DPRK that it can continue to rely unswervingly on the heroic and unflinching loyalty of the People's Militia and on the boundless love and unshakeable firmness of the entire people for the defense and further development of the socialist system.

The Central Committee, therefore, further calls on all the patriotic and peace-loving people of Korea to rally firmly around the banner of the Party and the whole nation in pressing forward the struggle for the peaceful unification of the motherland, the withdrawal of all US imperialist occupation troops, the disbanding of puppet troop formations, and the denuclearization of the entire Korean

peninsula including its maritime regions and the
establishment of the united Commonwealth of
Koryo and the deepening of the principle of
"one country, two social systems" by the new
revolutionary principle of "one country, many
solar systems."

May the continuing immortal presence of the Dear
Leader in our thoughts and memories and the
joyous and heart-warming certainty that he is
already at least one light-year away and forever
receding to ever greater distances console us for
his physical absence and inspire us all to new feats
of self-reliance!

PART FIVE

And the Salt Ocean Rolled

2 5

LIFE is elsewhere.

That was how Anne-Marie Chretien explained her abrupt departure to Bob Cartwright, when she called him from Paris some days after the international crisis passed. It has a more general application, in a universe where the Heim Theory has been proved. What happens on Earth no longer matters to the long-term future of humanity. It matters, however, to those of us who for whatever reason remain. The Execution Channel now shows scenes from new conflicts, and is in no danger of running out of material.

The full story of the ruthless and audacious FSB diversionary operation mounted after the capture of the Heim field generator—mistaken for an antimissile beam weapon—threatened to expose what was referred to, in the inner councils of the SCO, as the Exit Strategy remains untold. In general terms Travis's hypothesis was correct. The details, perhaps, must await the memoirs of Alain Gauthier, currently residing in Moscow.

Roisin Travis returned to England and took up post-graduate studies at SOAS. She has given a great deal of thought to her future career, and is at present undecided between politics and the Foreign Office. An oblique recruitment attempt by MI5 was rebuffed.

Maxine Smith still works for MI5, on a higher pay

grade. Her precise duties are classified, but are known to James Travis, who likes to keep in practice. James Travis lives in exile in Paris, where he works on complex IT projects for Électricité de France, as it struggles to install plasma focus fusion generators. He was debriefed by the DGSE and MI5 in a joint session, and gave them a complete audit trail of the damage he had done to various government IT systems at Result. He occasionally travels to the UK, using the identity of Kevin Levin, which—because of further hacking by James Travis—has not yet been exposed. He shoots rabbits with an air rifle at his cottage near Newcastle, and skins them with a Laguiole knife.

Mark Dark documented online the unfolding of the heartland isolationist mutiny that was launched, following a long-settled plan, within minutes of what its leaders—along with most of the world—believed to be a US first strike in a nuclear war. By the time their mistake was evident, it was too late to turn back. Tanks had rolled, blood had been shed, and things had been said that could not be withdrawn or forgiven. Some of them were said by Mark Dark. After his equipment was confiscated by the new authorities he had a long and painful conversation with his mother. He now works for a software company in Indianapolis, and posts to various overseas blogs under the name of Mark Hope.

Jeff Paulson continued to work undercover from the US consulate in Edinburgh until he was fatally stabbed in a back corridor of the Edinburgh music club Subway, by a woman whom witnesses could only describe as "some goth chick." Whether because of her black veil, her heavy makeup, or for some other reason, the club's CCTV cameras never recorded any recognizable image of her face.

Bob Cartwright's disinformation company lost its

contract after the new authorities—or the Regime, as he is wont to call them, privately—reorganized Homeland Security. He now works for a small neoconservative journal in New York, where he lives with Sarah Henk. Whenever he visits his family in Boston, he takes off for an hour or two to look at the Glass Flowers exhibit at the Harvard Museum of Natural History. It's in two large, dim-lit rooms, where the only sounds are the sideways shuffle and marveling murmur of visitors and the sough of the Leibert ventilation machinery maintaining a constant temperature and humidity. The models are delicate, and old.

Bob walks along the entire sequence of long glass cases, which contain life-size models of North American flora. The models are, for the most part, of hallucinatory precision. The minutest visible hair on a stem, the dots of pollen on stamens, the sharpness and size of every spike on a cactus, the slight drying and withering of some of the originals, are reproduced so well that it is, in some cases, almost impossible even on close inspection to distinguish them by sight from real plants.

He takes his time over these visits. He studies every model, every label with great care. And he leaves, shaking his head. After he has left, Bob sometimes finds himself looking at real plants—the grass and shrubs outside—as if they might be some uncanny simulacrum. In their final phone call, Anne-Marie told him that there was a message for him there, in that exhibit, but he still can't figure out what it is.